CRUCE

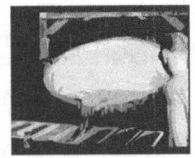

by
Brian Rae

ISBN 978-0-9863297-0-8 (print)
ISBN 978-0-9863297-1-5 (ebook)

printed by Createspace Independent Publishing Program

Book and cover design, prepress specialist:
Kathleen Weisel, Bellingham, WA (weiselcreative.com)

Dedication

CRUCE IS DEDICATED to those who helped shape my life: my parents and brothers; my friends, who graciously included me in their fun family activities like skiing, hunting, hiking; the nuns, who taught me how to read and write; those memorable, passionate English teachers, who taught me the importance of reading and the clarifying, creative joy of writing; the coaches, who taught me the fruits of hard work, competition and perseverance; the Jesuits who taught me the benefits of living a disciplined and ordered life. CRUCE is also dedicated to the men on D Shift at Kaiser Aluminum Mead Works, who taught me that caring, generous hearts often reside inside tough exteriors.

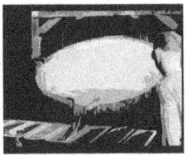

May 29, 1967

Dressed in cut off jeans, a white t-shirt and sandals, Bill Roberts glanced at his black and silver alarm clock on his desk. It was 2:10 PM. He eyed the stack of work clothes his mom had neatly folded for him and placed on his twin-sized bed in the basement and took a quick inventory: *long-sleeved shirt, long johns, pants, heavy socks, bandana, hat.* Satisfied he had all his work clothes, he began to pack them into a paper grocery sack from Rosauers that he'd grabbed from the kitchen pantry upstairs. The phone in the downstair's rec room rang but he made no effort to answer it. *Probably for Mom,* he thought tossing in his socks. But after three rings, he figured his mom must be outside so he hustled out of his room to answer the phone.

"Hello."

"Hey, congratulations on your graduation, Bro," Rod his older brother in Seattle offered. "Sorry I couldn't be there but had to start my new job last week. Are you still celebrating?"

"No," snickered Bill. "In fact I'm just getting my work

clothes together to head out to Kaiser. But you must have been celebrating all weekend; every time I called your place, you weren't there."

"Yeah, there were a lot of parties over here after graduation, and you know me—can't pass up a party. Well, I won't keep you if you're headed to work. I'll call you in a few weeks. I'd like you to come over. We need to celebrate our graduations together—drink some beer, and get you some pussy before you leave for the Novitiate in August."

"Sounds like a plan," replied Bill matter-of-factly knowing that plans with Rod oftentimes don't work out. "Well, I'd better get going; don't want to be late my first day back. Thanks for calling."

"You bet; talk with you soon. Just think...this is your last summer at Kaiser."

"I know; thank God! Bye."

Bill placed the rest of his work clothes in the paper bag and rolled down its top, put his safety glasses, sweat band, and cotton gloves inside his heavy, double-soled work boots that he'd laced together, slung the boots over his left shoulder and headed upstairs. Opening the door at the top of the stairway, he looked at the wood crucifix that hung on the hallway wall. *Please help me get through another summer at Kaiser, Lord.* Closing the door to the basement, he turned right and walked through the family room to the kitchen where he grabbed the sack lunch off the counter top that his mom had made for him. As he headed for the front door, he glanced at his diploma that his parents had placed on the fireplace mantel after his graduation from Gonzaga University on Saturday. *Lot of good that diploma did me. Still doin' the same job I've had the past four summers.*

When he opened the front door, his mom, Rachel was out

in the front yard enjoying a Winston filtered cigarette.

"Who called?" she asked exhaling a cloud of smoke.

"That was Rod. He wanted to congratulate me on graduating Saturday. Said he'll call back in a few weeks to invite me over to Seattle so we can celebrate our graduations together."

"Oh, that would be nice; hope it works out."

Bill placed a quick kiss on his mom's cheek then headed for his car. "Thanks for getting my work clothes together and for making my lunch, Mom."

Rachel Roberts smiled as she watched her son walk to his car. She couldn't help but admire his youthful, muscular body. His shoulders filled out his t-shirt nicely and Bill's calves were well-defined from all the running he'd done as a football player and as a sprinter. She took another drag from her cigarette. "Boy, it's hot today for May."

"I know! I wish my first day back wasn't starting at the hottest time of day," Bill replied tossing his work clothes, boots and lunch box into the back seat of his faded red 1961 Volkswagen Bug. *Man, it's like an oven in here,* he thought rolling down the windows. He was trying his best to block out the dread of another summer of weekly rotating shifts: Day, Swing, Graveyard. *At least I can pay off my college loan before entering the Novitiate in late August,* he thought in an attempt to minimize the dread.

Rachel waved to him as he backed out of the driveway into the street. She wore a pair of white cotton slacks and a floral blouse. *She still looks pretty darned good at 47, and for having raised five boys.* The afternoon sun illuminated her strawberry blond hair. Bill waved back. He knew she was proud of him and thrilled that at least one of her five boys would be a priest.

He drove west on 21st Avenue, and at University Road turned right to begin his familiar route to the Kaiser Aluminum

Smelter near Mead, Washington just north of Spokane. As he approached the stop sign at Sprague and Argonne Road, he couldn't believe this would be his fifth summer working at Kaiser.

Well, at least I had one day off after this graduation. He recalled how he had to begin his very first day at Kaiser the morning after he'd graduated from Central Valley High School in early June of 1963. An all night party at the local bowling alley followed that graduation, but he had to leave all the fun early so he'd be at Kaiser on time and alert the next morning. His buddies told him later how much fun they'd had that night: bowling, sneaking sips of booze they'd creatively procured, and gettin' all they could from the tipsy girls in their cars out in the parking lot.

As his Bug rumbled over the railroad tracks near Millwood, Bill remembered how scared he was at the beginning of his rookie summer at the plant, when the "lifers," particularly the carbon setters pushed him and the other new hires to see if they could last through the first week. The regular four man carbon setting crew would make the trainee change every other carbon anode rather than every fourth carbon as typical. This gave the crew an extra rest between their next carbon setting, and exposed the rookie to even more of the searing heat and pungent fluoride gas that roiled from the 1000 degree Celsius cryolite bath in the raised furnaces called "pots."

Each pot was a tall, narrow furnace with 12 carbon anodes secured to each side with sturdy clamps. Each of the 24 anodes consisted of a thick, heavy copper rod that was attached to a large block of carbon by an iron coupler. Atop each pot was a hopper filled with refined bauxite ore called "alumina," which was fed to the pots at designated times during all three shifts by pot men. Raised metal grates or "catwalks" between the pots allowed carbon setters to access the clamps that secured the copper rods of each anode to the pot, so the carbon blocks could be changed as they dissolved over time in the molten cryolite bath.

Until the rookies learned where to stand on the catwalk next to the exposed carbon anodes, how to efficiently use the crowbar, and when to breathe, their duration on the catwalk was very brief. In just seconds, the intense heat would cause pant legs to smoke and protective long johns worn underneath to burn legs. Even the double-soled working boots that all carbon setters wore wouldn't prevent feet from feeling like they were walking on hot sand. An ill-timed breath of the fluoride gas would constrict lungs and send a gasping worker down the three steps from the catwalk to the pot room floor below seeking the cool fresh air of the irrigated open courtyards. These extreme conditions were hard enough on an experienced worker, who'd learned all the tricks; they quickly took their toll on a green horn.

He thought of Jack Crenshaw, the cranky, no nonsense crane driver, who yelled and screamed at him and other trainees because they were too slow setting the crane's hook in the spent carbon anode rod, and too slow in releasing the hook after setting the new carbon anode into its slot in the pot's superstructure. "God damn it, release that fuckin' hook or I'll pull the carbon over the next pot and you with it!" Jack, a stocky man with short light brown hair and terribly stained teeth would continue his rampage at exhausted trainees as they walked to the break room or "waterhole" after completing the first setting, and even while they headed to the shower room at the end of a shift. Some summer hires didn't return to work the next day much to Jack's delight. "I knew that guy was a pussy!" Jack would gloat the following day.

How ironic, Bill thought to himself. *Five years ago, I was afraid of him; now I'm actually looking forward to seeing him again.*

As Bill accelerated from the four way stop at Argonne Rd and Upriver Drive, he remembered the afternoon Jack's attitude toward him changed. Bill had signed up to work a double shift after completing the second room of carbon setting on a sticky Day Shift in June, just three days into his carbon setting training. Jack was heading down to the shower room as Bill passed him heading up the alley to sign in for his double shift.

"Hey, don't you know you're headin' the wrong fucking way?"

"Yeah, I'm going to Line 4 to work a double," Bill answered tiredly, his face caked with carbon and ore dust. "It'll help pay for my tuition." Before Jack turned away and continued to the shower room, Bill noticed the slight nod and hint of a smile on Jack's lips. From that day on, Jack treated Bill with respect. Whenever Bill was assigned to Line 2 as an extra worker or "spare," Jack would even get on the foreman's case if he had assigned Bill an unreasonable work load. This was one of the reasons Bill was glad he'd be working D Shift again this summer; it was Jack's shift as well.

Bill looked forward to seeing the regulars again at the beginning of each summer. They always wanted to hear how college was going, and Bill enjoyed catching up on the Kaiser scuttlebutt since the previous summer. After brief conversations, however, it was obvious that not much had changed in their lives. He always wondered how these guys felt knowing that after just a 30-day probationary period, young whippersnappers like him would be making as much money as they were making, even though they had worked in the pot rooms for years.

After the forty-five minute drive to the large fenced parking lot at Kaiser, Bill joined the other D Shift workers walking from the parking lot to the guardhouse. He noticed how much quicker his step was compared to the other workers, whose pace seemed almost deliberately slow—as if they were attempting to delay their arrival at the guardhouse. He also noticed how thin, almost gaunt many of them looked compared to construction workers, who worked outside and typically sported muscular physiques.

After entering the exterior door of the guardhouse, he removed his time card from its 3961 slot on one side of the turnstile then inserted it into the clock. It made a loud "clunk" sound. Passing by the uniformed guards, who looked like policemen, he returned the card to another 3961 slot on the plant side of the turnstile before exiting another door that opened into a large courtyard. He remembered how nervous he was his very first shift five summers ago as he entered the large locker room filled with so many rough-looking characters. *I'm so glad I know what to expect now*, he exhaled heading to his assigned locker to dress down.

Even though well-ventilated, the locker room was steamy from the previous shift's showering. A variety of after shave and deodorant fragrances filled the moist air. These pleasant smells would be quickly replaced by a variety of gassy, pungent smelter-related odors as soon as he passed through a side door from the shower room and headed past the carbon plant to the pot rooms.

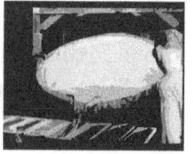

"Roberts?"

"Here!"

"Carbon setting Line 2," yelled Joe, the assigning foreman on Line 4.

Great, thought Bill has he trudged down to Line 2 in his heavy work boots. *I'll get to see Jack my first day back, and Ed Lewis, who is one of the regular Line 2 carbon setters now.* Bill had gotten to know Ed, who was a couple years older, during his third summer at Kaiser. Ed, tall and tan, liked to water ski, lie in the sun down at the river, and drink beer; so they got together periodically during the summer on their days off. Bill had shared with Ed his plan to enter the Jesuits at the end of August.

"I'll believe it when I see it," Ed had roared when Bill told him that spring. Ed was all too familiar with Bill's wild, sometimes destructive tendencies after having a few beers. Ed still gave Bill a bad time for ripping apart a picket fence in Ed's neighborhood when they came home after a keg party. Bill spent that night at Ed's. Fortunately, the resident, who had witnessed the event and recognized Ed's car, didn't call the police, but waited to call Ed the next morning. After answering the phone, Ed rousted Bill out of bed and they reinstalled all the pickets, not a pleasant task before a hangover is slept off.

"Oh shit, look who's back!" announced Jack as Bill headed to the Line 2 foreman's office. "Think you still remember how to set a fucking carbon?"

"I hope so," replied Bill shaking Jack's hand. "Just take it easy on me; I might be a little rusty."

"Bullshit! You'd better release my hook so we can finish at a decent time."

I'm sooo glad I've done this before, thought Bill as he met up with the rest of the carbon setting crew including Ed. But he knew it would take him several pots to get his timing back, and adjust to the strong magnetism that always tried to pull the crow bars and anode clamps from his hands. His biggest concern and dread was developing blisters from using the crow bar to break away the crust that formed over the molten bath, so that the new larger carbon anode could fit into its spot in the pot. He knew the blisters would pop and bleed before his hands became seasoned for the summer. This was a long, painful period because the blisters would reopen during the following shift. His sore hands looked forward to the first days off which would provide some healing time.

"Good to see ya back!" greeted Ed extending his hand. "If you start to suck gas a bit, just let me know and I'll take some of your pots," offered Ed when the rest of the crew was out of earshot.

"Thanks! I may take you up on that."

The first string of 14 pots went pretty smoothly as they were changing the Number 6 carbon anode located in the middle of the pot. He removed the heat shield to expose the Number 6 carbon, and loosened and removed the clamp that secured its copper rod to the pot. The strong magnetism always surprised Bill the first day back. When the crane's hook reached him, he inserted the hook into a hole near the top of the copper rod so

Jack could pull the anode from the pot. As soon as the spent anode was out of its hole, Bill grabbed the crow bar the other crew member had placed on the top of his pot, enlarged the hole for the new, larger anode, banged the tip of the crowbar against the pot to knock off any hot bath still attached, and placed the crow bar on top of the next pot away from the anode's exit. When Jack brought the new carbon anode to him, Bill guided its rod into the Number 6 slot, slammed the clamp home and simultaneously released the crane's hook for the next crew member.

"Not too bad for your first day back—a bit slow, but not too bad," yelled Jack from the cabin of his crane as his hands quickly moved between the three crane levers.

The crew's smooth pace continued into the next string of 14 pots until Bill's first "burn off." The copper rod attached to the carbon anode swung wildly when the crane's hook pulled it away from the carbon "butt" that sank quickly below the surface of the molten bath. *Aw fuck!* Bill thought to himself, moving his blue bandana over his nose to protect his face from the searing heat. He knew he had seconds to pry the butt to the bubbling orange surface with the crow bar so the crew could grab it with the large tongs and toss it down the three steps to the main floor. If his first couple of efforts to locate the butt failed, he'd have to head for the open courtyard to cool off and catch his breath, and this would hold the crew up. Fortunately, this butt had stayed in one piece, and Bill was able to pry it to the surface. *Whew!* sighed Bill relieved, as Ed grabbed the butt with the tongs, pulled it down the catwalk and flung it to the floor below the steps.

"I'll get your next pot," offered Ed noticing Bill standing near the open courtyard and filling his lungs with cool fresh air. "It takes awhile to get used to this shit again."

"Hey you lucked out; I'll see if I can find you another one," yelled Jack from the crane.

"Oh, that's okay," replied Bill looking up at Jack, who was concentrating on removing the carbon in the next pot. *How can he move the crane in so many directions at the same time* with *those three levers?* wondered Bill in amazement.

—⁓—

"Well, you should be graduated about now, shouldn't you?" asked Jack after climbing down the ladder from his crane and catching up to Bill and the rest of the crew heading to the waterhole after completing the first room's carbon settings.

"Yep. Graduated just last Saturday."

"Well, what the fuck are you doin' out here again then? Don't tell me after goin' to college for four fuckin' years, you're gonna work out here for the rest of your life!"

"No, this is my last summer; just need to pay off my college loan."

That seemed to satisfy Jack, who nodded then looked at him sideways. "Hey, is it true you're goin' into a seminary to become a priest!?"

Bill knew right away that Ed must have shared this with Jack.

"Yeah…at the end of August. Don't know how long I'll last, but want to give it a try," added Bill grabbing his lunch sack from the shelf above the table in the waterhole.

"Well, if that's what you really want to do…no way I could fuckin' do somethin' like that," mumbled Jack chewing on a mouthful of baloney sandwich.

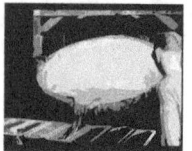

Heading into the last semester of his senior year at Gonzaga University, Bill was still clueless about what he wanted to do after graduation. He had no desire to enroll in law school like some of his buddies had, and he did not want to go to Viet Nam like other classmates who had joined ROTC. Not knowing what he wanted to do, and not having a job lined up after graduation made Bill feel very directionless and anxious.

During this semester, he got into the habit of attending the noon Mass in the student chapel. He enjoyed the Jesuits' stimulating homilies and the sense of community among the students who regularly attended. He was also hoping God would answer his prayers and help him decide what he wanted to do after graduation.

Between classes, he would often duck into St. Al's Catholic Church and make a short visit. He loved the stained glass windows, the faint smell of incense and the peaceful feeling he experienced when he was there. After kneeling and making the sign of the cross, he would briefly pray before heading to class or to the library to study. *Lord, please help me know what I want to do after graduation.*

During his last semester, he had also gotten to know a young Jesuit priest, Fr. Eric, who was teaching a philosophy course that Bill was taking. Fr. Eric had graduated from Santa

Clara University, a Jesuit college in California before he entered the Society of Jesus, a religious order founded by St. Ignatius of Loyola in 1539. Sometimes after class, Bill would hang around and chat with Fr. Eric, who as Bill discovered enjoyed many of the same things Bill did like running, hiking, skiing, writing, teaching and coaching.

"My life in the Jesuits provides me opportunities to do all the things I love to do," Eric mentioned to Bill in one of their chats.

—⁓—

"Want to go to lunch with me?" offered Bill after class one day.

"Sure! You buyin'?" kidded Eric.

"Did you know what you wanted to do by the time you graduated from college?" asked Bill as they walked to the commons area.

"No, not really. During my last couple of years at Santa Clara, I felt some attraction to the Jesuits and their lifestyle, but I wasn't really sure. I still felt this attraction near the end of my senior year, so I decided to apply to the California Province of the Society of Jesus. It really wasn't until I completed the Spiritual Exercises of St. Ignatius during the thirty day retreat while at the Novitiate that I decided the Jesuits were for me. What about you? What do you want to do after graduation?"

"Well…I really don't know," replied Bill picking up a lunch tray and handing it to Eric. "And I feel like I should know by now. All my friends have something lined up after graduation so I'm really feeling like I didn't plan or focus properly during college," added Bill paying for their lunches. "This one's on me."

"Thank you, Bill! Looks like a spot over there," nodded Eric. "Well, maybe God is calling you to do something you haven't even thought of yet. You know...the Spiritual Exercises you go through in the Novitiate are designed to help you clarify what you want to do with your life; to clarify what will make you happy in life. They're not just designed to help you decide if you want to be a Jesuit."

Bill and Eric continued their visits periodically after classes that semester, and Eric's explanation of how the long retreat during the early phase of his Novitiate had helped him decide what he wanted to do with his life after graduation began to resonate with Bill.

"Hey, want to come to lunch with me at Jesuit House?" asked Eric one day after class the following week. "It's on me this time, and it'll give you a chance to see where I live, and a glimpse of life in a Jesuit Community."

"Sure...but am I dressed okay?" asked Bill glancing down at his Carroll College letterman's jacket that he had earned his freshman year as a football player at the Montana College in Helena.

"No problem; we're not real formal at lunch."

Bill was impressed with how friendly most of the Jesuit priests were to him, and at how happy they all seemed. Lots of laughter and comradeship. After lunch, Eric showed Bill the beautiful Jesuit House chapel, the centerpiece of the Jesuit House residence. He also showed Bill his living quarters, a very small room furnished with only a twin bed and desk. Some framed photographs and a wood crucifix painted black and framed in sterling silver hung on the off-white cinderblock walls.

"This must be your family," guessed Bill looking at the photos.

"Yes, that's my mom and dad and my younger brother, John."

Then Bill moved closer to the crucifix. "This is really a unique crucifix."

"Yes, every Jesuit novice is presented with one of these crucifixes by the Provincial after professing his first vows of poverty, chastity and obedience. This marks the end of the two year Novitiate formation."

Eric noticed Bill scanning the rest of his small room, and could tell Bill wasn't impressed by its small size. "I don't really need that big of a room. I can access almost any room on campus if I need more working space, and I'm close to the library or gym," pointed out Eric.

After class one day in late February, Bill asked Eric if he would like to have dinner with him and his family on Sunday afternoon.

"Sure; I'd love to meet your family. Just give me directions and tell me what time."

—⟋⟍⟍—

Rachel was in heaven on Sunday. Having a young priest in her home for dinner, especially a Jesuit priest, whom Bill had invited was the ultimate for her. Bill's dad, Howard asked a few questions but was his usual quiet, reserved self. Bill's younger brothers were polite but quickly excused themselves after dinner so the older folks could visit. Rachel wanted to know all about Fr. Eric's family, where they had lived, where he'd gone to school, and what inspired him to enter the Jesuits.

"Well, I attended a Jesuit high school and university so the Jesuits had a significant influence on me. When I was at Santa Clara, their lifestyle of scholarship, teaching, coaching and performing priestly duties attracted me, and I didn't really have any strong attractions to other professional fields. So, during my senior year of college, I decided to see if I truly was being called by God to be a Jesuit priest."

Rachel looked at Bill. "Sounds a lot like what Bill has expressed to us this past year, and I've always just had a feeling that Bill would be a priest," added Rachel finishing her coffee and returning her cup to its saucer.

"Well, it's a big decision, and one that only Bill can make," emphasized Eric looking directly at Rachel; then at Bill. Eric glanced at the clock on the fireplace mantel. "Oh, I need to head back to GU." He rose from the couch and shook Rachel's and Howard's hands. "Thank you so much for the delicious dinner and wonderful visit, and thanks again for inviting me, Bill."

As Eric turned and headed for the front door, he noticed the thick wood crucifix hanging on the hallway wall. "That looks like a crucifix my folks have; is that a Last Rites crucifix?"

"Yes, it is," replied Rachel proudly. She removed it from the wall and laid it on the coffee table. She then slid the front section of the cross upward revealing two short candles, a small bottle of holy water, a purifier cloth and cotton ball. She placed the two candles in the small holes located at each end of the cross piece that had been bored out to hold them. "I'm sure as a priest, you would know how to use it," added Rachel.

"Yes," replied, Eric. "The responding priest would sprinkle the holy water on the sick or dying person. He would use the cotton ball to administer holy oil, and use the purifier to wash his hands prior to administering communion to the person. It's a good idea for Catholic families to have one of these…but hopefully you'll never have to use it," added Eric looking at Rachel. "Thanks again for dinner; see you in class, Bill."

"He seems like such a happy, nice young priest," offered Rachel after Fr. Eric left.

"Yeah, I've really enjoyed getting to know him this semester," Bill replied. "It's amazing how many interests we have in common."

—⟋⟍—

Going through the Spiritual Exercises at the Novitiate might be exactly what I need, thought Bill the following week while commuting back and forth to classes. So on Friday of that week when he had the opportunity to talk with Eric after class, Bill asked him what he'd have to do to enter the Jesuits.

Eric smiled broadly at Bill. "Well, just fill out some paperwork. When I applied, I had to complete a formal application, write a spiritual autobiography, participate in several interviews, submit a few references, my academic transcripts and sacramental records...I think that was about it. Then all these materials are presented to the Provincial, who makes the final decision regarding your admission to the Jesuit Novitiate. Since you're from Washington State, you'd apply to the Oregon Province. If you'd like, I can put you in touch with Fr. Wells here on campus, who works with Jesuit applicants."

"Yes, I'd like that, Eric; that would be helpful."

Over the next few weeks, Bill acquired and completed the application requirements with Fr. Wells's help, and he received an acceptance letter from the Oregon Province in early May three weeks before graduation.

"Congratulations, Bill! I'm so happy for you," responded Eric when Bill shared his good news after class. He gave Bill a big hug. "I'm confident your Novitiate experience will help you decide what you want to do with your life. I'll be on campus most of the summer so if you have any questions or want to get together and talk just call me," added Eric.

Deciding to enter the Jesuit Novitiate and receiving official acceptance brought Bill great relief and peace of mind. His step was much lighter now and he seemed happier than he'd been in a long time. He still attended the noon Masses in the student chapel and made short visits to St. Al's church between classes. *Thank you, Lord for hearing my prayers and for leading me to this decision.*

Rachel was thrilled of course, and enjoyed telling all her Catholic friends that Bill was going to be a Jesuit priest.

Now that he'd made this big decision and had started his last summer at Kaiser, he just wanted to enjoy this summer as much as possible, for he knew that the lifestyle and freedoms he was used to would drastically change on August 29 when he reported to the Jesuit Novitiate in Sheridan, Oregon.

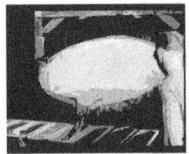

"Jerry Hendricks called earlier and wants you to call him back," informed Bill's mom as he emerged from the basement at 2 PM after sleeping off a Graveyard Shift.

"Thanks, Mom," he replied yawning. "I'll call him back later."

Bill was a starter on his high school football team and a star sprinter on the track team, so was pretty well known around school and had lots of popular friends. But he was also aware of and sensitive to classmates who seemed to be alone, and Jerry Hendricks was one of those students. Short in stature but stocky, Jerry always kept pretty much to himself. He was very quiet, almost shy, and when he did talk, he spoke in a very quiet, soft, monotone voice. Bill's locker had been next to Jerry's during their senior year in high school so Bill always made a point to say hi to Jerry between classes and in the hallways. A soft "hi" was the only response Bill usually received from Jerry.

Jerry was going steady with Sandy Frye, who was also very short—almost dwarf-sized.

However, unlike Jerry, Sandy was very outgoing and greeted everyone with her beautiful smile. Many in the senior class including Bill thought they were perfect for one another and had no doubts they would marry after graduation.

At the end of a school day in mid-April when Bill was at his locker, Jerry arrived at his locker and began to work his combination. "Are you gonna be free on Saturday, May 18?" asked Jerry quietly.

"Ah...I think so," replied Bill.

"Wanna be my best man?"

Bill looked at Jerry as if in shock. "You're getting married in May? Next month!?"

"Yep. To Sandy. Would you be willing to be my best man?" Jerry asked again in his typical monotone voice.

"Yes...of course," replied Bill still stunned but wanting to be supportive. "Just let me know the time and place, I'll be there."

Jerry smiled slightly and closed his locker. "Great. Thanks, I'll keep ya posted." Then he turned and sauntered down the hallway.

Even before school let out at the end of May, it was pretty clear that Jerry and Sandy had to get married. Sandy, who was beginning to show didn't bother to finish her senior year.

"I just got tired of using a rubber," admitted Jerry in his very matter-of-fact voice one day when Bill and he were chatting. "It was a hassle to put it on every time, and it felt so much better without one. Nothin' happened for a long time so we just kept screwin'. Then one day, Sandy told me she was pregnant."

This reminded Bill of what his brother Rod had told him once when he came home from college for the holidays. *Using a rubber is like wearing a glove. Screwin' feels so much better without one.*

"What did her parents say?" asked Bill, knowing that Jerry's folks could probably care less and wanted Jerry out of their home sooner rather than later.

"Oh, not much; they pretty much knew we were going to get married in the near future anyway."

—⟋⟍⟍—

About 3:00 PM, Bill returned Jerry's call from the downstair's phone. "Hi, Jerry, this is Bill; my mom said you called earlier when I was sleeping."

"Yeah, long time no see," greeted Jerry in his quiet voice.

"I know, I started working at Kaiser again a couple weeks ago."

"Your mom said you're on Graveyard Shift this week. Why don't you come by for a BBQ this evening before heading out to work? One of Sandy's friends from work is comin' over; says she remembers you from high school. We're gonna start about 6:30."

"Hmm…what's her name?"

"Barb Scott. She was two years behind us at CV. You probably remember her older sister, Teri."

"Yeah, she wasn't bad! Does she look like her sister?"

"Well, you can see for yourself tonight."

"Okay…meeting any girl this summer sounds good to me! See ya…I guess in just a few hours. Sorry; I'm still a bit rummy from Graveyard. Bye."

"I won't be here for dinner tonight, Mom. Jerry and Sandy are having a BBQ at their place and invited me to come over. I'll head out to work from their place."

"Okay, say hi to Jerry and Sandy for me. There are some eggs in the fridge if you want breakfast or there's sandwich stuff if you want lunch. I'm headed to the grocery store."

Coffee cup in hand, Bill headed down to his room to dig out his high school annual. *So she was a sophomore the year I was a senior,* he thought finding the sophomore class section. *Yep, there she is. She does look a lot like her sister—pretty good looking. And sophomore pictures aren't usually very flattering.*

—⟋⟍—

About 5:30 PM, Bill hopped in the downstair's shower to get ready for the BBQ. *It'll be fun to see Jerry and Sandy and to meet Barb,* he thought rinsing off. After drying off, he moistened his face, sprayed some *Barbasol* shaving cream into his left palm and dabbled it evenly to his face with his right hand. He began removing his two day's growth with his Gillette safety razor. *Better take my time; don't want any nasty nicks tonight.* After rinsing and drying his face, he looked at himself from different angles in the mirror making sure he looked okay. He applied *Old Spice* stick deodorant under his arms, then sprinkled some Avon *Oland* cologne in his left palm, rubbed his hands together and applied some to his face, chest and arms. His mom, who had tried her hand at selling Avon products the previous year, had given him the cologne for Christmas. He liked the smell and liked the unique bottle, which was shaped like an old Packard Roadster.

After brushing his teeth, he pulled on some underpants, a white t-shirt and his cutoff jeans; then stepped into his sandals. He returned to the bathroom to brush his short brown hair and gave himself one final check. *Well, let's see what happens,* he thought heading upstairs to grab his lunch and clean work clothes.

—⟋⟍—

"Bill, Hi! Good to see you," smiled Sandy giving him a hug. She then led him toward an attractive, dark haired girl standing nearby. "I'd like you to meet Barb Scott. Barb graduated from Central Valley a couple years after our class."

"Nice to meet you, Barb," replied Bill extending his hand.

Shaking his hand lightly, she smiled at him; her dark brown eyes looked into his deep blue eyes.

"Well, I'll let you two get to know one another a bit. Beer's in the cooler; hamburgers will be ready in about a half hour."

"You have to be Teri's sister; you look a lot like her."

"Yes, I'm Teri's sister. Everyone says we look alike," replied Barb taking a sip of beer from her tall-necked Bud. "Do you want to get a beer?"

"Yes!" replied Bill heading for the cooler.

"I remember you were quite the football player, and sprinter on the track team."

"Oh thanks; seems like a long time ago now," responded Bill removing the cap from his bottle with a nearby church key.

Bill liked the way one of Barb's cheeks dimpled when she smiled, and her dark shoulder-length hair was very attractive. He liked the way her tight shirt presented her breasts, and how the tattered cutoff jeans displayed her smooth, tan legs. Barb almost looked as if she could have some Indian blood in her. Bill had always been attracted to tan girls—perhaps because his light complexion didn't allow him to get very tan. During the summer months, he often wished he hadn't inherited his mom's light skin tone and strawberry blond hair.

The beer relaxed both of them as they talked a bit about high school; then about their jobs.

"Kaiser—that's a pretty good job isn't it?" she asked.

"It's been pretty good to me. It's allowed me to finish college, but at the same time, it's inspired me to complete college so I don't get stuck out there for the rest of my life. The rotating shifts and the unhealthy working conditions really take a toll on your health."

"I know what you mean about getting stuck in a job," Barb replied glancing downward. "I couldn't afford to go to college, so I went to work for J.C. Penney right after high school, and I think I'm probably stuck there for the duration," she added without enthusiasm. She looked back up at Bill and smiled as if wanting to change topics. "Sandy said you recently graduated from Gonzaga U—congratulations!"

"Thank you," replied Bill. "It's a good feeling to be done."

Bill and Barb visited with Jerry and Sandy and other guests, but they mostly visited with one another throughout the evening. Bill found Barb very attractive and easy to be with.

"Oh my gosh, it's almost 10:00," Bill suddenly announced looking at his watch. "I have to head to Kaiser. I'll have a couple of days off starting Friday; would you like to go out this weekend?"

"I'd love to!" she responded gently touching his left forearm with her right hand, and flashing a quick smiled into his blue eyes. Then finding a pen in the kitchen, she secured his right hand, turned it palm upward and wrote her phone number on his palm. "Don't work too hard," she said in a sexy kind of way, smiling at him.

"Thanks for inviting me, Jerry," said Bill as he walked toward his car. "Wish I didn't have to go," he added looking back toward Barb. "Tell Sandy thanks for introducing me to her—she's really good-looking!"

"We thought you'd like her," grinned Jerry.

Bill turned on his interior light several times on his drive to Kaiser in order to memorize her phone number. Knowing he would see her again soon made the drive to this Graveyard Shift almost pleasant.

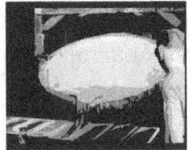

"Bob and Mary Ann are coming over about 6:00 for dinner tonight," his mom mentioned to Bill when he came upstairs on Friday about 3:00 PM. "They'd sure love to see you and visit for a bit before you leave in August."

"Oh, I'd like to see them too, but I'm going out tonight."

"Ohh, they'll be disappointed. Can you stay long enough to at least say hi?"

"Yes," he assured standing at the top of the stairs in the hallway, "but I need to leave by 6:15."

He nervously dialed Barb's number from the downstairs phone at 5:45 knowing that she got off work at 5:00. He wasn't sure why he always got so nervous about calling girls because he liked talking to them. He was fine once they started talking; it was just getting up the nerve to call. Perhaps it was the chance they wouldn't want to talk or would say, "no" to a date.

"Hello."

"Hi, Barb, this is Bill Roberts," he announced nervously twisting the phone cord around the index finger of his left hand.

"Hi! I was wondering if you were going to call."

"Well, I wanted to give you time to get home. I was wondering…if you don't already have plans would you like to go out tonight?"

"Yes! What did you have in mind?"

"Well, how about getting something to eat at Ron's about 7:00, hangin' out there for a bit; then we can head to the Drive-in to see *Bonnie & Clyde*. The show starts at 8:45."

"Sounds good; I've wanted to see *Bonnie & Clyde*. Let me give you directions to my apartment."

He excitedly wrote down the directions on a notepad by the phone. "Okay, thanks! I'll be there about 6:45. Bye." He headed for his downstair's bathroom to shower, shave, apply deodorant and slap on some *Oland* cologne. He wore a white t-shirt, jeans and white low cut Converse tennis shoes. *Think I'll take a light jacket just in case it gets cool*, he thought grabbing his blue cotton jacket from the closet. Taking one last look at himself in the bathroom mirror, he turned out the light and headed upstairs to say hi to Bob and Mary Ann before leaving.

"So nice to see you," greeted Mary Ann giving Bill a big hug in the living room where she, Bob and his folks were enjoying a cocktail.

"And congratulations on your decision to enter the Jesuits in August," added Bob with a big smile enthusiastically shaking Bill's hand.

"Thanks, Bob. Nice to see you guys. I'm sorry I can't stay longer and visit tonight, but I'm meeting some friends shortly."

"That's okay; we understand," replied Bob.

"Please tell Chris hi for me," said Bill heading for the front door.

"We will," answered Mary Ann.

Bob and Mary Ann were long time friends of his parents and devout Catholics. They had one son, Christopher, who was the same age as Bill, but Chris was extremely aloof and he and Bill just never developed a close friendship.

—ɯ—

Barb's apartment was on the second floor of a two story complex just a few blocks off Sprague about eight miles west of his parents' house. After parking his Bug, he walked up the stairs and nervously knocked on her door.

"Hi!" she said greeting Bill with a big smile.

"Hi! Wow, you look very nice!" Her dark brown hair was striking against the tight red v-neck shirt. He was glad to see her wearing cutoff jeans again tonight; sexy leather sandals completed her outfit.

"Let me grab my purse and a sweater and I'll be ready to go."

Ron's was the local hangout for students and graduates of Central Valley H.S. The hamburgers were good, and you could get a hamburger, fries and shake for 55 cents. It was a good place to catch up on the latest gossip, and admire the hottest cars in the Valley. Of course, guys also loved to show off a good-looking chick sitting close to them.

When Bill went inside to order, he spotted Tom Stevens, a fellow '63 graduate and football teammate.

"Hey, Bill, when did you start dating Barb Scott?" asked Tom looking out at Bill's car.

"This is actually our first date. Jerry and Sandy Hendricks introduced me to her just this week."

"Well, if she's anything like her older sister, you're in for a gooood time!?"

Bill paused briefly as he tucked this comment away. "Well, I hope so. We're headed to see *Bonnie & Clyde* at the drive-in; maybe I'll find out tonight!?"

When Bill returned to the car with their order, he asked Barb if she knew Tom Stevens.

"Yeah," she replied unenthusiastically. "He used to date my older sister. She said he was kind of a jerk."

"Really?"

"Yeah. She really liked him at first, but about the time they were seeing each other pretty regularly, he just suddenly stopped calling her. She was pretty upset at the time, but figured out he was interested in pretty much one thing."

"Hmmm," replied Bill handing Barb her hamburger and chocolate shake. He then unwrapped the first of the two hamburgers he had ordered for himself. They chatted about different classmates they knew while at CV as they finished their hamburgers and fries. Still working on their chocolate shakes, Bill started his Bug and headed west for the outdoor drive-in.

After Bill paid for their theatre tickets, he parked in one of the rows near the back, remembering what Tom had said about Barb's sister. He didn't want to park up close to the screen and be near families, who could hinder any action that might come his way.

"How's this?" he asked.

"Good! I'll toss our garbage on the way to the lady's room; I have to go freshen up a bit."

"Sounds good," he replied taking this opportunity to pop a stick of spearmint gum into his mouth to dilute the onion taste. As he waited for Barb to return, he thought more about Tom's comment about Barb's sister, and about Teri's assessment of Tom. *Probably pretty accurate,* thought Bill knowing Tom. *Will be interesting to see how my relationship with Barb goes.*

When Barb returned to the car, he could tell she had put on some more perfume; she smelled great. She was also chewing some gum probably for the same reason he was.

"I'm glad you called," she said smiling into his eyes as she had done at the BBQ.

"Yeah? I was looking forward to seeing you again too...and I have two full days off."

"Well...we'll have to make the best of that," she said, moving her face closer to his and lowering her eyes to his lips. He took advantage of this invitation to kiss her. He was glad the opportunity came so quickly, as it typically took him a long time to find the right moment with a new date. Her lips were so soft and full, unlike the last girl he had kissed, who had such thin, dry lips. He just hadn't been able to find the right way to kiss that girl.

"You kiss so nicely," he whispered when their lips parted.

"You do too," she answered not moving too far away from his lips. She approached his lips again this time touching his left cheek with her right hand as she caressed his lips with hers. Her kisses made him feel so warm inside, and so hard. The evening was off to a great start, and the movie hadn't even started yet.

But, *Bonnie & Clyde* was an action-packed movie; so much so, that there really wasn't another opportunity to resume the wonderful kissing that had been initiated before the movie began. Barb had continued to hold his hand throughout the movie.

The violent ending caused them both to watch the credits in silence for a bit.

"Man...did that actually happen to Bonnie and Clyde?" asked Barb still a bit stunned.

"Yes. I saw a picture of them one time after they were ambushed—I think it was in *Life* magazine, and they were pretty riddled." Bill rolled down his window and hooked the speaker to its pole.

As his Bug slowly edged toward the exit, Bill glanced at his watch; it was about 11:00.

"I'm not ready to go home yet are you?" she asked after seeing Bill check his watch.

"Me neither. I know a good place where we can park and talk about the movie a bit," offered Bill.

"Let's go," she replied smiling.

Barb continued to talk about the movie as they drove, but Bill's desire to kiss her soft lips again distracted him, and made his cock hard.

He pulled into a wooded area about a mile from his parents' place, and shut off the engine. He turned toward her and this time she put both hands on the sides of his face and worked her lips more aggressively against his. This kiss lasted longer than the others. He wondered how she'd react if he moved his left hand from her shoulder to her ribs. As he did so, she moved closer and taller into him, as if inviting him to touch her breast. When he moved his hand closer to her right breast, her lips hesitated and she moved slowly away from him.

"Sorry," he apologized.

She smiled at him, as if to say, it's okay, but just not so fast. They used this break to talk a bit more about the movie, and when they noticed it was approaching midnight, they agreed they should call it a night.

"I really enjoyed tonight, Bill. Will you call me again?"

"Yes, how about tomorrow!? There's a group getting together down at the river about 8:30 tomorrow evening, want to go?"

"I'd love to."

On the drive back to Barb's, she sat as close to him as she could with her left hand on his right thigh. Before stepping inside her door, she approached his lips and kissed him tenderly as if to say thanks, and to make sure he wouldn't forget how wonderfully she could kiss.

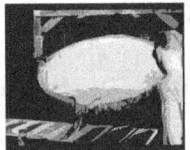

"Bob and Mary Ann were glad they got to see you but sorry they didn't get more time to visit with you last night," his mom emphasized as Bill poured himself a cup of coffee the next morning. "Your dad and I sure hope that we'll get to spend some time with you on your days off this summer. Summer always goes by so fast, and after August..." She stopped mid-sentence as if she didn't want to think about him no longer living at home. After an awkward moment of silence she asked, "How was last night?"

"Great! *Bonnie & Clyde* is really good; you and Dad should go see it."

"Who did you go with?"

"Jerry and Sandy and a girl that was a couple of years behind me at CV," lied Bill. "She's a friend of Sandy's."

"I hope you're not going to get serious about a girl now, just a couple months before you enter the Novitiate!" his mom stated looking at him sternly.

"Don't worry, Mom. I just had a chance to see this movie with some friends," he replied filling his cereal bowl with Cheerios.

Bill knew that his mom deep down always hoped he would become a priest. She had never come right out and said so, but her comments to him and her friends throughout elementary school at St. Charles, and his first two years of high school at

Gonzaga Prep made it pretty obvious to him.

At the end of his eighth grade year at St. Charles, a priest from the diocesan seminary in Spokane had come to their house to talk with Bill about enrolling in the seminary. Bill didn't really want to enter the seminary at that time, but didn't want to disappoint his mom either. His dad made the decision easy when he told the priest that eighth grade was just too young for a boy to make that type of commitment.

The following school year as a freshman in high school, Bill carpooled from the Spokane Valley to Gonzaga Prep, where he also played football. However, at the beginning of his sophomore year, he turned out for football at CV, as it was close to where he lived and that's where he really wanted to go. Bill's decision to do so greatly worried Rachel, who thought his leaving Prep would have all kinds of negative impacts on his life. She was convinced he'd start chasing girls like Rod did when he transferred to CV, and that Bill would lose all interest in becoming a priest.

While he was at football practice, his mom called one of the coaches at Gonzaga Prep, who told her that if Bill turned out at Prep for the afternoon practice, he would still be eligible to play at Prep that school year. After hanging up, his mom drove to CV and actually came out onto the field during the first practice, and told the coaches to get him "because he was going to Gonzaga!" Bill remembered how incredibly embarrassed he was, but in this public setting in front of coaches and players, he couldn't do much about it except ask his mom how she could do such a thing to him. She promised him on the drive into Prep that if he still wanted to go to CV for his junior and senior years, he could do so.

Rachel attempted yet again now to find out more about the girl Bill was with at last night's movie but gave up when Bill put his breakfast dishes in the dishwasher and headed down-stairs to his room. He decided to wash his car, which had gotten dusty last night on the dirt road where he and Barb had parked. Afterward, he lay in the sun in the backyard and kept thinking about Barb's soft lips on his; her gentle touch on his face, her tan legs. He analyzed her mild reaction when he moved his hand toward her breast, and thought about what he would do differently next time. Thinking of last night made him hard, and when his mom came outside to hang laundry on the clothesline, he rolled onto his stomach so she wouldn't notice the bulge in his swimsuit.

When he went in to shower, a strong urge to masturbate came over him. Thinking about Barb really had his juices flowing. But having been raised Catholic, he believed mas-turbation was a mortal sin, so he resisted the temptation to do so. Some of his non-Catholic buddies talked about how they would masturbate before they went out on a hot date so they wouldn't "cream their jeans" when making out.

At 6:00 PM he called Barb to finalize their date. "How was work today?" he asked.

"Not bad, but I kept thinking about you; I'm really looking forward to seeing you tonight."

"Me too!" he replied excitedly. "I'll pick you up about 8:00."

"What's on for tonight?" asked Howard looking up from his newspaper when Bill came up the stairs. Howard, a short, dark haired, handsome man of 51 kept pretty much to himself, and didn't like to get involved in confrontations unless he had to or Rachel insisted he do so.

"Not much; there's a get together at the river this evening, so I'm going to hit that for awhile."

"Do you have a date?" his dad probed.

Bill could tell his mom had talked to Howard about his date last night. "No…just meeting some friends there." Bill knew if he said, "yes" he'd have to answer more questions, and listen to a lecture about how dating at this point could compromise the important decision and commitment he had made to enter the Jesuit Novitiate in August.

Satisfied that he had asked the question that was on Rachel's mind, Howard resumed reading the newspaper.

"Have a good evening," wished Bill before heading out to his car. *Whew, that was close,* he thought flipping a U-turn in the street to head west toward Barb's.

—m—

Barb looked fabulous when she opened her door and invited him in. Her dark hair fell neatly onto her shoulders, her lipstick was so red, and the top two buttons of her paisley blouse were invitingly unbuttoned.

"Would you like to see my apartment?"

"Yes," replied Bill admiring her shapely apple butt when she turned around in her cutoff jeans. "It's really nice," he said though actually thinking how small the apartment was.

"It's not too bad. It's kind of small, and hot in the summer," she added fanning herself with her hand. "But it's okay for me." She showed him her small kitchen; then led him down a short hallway where the bathroom and her bedroom were. He made note of her twin-sized bed and wondered if he would lie in it with her at some point.

"Are you hungry?" he asked as they headed to his car.

"No, I just had something to eat."

"I picked up some cold Bud for the party on the way over."

"Great, that really sounds good after such a hot day."

Bill opened and closed the car door for her, and after he closed his door, she put her left hand on his right thigh, just as she had done last night.

Doesn't appear she's upset over my move last night.

When they arrived at the river, several cars were already there, and a crackling fire on the beach sent embers dancing skyward. He was glad to see Jerry and Sandy there, as they would help Barb feel more at ease. He introduced Barb to other friends who were there; then cracked open two cold Budweisers handing one to Barb.

Bill loved spending these warm summer evenings at the river with friends and drinking beer. He liked the taste of beer and liked how it relaxed him and helped him have a good time. He noticed that Barb was kind of the same way—she seemed to get chattier and more relaxed the more beer she drank.

About 10:30, it started to cool off and everyone moved closer to the fire to enjoy its warmth. Bill went to his car and brought Barb a blanket, which she eagerly shared with him. Sitting on a log snuggled together wrapped in the blanket, he placed his left hand on her right leg—it was so warm and smooth. As he lightly touched it, she nuzzled even closer to him. He could see the little dimple in her cheek when she smiled at him, and could tell she was enjoying herself.

When the beer was gone and folks began to leave, she turned to him and said, "Let's stay here awhile."

"Hey, Bill," shouted Sandy as she and Jerry walked to their

car. "Looks like you're the last ones here; will you put out the fire?"

"Got it; see ya later," assured Bill waving.

When the last car cleared the top of the gravel road that came down to the beach, it suddenly seemed eerily quiet. Bill and Barb both stared at the flames enjoying their hypnotic effect as well as the crackling sounds of the fire. To their left, the Spokane River glided by them.

"Sometime, it would be neat to sleep down here," Barb suggested.

"Yeah? You wouldn't be scared?"

"No—not if I'm with you."

He loosened the blanket so he could turn toward her, looked into her eyes, then to her lips and kissed her. He was so glad to be with her again; he had thought about her all day long.

After several long kisses, he said, "I don't know about you, but my butt's getting sore from sitting on this log. Let's move back to the car. If you get the blanket, I'll douse the fire." When he stood up to get some water from the river, he could tell he was pretty buzzed, and wondered if she was as well.

"Whoa, I'm feeling pretty good," she giggled, as she stood up and started to shake out the blanket. Bill filled two empty beer bottles with river water and poured them on the embers. He stirred them up just to make sure they were out, gathered up the rest of their beer bottles and headed back to his car with Barb. She held on to his right arm for stability then got in the car; Bill put the empties in his trunk.

When he closed his car door, she was facing him with her back against her door. "Come here," she invited looking at him with her dark eyes.

As he leaned toward her, she pulled him to her and kissed him. As she did so his left hand accidentally landed on her right breast, but the way she leaned into him assured him that this was okay tonight. As he explored its roundness and soft-ness, she made muffled little moans, as if to express how much she was enjoying his hand.

After a few minutes, she moved slightly away from him and looked into his eyes. "Would you like to really feel my breasts?" Seeing his nods, she unbuttoned a few more buttons of her blouse, and pulled him back to her.

Things were moving faster than he was used to with a girl on a second date, but he was so excited and anxious. He put his left hand on her breast which was now covered only by her bra. It was firm yet soft and warm. As she kissed him again, she thrust her torso towards him and moved so his hand moved on her breast. Her movements with the help of his hand soon worked her bra upward until her breast was bare in his hand. When his hand touched her rigid nipple, she gasped and moaned more deeply. Breathing heavily, she backed away slightly, finished unbuttoning her blouse and reached behind her back to unhook her bra. "There, that's better!" she sighed.

Instead of kissing him again, she leaned back against the door and watched what he would do next. The faint moonlight coming through the front window, revealed both her full, firm light-colored breasts and their dark nipples. For a moment, he admired them like a kid seeing something amazing for the first time. Then he slowly and gently placed both his hands on her breasts, softly caressing them. Leaning against her door with her eyes closed, she expressed her pleasure with hushed moans.

"Would you like to kiss them?" she asked softly.

"Yes," he answered with nervous excitement. When he moved, he could feel the wet spot in his shorts.

She placed both her hands in back of his head and guided him slowly toward her breasts. He kissed the top of her left breast first; then kissed around her nipple. She guided his face toward her nipple and when he placed it in his mouth and moved his tongue against it, she writhed wildly and gasped. When she couldn't stand it any longer, she moved him to her right breast. This time he started on the inside of her breast; then kissed underneath her nipple. Within seconds, her right nipple was in his mouth, his tongue moving against it. Again, she writhed against him and moaned with pleasure.

When she couldn't stand it any longer, she pushed him away, and still panting refastened her bra and buttoned up her blouse.

"What time is it?" she asked.

"About 12:45."

"I should probably get home; 7:00 AM is going to come way too early. I have to work the early shift tomorrow."

Both were still a bit buzzed from the beer, as they drove down the gravel road, rocks clanking against the undercarriage.

"Sorry, if I got a little too aggressive," Bill offered apologetically.

"Did I act like I was upset with you?" Barb replied looking over at him. "Do you start Day Shift tomorrow?"

"Yes; so I'll probably be able to see you at least a couple nights this week if that's okay."

"Well, I guess that's okay," she responded in an exaggerated tone.

When he walked her to her apartment door, she put her arms around his neck and looked up into his eyes. "I really enjoyed tonight, Bill; I know I'm going to have very pleasant dreams!"

"Me too," Bill smiled. He kissed her soft lips then quietly wished her good night.

—ɯ—

"What time did you get in last night?" his mom asked when he came upstairs about 6:30 AM.

"Oh about 1:00," he fudged. It had actually been closer to 1:30.

"Wow, pretty late the night before a Day Shift! Maybe this week we'll have some time to talk about what you need to purchase for the Novitiate. August will be here before you know it."

"I know!" he replied politely but trying not to think that far ahead.

—ɯ—

"Hi, hope you don't mind me coming by after work," said Bill stepping into Barb's apartment the next afternoon.

"Mind? I thought about you all day." She was wearing a t-shirt, shorts and no shoes.

"Yeah? How do you mean?"

"Well…you know…about how you made me feel last night," she replied grinning up at him.

"Well, I certainly enjoyed making you feel that way," he smiled looking into her eyes.

"So…you think I'll let you do that again?" she asked flirting with him.

"I hope so," he responded eagerly. He bent down and kissed her.

"Well, unfortunately you won't be able to tonight; my sister and mom are coming over in a bit. Want to stick around and meet them?"

"No, that's okay. I should probably get home before my folks wonder where I am...and I should probably spend an evening with them. Hey, I've been thinking about what you said about sleeping down at the river some night. Want to do that Saturday night? I could bring a couple sleeping bags."

She smiled. "Two sleeping bags?"

"Well...you know...one for the bottom and one for the top."

"Oh...so you've been thinking about this, huh?" She shot him a sexy look and smiled. "Sounds good to me!"

"See ya; have fun with your sister and mom," he said heading out her door.

"I know I'd have more fun with you. Call me this week."

Bill headed for his car with a smile on his face and hands in his pockets so no one would notice the bulge in his pants.

"Roberts?"

"Here!"

"Spare on Line 2," announced Joe.

Bill was kind of glad he was sparing because it was going to be really hot today, and sparing would definitely be cooler than setting carbon. Most of the time, sparing could be a pretty easy job, if the foreman didn't go overboard on the to do list he handed you. Breaking up and hauling away spent carbon anodes or butts, and sweeping pot room floors were typical sparing jobs, and most foremen let you work at your own pace as long as you pretty much completed their list. The downside of sparing was that you didn't get the long break that carbon setters did between the settings in the first and second rooms of their pot line.

Today, Bill was greeted by a sub-foreman, who was filling in for the regular foreman, and who must have been out to impress his supervisor. "Roberts is it?" Bill nodded. "Here's the list of items I need you to take care of this shift; if you finish before the end of the shift come see me." He then turned away and headed back to his office.

I've never been given a list this long! thought Bill as he scanned down the items: jackhammer a frozen corner in Pot 57, break all butts in Rooms 3 and 4 and haul them away;

sweep both rooms; replace the pokers in Pots 9, 21, 37, 46 and 64. *Holy shit, there's no way I'll finish all this in one shift!*

After jackhammering the frozen corner, Bill ducked into the waterhole across from the fifth string of pots in Room 3 to get a drink of water.

"Hey, Bill, what're ya doing today?" asked Jack, the Line 2 crane driver, who also served as a shop steward on D Shift.

" Just sparing," Bill replied unenthusiastically.

Jack could tell from Bill's tone that he wasn't in his usual upbeat mood. "Let's see what that sub-foreman know-it-all ass-hole has you doin' today.

Bill could see Jack's jaw tighten as he read down the list. "Jesus H. Christ; this is ridiculous! There's no way you can do all this in one shift! Sit your ass down in here, while I go get this straightened out."

Jack hustled out of the watering hole and within seconds Bill could hear him yelling at the foreman even over the hum of the pots. A few minutes later, Jack proudly returned to the waterhole and returned the to do list to Bill. Room 4 was crossed off the list for breaking butts and sweeping, and Pots 46 and 64 evidently no longer needed new pokers.

"Wow! Thanks, Jack," responded Bill in a stunned voice.

"Any time you're handed an unreasonable list like that, I want you to bring it to me; I'll take care of it! Savvy?"

"Yes sir," replied Bill gratefully.

Bill avoided the sub-foreman during the rest of his shift, but made sure he stayed busy because he wanted to maintain his reputation of being a hard worker. Over the course of the past four summers, the foremen on D Shift knew him as such. Before the shift was over, he had completed all of the items on his revised list.

Throughout the shift, he thought of Barb writhing and

panting as he felt her breasts. His heart raced and his groin stirred when he imagined being with her under the sleeping bag on Saturday night.

When the horn sounded to head for the shower room, Bill caught up with Jack, who was walking ahead of him up Room 3. "Thanks again for helping me out today, Jack."

"No problem; just remember to come see me anytime you're handed a list like that."

It always felt good at the end of a shift to wash off the carbon and ore dust that stuck to his sweaty body. The shower stalls were filled with a menagerie of characters, some decorated with unbelievable tattoos. One guy, who was always making crude comments had a propeller tattooed on each buttocks, and something on the end of his cock! Bill had heard via the grapevine that it was a spider. *Man, he must have been passed out drunk to get a tattoo there,* thought Bill to himself. This same character, whose nickname was "Stretch" would always whistle shrilly when someone would drop his bar of soap and bend over to pick it up. Stretch would then cackle loudly as the embarrassed worker hurried to complete his shower.

—ɯ—

"Roberts?"

"Here!"

"Spare on Line 5," barked Joe at the beginning of another Day Shift.

After replacing a couple pokers in a few pots, Bill took his first break in one of the waterholes. The water in the refrigerated drinking fountains always tasted so refreshing on a hot day, and workers drank a lot of water when working in the pot rooms.

"Someone told me you graduated from GU this spring, and that you're going to be a priest," said Bob, one of the Line 3 pot men, as Bill finished his drink from the fountain. This was the first time Bob had ever initiated a conversation with Bill. He was a quiet, slender guy, who was always reading some paperback when he wasn't feeding his pots.

Bill sat down across from Bob. "Well, I'm going into the Jesuit Novitiate at the end of August to see if that's what I want to do. Don't know if I'll make it all the way to the priesthood. It's a long process."

"Don't the Jesuits teach?"

"Yes, in high schools and colleges."

"I taught high school for a few years, but came here in 1959, and won't ever go back to teaching."

"You like this over teaching?"

"Yep! Here I punch in, do my shift, punch out and go home. And when I get home, my time is mine. When I taught, I was preparing lessons, putting up with sassy kids, and correcting papers—my time was never mine. The only time I miss teaching is in the summers. But enough of that. I wish you well; good luck."

"Thanks," Bill responded pressing the button on the fountain for another drink before heading out of the waterhole to begin the next task given him by his foreman. Several times during the rest of his shift, he reflected on what Bob had told him about preferring the pot rooms over teaching. Bill remembered well the teachers and coaches who had made a difference in his life throughout grade school and high school. He also recalled the teachers he didn't care for during those stages of his life. The latter teachers weren't able to connect with their students and seemed to be overwhelmed, unhappy, even angry at times. He wondered if Bob had been one of those teachers. *I think I'd find teaching and coaching much more stimulating and rewarding than working in the pot rooms,* surmised Bill.

On his way to the shower room at the end of his shift, he walked past the double shift board on Line 4 where several D Shift hopefuls were waiting to see if there would be enough openings on A Shift to reach their names on the doubles board rotation. *Sure glad I don't have to work any doubles this summer! I won't have any tuition to pay in the coming school year, and I'll be able to easily pay off my loan just working my regular shifts.* In past summers, he typically worked three or four doubles because he got paid time and a half, which really helped pad his savings account. He dreaded working them because he usually spared on a double, and the shift seemed to drag on forever. Then, he was right back to work after crashing for a few hours at home. Apart from the extra money, the only other perk of working a double was that he was brought a hearty and tasty meal that was prepared by some restaurant outside the plant. He liked the dinners on swing shift and the breakfasts on graveyard the best.

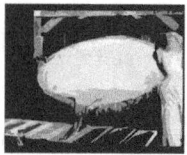

"Dad talked with Aunt Doris yesterday about staying at Newman Lake the first week in August. We're hoping you can spend some time with the family while we're there."

"I'll try, Mom; I'll have to see what shift I'm working that week."

Bill had loved going to Doris's cabin when we was growing up. It was an old two story log cabin with a wood stove in the small, narrow kitchen and a large rock fireplace in the living room. Above the rock fireplace a four point Mule buck stared blankly forward, and a black bear clung to the log wall to its right. Up a steep, narrow staircase opposite the fireplace was a loft with a full-sized bed on each side of a large glass-paned window that looked out at the lake. A screened-in porch wrapped around the front and north sides of the cabin. Bill and his older brother Rod loved to watch the occasional sheet lightening that occurred some nights after hot summer days.

A few times when Bill and Rod were young boys living in Spokane, Doris volunteered to drive them out to her cabin for a weekend probably to give Rachel some well-deserved rest. She drove a light blue 1952 Oldsmobile with a manual transmission on the column. She kept it in mint condition.

While at her cabin, she always made them follow her rules and assigned them chores like getting wood from the woodshed and pumping water from the well in back of the cabin, but she let them sleep out on the screened-in porch at night.

Before swimming in the lake, she made them use one of the two bathhouses on the ground floor of the cabin to change into their swimsuits. She changed in the adjoining one so she could swim with them and make sure they were safe.

One day after swimming, Rod discovered he could see her through a small crack in the wall. He motioned Bill over with his hand, and pointed to the crack. As Bill's eye adjusted, he could see her left bare breast as she pulled her panties up over her white butt. Bill turned away quickly and saw Rod grinning. "That's gross!" Bill whispered upset with Rod. From that time on, Bill would think of that image of his aunt when he looked at her. She had always been so nice to him and Rod, and he didn't like how this bathhouse memory now tainted the positive image he'd previously had of his special aunt.

The hammock that hung in the south corner of the front porch was one of Bill's favorite places to hang out. He'd use a small rope line that was attached to the wall to swing himself to and fro which created a welcome breeze on hot summer afternoons. His mind would randomly wander and sometimes he'd even fall asleep in the hammock.

Over the years, Doris, a spinster, had acquired all kinds of antiques: leather couches and chairs, unique tables, lamps, dishes; hand-sewn quilts and salt and pepper shakers from different countries. These shakers were displayed on a shelf below the windows in the dining area across from the kitchen. She had acquired an antique RCA Victrola that played big, heavy 78 rpm records. Bill enjoyed winding the Victrola up with its handle and playing the records which emitted old-time scratchy, cartoony sounds compared to the smoother 45s he was used to playing at home. She also had an antique foot-pump organ with stops that Bill loved to play. He liked opening and closing the stops to hear how they affected the tones of the music he played. He enjoyed the unique smoky, musty smell of the old cabin. But now that he was older and working, it was more of a hassle to drive all the way to the lake; then all the way back out to Mead.

As Bill thought about his mom's announcement that they'd be going to Newman Lake for a week an idea popped into his mind. *Hmmm, I could bring Barb over to the house when they're at the lake.* A smile came to his lips.

After dinner when his folks sat down to watch TV upstairs, he headed downstairs to call Barb. He took the phone into the back storage room for added privacy. "Hi, how was your visit with your mom and sister?"

"Fine. I hadn't talked to them in awhile so it was good to catch up. How's work going this week?"

"Ok, but I'm looking forward to Jerry and Sandy's party Saturday night. Are you still up for sleeping out at the river after the party?"

"Yes!" she answered enthusiastically. "Don't forget the sleeping bags," she added teasingly.

"I won't."

"Oh…just drive straight to Jerry and Sandy's Saturday night. I told Sandy I'd come over and help her get ready for the party after work."

"Sounds good; I'll be there about 7:00. By the way, my family's going to be staying a week at Newman Lake in a few weeks."

"Hmmm, we may have to take advantage of that week."

"Exactly! See ya Saturday."

After hanging up, Bill rummaged through the storage closet under the stairs to locate two sleeping bags. He checked to make sure the zippers worked; then rolled them up and bound them with their strings. He also grabbed a couple of old pillows, walked out the basement door and around the house so his folks wouldn't see him. He quickly tossed them into his car's trunk, where they joined the blanket he and Barb had used at the river.

—⟋⟋⟍—

As he drove to Kaiser Saturday morning, Bill felt certain he'd score with Barb that night. His stomach fluttered and his groin stirred when he thought about what it would be like.

"Roberts!"

"Here!"

"Line 7 carbon setter."

Bill was actually glad he'd be setting carbon today because the time would go by faster, and he'd be able to rest between rooms.

The Line 7 crane driver, Don Wilson was smoking a cigarette near the foreman's office when Bill arrived. "Hey, Roberts, is it true you're entering a seminary at the end of this summer?" Don, who sported several tattoos on his pasty white arms had the reputation of being a wild man, especially in local taverns after he'd had a few beers. He loved riding his decked-out Harley to work and one day after a Day Shift, he laid a long patch of rubber in the parking lot to show all the guys what his bike could do. But despite Don's wild, tough reputation, he had always been friendly toward Bill.

"Yeah, in August. We'll see how it goes."

"I have a distant cousin who is a priest back in Minnesota. Just met him once, but he seemed like a nice guy. In any case, I wish you well, and hope it works out if it's what you want."

"Thanks, Don, I appreciate it." As Bill headed up the aisle to put his lunchbox in the waterhole, he wondered what Don would think of him, if he knew his plans for the weekend.

Don wasn't quite as fast with the crane as Jack Crenshaw, but he was extremely smooth. Bill marveled at how steady Don kept the carbon anode when he brought it from the pot room floor up to the catwalk; then put the rod into its slot. Most of the time, Bill didn't have to exert much effort at all to guide the heavy rod to its slot.

"Great driving, Don," Bill remarked as they headed for the waterhole after completing the first room. "You are sure smooth with that crane."

"Well, guess I should be—been doin' it for a few years."

Don grabbed his lunch from the shelf in the waterhole and sat down to join two pot men and a carbon setter in a game of cribbage. Many of the regulars at Mead played cribbage in between pot feedings and carbon settings, and Bill enjoyed listening to their banter as they played: "...read 'em and weep"; "fifteen two, fifteen four and there ain't no more." Players continually ribbed one another and gloated when they came out on top. When duties called, they would head out of the waterhole until they were done; then resume play when they returned.

When the horn sounded at noon Bill joined the other carbon setters and headed for the second room of Line 7. Excitement built each time he thought of being with Barb tonight, and he had to remind himself to focus on what he was doing the remainder of the shift. *Don't want a careless injury to ruin tonight!* He vividly remembered the time a carbon setter, who wasn't paying close attention got hit in the head with an anode rod. The crane driver brought out a spent carbon anode and set it down on a small pile of bath lying on the pot room floor. The carbon setter, who was talking to another worker released the hook and pushed the rod toward the bay window expecting the anode to fall over on its side. However, he hadn't pushed it hard enough and when the anode righted, the rod struck him in the head. The result was a nasty gash on the right side of the carbon setter's head that required 35 stitches and two weeks away from work.

At the end of the shift, Bill headed for the shower room with Don and the other carbon setters.

"Enjoy your weekend," said Don as they neared the door to the shower room.

"I will!" replied Bill grinning. "You too."

—∾—

In the five summers Bill had been working at Kaiser, he hadn't ever been this excited after a shift. As he clocked out of the guardhouse and headed to the parking lot, he noticed a number of pick-ups with campers parked near the exit. These workers' wives had them stocked and ready for a weekend of camping over the shift change break.

I won't exactly be camping tonight, but I'm sure it will be incredible, he thought to himself.

Images of being with Barb darted through his mind as he drove home: her soft lips, her unbuttoned blouse, her dark eyes, tan legs; her tight ass, bare creamy breasts and dark nipples. The images made him hard and every once in awhile, Bill had to shake his head to make sure he was actually paying attention to his driving.

—∾—

"What are your plans for your days off?" asked his dad after dinner heading for his usual spot on the couch.

"Well, tonight I'm going to a party at Jerry and Sandy's, and will probably just stay at their place; so don't worry if I'm not here in the morning."

"Okay, but…I was hoping we'd have a chance to talk about your watchin' the place when we go to Newman Lake in a few weeks. Mom said she mentioned it to you?"

"Yes, she did. No problem. Let's talk sometime tomorrow."

"That works; be careful tonight," added his dad from behind the open newspaper.

His dad's last remark made Bill realize he hadn't bought any rubbers. He'd never bought any before, and knew he'd have to shop at a drug store where no one knew him. *I can't go to Halpin's; they know my folks too well. I know, I'll go to the drug store in Millwood that I pass on my way to work.*

As he was getting ready downstairs, he went through a mental checklist: *Let's see, I'll need a sweatshirt, oh…and a flashlight, money…okay, think I'm good to go. I'd better leave now 'cause I'll have to drive to Millwood first.*

A question Fr. Eric had posed to Bill in one of their conversations about decision making popped into Bill's mind as he was driving on Argonne Rd. and nearing Millwood. It was from one of St. Ignatius's meditations. *"Imagine yourself on your death bed. Would this be a decision you wish you would have made?"* This thought sent momentary anxiety to Bill's gut until he eliminated it by continuing to the pharmacy. *No backing out now,* he thought parking on a side street.

Upon entering the small drug store across from the paper mill, Bill browsed the aisles to see if he could find Trojans. When he couldn't, he waited until the pharmacist, an older guy wearing a white lab coat and wire-rimmed glasses wasn't helping anyone; then approached the counter.

"Yes, can I help you?" asked the pharmacist looking at Bill over his glasses.

"Well…I'm looking for Trojans," blurted Bill nervously.

"I'll get them for you," answered the pharmacist with a slight grin. "How many do you want?"

"Ahhh, can I get a dozen?"

"Sure; that'll be $2.50."

"Okay, thanks," responded Bill hurriedly. He caught the quick smile the pharmacist gave him before he turned to exit.

When Bill got into his car, he put two condoms in his pocket and the rest in his glove box.

—m—

"Hey, about time you got here," declared Jerry over the conversation din as Bill entered the back door. "Keg's in the back room."

As Bill headed to fill his glass, the door closed behind him. When he swung around, Barb, leaning against the door smiled at him and asked in a flirtatious voice, "Want to fill my glass while you're at it?" Bill could tell Barb had already enjoyed a beer or two, and that he'd have some catching up to do. The keg groaned from the dry ice that was packed around it in the cardboard box; a thin layer of frost covered its aluminum skin. "Did you bring the sleeping bags?" Barb asked moving close to him.

"You bet—and pillows! Just let me know when you're ready to leave."

She reached up to him and kissed him to assure him she was ready for tonight. "Okay," she replied smiling at him.

"Heeyy, Bill! Barb's been pretty anxious for you to get here tonight!" announced Sandy as he and Barb exited the back room. Sandy cocked her head at them. "You two must have some special plans tonight."

Bill grinned at Sandy. "Maybe, but I ain't tellin'."

Sandy laughed lecherously and winked at him before heading back to the kitchen. Sandy, who had introduced Bill to Barb was hoping he would change his mind about entering the Novitiate in August. Bill was one of Jerry's few friends—probably his best friend, and she knew how important this friendship was to Jerry. She also liked Bill, and Barb was a close friend and co-worker. Sandy even hoped that Bill and Barb would become a couple maybe even a married couple that she and Jerry could socialize with. Being married and raising a baby at such a young age excluded Sandy and Jerry from much of their friends' social lives. "Help yourself to pizza," added Sandy pointing to the kitchen table.

Bill enjoyed Jerry and Sandy's get togethers. Everybody got loose and had a good time. He could tell from the loud conversations and laughter that this party would go well into the night.

"Want another beer?" asked Barb noticing Bill's nearly empty glass. "You've got a ways to go to catch up with the rest of us."

Bill could feel the beers' effects after his second glass; so he started to pace himself a bit. He learned during his first summer working at Kaiser how quickly alcohol could sneak up on him after sweating so much at work. After just a few beers at a party that summer, he got sick, which brought a sudden, embarrassing end to a fun evening with friends. He didn't want that happening again tonight.

At 10:30, Bill whispered to Barb, "I suspect Sandy knows something about our plans, but why don't you tell her we're going to take off."

"Hey, Bill you just got here!" shouted one of his friends, as Bill and Barb headed out the door. "Better come back after taking Barb home!"

"Just might. Thanks, Jerry. Thanks, Sandy."

"We've still got a lot of beer left," Jerry reminded him.

Sandy quickly nudged Jerry, who wanted Bill to stay. "They want to be alone for awhile," she emphasized winking at Jerry then smiling.

Barb grabbed Bill's arm both out of excitement and to steady herself as they walked across the uneven lawn and headed to his car. When he opened the door for her, she turned and aggressively kissed him, until Bill's smile broke the passionate seal. "Hang on; we'll be at the beach shortly." Bill could tell she had had plenty to drink.

She nestled as close as she could to him while he drove, and rubbed the inside of his right thigh with her left hand. If she would have moved her hand just a bit, she would have felt his anticipation.

Perfect! No one else is down here, Bill thought to himself as his car lights revealed an empty parking area near the beach. He was so excited that this opportunity with Barb was finally here. He opened the trunk, handed Barb the pillows and the blanket; then he grabbed both sleeping bags. The moon-lit night made it easy for them to find their way to the beach.

Don't even need a flashlight, he thought leading the way. "How about here?" he suggested. "If you spread the blanket out, I'll put the bags on top."

While he was unzipping the sleeping bags and laying them on top of the blanket, he could see her taking off her sandals. She then knelt down on the top bag facing him. When he finished removing his sandals and turned toward her, she grabbed the bottom of his t-shirt and pulled it over his head. She paused a few seconds admiring his strong shoulders and hairy chest; then said, "Your move...."

Enraptured by her sexy pose and invitation, he reached over, pulled her shirt over her head, then hesitated as if unsure what to do next.

"Ever taken one of these off before?" she asked glancing down at her bra.

"No, but..."

"Here let me show you." She ushered his hands behind her back. "Do you feel where the ends come together? Now slide them toward one another."

As he did so, he could feel one end unhook from the other. Her bra relaxed, slid forward then fell off her shoulders onto the bag revealing her bare breasts. He was briefly transfixed by their fullness; then he carefully caressed them with nervous but excited hands. Her nipples were hard, and the scent of her body lured him closer.

"Come here," she urged as she crawled between the bags. When he did the same, he could feel her hands unbuttoning his cutoff jeans; then unzipping them. As soon as he found her jeans' button, she began kissing him lustfully, as if to encourage him to hurry. Removing her cutoffs, he could feel her smooth panties. Still kissing him, she began slipping off her panties. As he helped her move them downward, the back of his right hand made its first contact with her soft silkiness. He had never felt this part of a girl before. She completed the removal of her panties and cut offs with one of her feet.

Bill finished removing his cut offs, and as he began to slide off his underpants, she assisted as if desperate for him. "Oh my!" she exclaimed excitedly as she stretched them outward to free them. She then removed them from his ankles with her foot.

They were both naked together now for the first time. He wanted to feel her silkiness against him for awhile, but her wants were moving at a faster pace than his.

"Barb…should I use a…" Before he could finish, she introduced him to a warm, sensual paradise that he'd never experienced before.

"Oh, my God…you feel soooo good!" he gasped. He hesitated briefly realizing he wasn't using a condom.

"Barb…Do I need to pu …"

"Shhh!" she quickly interrupted. "Don't worry; just stay with me." She tightened around him and made passionate, muffled grunts in her throat as she stroked him.

"Oh, my God, Barb…!"

"Stay with me!" she urged, her eyes closed, her head thrust back.

He had never in his life felt so wonderful. *How can she make herself so…*

Then an exciting, hot rush began to well up in him and grew in intensity until…

"Yes, yes!" she gasped. "Come! Come!"

The river rushed by them as both enjoyed his explosive release—so wonderfully intense at first then less and less so. He stayed as close to her as he could, wanting this heavenly experience to last forever. Neither said anything while their rapid breathing slowed. Then he rolled on to his left side and brought his right leg up onto her, still firmly with her. "Oh my God, Barb. You feel so good!"

"So do you, Bill Roberts. Let's do it again soon!"

Barb's breathing began to relax now, and get deeper and he realized she was falling asleep. He felt sleepy as well, but wanted to relish this first, special life experience. *My first time…I'll never forget this.*

Before surrendering to sleep, he pulled down the top of the sleeping bag that was covering his right ear, lifted his head and intently listened to make sure they were still alone. Not seeing any car lights or hearing any partiers, he shrugged the sleeping bag over his exposed right shoulder, locked his right arm around her warm body and joined her in sleep.

—⟋⟋⟍—

Rachel Roberts sat out on her deck enjoying a cigarette before turning in for the night. She hoped Bill was just with friends and not some floozy who would get in the way of his entering the Novitiate in August. *I won't allow that to happen!* she assured herself exhaling.

Rachel had been raised in a devout Catholic family and after she delivered two sons, she dreamed that one of them would become a priest. By the time Rod her oldest was in high school, she knew he was not priest material. He stopped playing sports after his sophomore year at Gonzaga Prep, so he could get a job in order to buy a car. After he transferred to CV for his junior year, he got girl crazy. Rachel knew he was much too self-centered to be a good priest, but Bill was the perfect candidate for the priesthood in her mind. He was sincere, he cared about others, his Catholic faith had remained strong throughout high school and college, and he was eager to please others. With a look of determination on her face, she took one last drag, snuffed out her Winston in a beanbag ashtray and closed the screened slider behind her.

—⟋⟋⟍—

When Bill opened his eyes, it was beginning to get light,

but he could tell it was still very early in the morning. He was surprised they were still as one, and he felt himself beginning to get hard again. He knew he had to pee, however, so he very slowly pulled away so he could slip from underneath the top sleeping bag.

"What time is it?" Barb asked groggily.

"I'm not sure; I'll be back in a minute." He found his underpants outside the bag on the sand, and shook them before covering his privates and tip-toeing down the beach a ways. When he had finished and was heading back to the bag, he saw Barb naked heading up the beach a ways to relieve herself also. When he saw her, he realized it was foolish of him to cover himself after last night's intimacy.

He brushed as much sand as he could off his feet; then re-entered the bag. Soon, Barb sat down, brushed off her feet as well and wriggled in next to him.

"Was I dreaming or were we still together this morning?" she asked sleepily.

"We were still together when I woke up; it was wonderful!"

"Well, let's see what we can make happen before it really gets light." She invited him to her again. But this time she let him find his way; let him control the erotic pace, which to their pleasures lasted longer than last night. When she knew he was ready, she held him close; her toes grasping his legs as the tempo quickened.

"Yes; Yes!" she gasped relishing the wonderful climax.

"Oh, my God, Barb how do you make yourself so...

"Control," she proudly responded.

"Wonderful control," he added.

—◊—

They both dozed in one another's embrace until the heat from the 7:00 AM sun made it unbearable to be skin-to-skin between the heavy sleeping bags.

Bill reached out and thrust his half of the heavy, cotton-lined sleeping bag away from his sweaty body. The cool morning air soothed his clammy skin. He raised up and squinted into the bright sunlit morning. As his eyes adjusted, he peered out at the river.

"Looks like we have company across the river...some guy fishing."

Barb stirred. "What? Who? God, I'm so hot!" she complained putting one of her legs outside the bag.

"I'll put my shorts on then hold the sleeping bag up so you can get dressed," he said searching for his clothing.

"Thanks," she replied yawning. She gathered her scattered clothing and dressed while Bill held up the top sleeping bag to shield her from the fisherman. "Let's head back to my place for some breakfast," she suggested after zipping up her cutoffs.

"And a shower?" he added.

"Yes!" she agreed moving the pillows to a nearby log.

He moved the sleeping bags to the side, shook the sand from the blanket and handed it to her.

"If you can carry this and the pillows back to the car, I'll bring both bags."

"Okay," she yawned again then glanced across the river at the fisherman dressed in a red flannel shirt. "Wonder how long that guy's been there?"

"Who knows." *Eat your heart out*, Bill thought as he shook out the sleeping bags, gathered them in his arms and followed Barb to the car. Both sporting disheveled hair, shuffled slowly and stiffly to the car. He tossed the blanket, pillows and bags into the trunk of his VW and pressed them together so he could close the hood. As he did so, he saw Barb in the car looking in his rear view mirror and trying to comb her shaggy hair with her fingers. It made him smile.

—〜—

"Go jump in the shower while I get some eggs started," she offered after they entered her apartment.

As he enjoyed the warm spray against his back, images of last night ran through his mind like a slide show: Barb removing his shirt, her inviting pose, taking her bra off, seeing her beautiful breasts, feeling their nakedness together for the first time, her wonderful warmth. In a way, he didn't want to wash off any of their togetherness, but he was pretty confident that they would make love many more times over the next few weeks. This thought ended his fixed stare and he finished washing his body.

"Man, that shower felt good," emphasized Bill approaching the kitchen area dressed in his cutoffs and drying his hair with a towel. Barb was at the stove stirring the scrambled eggs. "That smells good; can I help you with anything?"

"Yes, you can butter the toast as soon as it pops up."

Bill put the towel around his neck, approached her and kissed the back of her neck. She shrugged acknowledging his kiss and smiled.

"Barb...you said last night that I shouldn't worry about anything..."

"That's right; you don't have to worry," she quickly replied. "Toast is up; there's the butter.

"So...what do you think now? Still want to go in the Jesuits?" she asked flashing him a flirty smile as they sat down to enjoy their breakfast.

"Aaa…well…I…" He had hoped Barb would elaborate more on why he didn't need to worry about not using a rubber but he didn't want to press. He didn't want to make her feel like he didn't trust her.

"Sorry, it's not fair to throw that at you right now…we'll just continue to enjoy each other's…company," she added taking another bite of her scrambled eggs. Bill tensed for just a second; he knew he would have to confront and answer Barb's question within the coming weeks. But right now, he didn't want to think about it. They finished their breakfast not saying much, just looking at each other and smiling, both enjoying this special time together.

"Mmmmm, that hit the spot," said Bill patting his tummy, "Let me help you clean up."

"No, I can take care of these before I shower. You probably need to get home before your folks start to worry; will I see you tonight?"

"Yes!" smiled Bill giving her a long hug at the door. "Last night was soooo amazing, Barb. I've never felt anything so…"

She leaned back and looked at him, "You liked that, huh! Well you made me feel good too." She moved close to him, closed her eyes and kissed him tenderly. "Call me later okay," she added flashing him a smile.

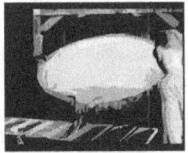

"How was the party?" his mom asked as he came in the front door late Sunday morning.

"It was good. Saw some old classmates I haven't seen for awhile."

"Want to go to Church with us?" she asked hopefully. "We're leaving in about 45 minutes."

"No, go ahead; it was a pretty late party. I'll go this evening at St. Mary's," he lied. He knew he'd be with Barb again during that time.

After his parents left for church, he pulled the sleeping bags from his car's trunk and carried them to the back yard, where he shook the sand from them. When he sniffed the soft cotton lining of the bags, he could smell her perfume. Wondering what they smelled like together, he found the still damp spot on the bottom bag that had spread a bit into the plaid cotton lining and sniffed. *Yeww. Not exactly pleasant, but…interesting…So, is this what a girl smells like inside?*

After he aired the bags out on the clothesline for about 30 minutes, he zipped them up, rolled and tied them, and tossed both bags back into the storage area under the stairs.

He checked his car to make sure Barb hadn't left anything visible on the seat; then headed for his bed to take a much needed nap. He didn't want to field a series of questions from his parents about last night until after he'd gotten some more sleep.

—〰—

"Well, it must have been a late night," his dad commented as he looked up from the Sunday paper. "It's almost 3:00 o'clock!"

"Yeah, I guess I was more tired than I thought; a combination of work and staying out late."

"Mom's cooking a nice roast for dinner; hope you'll eat with us tonight. It'll also give us a chance to talk about the week we're at Newman Lake."

"Sure, sounds good," he felt compelled to answer. He didn't want them to get too suspicious.

When he had the opportunity, he headed downstairs to call Barb. "I'll come over about 7:00," he assured her twisting the phone cord around his right index finger. "My parents want me to have dinner with them tonight, and I think I'd better before they start asking too many questions."

"I'll be ready," replied Barb in a suggestive tone. "Will you?"

"Oh, yeah," he quickly responded grinning. "See ya soon."

Bill headed down the hallway to his room. *Think I'll start getting ready for tonight now so I can chat at dinner and leave about 6:45. They'll think I'm heading to Church.*

—〰—

"Well, there's only six weeks left before you head for Sheridan, Oregon," his dad reminded Bill after they had dished up. "What do you need to do before leaving?"

"I have to shop for underwear, socks, black shoes, a couple

of white shirts and two pairs of black slacks. I'll do that after my next graveyard shift when I'll have 72 hours off."

"How long are you going to work this summer?"

"I think I'll work until two weeks before I leave—so probably until about mid-August. I'll see what the last shift day is around that time."

"Do you have to give two weeks notice?" asked his dad.

"Yeah; I'll be sure to do that."

"I hope you're going to be able to spend some time with us when we're at Aunt Doris's cabin in a few weeks," his mom reminded him again.

"I'll try, Mom," lied Bill. "It would definitely make for a long drive into work from Newman Lake," he emphasized.

"Well, at least on one of your days off," his mom urged. "Dad and I and your brothers aren't going to be able to see you again until the end of October!"

"I know!" he replied quickly hoping to avoid a lecture.

Bill wasn't really that close to his younger brothers. Phil was five years younger and had entirely different interests than Bill. He was very intellectual, liked listening to classical music in his room, and ran with friends who Bill felt were pretty effeminate. Don was ten years younger and George eleven years younger; so there wasn't much of a relationship with them.

George had attended several public schools for mentally handicapped children during his childhood. However, most teachers couldn't handle George, who would leave school and try to walk home because he missed his mom. Finally, a hard-nosed nun who operated a special needs Catholic school in Spokane was able to manage George and provide him some basic job skills.

As part of his daily commute to Gonzaga, Bill had driven George to this Catholic school each morning. Bill remembered well all the health issues George had as a baby: he couldn't hold down cow's milk so Rachel had to feed him goat's milk, his bowels weren't developed so Rachel had to give him daily enemas, he cried almost continually so Rachel spent a good part of her day attempting to comfort him. When Bill was in elementary school, he did much of the housework at his mom's pleading because he knew how much time she had to devote to George, and he felt sorry for her.

"George was given too much oxygen at birth," his mom once told Bill. "And that's what caused the mental and developmental damage." Some of the physical issues improved as George grew older but his mental age didn't develop beyond about eight years old. While George had an uncanny memory, he wasn't able to carry on a meaningful conversation, so Bill hadn't seen much development in their relationship over the three years of commuting together. But Bill gladly drove George to school each day knowing that it gave Rachel some hard earned and much needed private time away from George.

Bill also felt badly for Don, who was just 11 months older than George. Don shared a bedroom with George so had to endure George's frequent crying. He also didn't get much attention from Rachel, who had to spend so much time tending to George's needs. Fortunately, Don was a good natured kid, who was often placated with bottles of warm milk when he was little. One day when Bill was walking by Don's and George's bedroom, he saw Don lying inside the open bottom dresser drawer on top of the clothes. He was nursing a bottle of milk, seemingly unbothered by George's wailing in the bathroom where Rachel was attempting to give George an enema.

In any case, Bill was sure his brothers would not miss him when they were at Newman Lake. In fact, they would no doubt be glad when he was out of the house. Don would finally have a room of his own, and Phil wouldn't have to endure the comments Bill made about his effeminate friends and his interest in classical music.

This evening's Sunday dinner was typical. Because the roast was the most expensive dinner item, Howard sliced it as thin as he could and served meager portions. Potatoes, salad, vegetables and bread were passed around the table, and seconds of those were allowed if there was enough left. The boys could ask for more meat, but Howard always made them feel guilty for asking, and if more meat was served, the portion was even smaller than the first one. And there was the milk rule—one glass of milk per meal. Active and growing boys, Bill and Rod would frequently sneak sips of milk from the gallon milk jugs between meals when Howard wasn't around, and Rachel, who often saw them didn't stop them and never told Howard.

Ever since Bill could remember, his dad, a banker had kept his mom on a strict weekly grocery budget. Fights between his parents ensued when she would exceed the budget, which occurred almost weekly. It wasn't easy for her to feed a family of five boys on such a tight budget. These family dynamics made for nearly silent meals that were interrupted briefly by requests for more potatoes or another slice of bread.

Occasionally during dinners, his dad or mom would attempt to start some conversation by asking about a school event or a friend, but it rarely developed. Tonight during one of the conversation lulls, Howard asked Bill to water the lawn, pick-up the paper and mail and take out the garbage while the family was at Newman Lake.

"Sure; no problem, Dad. I won't be going anywhere except to work."

—m—

"Hey, Bill!" Phil shouted from across Sprague where he was gassing up his parents' car. "I thought you were supposed to be at Church!" he yelled sarcastically.

"Don't tell Mom and Dad or you're dead!" Bill responded emphatically as he topped off his Bug at the station across the way. He was glad Phil hadn't seen him outside of Barb's apartment, which was just a few blocks away. *Of all the luck,* Bill murmured to himself. *I hope he doesn't tell Mom and Dad he saw me; they'll definitely want to know what's going on.* He did not want to explain the recent choices he was making. Bill waited for Phil to leave; then headed for Barb's.

"What's wrong? You look worried?" noted Barb when she opened her door.

"Oh, it's nothing really…my brother saw me when I was gassing up a few minutes ago. I told my folks I was going to Church this evening."

"Do you think he'll say anything?"

"He'd better not!"

"Well…let's see if I can help you stop worrying," she said as her eyes and hands walked their way from his stomach, up his chest then to his face. She pressed her moist lips to his and with her arms around his neck walked backwards pulling him down the hall toward her bedroom. "It's only a twin bed, but I figure if we can do it in a sleeping bag, we can do it in my bed."

Sitting on the edge of her mattress, she unbuckled his belt then slowly unzipped his jeans. "Oh my; looks like you're glad to see me again," she said touching the bulge in his underpants and looking up into his eyes with eager anticipation.

He reached down and pulled her to a standing position so

he could return the favor of unzipping her cut offs and sending them to the floor. After stepping out of them, she slid both her hands beneath his t-shirt feeling the hair on his chest as she moved her hands upward. She then pulled his shirt above his head and flung it to the side. He began unbuttoning her blouse working from the top down. When he released the last button, she looked up at him and smiled. Using both hands, he removed the blouse from her shoulders letting it slide to the floor. Wanting him to remove her bra, she put her arms around his neck and leaned into him so he could easily access the clasps. He wasted no time reaching behind her to move the two hooks together. When her bra relaxed and joined her other clothing on the floor, he stepped back to admire her luscious fullness.

She let him enjoy her bare breasts for a few seconds then pulled him down to her bed and unto her so she could feel his hardness against her. He reached down with his right hand to remove her panties, but she stopped him and whispered, "Not yet; I just want to feel you against me for a minute."

As he pressed his hard cock against the mound in her panties, he could feel the wet spot in his shorts. Afraid he was going to come in his shorts, he once again tried to pull off her panties. This time, she didn't resist. He then raised up to remove his underpants revealing his long, hard cock. She fixed her eyes on it, then on his eyes and smiled. She slowly welcomed him to her warmness with her hands on his ass. "Slow," she coached. "Just hold it there for a second...now," she urged as she accepted him fully. "Is that better?"

"Yes! Oh, my God...you feel <u>sooo</u> good!"

He enjoyed being able to watch her in the daylight: her head on the pillow, her brown hair spread to the sides, her dark brown eyes looking into his, the curve of her breasts so light-colored, her nipples so hard. He couldn't resist raising up to peek at what was making such wet sounds. Each stroke was wonderful! The welcome breeze coming in the open bedroom window moved the draw string of the closed blinds from side to side like a pendulum.

"Look into my eyes," she commanded. As he did so, he could feel himself beginning to surge. He looked into her unblinking eyes as long as he could attempting to hold back his inevitable release. Then the erotic explosion. "Yes, Yes!" she gasped tightening around him and securing him to her depths with clenched fingers on his ass. His heart raced. "Come… come to me," she urged.

"Oh, my God; you feel so good!" he gasped between breaths.

As their breathing slowed, Bill thought about how peaceful it was lying there together—their breathing in tandem, the warmth of their united bodies.

"Your face doesn't look so worried now," she teased. "Did this beat going to Church?"

He nodded, "Yes!"

"You can even head home when you think Church will be over so your folks think that's where you were if you want to," she added.

"I don't want to; I'd like to spend all night here with you. But I suppose I should head for home soon so my parents don't grill me. Hopefully, my brother hasn't said anything to them.

"Tomorrow I start Swing Shift; so I probably won't see you 'til Saturday night. Unless…I could stop by some night after work about 12:30 if that's not too late?"

"I have an idea," she said climbing over him. "Let me give you a key. Just come in, take your clothes off and get into my bed. What a sweet awakening that will be!" She took a key from her dresser drawer and handed it to him.

"Perfect! I'll keep it in my glove box so my parents won't see it. I'll just have to make sure I don't fall asleep in your arms and get home after daylight," he chuckled pulling on his underpants.

"I'll look forward to you waking me up," she grinned before kissing him good-bye.

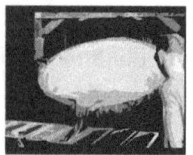

"Roberts?"

"Here!"

"Carbon Setter, Line 4."

"Hey, Stan, do you eat your fuckin' or fuck your eatin'?" asked Stretch when Stan, one of the carbon setters came into the waterhole after finishing the first pot room. Stretch was notorious for his foul mouth and gutter mind. His long, stringy hair always looked like it needed to be washed. He had a narrow, pock-marked face with sunken cheeks, and badly stained teeth from chewing tobacco.

Yuck! thought Bill to himself; *do those guys really do that!?*

"Neither!" Stan responded. "Not everyone's like you, Stretch," he added grabbing his lunch box from the shelf and walking out of the waterhole to get away from Stretch. Stretch wasn't the kind of guy you wanted to eat your lunch next to.

About midway through the break, the foreman suddenly appeared in the waterhole doorway. "Everyone to Pot 14," he ordered. "It's gettin' sick on us."

By the time the pot man and the carbon setters had arrived at Pot 14, three carbon anodes had already burned off and the molten bath, typically covered with a crust was an orange boil in the pot. "Get those carbon outta there so we can get new anodes in or we're gonna lose her," barked the foreman. Bill grabbed a crowbar and attempted to pry one burn off to the top of the boiling bath so another carbon setter could pull it out with tongs. It didn't take long before his shoes and pants were smoking. "Got it!" yelled the carbon setter pulling it to the stairs and tossing it to the floor. The crane driver brought in a new anode immediately so it could be set.

Other carbon setters and the frantic pot man pulled the other burn offs from the pot and new anodes were delivered by the crane driver. The foreman and pot man set the new anodes at the proper height and adjusted the voltage as the new anodes were installed.

"Good job, men; I think we may have saved this one," breathed the sweaty foreman. "Thanks for helping us out, Roberts."

After showering at the end of Swing Shift, Bill walked out of the steamy shower room into the cool evening air to wait for the official shift horn to sound. He enjoyed listening to guys' comments to one another while they waited to clock out. When Slim, a young single guy emerged from the shower room and approached the assemblage, one of the workers blurted, "Hey, Slim, I'll bet I know where you're headed tonight!"

"Yep, Wallace! Piece of butt, ham n' eggs, and I'll be all set for the next shift!" His laughter mixed-in with that of his co-workers.

Bill could understand why married guys didn't mind working Swing Shifts. They could get to bed before too late; maybe even have sex with their wives if they were still awake or willing. Then, they could enjoy most of their day before heading into work at mid-afternoon. This thought stayed with Bill as he headed for home and imagined Barb asleep in her bed—perhaps dreaming of him. It had been three days since he'd seen her, and he really wanted to be with her. *I think it's time I took advantage of the key she gave me,* he thought opening the glove box to make sure it was there. He grinned as he touched it.

It felt weird to be turning right on Sprague rather than continuing straight on Argonne Road for home after Swing Shift, but his anticipation of being with Barb quickly overrode any thoughts of guilt or consequences. As he pulled into her parking lot, he turned off his lights and ignition, coasting into a vacant parking stall. He quietly slipped the key she'd given him into the lock, slowly opened her door and listened to see if she was stirring. Hearing nothing, he tip-toed into her bedroom. As his eyes adjusted to the darkness, he could see that she was lying on her left side facing away from him.

Perfect! he smiled as he began undressing. She would awake to his hardness against her. When he slowly raised the sheet, he saw she was naked.

"I thought you'd never get here," she whispered turning toward him.

—⟋⟍—

Good, no lights on, Bill thought as he pulled his Bug into his parents' driveway at 2:00 AM. *If Mom hears me and gets up, I'll tell her I went out for a beer with friends after work.* He quietly opened then closed the front door, tip-toed into the kitchen to set his lunch pail on the counter then down the stairs listening for any sound—but no one stirred. *Whew!* he breathed as he closed his bedroom door.

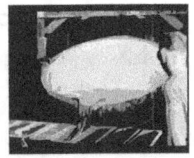

"Roberts!"

"Here."

"Spare Line 3."

Hopefully something low key and easy goin' today, hoped Bill still sleepy after getting to bed so late. *Glad I'm not carbon setting this afternoon in this heat.*

When Bill reported to Line 3, the foreman led him to Pot 17, where a jackhammer lie in a cart or "buggy" parked across from the pot. Bill's heart dropped because he knew exactly what he would be doing. The heat shield to the far corner anode was moved to the side exposing the anode which was missing its copper rod.

"I need you to jackhammer out the corner anode in this pot and remove the butt so we can install a new carbon. That corner's frozen pretty solid so it'll take some effort to clear that hole and widen it for a new anode. When you're done with that one return the jackhammer to the tool room and come find me."

"Will do," replied Bill attempting to hide his dread.

Having done this job before, Bill knew that you couldn't simply drag the heavy jackhammer up the metal stairs and across the metal catwalk. The magnetism was so strong it would grasp the jackhammer and make it nearly impossible to move. So, he picked up the jackhammer, cradled it in his arms and carried it up the stairs and across the catwalk to the Number 23 anode. He could see what the foreman was talking about. The carbon butt looked like it was encased in concrete. *No wonder, the crane pulled the copper rod off this anode.*

After securing the air hose to the nearest air supply line on the pot room wall, he pulled the lever activating the hammer. Even though he knew what to expect, the loud rat-tat-tatting still startled Bill. Because he was working between two pots, the noise was amplified. *Shit, that's loud!* Bill winced. He could tell from the reaction of the hammer's bit that the bath was very thick. Instead of penetrating the bath and exposing the molten bath below, the bit bounced along the surface producing occasional chips of bath. Bill held his breath while hammering; then released the lever and leaned out toward the breezeway to fill his lungs with fresh air. He knew from setting carbon that inhaling the putrid fluoride gas would send him gasping down the steps for air.

During his third attempt to break through the thick bath, Bill noticed his pants were beginning to smoke. He leaned the jackhammer against the pot and headed for the breezeway to cool off his pants and catch his breath. The irony of wearing long underwear in such a hot atmosphere made Bill shake his head. His non-Kaiser friends would always give him a bad time about wearing long underwear during the summer.

This hot, gassy, dusty routine of hammering for a few minutes, then cooling off near the breezeway continued until the jackhammer bit finally created a crack in the gray bath exposing the molten bath below. When Bill had created several cracks around the encased carbon anode, he schlepped the jackhammer across the catwalk and down the stairs; then fetched a crow bar and tongs. Using the crow bar, he chipped around the edges of the carbon butt, and as soon as it gave way and fell into the molten bath, he placed the crow bar under it, raised one edge so he could grasp it with the tongs. Then he flung the hot, smoking butt off the stairs and onto the brick floor below. He had learned from experience the importance of removing the carbon butt while it was still near the surface of the molten bath. If it sunk to the bottom and shifted, it could be a very frustrating, searing job to locate it and position it so it could be removed from the molten bath.

After cooling off in the breezeway, he returned to the pot and using the crow bar enlarged the hole where the spent carbon had been so it would be wide enough for a new, much wider anode.

When he was done, he tipped the buggy forward to make it easier to load the heavy jackhammer, righted the buggy and headed toward the foreman's office. When he reached the waterhole, he decided to enter and get a drink of cold water from the water cooler. A pot man was lounging on one of the benches leaning against what looked to be a homemade back rest. It was even painted the same green as the table and benches in the waterhole. Bill could see he was reading a *Playboy* magazine. He looked to be in his late 40s or early 50s.

"Man, what's the boss got you doin' today?" he asked lowering the magazine and looking up at Bill.

Bill could tell he was looking at his sweaty, dust-caked face. "Jackhammerin' out a frozen corner," replied Bill taking another drink from the water cooler.

"Oh, that job'll make a man outta ya," stated the grinning pot man. "Have a seat; take the load off," he suggested nodding at the bench on the opposite side of the table. "My name's Ed by the way—'Easy Ed' the crew around here calls me."

"Hi, Ed. My name's Bill—Bill Roberts." Bill made no

attempt to shake Ed's hand. It was obvious Ed wasn't going to move from his relaxed position on the bench, and he probably didn't want to shake Bill's sweaty, dirty hand. "Yeah, no kiddin'; sure wouldn't want to do that job everyday," emphasized Bill sitting down.

"It's definitely a job for young whippersnappers like yourself. That job's one of the reasons I don't work doubles anymore. It's possible to end up doin' that shit job or even worse, jackhammerin' out a cruce, if you work as a spare on a double. Are you workin' your way through college out here?"

"Well, I actually graduated from Gonzaga U this spring; so I'm workin' this summer to pay off my student loan."

"Good for you. I hope your degree allows you to get a good payin' job somewhere out there. But ya know—this job pays pretty good money too. Kaiser's been good to me and my family," noted Ed. "Being a pot man is a pretty easy job on most days. I make decent money doin' this, and the medical benefits are great. And, I've been here long enough now to qualify for the ten weeks paid vacation. How many jobs out there offer that?"

"Probably not many," agreed Bill while thinking that Ed would probably be doing this same routine until he retired. "And in support of what you just said, working here has been a great summer job for me too," added Bill. "It's allowed me to attend Gonzaga, a private college, without having to work during the school year. Not too many summer jobs in this area where you can do that. And I do like workin' with some of the carbon setting crews."

"Huh, carbon settin's another job for young guys; that's why I'm a pot man. Well, best of luck to ya in whatever you end up doin'," added Ed focusing once again on the *Playboy* magazine. It was obvious he was done talking.

Bill took another drink from the water cooler and headed out the waterhole door for the foreman's office. The foreman was reviewing paperwork at his desk. "The frozen carbon in Pot 17 is ready for a new anode," announced Bill from the office doorway.

"Great, I'll tell the carbon setters it's ready. Grab a sledge-hammer and broom from the tool room and work your way around the two rooms bustin' up any butts and wheelin' them to the spent carbon bin. That should get you through the rest of this shift."

"Sounds good to me," responded Bill. "Definitely better than jackhammerin' frozen corners."

During the rest of the shift while breaking up spent carbon butts, hauling them away, and sweeping the pot room floors, Bill thought about what Ed had said, *"Ya know, this place has been good to me and my family...."*

Shit, maybe I should continue working at Kaiser, considered Bill. *I don't have any other job lined up. I would eventually have enough seniority to bid a pot man's position, and like Ed said, it's good money. And if Barb and I do hit it off and decide to get married at some point, I'd be able to support her and any kids we might have.*

This line of thinking continued to run through Bill's mind in the shower room at the end of his shift, while he waited to punch out, and during his drive home.

—⁓—

"How's Swing Shift?" Rachel asked from the kitchen as he entered the kitchen about 8:00 AM. She was dressed in white shorts and a floral blouse that she often wore when she golfed.

"Looong," Bill replied, clearing his lungs. "Yesterday, I

jackhammered out a corner anode that was so frozen in place that the copper rod broke off when the crane tried to pull it out of the pot. My ears are still ringing from that damned hammer.

"Don't they give you ear plugs for a job like that?" she asked folding some towels and stacking them on the kitchen table.

"Yeah, some little foam ones that don't do much good."

"Hmmm, I think they should have to provide you more protection than that!" she declared exhaling a plume of tobacco smoke. "Sometimes, I think those big companies really take advantage of…" Her statement was cut short by the doorbell. "Oh, there's Rosemary. We're playing golf today at Liberty Lake. There's ham and eggs in the fridge; help yourself," she added snuffing out her cigarette.

"Great; have a good game, Mom. It's a nice day for playing golf."

As he enjoyed his breakfast out on the deck, he began to think about Barb and wished he could be with her. *I know, I'll swing by Penneys at noon and take her to lunch. I think she would like that, and it'll give me a chance to see what she does there.*

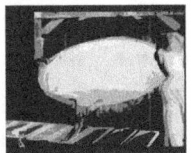

"Can you direct me to the women's department?" asked Bill approaching Barb, who was straightening a rack of women's clothes.

"Oh, my gosh, what a surprise!" Barb gasped putting her right hand to her mouth.

"Hope I remembered right—that you usually take lunch between 12 and 12:30."

"Yes! Let me just check with my boss, and we can hit some place here in the mall."

A couple minutes later, Barb returned. "Okay; let's go," she said taking his hand. She looked at him sideways and grinned as they strolled down the University Mall. "I missed you last night. I was hoping I'd wake up to you getting in my bed," she teased squeezing his hand.

"I wanted to, but I was hacking up so much dust from jack-hammering out an anode on a pot, that I just went straight home."

"Jackhammering!? Hmmm, I think I'm glad I do this kind of work. How about this place?" suggested Barb stopping out-side a sandwich shop. "They make their own soup and have good sandwiches."

"Sounds good to me." A waitress led them to a table for two near the far end of the restaurant.

"Thanks for taking me to lunch; it's very thoughtful of you," Barb said smiling at him.

"No problem; my pleasure," Bill replied leaning toward her and smiling. "So what do you do at J.C. Penney?"

The smile faded from her face. "Oh…you know…exciting things like restock clothes, take inventory, ring up sales," she replied looking down and straightening her silverware.

"Do you ever get bored working in the same department?"

"Yes! But it's a steady job, and I need the money," replied Barb tapping the handle of her spoon on the table as the waitress approached. "I'll have the vegetable beef soup and half of a roast beef sandwich," ordered Barb.

"And I'll get the chicken noodle soup and a turkey sandwich," added Bill. "Well, have you ever thought about going back to school and getting another job?"

"I'd love to, but there's no way I could afford to do that, and my mom doesn't have enough money to help me go to school."

"Well, maybe you'll marry some rich guy," offered Bill smiling at her with his blue eyes.

"Oh, that I'd be so lucky," she responded looking at him hopefully. When Bill didn't immediately respond to her comment, she quickly changed the topic. "So tell me about jackhammering out a …what was it called?"

"An anode," Bill answered filling in the details as they ate their soups and sandwiches.

It was obvious to Bill that Barb was more interested in hearing about his job at Kaiser than talking about hers. As soon as he answered one question, she asked him another.

"Will there be anything else?" asked the waitress stacking their empty bowls and plates.

Bill looked at Barb. "Would you like any dessert?"

"No, thank you; in fact I'd better head back to Penneys," she bemoaned glancing at the clock on the restaurant wall. When the waitress left the tab and walked away with their dishes, she reached across the table, touched his arm and looked into his eyes. "Thanks again for taking me to lunch, Bill."

After paying for lunch, Bill held Barb's hand as he walked her back to the J.C. Penney entrance and reminded her that tonight was his last Swing Shift.

"I know it is, and I asked for tomorrow off." She leaned back slightly still holding his hand and flashed him a sexy grin. "Think you might be stoppin' by tonight after work?"

"You got that right! I'll tell my folks that I'll be staying at Jerry and Sandy's place," he replied smiling at her.

—⁓—

"Roberts?"

"Here!"

"Carbon Setter, Line 4."

Bill closed his eyes in relief. *Whew! No jackhammering today! And carbon setting will make the time go so much faster!* Guys often called in sick the last day of a Swing Shift in order to extend the break between Swing and Graveyard shifts, so it came as no surprise that he would be setting carbon today. It also meant he could probably get in a nap between rooms, which could come in handy tonight.

A short time later as Bill and the rest of the crew members were heading for the waterhole to eat after finishing the first pot room, his foreman told them that Ed Lewis had put his foot in a pot on Line 2 while setting carbon. "They hauled him off in the meat wagon; no doubt he was highballin'," the foreman added. "Just wanted to let you guys know; be careful!"

"Highballing" was a way of life with carbon setters

particularly on Swing and Graveyard shifts, when the brass weren't around. A good crew could finish setting a room in 45 minutes, and have time to eat and sleep for a couple of hours before starting the second room. All carbon setters used their foot to guide the new carbon anode into its spot between the neighboring anodes and wouldn't typically release the crane hook until the anode was on the bottom. But when high-balling, some setters released the crane hook while the new carbon was still dropping into the molten bath so the crane driver could quickly move to the next pot.

Bill had seen the 1,000 degree Celsius bath immediately incinerate a piece of wood or a newspaper that guys had tossed into a pot. He winced as he envisioned Ed's boot riding the carbon into the pot and dipping into the molten aluminum—in a split second his boot would be aflame.

His window rolled down, Bill drove south on N. Bruce Road toward the Spokane Valley after his shift. The cool evening air felt good on his face, and the freshly cut alfalfa smelled so sweet after inhaling the putrid fluoride gas and ore dust for eight hours. Images of Barb waiting for him—naked under the top sheet aroused him. She turned to greet him; he could almost smell her perfume....

"Oh, shit!" he exclaimed aloud in frustration as he approached a slow-moving hay truck ahead of him. He knew from driving this curvy two lane route over the past five summers that it was an extremely dangerous drive when in a hurry—especially at night.

Bill remembered the roll over accident John Jackman, one of his high school buddies, was involved in as he was speeding to Kaiser one night in his little Sunbeam convertible. John had lingered too long at a party and was speeding to make the guardhouse in time for a Graveyard Shift. The Sunbeam clung to the curve on Bruce Road until it hit the gravel shoulder, slid off the road, rolled several times and lay upside down in a hay field. John's middle finger on his right hand was ripped off as he was ejected from his rolling car. He lay in the field until a passerby saw his errant car lights and stopped to investigate. John was one of those carefree guys that luck always seemed to shine on, and that night was no exception. He was thrown clear from his car as it began to roll. John liked to point out with a laugh that when he came to in the field, his radio was blaring, "Born to Lose."

Damn the luck; it'll take forever if I don't pass this asshole, thought Bill as he edged his Bug left in an attempt to look past the truck. He typically didn't see many vehicles this time of night, but knew that if he attempted to pass and a car was approaching from around a blind corner, it could be all over— especially in a Volkswagen Bug. But he was so looking forward to being with Barb tonight.

After rounding a curve, the driver moved his truck as far as he dared onto the right shoulder raising a dust cloud. *Thank you!* Bill estimated the distance to the next curve. *I think I can pass him before the next curve,* he thought jamming the Bug's accelerator to the floor. He held his breath as he moved into the oncoming lane. His Bug slowly inched past the truck's bed, its cab. Then he saw the approaching headlights. *Come on, come on...just a few more feet....*

He could tell the truck driver had applied his brakes because of how quickly Bill was at his front bumper. *Got to make my move **now**....*

Bill cranked the steering wheel to the right pulling directly in front of the hay truck. He passed through a cloud of dust *probably from the other car's being on the shoulder to avoid me,* guessed Bill. He could smell the burning rubber *probably from the truck driver slamming on his brakes,* he thought. His heart pounded. *Whew! Thank you, Lord! I'm not going to stop and thank that truck driver; he's no doubt very pissed at me, and I don't want to face that other driver either.* "Good job!" he said aloud slapping the dash of his Bug.

For the next few miles, Bill felt shaky from the close call. When he blinked, he could still see the other car's headlights approaching. He shook his head to erase the lights and the thoughts of what could have happened. The adrenaline racing through his body made him feel jittery but very alert. Even the street lights at the corner of Argonne Road and Sprague looked extra bright tonight as Bill headed west toward Barb's apartment.

He was so ready to be with Barb. He knew she could satisfy his wants and help him forget about his near miss. The sexy smile she'd given him after their lunch together flashed through his mind. He was glad that neither Barb nor he had to work tomorrow, and glad he'd told his mom that he'd be spending the night at Jerry and Sandy's after work. He and Barb could fall asleep together and resume their love-making in the morning like they had at the river. *Perfect!* he grinned.

Bill wasn't as cautious and quiet entering her apartment tonight, and he quickly undressed. "I got here as fast as I could," he whispered sliding beneath the sheet next to her. "Were you dreaming about me again?"

"Yes, very vivid dreams," she murmured rolling to him. "But just hold me for a bit while I wake-up okay?"

He breathed her in. "You smell so good."

"Good, 'cuz I took a long bath for you, in case you wanted to…"

"Wanted to what?" he asked curiously.

"Well, let me give you a hint." She kissed his lips, then his neck, then his nipples, then his belly; then she moved her mouth to his hardness, kissing it once, twice; then welcoming it all.

"Oh, my God!" he gasped. Every few seconds, she moved her tongue over him, making him writhe with pleasure.

She returned to his face and kissed his mouth with her wet lips. "Now do you get the idea?"

"I…think so," he replied hesitantly, not knowing exactly how to proceed.

"Just kiss me and I'll show you," she replied now lying on her back. Placing her hands on his face, she kissed him moving her tongue in his mouth. When she felt him relax a bit, she directed him to her neck. He could tell that kissing her neck excited her; her body writhed and her breathing grew louder.

After a few minutes, she moved him to her left breast, where he first kissed the sides, then her nipple. When she couldn't stand it anymore, she moved him to her right breast where he did the same.

Then she began pressing his head downward and raising her pelvic area to him. There was no doubt what she wanted now. Following her routine, he kissed her smooth, concave stomach, then above her silkiness, then the inside of her right thigh. He could tell by her movements and moans that she was enjoying his exploration of her body. For a moment he felt somewhat tentative about his next move. He remembered how the sleeping bag smelled—but Barb smelled so good all over tonight. She must have sensed his hesitation, as he felt her hands guiding his head toward her ultimate want.

Well, here goes, he thought trembling. He slid his arms under her legs to raise her to his mouth. When he met her, she writhed and moaned as she held him firmly to her and moved against him. He randomly explored her with his tongue, not sure exactly what to do. But it didn't matter; she was in ecstasy. After a few moments, she pulled him upward, and kissed his wet lips like she wanted to taste him. As she kissed him, she moved herself to welcome him—all of him.

"Just fuck me…fuck me, Bill!"

He hadn't seen her this passionate before; he had never felt anything so wonderful. He just wanted it to last all night. But all too quickly, he felt that inner surge beginning to build. He did his best to delay it, but it was like trying to hold back a breaching dam. He suddenly exploded. They both gasped in delight trying their best to muffle their climax.

"Oh, my God! You're still coming!" she exclaimed.

As their heavy breathing and rapid heart rates slowed, he rolled onto his side so their sweaty bodies could cool. They both enjoyed the peaceful recovery, not saying anything, just breathing together. Within minutes, they were asleep in one another's arms.

"I have to use the bathroom; be right back," she whispered. Bill stirred and tried to open his eyes. He didn't know what time it was, but could tell it was starting to get light outside. For a split second, he saw the oncoming headlights, but quickly pushed them from his mind. "Okay," he replied groggily. "Hurry back," he added rolling onto his stomach.

—⁓—

"Are you going to sleep all morning?" she asked from the doorway.

He struggled to open his heavy eyes. "Ohhh, what time is it?"

"Almost 9:00!"

"No! You're kidding!"

"How about some breakfast?"

"How about more lovin'?"

"Maybe after breakfast," she chuckled, as she headed back to her kitchen. "I guess I worked up an appetite last night."

The aromas of freshly brewed coffee and bacon and eggs made him realize how hungry he was as well. After finding his underpants and shorts, he headed for the bathroom to wash his face and thoroughly rinse out his mouth. His tired face and cow-licked hair peered back at him in the mirror, and attempts to flatten his hair with his hand and some water weren't totally successful. Stretch's gross comment to Stan shot through his mind; he quickly turned away from the mirror and headed to the kitchen.

As soon as Bill sat down, Barb wasted no time reducing the mound of scrambled eggs on her plate. She chased each mouthful down with a bite of bacon and toast; then a gulp of coffee. "I don't think I could've waited much longer for you to wake up," she announced after swallowing.

"Yeah, I can't believe I slept that long...mmm, this does taste great, Barb. Thank you!" *Is this what being married would be like?* he wondered. *I could handle this....*

Flashes of last night's new, orgasmic delights ran through his mind during breakfast: Barb's hands on his head guiding him to her, holding him against her, her passionate moans. He could feel himself getting hard again.

"What are you thinking about now?" she asked noticing his dreamy stare.

"Well...just how fantastic last night was. I didn't want it to ever end."

"It doesn't have to end, you know," she emphasized leaning toward him from across the table and looking into his eyes.

"I know...I know I'm going to have to make a decision soon; I just don't want to think about that right now," he replied leaning back in his chair. Then, reaching toward her and taking her hand in his said, "I just want to enjoy what we have going together now."

"Me too, and I'm fine with the way things are now, really. We can talk more about your decision in a few weeks. She paused and smiled at him through closed lips. "Hmmm, it is after breakfast now, isn't it," she reminded him.

He stood up and carried their plates to the kitchen counter. "Yes, it is."

Smiling coyly, she pulled the large sweatshirt she was wearing over her head, flung it at him and ran to her bedroom. In hot pursuit, he began unbuckling his belt and unzipping his cutoff jeans. Giggling, she wrapped herself in the sheets, and enjoyed making him work for what she knew he wanted.

Neither seemed interested in sexual explorations this morning, and wasted little time uniting. One thing he liked about having sex again after a brief period of rest, was how long the wonderful experience lasted. He knew he'd eventually come, and the sensuous progression would end, but he got to enjoy all the pleasures longer. *I wonder if she likes it more when it takes longer...?*

Satisfied in every way, they both fell asleep again, and didn't wake up until a little after noon.

Bill looked at his watch; then sat up in bed and stretched. "Man…I'd better head home for a bit or my folks might call Jerry and Sandy's; that wouldn't be good."

"Do you want to shower first?"

"No, I want to wear you all day," he chuckled lying back down and hugging her tightly.

"Yuck! Call me later and we can talk about what we're gonna to do tonight."

"You got it; talk with you soon."

"You look a bit rough," his mom remarked sternly as Bill walked through the door.

"Really? I actually feel great; got a good night's sleep at Jerry and Sandy's," he replied carrying his dirty work clothes to the laundry room.

She gave him the silent treatment for a bit while she put the groceries away in the kitchen. She wanted him to know she was concerned about his not coming home after work. When she felt she had made her point, she asked, "Fun time?"

"Yeah, although the party was winding down by the time I got there. Would sure be nice to have a day job like all my friends."

"Well, think of all the money you're earning to pay off your loan."

"Yeah, I suppose…. How was your golf game?"

"We both played great; one of our best rounds yet. Dad's requested salmon tonight; are you going to be here for dinner?"

"Sure, but will probably head out after dinner; some guys talked about seeing *The Graduate* tonight."

—⟋⟋⟋—

"Thought I'd better call you before I washed you off," he whispered from the downstair's phone about 5:00 PM. What have you been doing all day?"

"Laundry. Thought I'd better wash my sheets; they really needed it after last night's rowdiness. They got quite the workout!"

"Yeah? Well, it was the most enjoyable workout I've ever had…. Hey, I need to have dinner with my family tonight; want to do something say about 7:30?"

"Yes! Let's drive some place; I need to get away from this hot apartment for awhile."

"Sounds good; see you between 7:30 and 8:00."

Bill tried to think of where he could take her that would be fun but private…*Newman Lake!* He checked the trunk of his car to make sure his beach blanket was there. They could park at Mussie's Resort and walk along the beach to his aunt's cabin. She had a sandy, semi-private beach where they could lay a blanket down and look out at the lake.

—⟋⟋⟋—

"Good job on the salmon, Mom," praised Bill bringing dishes from the dinner table to the sink. "It was really moist. Reminded me of the salmon you'd fix for Geoff Jensen and me before our Friday night games in high school."

"Thanks," she replied rinsing off the dishes and putting them in the dishwasher. "At least there was enough to go around tonight. Remember when you and Geoff ate the entire salmon before leaving for the game? I had to go back to the store and buy another one for the rest of us."

"Well the salmon worked—we won the game that night," he bragged kissing her cheek. "See you later; I'd better get goin'."

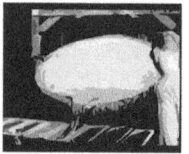

"Still want to go for a drive?" he asked stepping into Barb's hot apartment.

"Yes; it's such a nice evening and my apartment is so hot and stuffy."

"Well, how about Newman Lake?"

"Sure! I haven't been to Newman Lake in years!"

"I know a pretty nice beach there. I have a blanket we can use; do you have a couple beach towels we could take?"

"Yes; I'll get them."

"Perfect; let's go!"

Bill loved the smell of the warm summer air in the evenings. He felt so energized; so full of life. And having Barb sitting next to him as they drove to Newman Lake made the evening all the more special.

"You know, you made me feel amazing last night," she said positioning herself against her door to look at him.

Bill grinned. "My pleasure...but there probably won't be a repeat performance of...you know...we'll be at a sandy beach!" Barb smiled. He knew she understood perfectly.

"Which beach are we going to?"

"Well, we'll park at Muzzy's Resort and walk down the shoreline a ways. My aunt has a cabin on the east side of the lake and a nice, semi-private, sandy beach."

After parking at the resort, Bill carried the rolled up towels in his blanket, and they walked south past the resort. They came to a narrow dirt trail that separated docks from privately owned cabins along the beach. He was glad there would be a moon this evening, as it would probably be dark by the time they returned, and he'd forgotten to bring a flashlight. He inhaled deeply savoring the unique lake smells that took him back in time to when he and his family would come to the lake for one week each summer.

"Boys, we have to unload first!" Howard would yell, as Bill and Rod ran from the car down to the beach to look at the lake.

Now, as he and Barb walked along the beach trail, little waves lapped at the shoreline making their wet sounds. He was glad they had come here tonight. He just wanted to enjoy this beautiful evening; the summer was going by so quickly.

"There it is," he said pointing to a large, two story log cabin nestled back in the trees to their left. It was still light enough to see the "Hidden Lodge" sign above the screen door.

"Does she live here?" Barb asked.

"No, she lives in Spokane and only comes out once in awhile now. If she were here, her car would be parked in front." He spread out the blanket on the sand and handed her the towels. "Isn't this a nice beach!?" He was glad it would be getting dark soon, as it would give them more privacy while they gazed out at the lake and up at the emerging stars. It was so pleasant to hear the lake sounds: the frogs and crickets, an outboard motor off in the distance, the waves lapping at the shore, the laughter of children from neighboring beaches, and the voices carrying across the lake.

"This is so peaceful," reflected Barb sitting cross-legged on the blanket and looking out at the lake. "How long has your aunt had her cabin?" asked Barb.

"Ever since I can remember. She used to bring me and Rod out here sometimes when we were just little kids. I think she wanted to give my mom a break."

"Did she ever marry?"

"No…and I'm not exactly sure why she didn't. My mom told me once that when she was a young woman, a guy jilted her and that after that experience she became pretty bitter toward guys. It's too bad; she's a pretty good-looking woman." The image of his aunt's bare breast and white ass flashed through Bill's mind.

Barb was quiet for a few seconds; then turning to him said, "I'm going to really miss you when you leave for the Jesuits in August."

"I'll miss you too, Barb—a lot. I don't think I'll be able to take not being with you," he answered leaning forward on the blanket. "Right now, I don't really want to go, but I almost feel like I have to given what I've told my folks and my friends, and the commitment I made to the Jesuits. If I do go, I can't imagine that I'm going to stay very long," he quickly added. He turned and looked at her. "Will you be willing to wait at least a few weeks for me?"

She squeezed his arm. "Of course, I will."

They both sat in silence for several minutes just staring at the darkening sky and listening to the chorus of lake sounds.

"I love being with you," she said cuddling even closer to him. She then turned and gave him a long kiss. She pulled away just long enough to look into his eyes; then began to unbutton her blouse.

"Barb, we're pretty close to the lake trail; we'd better… not…make…love…here…," he attempted to say as she continued to kiss him.

"Shhh—I have an idea." She stood up, faced away from him and wrapped one of the long beach towels around her. In a few seconds, her cut offs and panties fell to the blanket. Wrapped fully in the towel, she turned toward him. "Stand up, face me and wrap your towel around your shoulders and do the same," she coached. When his cut offs and underpants slid to the blanket, she told him to lie on his back on the blanket.

As she lowered herself to straddle him, she opened each towel just enough to unite. His mind urged restraint, but once she began to welcome him, he didn't really care if someone walked by them on the nearby trail. *Nobody will know who we are anyway.*

She raised up a bit; then pushed against him. As soon as he was deep inside her, she began to stroke him, using her legs to raise herself; then lower herself, tightening with each upward stroke. A boat wake that had traveled across the lake moved the dock up and down; the water made a slapping sound against the dock.

As she quickened her stroking, he could feel his cock beginning to swell. With her on top this time, he would just let her take control...take all that she wanted.

"Oh, my God!" he gasped as he started to come. "Take it all...." She continued to stroke him, but he grabbed her and held her close to him as he finished climaxing.

As their passion ebbed, she bent down to kiss him, then reclined on top of him, her towel shrouding them. "Thank you!" she said still breathing quickly. "I just needed you so much tonight."

"My pleasure!" he grinned matching her breathing and enjoying her embrace.

As their heart rates slowed, he wondered how they were going to get dressed without getting any sand on places where it shouldn't be. "Hey, I have an idea," he offered. "Stand up; then pull me up."

As she did so, he removed his shirt; then removed her shirt and bra. Grabbing her hand, he bolted, pulling her into the lake with hoots and hollers. They didn't care how much noise they made now. Skinny dipping was very much a part of warm summer evenings at lakes in the Spokane area. Residents thoroughly enjoyed all the delights the summer seasons offered for they were so short, and the winters so long.

"I can't believe how warm the water is," she said delightedly dipping down so the water covered her shoulders.

"Yeah, this lake really gets warm in the summer; it isn't a very deep lake. When we were kids, we'd stay in the water all day long. We didn't even want to stop for lunch."

For several minutes they frolicked in the water laughing, swimming short distances then embracing keeping their shoulders beneath the warm water. Then not seeing anyone on the lake trail; Bill waded back to the beach, shook the sand from their towels and tossed Barb's to her as she neared the shore. Wrapped snuggly in their towels, they sat on the front edge of his aunt's dock, dangling their feet in the water and watching for shooting stars.

After about fifteen minutes, the cool evening air and wet towels became uncomfortable, and they hurried back to their scattered clothes. Bill held his beach towel up for her while she dressed.

"Thanks for bringing me here," Barb said zipping up her cut off jeans. "This has been such a perfect evening." She then held up her blanket while Bill dressed.

"I'm glad you enjoyed it," he smiled shaking the sand from the blanket. She helped him fold it. Before heading back to his car, he stopped for a moment and drew in the whole scene. He looked out at the lake, at his aunt's old rickety dock, the beach where he and Barb just made love, the rope swing hanging between two large trees and his aunt's cabin back in the shadows. *Yes, it has been a perfect evening,* he thought locking away its specialness. He knew this would probably be a once in a lifetime experience with Barb here and wanted to make sure he'd never forget it. He filled his lungs with the fresh, sweet evening air, closed his eyes and exhaled.

As they headed up the trail back to the car, he actually hoped she would get pregnant as it would provide him an understandable reason for not entering the Jesuits, and for staying at Kaiser. He made pretty good money there, and could support Barb and any kids they would have together. It would make his decision easy.

They didn't say much as they drove south on the dark, curvy, unpaved road around the lake. They were both reluctant to leave behind this idyllic evening. Finally, Bill broke the silence when they transitioned to the paved road that would take them back to East Trent Ave. and the Spokane Valley. "I'm kind of hungry after that swim; want to stop at Ron's and get a burger before heading back to your place?"

"Yes!" she replied. "I'm ravenous."

"I'd invite you in for some 'dessert,'" she said looking at him softly, "but I'm afraid I might have some sand where it wouldn't feel good to either of us."

Bill grinned. "I understand…and my getting home before midnight will avoid a bunch of questions from my parents. I think they're getting a bit concerned about me keeping my August commitment. I'll give you a call tomorrow." He leaned to kiss her then paused. "Hmmm—I could come by for some 'dessert' before I head into Kaiser tomorrow night. It would certainly help me face my first night on graveyard."

"I'll see what delight I can come up with," she teased before kissing him goodnight.

—⁓—

"You're home early for a change," his mother said as he came in the front door.

"Yeah; I'm kind of tired; so thought I'd just come home and hit the sack. Dad must already be in bed, huh?"

"He is, and I'm on my way; see you in the morning."

"Thanks, Mom; good night." *Whew! No questions tonight,* he thought pouring himself some Cheerios. He opened the screen slider onto the deck and sat outside in the warm evening air while he ate his cereal. *These summer nights in Spokane are so pleasant; I'm going to miss them.*

Setting his bowl aside, he put his head back, closed his eyes and listened to the frogs filling the night air with their music. His mind flashed back to Barb on top of him performing her rhythmic magic; then to the laughter that accompanied their swim. *How am I going to take not being with her!? But staying here with her would mean working in the pot rooms for the rest of my life. Just three months there during the summer is like an eternity.* Not wanting to confront this inevitable decision tonight, he picked up his bowl, put it in the dishwasher, and headed down the stairs to bed.

—⁓—

When he opened his eyes and looked over at his alarm, he couldn't believe the time. *Holy shit! It's almost 10:00 AM!* He jumped out of bed and headed for his bathroom before heading upstairs.

"You must have been tired!" his mom said as he entered the kitchen. "Do you want breakfast or lunch?"

"Oh…nothing yet; just coffee."

"It's such a nice day, we're going to head to Newman Lake for a swim and picnic; it'll also be a good time to check out the cabin to see what we need to bring with us when we go in a few weeks. Do you want to come with us?" she asked hopefully.

He had to suppress a smile. "No thanks. Tonight's the start of graveyard shift, so think I'll stay here and catch up on some things. Oh, I'm going to stop by some friends' place tonight on my way in to work, so I probably won't be here when you get back. Don't want you to worry. Have fun."

"We will; sure hope you'll spend some time with us in August when we're at the lake," she said in her reminding tone.

Turning down invitations from his parents, who sincerely wanted to spend some time with him before he left in August made Bill feel like a heel, and these feelings added to the guilt he felt about not telling them the truth about his seeing Barb. He recalled a question Fr. Eric had asked him in one of their conversations, *"Does this choice make you feel like your best self?"* Turning down this latest invitation did not.

—⁓—

"Hi," he greeted Barb sleepily over the phone. "I slept 'til 10:00 this morning!"

"Yeah, I slept in late too. Must have been all the exercise we got at the lake. What time do you want to come over tonight?"

"Probably about 6:00; I need to do some things here today. Hey, you won't believe where my parents are headed today— Newman Lake! They're going out to my aunt's cabin to enjoy the day and to check it out for their stay there in a few weeks. Hope we didn't leave any underwear on her beach."

"And I hope they don't check out the impressions we made in the sand," Barb added chuckling. "See you later; I've got to think up a good dessert for tonight! Bye."

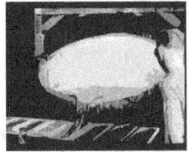

Bill didn't really want to spend time preparing for the Novitiate this far ahead of his departure date in August, but knew he had to. He pulled out the list he had received from the Oregon Province: 8 pairs of underpants and undershirts, 8 pairs of black socks, 2 pairs of black slacks, 1 pair of black shoes, 2 white shirts, 1 black tie, 1 black belt. His college wardrobe didn't contribute much to this list. *Man, I have some shopping to do.*

Looking at this list also made him think of what he was going to do with his belongings. He began to write down the articles he'd ask his parents to keep for him: his suit, a few favorite shirts, pants, sweatshirts and football jerseys, some books from college, his school yearbooks, his typewriter, his Enfield .303 hunting rifle, his Remington .22 rifle. The rest of his clothes, shoes, coats, etc. he would donate or toss.

When he completed his list, he began to go through his scrapbook and personal belongings tossing items that didn't really mean much to him any longer, like athletic awards he'd received in elementary school. He placed items he wanted to keep in a rectangular Bon Marche gift box on the top shelf of his closet, taped it closed and labeled it: **Bill's Personal Stuff**.

Let's see, what else will I have to do before August 29…? Oh, my car, I'm going to have to sell my Bug before I leave. And I'll

ask Dad to keep my savings account active until further notice.
Feelings of uneasiness, doubt and a bit of fear came over him.
*Do I really know what the fuck I'm doing? What if I decide to
return home after a few weeks? I won't have a job, a car...perhaps
not even Barb anymore.... Maybe I should just keep my job at
Kaiser and stay here....* But another voice kept telling him that
he needed to stick with his commitment to enter the Novitiate
at the end of August. *Right now you're aimless, and heading
down a path that will result in you working at Kaiser the rest of
your life—and perhaps feeling trapped in a relationship or marriage you might not want to be permanent.* He lay down on his
bed and stared at the ceiling trying to think his way through
this troubling maze.

When he opened his eyes, he realized he'd fallen asleep...*Oh
man, 3:00!* He thought about going shopping for the clothes he
needed, but decided to wait a few weeks more—*just in case I
change my mind.* Not wanting to think about these decisions
and responsibilities any longer, he changed into his running
shorts and jogged down the street to nearby Bowdish Junior
High where he liked to run in the summer. He had always
been in good shape, and this was one thing he was determined
to maintain no matter what he did. Being out of shape and getting fat were big fears for him.

The smell of the grass as he ran wind sprints on the football field reminded him of all the years he'd prepared for football season during the summers. He loved the sun, the heat,
the smell of the grass, sweating, the breeze on his face and the
feeling of freedom when he sprinted. The other thing he loved
about running was that it helped him forget about things he
didn't want to think about. He just felt healthy, young, alive, in
control, in shape.

When he'd worked up a good sweat, he jogged back home

and jumped in the shower. As the water massaged his back, he wondered what delight Barb would have for him tonight. His groin tingled and he began to get hard. *Better plan something for dinner and for my sack lunch,* he thought in order to refocus.

Perfect, 5:30. I'd better leave the folks a note to remind them I'm stopping at a friend's before heading to work. He knew if his mom forgot, she'd start worrying about him, and call some of his friends to see if he was there, and he didn't want that to occur.

—m—

When Barb opened her door, Bill stared at her in amazement scanning her from top to bottom. She was wearing an apron over—nothing!!

"Hi," she greeted with a big grin. She put her arms around him, and kissed him pulling him into her apartment. "Have you been wondering what I made you for dessert?"

"Yes, all day," he lied.

"Well, you'll have to take your clothes off and get into my bed to find out. I'll be there in just a few minutes—with your treat."

Complying eagerly, he removed his clothes and hopped into her bed quickly so she wouldn't see his erection. *I wonder what she prepared?* "Okay, I'm ready!" he announced.

When Barb entered the bedroom, she lifted the apron's top loop over her head; then looking at him, slowly untied the apron and let it fall to the floor revealing her nakedness. Before getting on her bed, she sprayed whipped cream on her nipples.

"I hope you like whipped cream," she teased.

"I love whipped cream!" he responded with an eager grin.

She knelt next to him on the bed so her nipples would be

easily accessible to him when he sat up. When he did so, he admired her breasts for a few seconds like a young boy being offered two decorated cupcakes— not sure which to enjoy first. Sensing his indecision, she placed a hand on each side of his head and led him to her right nipple. She flinched and gasped with pleasure as he slowly licked off most of the whipped cream. To make sure he removed all the cream, she pulled him closer to her and pressed her entire nipple into his mouth moaning with delight as he removed the last bit of sweetness. Then she moved him to her left breast and encouraged him to do the same.

When she was satisfied, she moved him away from her, looked into his eyes and pushed him down onto her bed. "Now it's my turn," she announced.

She swept the top sheet to his feet with her right hand admiring his alertness as she did so. She grabbed the can of whipped cream from the nightstand, raised his hard cock with her left and covered the head with cream.

She began licking the cream off little by little, and as she did so, he could feel her soft, warm tongue on him. Each lick sent sensual shivers deep into his body. When just a little cream remained, she took him into her mouth, as if not wanting to waste any. Her tongue which moved on him was even more sensuous now that the cream was gone. He could hardly stand it. His entire body stiffened into the mattress.

She then crept upward toward his mouth, stared at it briefly then kissed him with her juicy, sweet lips. She began moving her tongue in his mouth, and he knew what she was asking him to do. When she pulled back and looked at him, he rolled her onto her back, grabbed the can of whipped cream from the nightstand, and sprayed some where he knew she wanted it. Before moving southward, he looked into her eyes, smiled, then kissed his way to her. Her entire body trembled with anticipation as she raised herself up to him. She wanted him desperately. First he carefully licked away the cream with the tip of his tongue. He wanted to see what a pussy actually looked like. *It's so pink,* he thought when he had removed all the cream. He began to explore her with his tongue now, and as he did so, she gasped and thrust her head back into the pillow, slapping the mattress with her hands.

"Oh my God, that feels so fucking good…."

When her ecstasy became too much for her, she grabbed his head in her hands, pulled him upward to her mouth and kissed him passionately. After a few seconds and eager to excite her again, he began moving downward but she stopped him. She was done with that; she wanted all of him now. Her readiness combined with the helpful lubricants made their uniting easy and smooth, and both experienced new levels of delight.

For Bill, the intense foreplay shortened the time it usually took him to climax, and she could tell. She grabbed his ass and held him close to her. When he came, she tightened around him and moved with him as if to capture everything he could give her. Aware of the poorly insulated apartment walls both attempted to muffle their rapture as best they could; then recovered from the intense bliss together.

"That's the best dessert I've ever had," Bill said still breathing heavily.

"Glad you liked it. I worked on it all day in my hot kitchen," she smiled.

"It will certainly help me get through graveyard tonight; the first night is always the hardest."

"'Hard'—even after this?" she teased jabbing him in the ribs. "Hey, let's shower together," she suggested as she got out of bed. "You can wash my…back."

The cool shower felt good after such intimate passion. Lathering her hands with the bar of soap, she began washing his now limp cock. "How come it's no longer hard?" she teased.

"'Cuz you took it all out of me." Bill flashed an embarrassed smile, lathered his hands with soap and gently washed her firm breasts. "Does that feel good?"

"Very!" she replied with her eyes closed. "Turn around; I'll get your back," she directed lathering a washcloth. This was the first time he'd ever showered with a girl, and he loved it. *I could get used to this real fast,* he thought wishing he didn't have to leave for work in a couple of hours.

They enjoyed washing each other until the warm water began turning cold; then they dried one another off.

"I actually did pick up some dessert for us," admitted Barb as they finished dressing. She walked ahead of him into the kitchen, opened the refrigerator and removed some strawberries to put on top of shortcake. "Would you like some whipped cream on top?"

"Sure! A guy can't ever get too much whipped cream," he chuckled kissing her on the back of her neck.

Later that evening as he prepared to leave for work, he gave Barb a big hug. "Thanks so much for tonight, Barb; your dessert was wonderful! I'll be thinking about it tonight and all week."

"That's the idea," she grinned.

"I'll give you a call later in the week."

"Bye," she said; then kissed him. "I'll serve you dessert anytime."

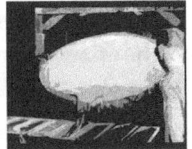

"Roberts."

"Here."

"Pots, here on Line 4. You'll be with Jim Bingham, who has the first string."

Wow, pots! I've never been a pot man before, he thought heading up the line to find Jim.

"You must be my trainee," guessed Jim as Bill entered the waterhole. Jim was a little taller than Bill but not as muscular. Like most pot men, he wore an old, unbuttoned long sleeved shirt over a t-shirt. He had a calm, kind face and sincere smile. He didn't attempt to display his tough guy look like some of the lifers do when they meet a trainee.

"At least you got a good one," said the crane driver. "He's one of the better spare carbon setters we get during the summers."

"Thanks," Bill replied acknowledging the crane driver. "I appreciate the chance to learn about being a pot man; I've never had this opportunity before," added Bill looking at Jim.

"I'll teach you what I know," stated Jim matter-of-factly.

Bill knew that pot men had an important job because it was their knowledge, skills and attention to their pots that determined the high quality of the aluminum produced at Mead. He also knew it was a pretty sweet job, as they fed their string of 14 pots once each hour. If their pots were all running smoothly, they could finish a feeding in about 25 minutes then spend the rest of the hour in the waterhole playing cards, reading or snoozing until the top of the next hour.

"Okay, let's go feed my string," directed Jim. "We'll feed the front sides of Pots 1-14 on the even hours and the back sides on the odd hours." He stopped in front of Pot 14. "Always look at the voltage meter on each of your pots. The needle should be between about 4.7 and 5.0 volts. To decrease the voltage, you pull this chain counterclockwise; to increase the voltage, you pull the chain clockwise. The wheel that the chain turns lowers and raises the carbon anodes in the pot thus affecting the pot's voltage."

Jim then slid the front cover of Pot 14 to the side and showed Bill how to remove the long poker from its hanger inside the pot. "Here now you try it."

"Man, the poker's really heavy!"

"Yeah, you have to learn how to use the roller for leverage— like this...." Jim moved backwards to balance the long poker on the roller at the base of the opening. When he had adequate leverage, he rotated the poker so its hooked end was facing upward, raised the front end of the poker then lifted the handle letting the full weight of the poker drop onto the crust that had formed on top of the molten cryolite bath.

Sometimes it took Jim several drops to fully break the crust and expose the molten bath inside the pots. Once this occurred, he turned the poker end sideways and moving it back and forth on the roller bar removed any refined bauxite ore or alumina that was covering any of the iron couplings that connect the copper rods to their carbon anodes. "You need to make sure no anode connections are glowing red because a red connection can result in a burn off if the carbon isn't adjusted in time. You know from carbon setting what a hot, gassy, miserable job it is to remove a small, spent carbon from the pot. Imagine trying to remove a large carbon that's been recently installed. You'd have to get the foreman and maybe even the carbon setters and crane driver to help you, and they don't appreciate that."

After Jim had exposed the anode connections on that end of the pot, he reached up, grabbed the ore hopper handle and released one dump of bauxite ore into the molten cryolite bath. "The ore mixes with the cryolite bath to produce aluminum metal. But you don't want to feed your pot too much ore at once or you'll wind up with a 'cold pot' that will give you fits," Jim explained. "It's better to return a bit later after the crust begins to form on top of the bath, then add another dump or two of ore."

After they had fed Pots 1-14, they walked around to the back sides of the same pots. "After each feeding, always glance inside the opposite ends of your pots to see if there are any glowing anodes; then add a dump of ore on top of the crust. This will help keep your voltage up where it should be."

"Thanks, Jim; now what do we do?"

"We relax in the waterhole until the top of the next hour when we feed the back sides of the pots or until we hear the carbon setters. Do you know how to play cribbage?"

"No, but I enjoy watching you guys play it."

"Well, you'll have to learn how to play."

After they had been in the waterhole for about 15 minutes, Jim heard the overhead crane heading up the line to his first string. "Here come the carbon setters; this shift they're changing the Number 8 carbon in my string." Jim grabbed some type of measuring stick, then showed Bill a chart in the waterhole that indicated which recently set carbon anode they'd use as a reference for setting the Number 8 carbon. The chart also indicated how much more height they'd add to this particular reference carbon. "So first find Carbon Number 8 on the chart...then its reference carbon...then add the indicated adjustment. How much does it say to add to our reference carbon?" asked Jim.

"Plus 3/4."

"Yep; that's 3/4s of an inch. So we'll take a measurement from the mark that's on the rod of our reference carbon; then add 3/4 of an inch and secure our measuring stick. Why do you think we have to add 3/4 of an inch to the reference carbon?"

"Well, probably because the reference carbon has already lost 3/4 of an inch since it was set."

"That's right; very good. Now, let's head out, and I'll show you how to set the measuring stick and how to adjust the Number 8 carbon."

On the way to the first string, Jim grabbed another piece of equipment. "This is called a 'jack'; we use this to raise or lower the new carbon to our setting. But first let's set our measurement." Jim placed the measuring stick over the recently set reference carbon in Pot 14, adjusted the stick to the mark on its copper rod, then added 3/4 of an inch to the measurement. He then tightened the measuring stick to that setting. "Now we're in business," Jim added.

After the carbon setters removed the old Number 8 carbon and inserted a new one into its slot, Jim led Bill up the stairs onto the catwalk. He placed the measuring stick over the rod of the new Number 8 carbon then affixed the jack to the side of its rod. Using the jack, Jim raised up the new carbon until the mark on its copper rod matched the measurement on their stick; then tightened the clamp that secured the rod to the side of the pot.

"There. This places the new anode at just the right height

from the bottom of the pot."

"Do we have to adjust the other carbons as well?"

"No; not unless we'd discover an anode that has been set at the wrong height or has dropped, and that does happen occasionally if someone didn't adequately tighten its clamp.

"One thing you'll quickly learn as a pot man is that the quality of your string of pots is determined to a large extent by the quality of the pot men who operate your string. If one of the pot men on another shift is lazy or doesn't know what he's doing, the other two pot men will be negatively impacted. That's one of the reasons I want you to learn everything well. You don't want to be the one who screws up someone else's string of pots."

Bill closely watched Jim align the first few new carbons.

"Okay, your turn," directed Jim handing Bill the jack and measuring stick. He let Bill finish aligning the remaining new carbon anodes in his string, checking each one to make sure Bill had set them to the proper mark. "Good job; I think you've got it down. Now we're done with the carbon setters until our next scheduled carbon change. But it's just about time for us to feed the back sides of our pots, so we might as well do that. We'll do the same thing we did on the front sides. You want to make sure you carefully check your voltages because a carbon change can sometimes affect a pot's voltage."

"Man, you sure stay a lot cleaner and sweat a lot less than when you're carbon setting," emphasized Bill after they finished the feeding.

"Yeah, but don't get sucked into staying on out here like so many of you young bucks do," Jim cautioned. "Just remember that this is what it's going to be like for the next 30 years: changing shifts every week, same routines, breathing gases and dust that aren't good for your lungs. Take advantage of your college education and find a job that challenges you and offers advancement opportunities. If you get stuck out here in the pot rooms, you'll regret it!"

"Other guys out here have given me the same advice; thanks, Jim."

Bill watched Jim closely for the rest of the shift, asking a lot of questions and making sure he knew how to do the various tasks Jim performed with his pots.

"See ya tomorrow," waved Jim as they headed to the shower room at the end of the shift. "I'm told you'll be with me for the rest of graveyard shift."

As Bill headed for his car after clocking out, Don, the Line 7 crane driver asked Bill if he'd seen Ed Lewis since Ed stepped in a pot a few weeks back.

"I haven't yet, and I heard he can have visitors now that there's less chance of infection. Thanks for reminding me."

I should go see Ed this morning; otherwise I'll just put it off, thought Bill. So instead of heading east for home, he drove west to Division Street and headed south toward Sacred Heart Hospital. When he reached E. Boone Ave., he glanced to his left toward the GU campus. *Man, I'm so glad I'm done with that part of my life!* He then continued south and up Grand Boulevard to Sacred Heart Hospital.

"Well, if it ain't Bill Roberts," greeted Ed as Bill peeked into Ed's room. Ed was sitting up in bed reading a paperback; his right foot was wrapped in lots of white gauze.

Bill walked closer to Ed's bandaged foot; then shook his hand. "How's it healing up, Ed?"

"Pretty good. The docs are pleased with how the skin grafts

are taking." Ed showed Bill where doctors had removed healthy skin from his thigh to use on his foot.

"Man, I can't begin to imagine how painful it must have been," winced Bill.

"Well, it happened so damned fast, and you know what's strange? The Doc said my sweaty foot actually saved my foot. The steam from the sweat is what really burned my foot, but it actually helped protect my foot as well. He said the sweat acted like a cushion and kept my foot from getting as hot as the molten metal."

"Oh, that explains why your boot looked like it had exploded outward. After we heard about your accident we went down to Line 2 and your foreman showed us your boot."

"Yeah, for once I was thankful for sweaty feet!" chuckled Ed. He filled Bill in on what happened after the accident, and his hospital stay thus far; then Ed wanted to know the latest scuttlebutt at work. While they were visiting, a couple different young nurses came in to check on Ed.

"Now I understand why you're still in here!" ribbed Bill.

"No kiddin'; I might ask one or two of them out when I'm outta here."

Bill could tell Ed was hungry for company and updates from Kaiser; so he visited with Ed for over an hour.

"Thanks for comin' to see me. Keep in touch, and in the meantime, don't step in any pots."

"I won't," promised Bill glancing at Ed's foot again before heading out the door.

As Bill headed for his car he wondered if Ed would stay at Kaiser and become a lifer. Ed, who was just two years older than Bill had decided to continue at Kaiser after his first summer there. Ed then bought a brand new red 1961 Pontiac Bonneville two door hardtop—*probably one of the reasons Ed stayed at Kaiser,* surmised Bill. *I imagine the payments were pretty hefty.*

—w—

"Where you been?" asked his mom, as Bill entered the front door about 10:30. She was folding laundry into individual stacks on the kitchen table.

"I stopped by Sacred Heart Hospital to visit Ed Lewis. He's the guy who stepped in the pot a few weeks back. I've been meaning to visit him, and thought this morning was as good a time as any."

"Oh, that was nice of you; I'll bet he appreciated your visit."

"Yeah, he did. He's pretty fortunate he didn't lose his foot."

His mom winced. "Well, you had two calls this morning. One was from Fr. Eric. He said he's going to be gone during July and August so wanted to just call and see how you were doing. That was sure thoughtful of him. The other call was from Jeff Zarillo; he wants you to call him back."

Bill's gut tightened when he heard that Fr. Eric called. "Thanks, Mom, I'll call them back after I grab a bite." As he fixed his breakfast, he wondered what he would tell Eric. *What if he asks if my novitiate plans have changed since graduation? What if he wants to get together and talk before he leaves?*

Bill was glad Jeff, who was one of his closest friends at Gonzaga University, had called. He definitely wanted to see Jeff before he left for the Novitiate in August.

After enjoying his scrambled eggs and toast, Bill decided to call Eric back first. If Eric wanted to get together, he knew that should take precedence. He picked up the phone from the upstairs family room and carried it into the living room.

"Hi, Eric; this is Bill. Mom said you're going to be gone the rest of the summer."

"Yes, I'm heading to Berkeley for a retreat; then I'll be filling in at a nearby parish while the pastor is on vacation. Just wanted to call and give you the phone number where I'll be staying in case you need to call me about anything.

"Thanks, Eric; got it," replied Bill after writing it down on the back of an envelope.

"How's your summer going so far?"

"Pretty good; just workin' at Kaiser."

"Any second thoughts about entering the Novitiate in August? I know I had a few during the summer before I entered. It was such a significant decision for me."

"No…not really; I still think it's what God's calling me to do at this point in my life."

"Just remember, Bill that God wants you to be happy and at peace with your life. Listen to His voice when you pray over your decision. Which decision gives you a sense of peace and consolation? Which decision brings with it a sense of disquiet and desolation?"

"I will, Eric. That's good advice. Thanks for calling me, and thanks for giving me your phone number. I hope you have a good retreat. Bye."

Whew! Bill sighed relieved that Eric hadn't suggested they get together. He didn't want to mention anything to Eric that could jeopardize the option he had with the Jesuits—the option that could provide him the direction he knew he really needed in his life right now. At the same time, he wasn't ready to give Barb up at this point in the summer. He headed to the downstairs phone to return Jeff's call.

"Hey, where you been all summer?" scolded Jeff over the phone. "You gonna leave for the Jebbies before sayin' good-bye!?"

"No, I was going to call you for sure; just been busy workin'."

"What shift are you working now?"

"Graveyard until this Friday."

"Perfect! I'm having a party Friday night starting about 7:00, and I'd like you to come. My folks are in Eastern Washington with my brothers and sisters. Bring a friend if you'd like to."

"I'll be there, Jeff; count me in, and thanks for calling!"

"Don't even need to bring any beer; I'm getting a keg."

Jeff Zarillo had been a classmate during Bill's freshman and sophomore years at Gonzaga Prep; then again while Bill attended Gonzaga University. They both belonged to the Spokane Elks Club during college and played a lot of handball together. Jeff and Bill were about the same height and build and both had good quickness so they were well matched on the handball court. *It'll be great to see Jeff and some of the GU gang*, thought Bill after hanging up the phone. He was already looking forward to Friday night.

Bill wanted badly to leave early for work to see Barb, but he knew if he did, he wouldn't be sharp for his pot training with Jim Bingham. So, he decided he'd just call and ask Barb if she wanted to go to Jeff's party Friday night.

"Sure; what time should I be ready?"

"I'll pick you up about 7:00; that will get us to Jeff's about 7:30. It should be a good a time; Jeff always throws great parties, and his family's out of town."

"Do I have to wait 'til Friday night to see you?" she asked disappointedly.

"I'm afraid so. I'm being trained to be a pot man this week; so I really have to be alert and on my toes. It's a lot of responsibility. I promise, I'll make it up to you Friday night!"

"Darn! Okay—as long as you'll keep your promise."

—ⱲⱲ—

As Bill walked to the Line 4 waterhole on Thursday night, he noticed Jim working on Pot 9. Its warning light was on and a bell was persistently ringing. Jim was attempting to silence the annoying bell by running the poker under the anodes.

"What's going on?" asked Bill approaching the pot.

"Some dumb shit on the previous shift overfed this pot; so now I'm trying to break up the 'sludge' that built up under the anodes." Jim had already worked up a sweat and was breathing hard. "The sludge decreases the electrical conductivity. Most of the time you can disperse the buildup by placing the poker hook sideways under the anodes and raking it back underneath them. If this doesn't work and the pot gets sicker, the entire pot may have to be shut down, and you want to prevent that from happening at all costs. Watch how I position the poker and how I pull back on it." Jim positioned the hook end of the poker under the anodes on the right side of the pot, put his left foot on the front of the pot, then pulled the poker toward him in a quick fashion with both arms. The bell stopped ringing for a few seconds, but came back on. "Here; now you try it on the left side of the pot!"

Bill knew he was a lot stronger than Jim so thought he'd impress Jim by how hard and quick he could pull the long poker underneath the anodes. But to his surprise, he couldn't pull it nearly as effectively as Jim, and the bell just kept ringing.

"Harder than it looks, huh!" jabbed Jim. "It gets easier as you learn how to use the roller. Do the same thing one more time on the left side. If the bell keeps ringing then we'll do the same on the other end of the pot."

After a couple tries on the opposite end of the pot, Bill was finally able to disperse enough sludge under the anodes to re-establish effective current distribution in the pot. The bell stopped ringing and the pot's warning light flickered—then turned off.

"Good job. Now check your voltage to make sure it's between the two numbers we talked about."

Jim let his foreman know what had occurred with Pot 9. "If you can't get the bell to stop ringing after several attempts on both ends of the pot, contact your foreman right away," emphasized Jim as they walked back to the waterhole. "He has to make the call on what to do at that point. If a pot 'turns over,' it's an ugly situation, and guess who gets the blame!"

"I hope that doesn't happen to me on my watch," declared Bill.

"Yeah, you and every pot man out here," added Jim. "The pot has to be shunted and rebuilt, which costs the plant money. So pot men and their foremen use all their skills to not lose one on their shift," elaborated Jim as they entered the water-hole. "But every now and then a pot cell will develop a leak in its lining and once the aluminum metal breaches the cell's iron outer shell, there isn't really anything even the best pot man can do to stop it," he added sitting down on the near bench.

Jim's last comment reminded Bill of a scary scene he'd witnessed while sparing a few summers ago. He was sweeping the floor in a pot room and watching a crew attempt to shunt a "sick pot." Smoke was roiling from the pot and the carbon anodes were burning off their copper rods. He could feel the searing heat standing 20 feet away from the pot. Suddenly some orange liquid aluminum metal began to leak out of the pot cell and as soon as it hit the much cooler pot room floor, all hell broke loose. Hot aluminum shrapnel began to shoot in all directions amid thunderous reports that were every bit as loud as his hunting rifle.

"Run!" the pot man yelled to warn everyone in the area. But before Bill could react, a piece of the hot metal struck one of Bill's safety glass lenses, and when he turned to run toward the alley, another piece hit him in the back immediately burning through his shirt and into his skin. He wondered if this is what it would feel like to get shot. There was no way even with his sprinter's quickness he could escape these speeding bullets. When he was safely around the corner in the alleyway, he removed his safety glasses and noticed a divot in the left lens. *Boy, I'm sure glad I was wearing my safety glasses! I would have lost my left eye!* He knew from experience that the burn on his back would scab over and heal leaving a barely noticeable scar, but right now it was a searing pain.

When he peeked around the corner of the alley, he saw the crane operator positioning the crane above the sick pot. A crew attached cables to the pot; then the crane's block raised the pot up enough so men could hammer shunts into the "bus bar." Electricity would now bypass that pot.

Days later, after the pot's bath and metal cooled sufficiently, the pot was disassembled, and its cell was jack hammered out by a maintenance crew. After the cell was clean, a new cathode lining of refractory bricks and carbon was installed over time; then when the pot was reconstructed, the shunts were removed so it could be brought back on line.

"Is there any indication that a pot's lining is developing a leak?"

"Yes, if the Quality Control guys catch it in time. Periodically they come around to take samples from the pots. When an unusually high level of iron shows up in the sample of an aging pot, they know there's probably a crack in the cell's lining, which has allowed the molten aluminum to weaken the steel cell. In that case, they'd order the pot tapped to get as much aluminum out as possible; then have the pot shunted. The brass in the head shed don't blame the pot men or the foremen when a pot reaches the end of its normal life span. They know each pot will eventually need to be shut down and rebuilt."

By mid-shift, Pot 9 had settled down and the rest of Jim's string ran smoothly throughout the shift.

"Thanks for all the training this week," said Bill as he and Jim headed for the shower room. "If I ever have to sub as a pot man, I hope it's on your string."

"You should do fine," replied Jim. "Just watch your voltage, check for red anode connections, don't overfeed and make sure you set your new carbon correctly."

It was a beautiful July morning as Bill headed home on N. Bruce Road. He was always tempted to stay up and enjoy such sunny days rather than go to bed the morning after his last graveyard shift, but he knew he'd be sorry by tonight if he stayed up. He wanted to enjoy a fun evening at Jeff's, and he knew Barb would hold him to his promise. So after some breakfast, he headed downstairs to his cool bedroom, closed the curtains, and fell into a deep sleep.

"I'll bet you're glad graveyard is over," his mom said as Bill shuffled into the kitchen at 3:30 that afternoon.

"I'll say, and I'm really looking forward to seeing Jeff tonight. Should be a fun time; I haven't seen him since graduation."

"Are you going by yourself or with someone?"

"Just by myself," Bill lied wanting to avoid a discussion about his commitment in August.

After fixing a fried hot dog on toast, Bill headed out to the deck to enjoy the sunshine. He loved being in the sun but it was tough on his light complexion. He typically got sun burned early in the summer; then attempted in vain to get some semblance of a tan. He always looked so white next to most of his friends. But he loved days like this when he could just enjoy the warmth of the sunshine, the blue sky, and not have to think about going to work.

After washing his car and cleaning its interior, Bill jumped in the shower. It had been five days since he had seen Barb, so thoughts of being with her made him stand at attention.

—⧜—

"Oh, I've missed you this week!" greeted Barb hugging him; then kissing him. Hopefully you've missed me too."

"Yes, and you'll find out just how much later," he assured her as they headed for his car.

She cocked her head and looked up at him. "I don't know if I can wait that long," she replied with a hint of seriousness in her voice.

On the way to Jeff's, they shared their work weeks. "Tell me about your pot man training," Barb asked. "Do you like it?"

"I think so. It's a more responsible job, and you sure stay a lot cleaner compared to carbon setting," replied Bill.

Barb smiled at him. "Is that the job you'd want to have there if you decide to stay at Kaiser?"

"Probably...I think it's a little healthier than carbon setting too because you're not spending as much time standing directly over the exposed anodes."

Bill exited the freeway and headed for Hamilton Street. "I think you'll really like Jeff," Bill said wanting to change the topic. He's very friendly and likes to have a good time. I'm not exactly sure who will be there tonight, but probably some of my college classmates and their dates." Bill could detect some nervousness on Barb's face. "You'll feel very welcome at Jeff's and will have a good time," assured Bill.

"What's Jeff going to do now that he's graduated?"

"Jeff's got it made. His dad owns an electrical business, and Jeff will help his dad run it. He'll eventually take over the business and knowing Jeff, he'll expand it. He's already developing some new electrical circuit that he thinks can be used in manufacturing computers. I have no doubt Jeff will be very wealthy some day," added Bill hanging a left on E. Sinto and parking on a side street near Jeff's home. As they approached Jeff's house across from Mission Park, they could hear the player piano rockin' in the basement; so they let themselves in the back door and headed downstairs.

"Bill! Glad you could make it!" yelled Jeff coming over to greet him. "And who is this good lookin' gal?"

"Barb Scott; she's a CV grad as well."

"Those CV gals are all pretty hot!" teased Jeff. "Let me get you two a beer," offered Jeff leading them towards the bar. He filling two red milk shake cups from the keg located behind the bar. "Just help yourself to more beer and food; there's plenty."

It was so good to see guys he hadn't seen for a long time—some since he attended Gonzaga Prep his freshman and sophomore years in high school. They were glad to see Bill, too, and wanted to reminisce about school, sports and everyone's post-graduation plans.

Bill did his best to introduce Barb to friends and involve her in various conversations, but it was clear that she was out of her social element in the presence of college graduates. She stayed pretty close to his side smiling and pretending to be interested while sipping her beer. Some girls attempted to involve her in their conversations, but after a short period of time, Barb was back at Bill's side.

After a couple hours had gone by, she periodically squeezed his hand or nudged him, then looked at him like she was ready to go. But for Bill, the cold draft beer tasted so good and went down easily after a week of graveyard. And he was thoroughly enjoying seeing old classmates again and catching up. At one point after yet another nudge from Barb, Bill realized that she just didn't seem able to socialize with his friends, and he tucked this awareness away.

"I'll be right back; I have to use the bathroom," Barb announced to Bill. "Where is the bathroom?"

"Upstairs," replied Bill nodding toward the stairs.

"If the one off the main hallway's occupied, there are two bathrooms upstairs," added one of the girls within earshot.

When Barb returned, she refilled her cup for the fourth time. Bill could tell she was definitely feeling the effects of the beer by the way she carefully navigated back toward him. She resumed her position standing to his right teetering a bit from time to time. After a few minutes, she grabbed Bill's arm and pulled him toward the stairs.

"What!?" Bill asked puzzled.

"Come here; there's something I want to show you," she insisted slurring her words.

At the top of the stairs, she led him through the kitchen, through the living room and to the stairs leading up to the second floor.

"Barb, where are we going?" asked Bill uncomfortably.

"You'll see; just follow me," she responded in a low voice.

At the top of the stairs, she led him into a dark bedroom, closed and locked the door. As his eyes adjusted, he determined that it was the master bedroom because there was an adjacent bathroom dimly lit by a night light. She turned to him, kissed him and began unbuckling his belt.

"Barb, we can't…now…here," he mumbled as she kissed him and slid off his shorts.

"Shhhh," she whispered. "I can't wait any longer. I didn't see you all week and you promised that you'd make it up to me," she added unbuttoning her cutoffs.

Bill paused to listen for anyone who might be coming up the stairs; then decided he'd comply so they could get back downstairs before Jeff came looking for them. And he really didn't want to leave the party yet. He removed his underpants as she was stepping out of her shorts and panties. She lay down on the carpet, pulled him to her and within seconds eagerly greeted him.

He knew he would probably come quickly as he hadn't been with her all week. But unexpectedly, she moved him away, rolled onto her hands and knees facing away from him and told him to enter her. She could tell he wasn't sure what to do, so she reached back and guided him to her while she backed against him. This new experience with Barb was amazing! It made her feel so incredibly tight. Her movements against him were measured as she didn't want to lose him. Her small, round ass bumped against him. Bump, bump, bump.

"Oh! Oh, my God!" Bill gasped. Each mini-stroke was so tight and sensual and as she moved toward him, he could smell her essence. She was like a female animal in heat wanting, needing relief now. She tossed her head from side to side and made deep rhythmic grunts with each stroke. It made him feel animal-like as well. All that mattered to him now was enjoying this tight pleasure. Bump, bump, bump…

"Oh…my God, Barb!" When he began to swell, she lowered her face to the carpet as if to invite him deeper, and to brace herself for his surge.

"Yes! Yes! Yeeess," she moaned each time he came.

"Oh, my God, Barb you feel sooo tight that way," exclaimed Bill breathing heavily over her. He wanted to just remain in her, relishing her tightness until they had fully recovered, but he also wanted to head downstairs before someone else discovered them. He spotted a Kleenex box on an end table and after exiting her, wiped himself off before putting his underpants on. She also used some Kleenex, grabbed her shorts and panties, entered the master bathroom and closed the door. He heard her peeing; then the toilet flush and the sink run before she re-emerged into the dark bedroom.

"I missed you sooo much all week, Bill," she whispered. "I just couldn't wait any longer!"

"I'd love to do that again soon!" he declared, "but we'd better get downstairs before someone comes looking for us."

—ɯ—

"Where you two been?" asked Jeff as they re-entered the basement. "I thought you'd left without saying good-bye."

"No, we just went outside for a bit; Barb was getting a bit... light-headed."

"Well, glad you're still here; have another beer, and eat some more of this food!"

It was difficult for Bill to get back into the same visiting mode after such an amazing sexual experience, especially when Barb would look at him and smile. Both enjoyed a couple more refills.

"You ready to do that again later?" he whispered to her after one of her glances.

"I'm ready anytime you are!" she grinned taking another sip of her beer.

After making a point to visit with Jeff and his girlfriend a bit more, Bill knew it was time to not only rescue Barb, but get her to her place where he could enjoy again the incredible new position she had just shown him.

"Thanks so much, Jeff for inviting us. I've got to get Barb home because she works early tomorrow."

"Bummer; seems like you just got here!"

"Ya hafta help us drink the rest of this keg!" added another GU classmate standing nearby.

"I'm sure you guys will manage," Bill chuckled. He looked at Jeff. "I'll call you before I leave in August."

"You'd better! Hey, great to see ya," said Jeff shaking Bill's hand, "and nice to meet you, Barb."

"Thanks; nice to meet you too," she smiled relieved that she would now be just with Bill.

Barb wrapped her left arm through Bill's right arm for support as they walked to his car. While his body urged him to hurry to Barb's, his mind was still back at the party. It had been so good to see his friends again, talk about old times and what their plans were now that they'd graduated. But it concerned Bill to see how uncomfortable Barb had been the whole time they were at Jeff's. Jeff and his girlfriend really tried to make Barb feel welcome, as had several other girls who had attempted to initiate conversation with her. It began to dawn on Bill that their social life might very well be limited and awkward if they were married. *She would have difficulty relating to my friends; them to her,* he thought closing her car door.

"Sorry if it was a bit awkward for you to be at Jeff's party," Bill remarked as they headed toward the freeway.

Barb shrugged. "That's okay. I couldn't contribute much to the conversations, but it was kind of interesting to hear about their plans now that they've graduated. And I'm glad I got to meet some of your friends. Jeff seems like really a nice guy."

"He really is; it was great to see him and catch up."

Barb looked over at Bill and grinned at him. "But what I enjoyed most was what we did upstairs."

He looked over at her. "Barb, that was amazing! I can't wait to do that again—soon!"

"Glad you liked it. Hopefully you'll be 'up' for it when we get back to my place—we can take our time this time."

—⟋⟍⟋—

Bill's groin tingled with anticipation when he thought about stroking her from behind, and by the time they reached her front door, he could hardly wait to enjoy that incredible tightness again. They began to undress each other as soon as they stepped into her apartment. Shirts were pulled off, shorts were quickly unzipped, underthings were left where they fell. As soon as they lay down, Bill wanted to mount her from behind, but she delayed his eagerness.

"Slow down," she coached. "First, enter me this way," she directed pulling him to her. "I'll roll over when I'm ready for you," she gasped as he entered her.

He knew it would take him longer to climax this time, so he stroked her slowly until she pushed him away and rolled onto her hands and knees. This time, he found his way without her guidance. She always felt tight to him when they made love, but he couldn't believe how incredibly tight she was this way, and how deeply he could reach, especially when she lowered her head to the pillow.

"Ugh, ugh, ugh," she grunted with each thrust. The position, the sounds, the smells made him feel animal-like again— like he was breeding her. And when he came, he didn't care if he impregnated her. He wanted to impregnate her. When he finished coming, they rolled onto their left sides, Bill embracing her from behind, recovering with her; then falling asleep with her.

They were still together when he awoke and realized he had to get rid of some of the beer he'd consumed earlier. She stirred when he moved from her.

"I'll be right back," he whispered.

After he peed and before re-entering the bedroom, he glanced at the wall clock in the kitchen. *Oh shit—almost 1:00 AM!*

"Barb, I have to get home so my parents don't call Jeff's. I'll call you later…."

"…'kay," she slurred quietly from her slumber.

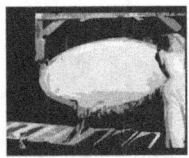

"How was the party?" his dad asked from the kitchen table as Bill entered the family room from the basement about 9:15 AM. Howard was working on some paperwork he had brought home from the bank for the weekend.

"Great! I hadn't seen Jeff since graduation, and some of the guys who were there since I was at Prep."

"Well, that's good…say, I talked with Aunt Doris again this morning, and we're all set for her cabin the first week in August. Hope you can spend some time with us that week. The 29th of August will be here before you know it," reminded Howard taking a sip from his coffee cup.

"I'll try to, Dad."

Bill finished a bowl of cereal and two slices of toast with peanut butter out on the deck while Howard continued to review his paperwork at the kitchen table. Then, Bill headed downstairs with his coffee and dialed Barb's number from the storeroom.

"Mornin'," he greeted quietly into the phone. "Sorry I had to leave you last night, but I hadn't told my parents that I wouldn't be home. Didn't want them to call Jeff's place looking for me."

"I didn't even hear you leave last night; I slept so hard. Speaking of 'hard' are you coming over today?"

"Better believe it; I'll be there in two hours. Want to go to the river and lie in the sun?"

"Sounds good; I'll be ready when you get here."

— m —

When Barb opened her door, she was holding her red beach bag and was ready to go. "I'd invite you in but I'm a little tender from last night. Maybe I'll be okay in a few hours," she said teasingly. "Think you can wait that long?"

"Hmmm, I'll try. Want to get a burger on the way to the river?"

"Yes; I'm really hungry."

On the way to Ron's, Bill asked her if she felt anything different after last night.

"Well, other than a bit sorer than usual—no. Why do you ask?"

"Well...last night you felt so—tight—you were amazing, Barb. And I had this feeling that I was getting you pregnant. So, just wondering if anything happened...if you feel any... different."

She looked at him intently. "What would you do if you did make me pregnant?"

"I'd take care of you and the baby."

"Really!? You wouldn't go into the Jesuits?"

"If you get pregnant, that will take priority over my going into the Jesuits."

"What would your folks say?"

"They'd be upset, but it wouldn't be their decision."

Barb was silent for a few seconds as if thinking about what Bill had just said. "Well, so far, I don't think you have anything to worry about."

"Will you tell me if you do get pregnant?"

"Of course," Barb replied as they pulled into Ron's.

It felt good to lie on the sandy beach just west of the Sullivan Bridge and feel the hot sun on their bodies. When they got too hot, they'd plunge into the Spokane River and swim out to "the rock" as everyone referred to it. It was about thirty yards from shore or a quarter of the way across the river. During the summer about six feet of its nose was above the water, which made this beach so popular. It offered several natural toe holds so you could climb your way to its top then dive off. Strong swimmers would spring off and swim madly against the river's steady current to get a few yards upstream, then dive towards the bottom and let the current take them through an underwater "arch" on the beach side of the rock. Today, however, both Bill and Barb just climbed to its top, dove off and swam back to their beach towels. Their rowdy lovemaking had sapped their energy.

After a couple hours of sunning and cooling off in the river, they folded up their beach towels and headed for Barb's.

"My dad reminded me this morning that they'll be at Newman Lake during the first week of August," informed Bill after turning west onto Sprague from Sullivan Road. "They're leaving on Saturday after breakfast."

"Think we'll get any sleep?" she asked glancing sideways at him and chuckling.

"Just between sex!" Bill grinned.

"Speaking of sleeping, will we sleep in your bed?" asked Barb as they neared her apartment.

"Well, we could—it's a twin bed like yours and it's in the

basement where it's cool. Or...we could sleep in my parents' bed—it's a queen-sized bed," he emphasized with a grin.

"Hmmm, that would be fun!" she responded as Bill pulled into her parking lot.

"Let's shower together again," she suggested as he closed the door to her apartment. "We can wash off all that nasty river water, then see what happens."

He enjoyed having her wash him with her soapy, gentle hands. He wondered if she enjoyed it as much when he returned the favor.

"Gentle," she urged when he began to wash her. "Guess I'm still a bit sore."

When they had dried off, she took his hand and led him into her bedroom. She pushed him back onto her bed; then knelt over him. She looked into his eyes then began to kiss him starting at his neck and slowly working her way to his chest, his belly, his thighs, then his erectness. He loved this sensuous anticipation. She took her time—first kissing different parts of him; then finally giving him what she knew would please him. She enjoyed making him writhe with pleasure as she moved on him. Periodically, she would stop and look up at his face as if to let him catch his breath. Then she would resume her wonderful movements.

He knew she could tell when he began to swell because she used a hand to control his enthusiasm. He grabbed her head to stop her movement during his climax. His whole body tensed. "Oh!...oh!," he gasped as he came.

When he finished, she kissed his mouth sharing some of what she had taken from him.

"Does that make up for not fucking you?" she asked looking into his eyes.

"Oh, my God, Barb," he replied still breathing heavily. "You have so many ways of making me feel good. You're amazing!"

She smiled at him then lay her head on his outstretched left arm and looked at the curtain shadows dancing slowly on the ceiling. Their eyes soon grew heavy in the peaceful silence, and within minutes they both dozed the rest of the afternoon away.

"Rod called this afternoon and wants you to call him back," his mom said as he came in carrying his towel and bathing suit. "He wants you to come visit him in Seattle," she added enthusiastically, slicing stalks of celery for a potato salad.

"He does!? Thanks, Mom, I'll call him back," replied Bill pondering this invitation. Bill wasn't particularly close to his older brother, as Rod had teased him a lot when they were young. In fact, Rod had been downright mean to him at times. Rivalry remained pretty fierce until Bill was a sophomore in high school and surpassed Rod in strength. Rod, who was two and a half years older, had quit athletics after his freshman year in high school to earn money to buy a car, so Rod wasn't very fit during his last few years of high school.

When Rod enrolled in college at Eastern Washington as a freshman, he followed Bill's athletic success in football and track at CV, and proudly bragged about Bill to his roommates and friends. The icy relationship they had during their youth began to thaw, and now when Rod came home on holidays they looked forward to catching up on one another's adventures.

"Down at the river, huh? Lots of chicks still go down there?" Rod was familiar with the river's beaches in the Valley and used to enjoy them during the summers as well.

"Oh, a few. What's goin' on in Seattle?"

"Well, I'm going to throw a party at my place on Saturday the 22nd, and want to invite you to come over and spend that weekend here."

"Hmmm, I don't know if my ol' Bug would make it. Anytime I've taken a long trip with it, I've burned a valve or two."

"Well, think about it; I know we'd have a good time. I can almost guarantee that you'll get laid given the girls who will be at the party. And, it may be the last time we can party together since you're going into the Jesuits. You are still going aren't you? Mom said she's beginning to wonder."

"Yeah, I'm still goin'; don't know how long I'll last though."

"Well, give me a call sometime next week if you decide to come over okay?"

"Will do. Talk with you soon, and thanks for inviting me."

On Monday afternoon after Barb got off work, Bill called her. "My older brother Rod phoned me yesterday, and wants me to drive over to Seattle for a party he's having on the 22nd. I'm tempted to go, but don't know if my Bug will make it," he said working the phone cord with his left hand.

"You should go; it may be the last time you'll be able to be with him in Seattle before you enter the Novitiate. I know I'd go if I had the chance; I've never been to Seattle."

"You've never been to Seattle!? You gotta be kidding! Would...would you go over with me?"

"Sure, I don't have to work that weekend, and I might be able to get that Monday off too—or at least the morning off."

"Okay; I'll call him and tell him we're driving over. I'm sure you'll have a good time; Rod loves to party! We'll have to leave pretty early that Saturday morning though to get there by mid-afternoon."

"That's okay…ohhh, I'm so excited!" blurted Barb. "I've always wanted to visit Seattle."

—ⵡ—

The next evening after Day Shift, Bill called Rod. "I've decided to come over on the 22nd!" Bill announced enthusiastically over the phone. "And I'm going to bring this gal I've been seeing this summer, but please…don't say anything to the folks. They don't know about her, okay!?"

"Well, I think they suspect you're seeing some girl, but don't worry, I won't say anything. About what time do you think you'll get here?"

"Well, assuming I don't burn a valve, we should get to your place about 3:00 PM."

"Perfect! That'll give you time to rest up a bit before people start coming around 6:00. Guess I don't have to worry about gettin' you laid while you're here. See ya then!"

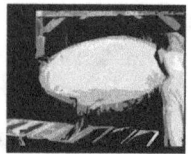

"Roberts!"

"Here."

"Pots, Line 7."

Bill couldn't believe it. *The first time in five summers I've ever subbed for a pot man,* he thought as he headed up to Line 7 the first day of Swing Shift a week later. *I'll finally get a chance to use the skills that Jim taught me, and what great timing—the week before I drive to Seattle. Assuming there aren't any serious problems with any of the pots, I should be well rested before heading to Seattle.* He was a bit nervous, however, as he knew being a pot man carried with it a lot of responsibility.

"You're going to be in charge of the first string in Room 13 for the next week," the Line 7 foreman told Bill. "It's typically a good string, but keep a close eye on Pot 6. And let me know if you have any questions okay?"

"Will do," replied Bill heading for the waterhole.

As Bill looked up the floor to his string, he could see a light flickering on one of his pots and could hear the bell ringing; so he knew he had to get right to work. He put his lunch sack in the waterhole then headed to the troubled pot. It was Pot 6. The voltage looked a bit low; so he raised it, pulling the chain to the right. Next, he unhooked the poker on the front end of the pot and used the roller to gain leverage on the poker to break the top layer of crust that had formed over the bath. He then ran the poker hook underneath the anodes on each side. On the second pull, the bell stopped ringing. *Whew!* He remembered what Jim had said about someone overfeeding a pot to cause this problem, so he didn't give it anymore ore. He rechecked the voltage to make sure it was between the numbers Jim had shown him. *Well, might as well continue feeding the front sides as it's almost time to feed anyway,* he thought.

"You must be Tom's sub this week. My name's Rick; I have the third string." Rick was a short man, who wore an unbuttoned long-sleeved shirt over a soiled white t-shirt that struggled to cover his large belly. He wore a black welder's cap and chewed gum incessantly.

"Nice to meet you, Rick," replied Bill extending his hand. "This is the first time I've subbed for a pot man; so I'll do my best. Don't hesitate to give me any advice if needed."

"No problem; just ask away if you have any questions. The regular who operates your string is a good pot man; so they should be in pretty good shape assuming no one screwed them up last shift."

"The voltages look pretty good," added Bill. He was glad he had someone to talk with, as the clock moved more slowly than when he was setting carbon.

"Well, here come the carbon setters," indicated Rick getting up from the bench in the waterhole. "Any questions on how to adjust your carbon?"

"No, I think I've got it," replied Bill.

"Easy money today, huh!" yelled Bud, one of the Line 7 carbon setters Bill had worked with on occasion.

"Yeah. Can't believe how clean I still am!"

Later in the shift after Bill had adjusted all the new anodes that had been set in his string, he heard the overhead crane hauling the crucible up to his string of pots. He could always tell when the crucible was coming. The crane moved at a slow, steady pace up the pot line, and the heavy weight of the cruce made a different, almost ominous sound on the crane rails.

It had always fascinated Bill to watch the "tappers" remove the liquid aluminum metal from a pot. Prior to the cruce's arrival, one of the two-man siphon crew would break the crust at the front end of the pot to be tapped using a crowbar, and skim out any chunks of bath that might block the siphon. Then using a metal "dip stick," which looked like a long rod with a right angle bend, he stuck the end into the molten bath to see where the metal that resided at the bottom of the pot cell interfaced with the bath. There was a definite color difference between the metal and the bath.

When the hole was cleared, the crane driver would position the heavy cruce in front of the pot; then pick up the big siphon from the pot room floor so the siphon crew could guide one end of the siphon down into the bottom of the pot where the aluminum metal resided. The crew members positioned the other end of the siphon, which contained an aluminum foil plug or "teat" into the cruce. Once in place, a crewman would attach an air hose and open an air nozzle on the siphon allowing air pressure to build in the siphon in order to create enough suction to begin the siphoning process. The molten aluminum metal coming from the bottom of the pot's cell through the siphon quickly melted the foil plug, and continued its flow into the crucible.

When the tappers had established a good siphon and the aluminum metal was being drawn out thus lowering the level of the molten liquids in the pot, the crane driver exited his crane and standing on the crane side of the pot carefully watched the pot's voltage meter. The voltage meter would tell him how much he should pull the chain to the left, which lowered the anodes so they maintained their critical distance from the bottom of the pot.

When the tappers had removed the designated amount of aluminum metal from the pot, they turned off the air to the siphon, disconnected the air hose and readied the siphon to be lifted by the crane driver, who had climbed back into his crane. As the crane driver carefully lifted the siphon, one of the tappers using a chain attached to the siphon would pull back on the chain and guide the siphon from the pot and position it so the crane driver could set it on the pot room floor for the next pot to be tapped. It typically took three different pots to bring a cruce to its fill level.

When the cruce was at its fill level, the crane driver slowly and cautiously hoisted the cruce above the pots and headed toward the far end of the pot room, ringing his bell as he rolled to warn workers below to not stand beneath the crucible. Bill often cringed when he thought about what would happen if the crane driver accidentally hit the top of a pot or had to abruptly stop. Some of the molten aluminum, which was about a thousand degrees Celsius would no doubt slosh over the edge of the cruce and immediately ignite anything or anyone it landed on.

After the crane driver lowered the crucible at the far end of the pot line, it would be picked up by a large, specially designed fork lift vehicle and taken to the casting room. The molten aluminum it contained was poured into molds to form "ingots" or "pigs," which were later trucked to the Trentwood Mill in the Spokane Valley. Here they were remelted and rolled into thinner sheets of aluminum to be sold to different industries.

Bill already greatly admired the crane drivers' skills from carbon setting. Sitting in an open metal cage about 15 feet above the pot line floor and looking down through the smoke, dust and gas that rose from the pots, these guys could place the carbon anode hook which was attached to the large hook on its hoist very close to the one inch diameter hole in the anode's copper rod which was located on the pot room floor at the far end of the crane's bridge. They could bring the anode from the floor up between the pots to the carbon setter, and place the anode's copper rod into its three inch receptacle on either side of the pot. And they could do this in a smooth, continuous motion. But after watching the crane driver manipulate the siphon in and out of the small opening at the front of the pots, and carefully haul the nearly full crucible down the line, Bill had even more admiration for their skills. The eye-hand coordination, depth perception and timing needed to operate the three levers in front of them took hundreds of hours of driving experience and fearless patience. An experienced, smooth crane driver was worth his weight in gold.

For the next week, Bill enjoyed the break from setting carbon and sparing. *Being a pot man wouldn't be a bad job, and it's pretty good money,* mulled Bill. When he thought about submitting his two week notice in just a few weeks, his gut churned. *Do I really want to do that? If I quit, and the Jesuits don't work out for me, I won't have a job—and maybe not Barb either!*

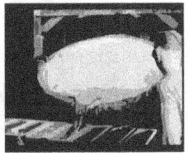

"Are you pretty much packed for tomorrow morning?" asked Bill when he called Barb on Friday.

"Yes, I'm so excited for this trip! Why don't you spend the night here and we can leave early tomorrow?"

"I'd love to, but I'm having my car's valves adjusted now, and I have to pack. I'll be at your place by 7:45 tomorrow morning." Bill knew he'd be wiped out if he spent the night with Barb, and he knew how long the drive to Seattle would be in his underpowered Bug.

"Okay," she sighed teasingly. "See you tomorrow morning. Bye."

"Have a great time in Seattle," his mom said as Bill headed out the door with his small suitcase.

"Thanks, I will. Just hope my Bug makes it over the pass okay."

"You know the rule; be sure to call and let us know you arrived safely," reminded his mom following him unto the porch.

"I will," he promised kissing her on the cheek.

As he drove to Barb's, he could tell his Bug was running

better and had a bit more get up and go than usual. *The real test will be the hills and, of course, Snoqualmie Pass,* thought Bill.

When Barb opened her apartment door, she was ready—suitcase in hand. Like Bill, she was dressed in cutoffs, a t-shirt and sandals and was wearing sunglasses. "Let's go!" she said excitedly.

Driving up the steady grade on I-90 east of Spokane, Bill could tell his Bug was beginning to labor a bit. *Not a good sign,* he grimaced to himself. As he neared Cheney, the highway flattened out, and he was able to increase his speed a bit. "Hey, want to see where I lived when I was really young?"

"Sure! You lived in Cheney?" she asked as he exited I-90.

"Yeah. My dad got transferred there shortly after I was born in Spokane. We lived here until I was in kindergarten—so about five years. I really don't have too many memories of Cheney; the clearest ones are of traumatic experiences." As they approached the crest of a gradual hill Bill pointed to his right. "There—that's it. The yellow brick house on the corner."

"Wow! That's a nice house."

"Yeah—it was brand new when we moved in. It still looks pretty much the same as I remember it."

"So what terrible things can you remember?" asked Barb as they turned around and headed back toward I-90.

"Well, I kind of remember flashes of when I drank some oil of wintergreen that was in our bathroom. I remember it was such a pretty green color, and I remember climbing up to get it. I remember how hot I was in my bed that night, how I couldn't sleep, and of course the never ending smell of wintergreen. To this day, I still don't like the smell or taste of wintergreen. I guess the doctor, who stayed with me at the house most of the night, wasn't sure I would make it through the night."

"Oh, my gosh!" exclaimed Barb looking at him seriously.

"Your folks must have really been worried sick."

"Yeah, I guess they were…but they don't like to talk about it much. They probably feel guilty about leaving the bottle within reach.

"I remember another time, I was trying to cast a fishing line standing out on our side street—the street we were just on. At one point when I picked up the hook, our dog, Rusty grabbed the pole and began running in the opposite direction. The hook of course went into my finger; so I had to run toward the dog screaming for him to stop. I can't remember who finally rescued me, but it hurt like hell when they took the hook out of my finger."

"Ouch!" Barb winced while looking out her window at the treeless, desolate terrain near Sprague, Washington.

"Oh, two other finger memories. One happened when I was waiting for my mom to finish getting ready in the bathroom. We were headed into town to shop. Well, I stuck my little finger into the opening of a can of tooth powder. When neither I nor my mom could get my finger out, she took me over to our neighbor's house. He had to cut the can off my finger using tin snips. I can't remember now if we ever made it to town, but I remember how frustrated Mom was with me."

"I can just imagine," chuckled Barb shifting to a more comfortable position in her seat.

"But the worst finger disaster, and fortunately one that I can't remember, happened shortly after we moved to Cheney when I was just a toddler. My older brother, Rod shut the back door on my little finger." Bill held up his right hand to show Barb his stubby little finger.

"Oh my God, I've never noticed that before." Barb grabbed his right hand with her left so she could have a good look. "That must have really hurt!" she grimaced. "Good thing you can't remember it!" she added releasing his hand.

"The doctor told my folks I'd probably have only a stub. But at some point, the fingernail actually grew back—well, kind of," he added holding up his finger again and chuckling.

"Let's see...what else can I remember about Cheney," Bill thought aloud, looking ahead to see if any large trucks were heading west. "Oh, I remember a man knocking on our back door and showing us our dog lying on its side on our concrete porch. Rusty's mouth was moving slightly but he couldn't hear me when I called his name. The man said he didn't mean to hit our dog, but it ran out to chase his car. Rusty did like to chase cars."

"Ohhh, that's so sad; did you cry?" she asked leaning toward him.

"Not when I was lookin' at Rusty. I don't think I really understood he was dead 'cause his eyes were open and he was still movin' a bit. But I did cry hard after the man took him away, and my mom told me that Rusty was dead and would never be coming back."

Barb glanced at an old, abandoned homestead off the Interstate then leaned back against her door.

"I also remember some kid running over my throat while he was riding his bicycle. I think he knocked me down; then his back tire ran over my neck. I remember screaming bloody murder, and my parents taking this up with his parents. My parents probably never knew that Rod had talked me into trying to put a stick through the kid's spokes when he was riding by. I remember Rod acting like he didn't have anything to do with it."

"Oh, my gosh, how old were you?" asked Barb shaking her head in disbelief.

"I can't remember, but pretty young. I remember Rod

climbing a big pine tree one summer that was in a field next to our house, and then not being able to climb down. I think some neighbors using a ladder helped him get down."

"Did you and Rod get along very well when you were little?" asked Barb as they passed the exit to Ritzville. She lowered her window a bit to match Bill's window and create additional air flow. It was definitely starting to warm up outside.

"No! He teased me all the time. One time, when we had company in Cheney, he was teasing me through the garage door window; so I tried to hit him putting my fist through the glass. Rod just laughed at me through the broken window, and I was the one who not only got cut but sent to my room."

"Don't you have any pleasant memories of Cheney?"

"Hmmm, let me think…Well, Cheney is where I had my earliest awareness. Have you ever tried to recall your first memory?"

"No, I don't think so."

"Well, mine was while I was lying in my bed. I remember hearing the drone of a small airplane flying over our house. I remember it was sunny in my bedroom—so maybe summer time. My guess is that I had just awakened from a nap."

"Hmmm, I'll have to try to remember what my earliest memory is," reflected Barb looking out the windshield.

Bill reached back in his memory to recall any other Cheney experiences. "Oh, I also remember Rod and I listening to 'The Lone Ranger' and 'Sgt. Preston of the Yukon' on the radio every afternoon before dinner. We loved those radio shows.

"And I remember some woman who lived across the street from us on the corner, who would fix me a buttered piece of home baked white bread with honey on it. I would always ask her for another piece—it was soooo good," emphasized Bill spotting a semi truck up ahead.

"And I do kind of remember my kindergarten teacher, Mrs. O'Brien. She had black hair. I remember that it took me a long time to get the concept of tracing letters over and over to learn how to print the letters of the alphabet. Instead of tracing over the letter already there like she wanted me to, I would print a new letter beside it. I guess I didn't see a reason for not making my own letter. She had to explain it to me several times before I finally got it. I think I've always been a slow learner."

"What were your parents like back then?" asked Barb attempting to find a more comfortable position. She lifted each leg up from her seat to get some air on the backs of her legs.

"Well, I don't remember us being a particularly happy family—I think my dad spent a lot of time at the bank. But I don't remember my parents arguing or fighting in Cheney as much as they did in later years when we lived on Cleveland Street back in Spokane."

Bill had finally gained on the semi enough to utilize the truck's "slip stream," which he knew from experience would pull his Bug along, saving wear and tear on his engine. He could tell when he had broken through the truck's tail wind and into its slip stream because he could feel his car being pulled along and buffeted a bit from side to side.

"Isn't this a bit dangerous to be following so closely?" asked Barb nervously staring at the back of the semi trailer.

"Yeah, probably, but using the truck's slip stream is probably the only way we're going to make it all the way to Seattle. I've done this before; it will be okay." He could tell by the look on Barb's face that she wasn't assured by his answer.

"Well, tell me more about Rod; how much older is he than you?"

"He's about two and a half years older."

"Did he graduate from CV as well?"

"Yeah, in 1961."

"Why did he tease you so much when you were little?" she asked with a puzzled look on her face.

"I'm not really sure. We played pretty well together when it was just the two of us, but when he was with his friends, he teased me a lot, and was even pretty mean to me sometimes."

"How so?"

"Well, like the time he and one of his friends were teasing me when we lived in Spokane. I wrestled his friend to the ground telling him to knock it off; then Rod pulled me off him and held me so his friend could punch me in the face. When I started to cry, they both laughed and continued to tease me until I went in the house."

"What!?" Barb gasped in disbelief.

"Another time when a group of us were riding our bikes home from elementary school, Rod slowed way down and kept weaving back and forth in front of me so I couldn't pass him. When I tried to go around him, my front wheel spokes caught in his three-speed gear sprocket and down I went onto the pavement scrapping the skin off my arms, knees and the right side of my face. Instead of stopping to help me, he just kept riding home with his friends laughing."

"Oh, my God, that's terrible! How did you get home?"

"Well, my front wheel was out of alignment so I couldn't even push my bike home. So I asked some older guy, who was working in his yard if I could leave it at his place until my mom could come get it.

"When I got home and my mom saw me, she was horrified. When I told her what happened she really got angry at Rod, who hadn't even told her what had happened. After cleaning the dirt out of my wounds, she took me to get my bike, and made Rod pay to get it fixed."

Barb looked out at the giant sprinklers watering crops as they neared Moses Lake and shook her head as if trying to fathom how an older brother could be so mean to his younger brother. "Did you get along better when you were older?"

"Yeah, but only because I got stronger than him. I continued to play sports in high school, and he stopped after his freshman year. One time when I was a sophomore at Gonzaga Prep and he was a senior at CV, my mom asked him to drive in to pick me up because my ride home wasn't available that day. Rod didn't want to drive his car all the way in to Spokane so he was very angry, and took it out on me. A classmate, who commuted with me, also needed a ride to the Valley, so he witnessed Rod's barrage of put downs and complaints all the way back to the Valley. I was so embarrassed, hurt and angry. When we finally got home after dropping my classmate off, I tore into him something fierce in our front yard. My mom had to turn the garden hose on me to make me stop hitting him in the face. I literally wanted to kill him. That was the last time he ever teased me or put me down. When he started college at Eastern Washington, he'd come to my home football games and cheer me on. I know he was proud of me; he's just always been a bit odd."

"Oh good, and we're staying at his place!? I'm almost afraid to be around him after what you've told me."

"Everything will be fine," assured Bill. "He treats me fine now, and is actually a lot of fun after he's had a few beers. We'll have a good time."

As they approached a long grade outside Moses Lake, the truck slowed, and Bill pulled out of the slip stream to ease his way around the semi. Without the aid of the slip stream, his car labored against the persistent head wind, and it took a couple of minutes to inch past the truck. Bill began to look for another semi.

"Well, enough about me and my past; tell me more about you and your family. Have you always lived in the Valley?"

"No, we originally lived in Kennewick. That's where Teri and I were born. We moved to the Valley when I was in 7th grade."

"How old were you when your parents divorced?"

"My dad left my mom when I was about two; so I don't have any memory of him, and I have no desire to ever see the bastard. Mom had to work long hours to support Teri and me, so Teri and I played together a lot growing up. I think that's one of the reasons we're so close."

"Are you and Teri pretty close to your mom?"

"In some ways. We keep in close touch with her and would certainly come to her rescue if she needed us for anything, but we don't like most of the guys she hangs out with. When we were younger, we had to watch how she acted with men she invited over; when we were older, we tried to spend as much time as we could at friends' homes."

"What do you mean, how she acted with her dates?"

"Well, imagine watching your mom making out with some strange guy, or hearing bedroom sounds through her door, or overhearing telephone conversations with her friends about her dates."

So that's how Barb learned how to please a man, thought Bill as Barb described some of the bedroom scenarios and phone conversations she and Teri overheard.

"And Teri and I really don't like how my mom flirts with our dates when she's around."

"Really? She flirts with your dates!?"

"Yes, it's so obvious—especially if she's been drinking. If she came over to my apartment sometime when you were there, and I had to leave for awhile, I'm sure she would try to seduce you. It's like she can't help herself."

"Does your mom still work?"

"Yes, she tends bar at The Plantation currently, but she's tended bar at several different bars in the Valley over the years. She's always made pretty decent money and made sure we've had an okay place to live and food and clothing. But she never encouraged us to attend school beyond high school. Teri and I will probably be locked into dead end jobs for the rest of our lives—me at J.C. Penney, Teri at the bakery." Barb looked out her window and grew quiet as if she was finished talking about her family.

"Pretty soon we'll be heading down a steep grade; then we'll cross the Columbia River at Vantage. It's a pretty impressive view," Bill said breaking an awkward silence.

As Bill's Bug picked up speed down the grade to Vantage, he shifted into neutral to give the engine a rest. Barb peered out her window looking down at the Columbia River framed by the steep canyon walls.

When they reached the bridge, Bill put his Bug back into gear to fight through the buffeting side winds.

"Wow, that is an impressive view," stated Barb looking upriver as they crossed the bridge."

"Have you ever been to Grand Coulee Dam?"

"No. Where's that?"

"North of here. It really gives you an idea of how mighty the Columbia River is." His Bug began to slow significantly as it headed up the steep grade west of Vantage and battled the incessant head wind. He tried to distract Barb, who had also noticed how slowly they were going up the grade. "When we lived in Omak, we'd always stop at Grand Coulee Dam on our way to visit my grandparents in Spokane. There was a restaurant that had a view of the dam and served great hamburgers.

When the dam's gates were open, you could hear this deep roar and actually feel the ground shake."

With a concerned look on her face, Barb leaned over to look at the speedometer which now registered about 35 mph. "Man, how much longer is this hill?"

"A few more miles unfortunately. When we get to the top, we'll start to descend into Ellensburg, which is where we'll get something to eat and top off the gas tank."

"Good! I'm ready to eat something, and I really have to pee." Barb was pretty quiet over the next few miles to Ellensburg. Bill could tell she was ready to rest; he was too.

"Why don't you use the restroom while I fill up," recommended Bill pulling in next to a gas pump in Ellensburg just off I-90. "I'll rest when you get back."

"Thank you!" responded Barb opening her door and heading to the restroom located on the east side of the gas station.

After filling up, Bill pulled his car to the restroom side of the station and waited for Barb to come out. After he'd rested, he drove across the street to the A&W where they each ordered a hamburger, fries and root beer in a frosted mug.

"Oh, this tastes so good!" remarked Barb after her second bite of hamburger. "And this ice cold root beer really hits the spot. I didn't realize I was so thirsty."

"Yeah, this is usually where I stop when I come to Seattle," replied Bill swallowing a cold gulp of his root beer.

After they finished eating and the carhop had removed the tray from Bill's window, Bill started the Bug and they headed toward I-90 to begin the last leg of their drive to Seattle.

"You'll really start to see the scenery change as we head toward Snoqualmie Pass," said Bill after merging onto I-90. "Western Washington is so green compared to what we've just driven through." *Just hope my Bug can handle the stiff headwind and steady climb to the summit.*

"I see what you mean," mentioned Barb as they headed west toward Cle Elum. "The trees and rolling hills remind me of the Cheney area west of Spokane."

"Yeah, isn't that something how the middle part of Washington State is so dry and barren while Eastern Washington and Western Washington have trees."

As they began the climb up the eastern flank of Snoqualmie Pass, Bill could tell his car was losing power. About half way to the summit, he shifted into second gear and was going only 35 mph even with the accelerator to the floor. *Come on; just a few more miles and we'll be at the summit.* He didn't want to say anything that would worry Barb, who was taking in all the new scenery.

"Oh, my God. Everything is sooo green and beautiful!" remarked Barb gawking at the craggy Cascades near the summit. "It's so different than the Spokane area."

"I'm glad it's a nice day so you can see everything; a lot of times, it's cloudy and rainy by the time you reach the pass. "Look there's the ski lifts." Barb ducked her head so she could look out Bill's window as he drove by the ski area.

Whew! Now we can coast for awhile, sighed Bill to himself as they crested the summit. He took his car out of gear and relaxed as his Bug picked up speed down the west side of the summit. He let it coast as far as he could down the western flank then shifted into fourth gear to maintain his speed.

"Where are we now?" asked Barb noticing what looked like a small town. Is this the start of Seattle?"

"No, this is Issaquah. There's a great chocolate shop over there," added Bill pointing to his left. "Maybe we can stop there on our way back to Spokane."

"Wow, what lake is that?" asked Barb looking out her window.

"Lake Sammamish, and in a bit we'll cross Lake Washington on the floating bridge. Wait 'til you see that scene. That's one thing you'll notice about this side of the mountains—all the different bodies of water."

"Oh, my gosh, that is a huge lake!" declared Barb as they crossed Lake Washington several minutes later.

Bill pointed out her window. "See that stadium over there? That's Husky Stadium."

After passing through the Mt. Baker Tunnel, Bill exited onto northbound I-5. Both were amazed at how much busier the traffic was compared to Spokane, and Bill, not real familiar with Seattle, began to intently look for the exit Rod had told him to take.

"Oh! There's the Space Needle!" Barb blurted. "I've seen pictures of it, but I've never actually seen it. There is sooo much more to see here!" she gushed as they passed over Lake Union.

"There's the UW campus off to the right; I'll have to take you there this weekend."

"I'd love to see it," smiled Barb.

"Okay, there's the N.E. 45th Street exit," announced Bill with a sense of relief. "Now I know where I am." After exiting, he headed east to 20th Ave. N.E. and turned left. "Not bad, 3:15—pretty close to when I told Rod we'd arrive," Bill boasted as they stopped in front of an old two story house on 20th Ave. N.E. Bill beeped "Shave and a Haircut" on his horn to signal their arrival.

Emerging onto the front porch shirtless and in shorts, Rod

raised a stein in a salute then sauntered down the front steps between two overgrown shrubs to greet them. He gave Bill a big hug and slap on the back with his free arm, then asked, "… and who is this?"

"Barb Scott," Bill responded putting his right arm around Barb both to ease any fears she might have and to show her off. "Barb's a CV grad—two years behind me."

"Well, any CV grad is welcome here!" Rod boomed shaking her hand. "Bring your stuff in; I'll show you where you'll be crashing tonight. Good to see ya, Bro."

The house Rod was sharing with two other roommates was about a mile from the UW campus. Rod, who had transferred to the UW after two years at Eastern Washington State College, had graduated in early June with a degree in pharmacy. He had pretty much put himself through college, as had Bill because Howard, who hadn't graduated from college, wasn't sold on its importance. One Christmas he gave both Rod and Bill 100 one dollar bills in an envelope from Seattle First National Bank, the bank he worked for. Both were shocked and thrilled by Howard's very unusual generosity, but this was the extent of his financial assistance to each of them during their college years. Rod never forgot Howard's meager support and would frequently mention in conversation that he had to eat hotdogs for breakfast, lunch and dinner in order to afford college. However, Rod always seemed to have enough money for beer on the weekends. Recently, he had been hired by Bartell Drug; so from now on, he would be making good money, and would be able to afford a place of his own by the end of the summer, and a healthier diet.

Rod led Bill and Barb to a bedroom located in the basement of the old house. "Here ya go; make yourselves at home. Folks should start arrivin' in a couple of hours so you have time to relax, shower and get ready. Hope you don't mind BBQ'd hotdogs and hamburgers; I'll fire up the grill in a bit," Rod rattled on. He turned to head back up the stairs. "In the meantime grab a cup of Bud in the kitchen—keg's ready!" he added raising his stein.

"Why don't you shower first," Bill suggested to Barb as they opened their luggage; "I'll go upstairs and get us some beer."

"Okay," replied Barb scoping out the dark, damp room and small bathroom, as Bill strode up the stairs.

"Hey, I want to introduce you guys to my little bro," slurred Rod to his roommates waving Bill into the kitchen. "Pour him a cup; he needs to get started. This may be one of his last big parties; he's joining the Jesuits next month."

Steve, one of Rod's roommates and a CV classmate of Rod's was sitting on a kitchen countertop. "Hats off to ya," congratulated Steve hopping down to shake Bill's hand. "No way I could do that, and give up pussy."

"Well, he hasn't given it up yet," clarified Rod; "he brought over a girl he's been seein' this summer." Rod lowered his voice and nodded toward the basement. "Bet you been gettin' a little too, huh, Bro?"

"Well…," Bill replied shrugging his shoulders. Rod and his roommates laughed approvingly.

"Where is she?" asked Rod.

"Down showering; I'll take her a cup if that's okay."

"Fuck yes, it's okay!" asserted Rod loudly, "the first of many!"

Bill chuckled when he noticed Rod's calendar hanging on the kitchen wall: "Class," "Study," "Test" were written in the weekday dates, but "DRINK BEER" was written in all the weekend dates. "Glad you have your priorities straight, Rod," stated Bill nodding to the calendar as he drew Barb's beer.

"Well, hell yes!" laughed Rod.

It was obvious to Bill that Rod had been sampling the keg for some time before he and Barb arrived. *He won't make it through the evening,* Bill predicted to himself. "Oh, I'd better call Mom and tell her I arrived safely; you know how she worries if we don't call. Okay if I use your phone?"

"Sure. Go ahead, it's in the living room."

Bill noticed how dimly lit the living room was even though the front window curtains were open. Shrubbery, which hadn't been pruned for years blocked most of the large front window, the outside of which hadn't been washed for some time. An old cracked red leather couch sat along the wall opposite the front window. A reddish brick fireplace centered the south wall; two large, mismatched stuffed chairs were on either side of the cloudy window. The black phone was on the lamp table between the two chairs.

"Hi, Mom. Just want to let you know I arrived safe and sound.... Yep, Rod's doin' fine."

"I'm so glad to hear you're there safely," replied Rachel. "Have a good time and we'll see you Monday afternoon or evening before you head into Graveyard?"

"I hope so unless I have to get my car's valves adjusted; it's runnin' kind of rough.... Love you, too. Bye."

Bill returned to the kitchen to get Barb's beer and headed downstairs closing the bedroom door behind him.

"Anybody here yet?" asked Barb as she came from the shower wrapped in a towel.

"Not yet, just Rod's roommates," replied Bill handing her a cold cup of Bud. He lowered his voice. "Boy, Rod's already well on his way; no way he's going to make it through the evening. It's so typical of what happens when he drinks. He enjoys his beer so much, and has such a good time, that he drinks too much too fast; then passes out."

"Hmmm, sounds like he has a drinking problem."

"Probably does…. Well, I'll hit the shower while you're getting dressed," he said kissing her; then peeking at her cleavage.

"Later," she chuckled. "Go shower."

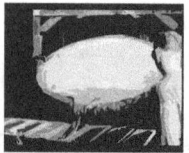

"Ahhh, shower felt good, and the beer's nice 'n cold," stated Bill smacking his lips as he toweled off. He pulled on clean underwear and white socks, a green polo shirt, zipped up his khaki shorts and laced up his white low cut Converse tennis shoes. "Let's head upstairs and I'll introduce you to Rod's roommates. We should probably eat a burger or hot dog once they're ready because the beer will be flowing all night. We don't want to get sick.

"Hey, guys, this is Barb Scott," introduced Bill as he and Barb entered the kitchen.

"Nice to meet you," replied Steve. "And you're givin' this up for the Jesuits!?" kidded Steve admiring Barb's dark skin and shapely breasts displayed by her tight yellow t-shirt. Barb, noticing Steve's narrow focus smiled politely and put her arm through Bill's.

A few minutes later, the roomies' girlfriends arrived carrying a few snacks. Tom, Rod's other roommate made the introductions. "This is Rod's brother, Bill and his girlfriend, Barb from Spokane; this is my girlfriend, Sarah, and Steve's girlfriend, Karen."

"Nice to meet you," replied Bill.

"And nice to meet you both," echoed Sarah. "Glad you could come all the way from Spokane for Rod's party; I know it means a lot to him," she added. Karen's welcome was cooler than Sarah's because she had observed Steve looking at Barb's breasts. When Steve noticed Karen's glare at him, he tried to recover by moving closer to Karen and putting his arm around her.

"Hot off the grill; help yourselves to a hotdog or burger if you're hungry," announced Rod as he placed a plate of each on the kitchen counter next to the ketchup, mustard and buns.

"Thanks," said Bill handing Barb a paper plate. "We're really hungry from the drive over."

After finishing their hot dogs, Bill announced that he'd like to drive Barb around the UW campus before it got too late. "Believe it or not, this is Barb's first time in Seattle; so she wants to see some sights. Just don't drink all the beer; we'll be back soon."

"Yeah, I know, you just wanna...just kiddin'," slurred Rod topping off his half-empty stein.

"Thank you!" whispered Barb squeezing Bill's hand as they walked to the car. "Man, I see what you mean about Rod's drinking; he's liable to be passed out by the time we get back."

Barb was like a little kid staring at the big brick buildings covered with ivy, as they drove through the UW campus. "It's so beautiful!"

"You'll love the view of Drumheller Fountain," Bill assured her as he parked the car.

When they reached the steps and looked down at the fountain, stately Mt. Rainier was in the background. "If you stand just right, it looks like Mt. Rainier is sitting atop the spray," Bill pointed out leading her down the steps to the fountain.

Barb stood motionless taking in the scene: Mt. Rainier atop the fountain's spray, students sitting on the edge of the fountain cooling their feet in the water, the nearby rose gardens. "This is such a pretty campus!"

"Wanna walk through the campus a bit?" asked Bill after several minutes.

"Yes! I can't wait to tell Teri how beautiful this campus is. It makes me want to go to college here."

"Well, you can if you want to badly enough."

"Yeah right. Not with my smarts. And there's no way I could afford it," Barb said looking down. "But right now...I just want to enjoy this," she added quickly as she looked up at the surrounding brick buildings.

When they returned to the car, Barb turned to him and kissed him tenderly. "I'll always have this memory of us here in this gorgeous place," she murmured. "Thank you!"

"You're welcome. I knew you'd love seeing this campus. On the way back to Rod's, I'll drive you by some of the frat houses and the sororities. They'll make you really want to come here for school."

"Oh my gosh!" Barb blurted staring at the big, impressive homes and the bare-chested guys tossing a Frisbee in front of one of the fraternities. A live rock band played on the balcony of another frat.

"Rod tells me that some studying actually does occur at this place once in awhile," joked Bill turning right on a side street that took them back to Rod's.

"Man, a few people have arrived since we left," exclaimed Bill driving past Rod's apartment searching for a place to park on 20th.

"Come on Baby Light My Fire" by The Doors, one of Rod's favorite rock groups could be heard even several houses away from his house. "I imagine the neighbors aren't too thrilled," commented Bill shaking his head.

"Hey, there he is—my little brother!" yelled Rod above the blaring stereo and loud conversation as Bill and Barb entered the crowded living room. "Get him and his girlfriend some fucking beer!" he bellowed. Bill could feel Rod leaning on him for support, as they wove through the guests toward the kitchen to fill two more cups. Bill estimated about 25 people crammed into the downstairs area, and he could see several more couples in the back yard. The pungent smell of marijuana permeated the house. Several couples sitting in the living room shared joints with one another.

This was a much different crowd than Bill and Barb were used to in Spokane, and they both enjoyed just taking it all in—people getting high on beer and pot, couples making out, people laughing and trying to talk over the loud music. They stuck pretty close together and turned down several offers to try marijuana.

"Hey, want to see a neat ravine?" asked Bill after he and Barb had finished off a couple more refills.

"Yes! It's so smoky and loud in here."

They both filled their lungs with fresh, cool air as they escaped the humid, stuffy house and stepped off the front porch about 9:00 PM. It was still light and warm, but they could feel the coolness of the approaching evening. Bill led her south on 20th. About a block away was a narrow two lane bridge that spanned a deep ravine. At the south end of the bridge, there was a path that extended down into the dark green canopy.

"It's like a jungle down here," exclaimed Barb as they descended. The buzz from the beer, the coolness of the evening, the youthful freedom of being away from home energized them both as they strolled hand in hand down the gravel path at the bottom of the ravine. "I'm so glad you decided to come to Seattle and bring me along!" Barb gushed taking in the damp smells and luscious greenery.

"Me too!" Spotting a low hanging tree branch, Bill ran toward it, pulled himself up onto it, and began beating his chest like a gorilla. "Aaayayayaya," he yelled mimicking Tarzan. An elderly couple out for an evening walk glanced nervously at Bill, and quickened their pace up the path shaking their heads.

"Stop!" laughed Barb hysterically. "You're crazy!"

When Bill jumped down, she grabbed his arms, and kissed him. "Ouch—a mosquito," exclaimed Barb slapping her right calf. "We'd better head back." She pivoted and began running up the darkening path. "I'll race you to the top!" she challenged looking over her shoulder.

Bill gave her a generous head start then sprinted by her about halfway up to the bridge. "Caught ya!" he yelled grabbing her waist. She screamed in delight. He spun her around and kissed her. "Let's go see if anyone's in our room."

The music was still blaring when they approached the house. There were fewer people in the living room now. Two couples were making out hot and heavy—one on the leather couch; the other in one of the large stuffed chairs. And next to the couch on the floor was Rod—passed out. His roommates were nowhere to be seen; *probably in their rooms with their girlfriends*, guessed Bill. A small group of very loud drunk people were in the kitchen, and when Bill entered to scope out the situation, he spotted the ketchup that someone had flung onto the ceiling. It was obvious to Bill that the party was getting out of hand, and Rod was oblivious.

"OK, party's over!" Bill announced loudly.

"Who are you?" asked one of the guys with a sneer.

"I'm Rod's brother, and he's passed out; so I'm tellin' you the party's over," Bill shot back getting in the guy's face.

"Awww," one of the girls complained as she headed for the front door pulling her intoxicated boyfriend by the hand. The couples in the living room followed them out overhearing Bill's directive from the kitchen.

As soon as the last guest exited the house, Bill turned off the blaring stereo in the living room then locked the front and back doors. He then headed downstairs to check the room they'd be staying in. "No unwanted guests downstairs. I'd better see if Rod's roommates are still here," he said to Barb, who had waited in the living room. Bill put his ear to Steve's bedroom door upstairs and could hear passionate moans. *I don't have a problem with that*, Bill thought to himself.

"I'm going to just put a blanket on Rod and let him sleep it off here," declared Bill placing a cushion under Rod's head. "No way I'm gonna try to carry him up to his room; if I wake him, chances are pretty good that he'll get sick—on me. Better to just leave him be."

He then approached Tom's bedroom door on the main floor which was slightly ajar and slowly pushed the door inward. The mixed odor of incense and pot emanated from the room. He could hear music playing and could see candle light shadows flickering on one of the bedroom walls. Sticking his head into the room, he saw Sarah straddling Tom moving up and down. Her long dark hair hung down her naked back. He motioned for Barb to come take a look. As she stepped back into the living room, both covered their mouths to keep from laughing aloud.

"I guess it's time for us to go to bed," whispered Bill leading her toward the basement.

—⟋⟍⟍—

Barb pulled her shirt over her head. "What a crazy night this has been! Wanna take a shower with me before getting into bed? I smell like pot smoke and sweat, which probably means you do too."

"Sounds good; you know how I hate showering with you!" grinned Bill removing his polo shirt. "Allow me," he added reaching around her to unhook her bra. She looked up at him, smiled then kissed him passionately. He loved the feeling of her warm soft breasts pressed against his bare chest.

"Oooh...what's this?" she asked grabbing his erectness as he entered the shower. The warm water raining down on them felt great, and they took turns lathering the soap and washing one another. He felt a bit embarrassed standing at attention so, but Barb just smiled when she'd glance at his hardness.

"Oh, I feel so much cleaner," she sighed drying her hair with her towel.

"Me too—good idea!" he mumbled brushing his teeth.

"I'm going to leave the bathroom light on and the door slightly ajar," added Barb. "It is so fucking dark down here!"

When Barb joined him in bed, she had a little jar with her. "Let's try some of this," she suggested slowly removing the lid. It was some type of gel that she placed on her fingers and applied to him. "Now come to me," she invited.

Bill was amazed at how smoothly they united. "Ooooh, myyy...that's nice!" he breathed. Their movements were so effortless and he loved the liquid noises they made together. She put her legs up on his shoulders so he could enter her deeply.

When her legs tired, she lowered them and secured herself to him with her feet, while she exerted her wonderful control. Bill was in heaven and tried his best to prolong his intense pleasure. But much sooner than he wanted, he felt himself beginning to swell. He knew Barb could feel it too for she quickened her pace, grabbed his ass and held him deep.

"Yes, come baby!" she commanded as he swelled inside her. "Come, come," she gasped confident the basement would contain their ecstasy.

After enjoying the wonderful rush, Bill relaxed into her arms relishing the warmth of their bodies and unified breathing. When Bill rolled onto his left side, she did as well and Bill snuggled her in his arms.

"Thank you for showing me the UW campus today; I enjoyed seeing it so much."

"You're welcome," Bill whispered kissing her right shoulder.

After several moments of silence, Bill heard Barb emit a heavy sigh. He rolled her onto her back so he could face her. "Are you okay?"

"Yes...I just...I'm going to miss you so much after you're gone," Barb shared wiping a tear from her cheek. "I have so much fun when I'm with you, and you're such a wonderful lover. I'm going to feel so lonesome and empty when you're gone."

"I'll miss you too, Barb. Listen, I'm sure I'll only be gone for a few weeks. Will you wait for me...at least for a few weeks?"

"Yes, of course I will," she replied reaching up to hug him.

"And I want you to tell me if you get pregnant, okay?

"Okay."

Spooning again, they reminisced a few scenes from the party until Bill fell asleep. Sleep didn't come as quickly for Barb, who was attempting to quiet the myriad thoughts and emotions running through her mind: the drive from Spokane, her first time in Seattle, the beautiful UW campus, Rod's wild party, Bill's departure in just a few weeks—maybe forever; her future.

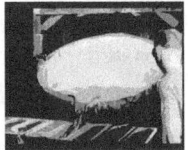

At first Bill thought he was dreaming when he heard "Light My Fire," by The Doors. He rolled over attempting to fall back to sleep, but the music made that impossible. *Where in the hell is that coming from?* he wondered as he tried to open his eyes. He squinted at the dim light escaping from the bathroom and headed to the toilet to relieve himself. When he finished, he left the bathroom door open enough so he could find his underpants and shorts. Then slipping on his sandals, he carefully worked his way up the dark basement stairway to find the stereo switch. When he entered the living room, the music was louder, but he remembered turning off the stereo before going to bed. He panned the room then determined the source of the loud music. It was coming from the house next door! When he peered out the window on the north side of the house, he could see a stereo speaker pointed directly at Rod's house through an open window next door.

"What the hell!" mumbled Rod stirring. He had somehow moved from the floor to the couch during the night.

"Your neighbor's getting even with us," Bill asserted pointing next door. "He must have recorded the music you were blasting last night." At times, you could even hear laughter and voices from the party on the recording.

"Aw, fuck!" Rod complained trying to sit up. "I feel like shit!"

"I can imagine; you passed out on the floor well before the party was over. Barb and I went for a walk in the ravine, and when we returned some assholes in the kitchen had flung ketchup on the ceiling; so I kicked everybody out."

"No shit!? Thank you; I'm sorry you had to deal with that," Rod apologized holding his head in his hands. He slowly stood up on wobbly legs. Let me take you and Barb to breakfast so we can get away from this noise. Maybe by the time we get back, 'numb nuts' next door will have turned his recording off." He slowly trudged upstairs to pee, wash his face and change his clothes.

"Breakfast sounds good to me," said Bill when Rod came down from upstairs. "I'll drive; I want you to listen to my engine. I think I might need a valve adjustment before heading for Spokane. Let me see if Barb's awake and wants to come along."

"What the fuck is that noise?" asked Barb when Bill asked her about going to breakfast.

"The guy next door taped the music last night and is aiming his speakers toward Rod's house; we're hoping he'll turn it off when he sees us leave."

"Go ahead and go to breakfast with Rod; I'm gonna try to sleep a bit more if I can," muttered Barb wrapping her pillow around her head and curling up in a fetal position. "If you could bring me back a coffee and a pastry of some sort that would be great," she mumbled from beneath the pillow.

—◊◊◊—

As Bill drove toward the U-District, Rod listened to the engine through his open window. "Yeah, sounds pretty rough," agreed Rod. "I think you'd better get a valve adjustment before driving back over the pass. You don't want to break down on I-90 in the middle of nowhere. There's a Volkswagen dealership nearby in the U-District; you can take it there first thing tomorrow morning."

"Shit, that's going to be a problem for Barb. She has to be at work Monday afternoon. I can always call in sick Monday evening for Graveyard Shift if I need to."

"She could fly to Spokane. I can follow you to the VW dealership tomorrow morning, then take you guys to the airport, then drop you off at my place before heading to work. Can someone pick her up from the airport in Spokane?"

"Yeah, her sister, Teri probably can," replied Bill as they entered the restaurant on Roosevelt Way N.E. "Let's call for flight times when we get back to your place."

"Sit anywhere you want," directed the hostess. "Your waitress will be right there."

"Man, I'm kind of hungry," Bill noted rubbing his hands together.

"Lucky you," replied Rod rubbing his forehead.

"Coffee?" asked the cute young waitress filling their water glasses.

"Yes!" they responded in unison.

"I'll be right back to take your orders," the waitress smiled giving each of them a menu, turning their cups over and pouring them coffee.

"I can't believe Barb's never been to Seattle before!" Rod said in amazement after testing his first sip of coffee to see if his stomach was okay with it. He wasn't ready for food yet. "Man, she's had a pretty sheltered existence."

Bill savored his first gulp of coffee. "Well, her family didn't have much when she was growing up. Her dad left her and her sister when Barb was just two, and her mom worked different jobs as a bartender."

Their waitress returned and Bill ordered. "I'll have two eggs over medium with bacon and toast."

"Just coffee for me now," added Rod. "Nice ass!" Rod commented as she swished away from their table. "Hey, after we get my place straightened up a bit, let's show Barb around Seattle: Pike Place Market, The Ballard Locks, Green Lake, Golden Gardens; then tonight let's take her to Ray's Boathouse for dinner. We need to celebrate our graduations and you going into the Jesuits, and it would be a real treat for her."

"Oh, she'd love that, Rod," replied Bill adding more cream to his coffee.

"Now tell me the truth. Are you really going to be able to give her up in a few weeks when you leave for the Novitiate?"

"I don't know," Bill sighed stirring his coffee. "We do have a great time together—and the lovin' is incredible!" he added grinning at Rod. "But I just feel like I need to give the Jesuits a try. All during my senior year at GU, I felt so aimless, and had this feeling that God was calling me to the Jesuits." Bill looked at Rod. "And I don't have any job lined up that I'm really interested in."

"You could stay on at Kaiser couldn't you? Isn't it pretty good money?"

"Anything else I can bring you guys?" asked the waitress after bringing Bill's order and refilling their cups.

"No, not now anyway," replied Rod flashing her a smile.

"It is pretty good money," replied Bill dipping his toast into one of his eggs. "But...I don't want to get stuck out there in the pot rooms. The working conditions are really unhealthy and the guys I work with have all warned me not to stay and get stuck out there." Bill paused and took a gulp of coffee before taking another bite. "And I've told Mom and Dad and all my friends that I'm entering the Novitiate at the end of August. Fr. Eric, a young Jesuit teacher I had this year and got to know pretty well, told me that the long retreat you go through at the beginning of your Novitiate is designed to help you figure out what you want to do with your life. I guess I'm hoping it will help me decide. And if I leave after the long retreat, which'll probably the case, at least everyone including me will know I tried it."

Rod took another sip of his coffee and holding it with both hands as if warming them said, "Well, then you'd better go." Rod looked directly at Bill. "Just don't get her pregnant before you leave."

"I've told her if that should happen, I won't go," Bill replied enjoying his last bite of toast and bacon.

"Not hungry this morning?" asked the waitress smiling at Rod like she knew he was hung over.

"Unfortunately, no," replied Rod with a sheepish smile as she placed their tab on the table and removed Bill's empty plate. "But I'll be sure to come back again when I am. Is this your section?"

She grinned at Rod. "Most of the time," she responded before walking away.

"I'll definitely be coming back here in the near future," stated Rod admiring her ass again. "Breakfast is on me," insisted Rod grabbing the tab. "Thanks again for watchin' out for my place last night."

"No problem. Hey, while you're paying for breakfast, I'll order a coffee and pastry to take back to Barb."

When they pulled in front of Rod's apartment house, it

seemed eerily quiet after the noisy, rude alarm they awoke to. The neighbor had turned off his recording, and his speaker was no longer sitting on the window ledge pointed at Rod's house. "Thank God!" sighed Rod. "I don't think I could have taken it much longer with my hangover."

Barb was just getting out of the shower as Bill came downstairs. "Here's your coffee and pastry, Barb. Did you manage to get any more sleep?"

"A bit more. The guy did turn off the recording shortly after you and Rod left for breakfast—thank God!"

"While you're getting ready, I'll help Rod clean up the place a bit; then we'll take you to some places in Seattle we think you'll really like."

"That would be great! And thanks for the breakfast," she added enjoying the first bite of her Danish.

"Oh, I talked to Rod about my car. He agrees that I should get my engine's valves adjusted before heading back to Spokane, which means you'll have to fly back to Spokane tomorrow morning so you can make it to work on time. Can Teri pick you up at the airport?"

Barb stopped toweling and looked at Bill a bit worried. "Probably...but...I didn't bring enough money for a plane ticket...and I'd have to call Teri."

"Don't worry, I'll pay for your ticket, and you can use Rod's phone to call your sister."

"Oh my gosh...I've never flown on a plane before."

"You'll love it; it's sooo fast. I guarantee it will be more fun than riding back in my slow Bug in the heat of the day. When you come upstairs, we'll make some calls and see about flights to Spokane tomorrow morning. Rod said he can drive us to the airport and me back to his place before he leaves for work."

"Hey, Bill come up here a sec," called Rod from his second

floor bedroom. When Bill entered Rod's bedroom, Rod displayed a small brown prescription bottle in his left hand. "This is Benzedrine, which is a stimulant," he explained removing the lid to reveal a white powder. "You only take just a tiny bit, as it doesn't take much," he emphasized sprinkling a small amount of the powder into his right palm. He then licked it with his tongue and drank some water. "This will help me get through the day after such a rough night. Want to try some?"

"Naw, I'll pass for now; maybe later."

"Well, if you need some, it's right here in my top drawer. Just remember, take only a tiny bit or it can really kick your ass."

—⁓—

"You can catch an 8 AM Northwest Airlines flight to Spokane from Boeing Field tomorrow morning," Bill announced to Barb when she came upstairs. "That should get you home well before you have to be to work in the afternoon."

"Okay, I'll call Teri. She's not going to believe it—me flying home from Seattle! Neither one of us has ever flown before."

"Well, then it's about time you did!" grinned Rod washing some dishes in the kitchen sink.

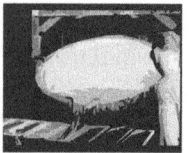

In front of the Pike Place Fish Market, Barb stopped and stared wide-eyed at the huge salmon that were displayed on ice. "Oh, my God, look at the size of those fish!" she exclaimed. Then, one of the vendors yelled something and flung one of the big salmon to another vendor. Barb's jaw dropped. "Did you see that!?" Bill and Rod enjoyed watching her first time reactions; she was like a little kid.

"Pick out a necklace or earrings to remember this trip by," urged Bill as they shuffled by several jewelry vendors. "My treat."

"Oh, my gosh—are you sure?" asked Barb looking at Bill.

"Yes, I'm sure."

After trying on several different necklaces, Barb decided on a sterling silver cross with turquoise inlay. "I think I like this one the best."

"Let me fasten it around your neck," suggested the dark-haired lady behind the table.

"What do you think, Bill?"

"Perfect! The color looks great on you, Barb," smiled Bill.

"Thank you sooo much!" she exclaimed kissing him, then admiring the cross in the mirror on the table. "This will always remind me of this special time with you in Seattle. And…if you decide to stay in the Jesuits…I'll always think of you when

I wear it," she added looking at him.

When they reached the far end of the market, they gazed out at Puget Sound. "This is sooo beautiful," Barb uttered watching a ferry pulling out from the terminal. Bill didn't rush her; he let her just soak it all in. "And there's Mt. Rainier, oh my God!"

"If you like seeing ships, you'll love the Ballard Locks," assured Rod. "You won't believe some of the yachts you'll see."

—◊◊◊—

"Where are we now?" asked Barb as Bill found a vacant slot in a parking lot.

"This is Ballard," replied Rod, "and we're at the Ballard Locks. These locks allow boats to pass between Puget Sound, which is salt water and the Ship Canal, which connects to Lake Union and Lake Washington, which are fresh water bodies. We'll stay long enough so you can see how the locks work."

It was a joy to watch Barb taking in this new experience. "I can't believe the size of those boats!" gasped Barb.

"Those are called yachts," clarified Rod. "Gives you an idea of how rich some people are doesn't it?" Rod enjoyed explaining to Barb how the locks worked. "See how the vessels waiting out in Puget Sound are lower than the those in the locks below heading toward the Ship Canal? When all these vessels have headed into the Ship Canal, the locks will be closed and the water lowered to accommodate the vessels waiting their turn out in Puget Sound. Notice how the attendants toss ropes down to the vessels so the people on board can secure their vessel."

"I could spend hours watching this," exclaimed Barb from behind the railing as she watched all the different sized vessels tying up to one.

"I know what you mean," replied Bill. "I was the same way when I saw this for the first time. It's so different from anything we have in Spokane!"

"Man, I think I'm finally getting my appetite back after last night," declared Rod after about forty-five minutes at the locks. "How about grabbing a burger at Dick's; then we'll head to Green Lake," suggested Rod.

"Sounds good to me!" Bill responded. "That breakfast didn't stay with me very long."

Barb's head was on a swivel as they drove past bridges and old brick homes on their way to Dick's Drive-In on 45th.

"Quite a bit bigger than Ron's isn't it," pointed out Rod as they pulled into the parking lot. "And it's always busy like this."

"Not bad prices either," added Bill after ordering. "A burger, fries and milk shake for 55 cents!"

"Let's take our food back to my place. We can clean up, change and head to Green Lake," recommended Rod. "After a couple hours at Green Lake, we'll head for Golden Gardens then Ray's Boat House for dinner. Their food is amazing!" he added looking at Barb.

—⁓—

After slurping the last of his chocolate shake, Bill began to feel the effects of yesterday's long drive, the late night and the rude alarm that woke him way too early.

"You know, I think I will try a little of your Benzadrine," Bill said when Barb had headed to the bathroom in the basement. "I'm really starting to fade."

"Sure; let me show you how much to take," replied Rod as they headed up to his room. "Hold out your palm," he directed; then he carefully portioned out a small amount of the white powder. "Just lick this off your palm and drink some water. You'll definitely feel like you have more energy in a bit," assured Rod replacing the cap and returning the bottle to his top drawer. Sure enough, in a few minutes, Bill no longer felt sleepy, but noticed that he felt a bit jittery—like he'd had too much coffee.

—⁓—

"You'll like Green Lake," Bill guaranteed Barb as the three of them headed west from Rod's after finishing their lunch. "It's fun to just watch all the people walking around the lake, riding their bikes, sun bathing, boating."

"Some of these old brick homes remind me of the brick house Grandma Roberts lived in on Washington Street in Spokane," pointed out Rod to Bill as they neared Green Lake. "This would be a neat area of Seattle to live in," he added.

"Look at all the people!" remarked Barb as they walked toward Green Lake after parking the car. While walking counter clockwise around the lake, they were passed by myriad characters Bill and Barb didn't typically see in Spokane. A shirtless hippie-looking guy in his 40's with long scraggly hair, wearing beads and cutoffs roller skated by them. He was singing the song that blared on his transistor radio. Bicyclists wove in and out of walkers and skaters. Canoeists paddled slowly across the lake enjoying the sunshine. Sun bathers rubbed sun tan lotion on one another. Bill noticed Barb looking at the young couples holding hands, laughing, embracing, and he wondered what she was thinking about. *Is she wishing this was us? Will she eventually move to Seattle and find a boyfriend who will bring her to Green Lake?*

About halfway around the lake, Bill bought a bag of

popcorn from a vendor. They watched toddlers scampering about in a play area while their parents watched in delight.

"If you need to use the restroom, now's the time," suggested Rod heading to a concrete building nearby. "The next one isn't until we get back to the parking area."

"Sounds like a good idea," replied Bill joining Rod. "Do you have to go, Barb?"

"No, I'll wait here for you…and finish the popcorn," she chuckled.

While using the restroom, Bill realized again how jittery he felt. *Must be the effects of the Benzedrine.* While he appreciated the lift it had given him, he didn't like feeling this way. It was hard for him to concentrate on any one thing for very long.

After using the restroom, Bill and Rod rejoined Barb, and the three of them completed the circuit around the lake taking in the beautiful scenery and the stream of activity along the way.

"I wish I lived in this area," sighed Barb as they headed for Bill's Bug.

"Well, you could always move here," replied Rod. "There are lots of J.C. Penney stores in the Seattle area."

"And you could see about enrolling in a community college," offered Bill.

Barb took one last look at Green Lake before climbing into the back seat. "Maybe I can talk my sister into moving here with me; it would be good for her to get away from Spokane, too."

As Bill's Bug headed up a steep grade on NW 85th Street toward Golden Gardens Park, it was obvious it wouldn't make it over Snoqualmie Pass without a valve adjustment.

"Man! Not much power. Good thing you're getting a valve adjustment before attempting Snoqualmie Pass!"

—ᴟᴟ—

The view of Puget Sound from Golden Gardens Park was breathtaking, and so much more expansive than the Eastern Washington lake scenes Bill and Barb were used to seeing.

"Wow, what mountains are those?" asked Barb looking west across the water.

"Those are the Olympics," replied Rod. "You don't see anything like that around Spokane, do ya!"

For the next couple of hours, they walked on the low tide beach looking for shells, colorful rocks and sea creatures. Bill and Rod periodically skipped rocks near the shoreline. Barb selected several shells and rocks to take back to Spokane. "Look! Here's a small crab," declared Barb peering down at the beach from a couched position. Bill looked at Rod and both smiled. They were delighted to see Barb having so much fun.

"Well, I'm ready for a beer," announced Rod. "Let's head back to the car and drive to Ray's Boathouse."

"Sounds good," replied Bill.

"Park out here; you don't want to pay for valet parking," coached Rod as they pulled into the parking lot. "You will love this restaurant," Rod assured Barb as they walked toward the entrance. Two of the valet attendants admired Barb as she passed by them. "We'll try to get a table on the deck so we can enjoy the view of the water and the mountains," advised Rod opening the restaurant door for Barb and Bill.

Barb couldn't believe how lively the bar and restaurant were. A hostess led them through the crowded bar to a table on the deck and provided them menus. "Oh, my gosh, look at all the sailboats!" gushed Barb before taking her seat on the deck. "And the size of some of those boats…."

"Yachts!" reminded Rod.

"I'm sorry, yachts!" Barb repeated smiling. "There must be a lot of rich people who live here," she added scanning the marina.

"Hi, I'm Diane and I'll be your waitress," smiled a young lady with short blond hair. "Can I get you guys something to drink?"

Rod smiled at her and asked her to bring them a pitcher of Bud. Bill was glad she didn't ask to see their ID's as Barb wasn't of age, and he knew Barb would be ready for rowdy sex after having a few beers.

"You have to order seafood," declared Rod opening his menu. "It's so fresh here."

"Okay, what would you recommend?" asked Barb opening her menu.

"I think we should all get something different so you can try some of each. That way you'll know which you like best," Rod suggested.

"Good idea," Bill added perusing the dinner options. "I'll order the scallops."

"Okay, I'll get crab cakes," Rod said. "Barb you should get either halibut or salmon."

"I've had salmon before; what is halibut?" she asked looking up from her menu.

"Halibut is a white fish—very tender and delicious. You'd like it!"

"Okay, I'll try it," she agreed closing her menu. "This is sooo much fun! Thanks for showing me all these beautiful places. I definitely want to come back to Seattle sometime."

"Well, when Bill's in the Novitiate—praying for us in his cubicle, bring your sister over. You gals are welcome to stay at my place while you visit," Rod invited filling their glasses. Rod raised his glass. "Here's to our futures."

Bill enjoyed hearing Barb rave about the new sights she'd seen earlier in the day, and seeing Rod so happy now that he'd graduated and landed his first pharmacy job. *What a perfect evening*, reflected Bill savoring his beer and looking out at the water and the Olympics. *Times like this are so special!* He wanted to just relish this experience but uninvited questions and thoughts began to flit through his mind. *Do I really want to enter the Jesuits and give all this up? Are You calling me to something even better, Lord? Please help me decide...maybe I should just stay at Kaiser...but so many workers there have warned me not to get stuck there.* He recalled Jim's caution, *"If you get stuck out here in the pot rooms, you'll regret it!"* Please help me decide, Lord.

"Are you ready to order?" asked the waitress refocusing Bill's thoughts.

"I am," replied Rod confidently. "How about you, Bro?"

"Ah...yeah...Barb, you go first."

"I think you'd better bring us another pitcher," suggested Rod after the waitress had taken their orders.

"So, where do you think you'll move to, Rod?" asked Bill.

"North of here...probably somewhere near Bothell or Kirkland. The pharmacy I'm working at is on Juanita Blvd, which is between those two areas. If you were going to be here longer, we could drive out that way and I'd show you where my pharmacy is. I'll probably rent for the first year or so; then I'd like to buy a house for investment purposes."

"You'll have to give Barb your phone number after you find a place so she can contact you when she returns to Seattle," suggested Bill.

"Darn rights," agreed Rod smiling at Barb. "Has your sister ever been to Seattle?"

"No, and I know she'd love it."

"Well, bring her with you so we can give her the Seattle tour. Where does she work?"

"At Rosauers in the bakery," replied Barb.

Rod attempted to find out more about her sister and her mom, but could tell quickly that Barb didn't want to go into much detail.

"Oh, look at my halibut!" exclaimed Barb as the waitress placed her dish in front of her. The generous slice of Halibut on one side of her plate was topped with an Asian-looking sauce and sesame seeds were sprinkled on top; rice pilaf and green beans balanced the other side of the plate. "I can hardly wait to try it. And your dishes all look so good, too! Mmm… this is sooo tasty!" savored Barb after her first bite of halibut. She nodded at Rod and pointed her fork at her dinner. "Good advice!"

"Here, try a bite of scallop," offered Bill extending his fork.

"Oh, that's sooo good…it's really rich," replied Barb enjoying the new taste.

"Okay, now you have to try a bite of my crab cake," insisted Rod moving his plate toward Barb.

"Yumm, that's very good, too. Now I have a better idea of what to order next time I come to Seattle."

The conversation slowed as they enjoyed their dinners, the views of the marina, the Olympics and the colorful sky as the late afternoon sun began its descent.

"Looks like each of you enjoyed your selection," observed their waitress as she cleared their plates. "Did you save room for dessert?"

"Oh, I didn't," stated Barb placing her hands on her stomach. "I am so full."

"I think I'm fine as well," added Rod draining the last sip of beer in his glass.

"I'm good, too," added Bill with a smile. "I think we're ready for our bill."

"This has been such a great day," mused Bill aloud. "Thanks for showing us all these neat places today, Rod."

"No problem; I'm glad you guys could make it over."

Their waitress returned placing the bill on the table. "Thank you and come back again."

"I definitely will!" replied Barb enthusiastically.

"Well, the next challenge is to get you two back to Spokane! But first, let's walk along the marina for a bit and drool before we head back to my place," Rod suggested figuring out his share of the tab and tip.

After leaving Ray's Boathouse, they walked along the Shilshole Bay Marina pointing out boats they'd choose if they could afford them.

"Given all the money you'll be making as a pharmacist, you'll probably have a yacht moored here someday, Rod," speculated Bill.

"Ah, I don't think so. I would like to have a ski boat someday, though. I'd love to learn how to slalom ski."

"Wow, look at the size of that one!" stated Bill in amazement pointing to a yacht named *My Eden*. "I wouldn't even be able to afford the moorage costs."

As Bill watched the sun set with Barb and Rod, he tried to relish each remaining minute of this special day, and he could tell from Barb's gaze that she was doing the same. When the sun slipped from sight below the horizon and the vivid, golden colors began to fade to gray, Bill hoped this extraordinary scene would never fade from his memory. *Thank you for this very special day, Lord!* They turned and walked back to his car.

—ɯ—

"Turn right here and I'll show you where the Volkswagen dealership is," directed Rod as Bill drove them back toward Rod's apartment. "This way, you'll know how to find it from my place. We'll drop your car off here at the Service Department tomorrow morning," Rod said after they pulled into the dealership lot on Roosevelt Way N.E. "Then we'll drive Barb to Boeing Field in my car. I can drop you by my place on my way to work, and you can either walk here from my place or take a cab to pick it up when it's ready. I'd drive you back here but I have to work until 6:00 PM."

"No problem, I can just walk. It will be good for me before the long drive back to Spokane."

"Thanks again for such a great day," repeated Barb to Rod as they exited the car and headed for the house. She gave him a hug.

"You're welcome; it was my pleasure. Now you can tell people that you've been to Seattle. Hope you come back sometime."

"I will come back," vowed Barb scanning the neighborhood.

"We'll have to get up about 6:15 so we can drop off your car and get to Boeing Field by about 7:20. Right now I'm going to crash. See you two bright and early," Rod yawned heading up to his room.

—ɯ—

Hope I can sleep tonight, thought Bill to himself as he headed downstairs with Barb. He still felt the effects of the Benzedrine—jittery, like he'd drunk way too much coffee. But he was pretty sure he'd feel sleepy after having sex with Barb.

"Oh, no!" he heard Barb exclaim from the bathroom off their bedroom.

"What's wrong?" asked Bill from outside the closed door.

"Oh, my damn period started; what a mess! I'll be out in a bit."

After a few minutes, Barb came out to get something out of her bag; then headed back into the bathroom. "Sorry. I'll be out soon."

"Well, the good news is I'm not pregnant," Barb assured him as she exited the bathroom. "The bad news is we can't make love tonight."

"Oh...?" replied Bill looking surprised.

Barb could tell from his reaction that he was disappointed, and that he didn't fully understand the issue. "Believe me, you wouldn't want to have sex with me tonight, Bill. We'd really make a mess, and I don't want to stain Rod's sheets and bedding."

"Darn, I was so looking forward to making love with you after such a wonderful day, and I feel so wound up.... What if we put a towel under us? I can wash everything when I get back from the airport," assured Bill.

"You don't understand, Bill. I'm really messy right now, and...I don't smell good."

"I don't mind, Barb; I just want...I really need you tonight!"

"Bill, you.... Okay," she reluctantly agreed letting his disappointed face sway her. "See if you can find a couple dark-colored towels; we're going to need them," she added heading into the bathroom again.

After a few minutes, Bill emerged from the laundry room with a large red and black beach towel. Barb folded it in half and placed it on top of the bottom sheet.

When he approached her, he could tell Barb wasn't eager like she usually was.

"Slow, slow," she urged grimacing slightly as he began to penetrate her. She felt different to him tonight. The normal smooth entry felt almost rubbery, and he could tell his movements weren't comfortable to Barb. The smell wafting up to him was very different as well. Once she had fully accepted him, he could feel her relax a bit. She wrapped her legs around his waist and urged him to stay close to her as they moved as one. He could tell she didn't want him to move independently. When she could feel him begin to surge, she squeezed him with her legs to keep him close.

"Yes, yes!" gasped Bill as he climaxed. He wanted her to enjoy the ecstasy as she typically did, but her usual passionate sounds were missing. It was like she was doing her best to please him, but just wanted him to come and be done. As his rush eased, she released her legs from him and relaxed.

"Are you okay?" he asked stroking her forehead.

She nodded her head slowly, "But I'm very sleepy."

Within minutes, she began to breathe heavily; then to snore lightly lying on her back. The day's activities, the beer and rich dinner had caught up with her. He was envious; he knew he needed to sleep long and hard tonight too. Tomorrow was going to be a busy day, and a long, hot drive back to Spokane. But his heart still pounded away from the effects of the Benzedrine. It felt like his whole body was pulsing.

When he retreated from her, he felt sticky, and he could smell the mess she had warned him about. But he wasn't about to clean up anything at this point, so he lay there for what seemed like a long time before he fell into a shallow on and off doze.

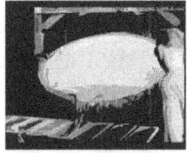

Both awoke with a start when Rod rapped lightly on their bedroom door. "It's 6:25 you guys," he announced before heading back upstairs. Barb was up first and headed for the bathroom. "Oh my God, what a mess, Bill! I tried to tell you," she complained anxiously but quietly so Rod wouldn't hear her.

Bill reluctantly rolled out of bed and turned on the bedroom light. As his blurry vision cleared, he was shocked by the extent of the blood that covered the white sheets and him. Barb had bled through the folded beach towel, the bottom sheet and into the mattress pad. Now he was wishing he had heeded her caution last night. He wondered how he was going to be able to clean it all up before he left for Spokane.

He tried to calm Barb's anxiety through the bathroom door. "Please don't worry about it right now, Barb; I'll clean up everything while I'm waiting for my car to get fixed. Just shower and get ready so we can get you to the airport in time."

While Barb was showering, Bill removed all the soiled bedding and put it in the laundry sink that was adjacent to their room in the basement. He filled the sink with cold water so everything could soak until he returned. Then he showered while Barb was dressing and packing.

—⟳—

"Mornin'," greeted Rod with a yawn. "Man, 6:15 came way too soon for me. Got everything?"

"I think so," answered Barb meekly.

"You'll have to push my Bug a bit so I can start it," Rod explained to Bill as they loaded Barb's bag into the back seat of his faded black 1955 VW Bug. "Then just follow me to the dealership."

No wonder he keeps it parked facing downhill, thought Bill pushing against the motor's hood until Rod popped the clutch. The old engine coughed and sputtered to life, and Rod kept revving it while he flipped a "uey" on 20th and drove back toward the house.

"Thanks!" yelled Rod from the open passenger-side window. "Someday these old VW's will be worth some bucks. You don't see too many anymore with the small rear window."

Probably for a reason, thought Bill wondering if it would get them to the airport and back.

—⁂—

"Okay, we'll take care of it," assured the slender service manager dressed in a blue shirt with a VW insignia. "It'll probably be ready about 2:00 this afternoon. You might want to call first to make sure though."

After Bill emerged from the dealership and hopped in the passenger seat, Rod headed for the freeway. *Rod's Bug sounds worse than mine,* thought Bill listening to the noisy valves.

Barb quietly took in the Seattle skyline from the back seat, yawning every few minutes as they drove south on I-5 toward Boeing Field. "The weekend went way too fast," reflected Barb aloud. Bill could tell she wasn't ready to leave such a vibrant city and return to her boring job in the Valley.

"I'll let you guys out here," informed Rod as they pulled up to the passenger loading zone. "I'll drive around a few times and pick you up Bill, once Barb has her ticket; I don't want to shut this thing off. Nice to meet you, Barb. Enjoy your first flight, and I hope you get to Seattle again."

"Me too; thanks again for the great time, Rod."

"I'm kind of nervous," Barb admitted as they approached the Northwest Airlines ticket counter. "But kind of excited, too. Are you driving back to Spokane this afternoon?"

"If my car's ready by early afternoon. If it's not done until late afternoon, I'll stay another night and leave early Tuesday morning," replied Bill writing a check for Barb's one way ticket.

"Don't you have to go into work Monday evening for grave-yard?" asked Barb.

"Yeah, but Mom can call in for me if I can't make it."

She kissed him and gave him a hug. "You look pretty tired; drive careful, okay? Sorry you have to drive all that way by yourself. Give me a call when you get back to Spokane," she added getting in the line to board her flight.

"Okay. You'll really enjoy your flight, and you'll be amazed at how quickly you get to Spokane," he replied flashing her a reassuring smile.

When Barb disappeared through the departure door, Bill turned away and exited the terminal to wait for Rod. He took several deep breaths. The cool, fresh morning air helped him wake up a bit.

"She'll be in for quite a thrill flying for the first time," said Rod after Bill closed the passenger side door. "She seems like a nice girl." Rod headed for the parking lot exit. "Man, how in the hell are you going to make it in the Jesuits after screwing her all summer?"

"I don't know…I'll probably be back after a few weeks,"

replied Bill staring blankly out the front window, and trying not to think about how sleepy he was. "It must be a great feeling to have worked so hard through pharmacy school and now have a good job with Bartell Drug." Bill wanted to change the direction of Rod's conversation.

"Yeah, it is. I'll finally be able to afford a nice place to rent and I can purchase a newer car. Then I want to put enough money aside over the next few years to be able to buy a house. It's not very smart to rent for too long."

"Man, owning your own house—that's exciting to think about! Hey, not to change the subject but I've overheard Dad and Mom talk about throwing a going away party for me in August. If they do, think you'd be able to come over?" asked Bill completing a yawn.

"Well, let me talk with Steve. I know he's planning to drive to Spokane sometime in August to see his folks; maybe it will work out. As you can probably tell, my Bug certainly wouldn't make it over and back."

Rod pulled up in front of his rental house and got out with Bill, leaving his car idling. He gave Bill a big bear hug. "Thanks for driving over, Bro. The side door's open; help yourself to whatever you can find. I've got to get to work. You're welcome to stay another night if your car isn't ready this afternoon. But if it is, maybe I'll see you in a few weeks."

"Thanks for the great time," replied Bill as Rod ground his Bug into first gear and drove north on 20th Ave N.E. Bill headed for the side door and immediately thought about the mess he had to clean up in the basement.

"Did you get her to the airport on time?" asked Steve as Bill entered the kitchen.

"Yeah; she's pretty excited about flying for the first time."

"I'll bet she is. I just made some coffee, help yourself. I have to head to a summer school class I'm taking."

"Thanks, Steve. I'll definitely need some coffee to keep awake on the drive back to Spokane," he admitted pouring himself a cup. "For some reason, I didn't sleep for shit last night. Is Tom still sleeping?"

"No, he had to work today."

Whew! At least they won't be around to see me cleaning up, Bill thought as he headed down stairs with his cup of coffee.

—⋘—

Bill couldn't believe his eyes when he saw the sink full of red water. *Oh my God, how in the fuck am I going to get these sheets and pad white again?* He emptied the sink and realized he'd have to wring out the bedding in the back yard as there just wasn't enough space in the laundry room sink. He found a bucket, rinsed it out, and carried the wet bedding into the back yard where he did his best to wring out as much water as he could. He then refilled the sink with cold water and soaked the items again to remove more of the blood. After three additional rinses in the sink, he threw the pile into the washing machine. He then went upstairs to see what he could find for breakfast. He peered into the messy refrigerator. *Hotdogs! No surprise,* he thought well aware of Rod's typical hot dog diet. *Two fried hot-dogs, eggs, toast and coffee. I can live with that.*

After breakfast he washed his dishes; then headed for the living room and closed his eyes to see if he could nap for awhile. But his body still felt like it was pulsing from the Benzedrine. A semi-doze was the best he could do.

When he heard the washer shut off about 10:30, he went downstairs to check the bedding. *Fuck, everything's still pink!* He decided to wash the load again and this time used a little bleach. *Hope this will help whiten everything.*

While he waited for the second washing cycle to finish, he thought about Rod starting his new job as a pharmacist. *How exciting for him. He'll make good money and should have a good life ahead of him. I wish I would have known what I wanted to do like he did. I still have no idea.* Then something Father Eric said popped into his mind. *"Maybe God is calling you to something you haven't even thought of yet.... I know that your Novitiate experience will help you decide what you want to do...."*

Bill once again began to feel anxious and uneasy, and he knew he had to move about. *Got to get some fresh air...I know, I'll go for a walk in the ravine. Can't be gone too long though.*

As long as he was moving, he felt like he was making headway and had some control over the heavy thoughts invading his mind. He filled his lungs with the fresh, cool ravine air; then slowly exhaled. He loved the damp smells, and the cooler air made him feel less sleepy. He enjoyed listening to all the bird sounds coming from the trees which formed a green, shady canopy over the ravine. After walking about a mile, he turned around and headed back to the house.

Whew! Everything looks a lot whiter this time. I'll hang them outside in the sun then call the dealership.

—〰—

"Service Department," answered a man who sounded way too busy to be answering the phone.

"Hi, my name is Bill Roberts and I'm calling to see if my car's done yet—I'm getting a valve adjustment done on my '61 Bug."

"Hang on, I'll check," he replied laying the receiver down hard on the counter. "Should be done within the hour. You really need to have a complete valve job done, but the adjustment will definitely improve how it runs for awhile."

"Thanks, I'll be down shortly," responded Bill. He hung up the phone, breathed a sigh of relief and headed downstairs to grab his check book. *At least I can head back today.*

Walking with a lighter, quicker step, he headed toward the U-District. *I love these old houses and neighborhoods. Reminds me of parts of the South Hill in Spokane. But it's so different over here: the vegetation, the smells, and the humidity,* he thought wiping the beads of sweat from his forehead. *Don't know if I'd like to live here though…if you're not wet from the rain, you're wet from the humidity. And there's so much more traffic!*

The air conditioning felt wonderful as he entered the dealership and headed back toward the Service Department. "Hi, last name is Roberts; I'm here to pick up my Bug when it's done."

"Okay, have a seat; shouldn't be too much longer," replied a middle-aged guy wearing a blue VW shirt.

Unable to sit still, Bill headed for the showroom to scope out the new Bugs.

"Pretty nice aren't they?" declared a heavy-set bald guy in slacks, white shirt and tie.

"Yeah, wish I was driving one of these to Spokane rather than my '61," replied Bill. "Every time I drive it to Seattle, I need to get my valves adjusted."

"Well, these new Bugs have so much more power than your '61, and the valve adjustment problems are pretty much a thing of the past. Would you like to test drive one?"

"Oh, no; I can't begin to afford the payments at this stage of my life. But thanks for the offer."

"Well, come back and see us when you're ready…and hope your drive back to Spokane is uneventful."

Nice guy, Bill thought to himself as he headed back to the Service Department.

"Ok, Mr. Roberts, your car's ready," announced the Service Manager standing behind the counter. "Total comes to $86.45 with tax," he stated handing Bill a copy of the invoice. "Cashier has your key; you can settle up next door. Thanks for coming in."

"You're welcome," responded Bill breathing a sigh of relief that it wasn't more money. *Now if the sheets are dry, I'll be in good shape time-wise,* he thought noting 1:10 PM on the showroom clock. Bill started his Bug and smiled. *Wow, sounds so much quieter and smoother.* He pulled out of the dealership and headed back to Rod's.

—⁂—

Thank God! he said to himself relieved. The sun and the light breeze had dried the sheets and mattress pad nicely.

After re-making the bed and straightening up the downstairs bedroom and laundry room, he shaved, brushed his teeth and packed his bag. As he scanned the room to see if he had forgotten anything, he realized how tired he was. The lack of sleep from the Benzedrine rush had really taken its toll, but remembering what Rod had told him about its ability to keep you going, he went upstairs to Rod's room, opened the pill bottle and poured just a tiny bit of the white substance into the palm of his left hand. He licked it away; then went into the bathroom to wash the bitterness down with water. *That should help me keep awake for the next six or seven hours. I know I'll be a zombie by the time I get home and to work, but I'm just too fucking tired to drive all that way without some help.* He found himself being extra cautious as he descended the narrow stairs from Rod's room to the phone in the living room. He wasn't used to being this tired and jittery.

"Hi, Mom. Just wanted to let you know that my car's valves are adjusted and I'm heading home now."

"Okay, did you have a good time?" she enthusiastically asked.

"Yes. I'll fill you in when I get home."

"You sound really tired. Will you be ready for Graveyard Shift tonight?"

"I hope so," he replied knowing he'd probably call in sick when he got home.

"Okay...drive carefully."

"I will, Mom; probably see you between 8:30 and 9:00. Bye."

He then wrote Rod a thank you note that he left on his dresser upstairs, threw his bag in the back seat, and headed for I-5. It was 2:05 PM.

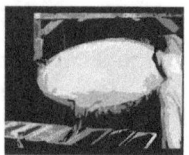

His lack of sleep, and nervousness from the Benzedrine high made Bill all the more anxious driving south through Seattle on I-5. *Shit, I can't remember how far south the exit is…I know it's past the downtown area…don't panic…just watch for the I-90 sign,* he told himself. *There's the sign for I-90…whew! Once I get across Lake Washington, traffic will start to thin out. I should be in Spokane by 8:30 if I don't have any car trouble.*

He could tell his Bug was running smoother and had more power as he headed east across Lake Washington. A slalom skier kicked up spray north of the bridge. It reminded him of when he learned to ski on Lake Coeur d' Alene in Idaho. John Thorson, a 7th grade classmate at St. Charles Elementary in Spokane invited Bill to his family's cabin one weekend during the summer, and John and his dad, Bob taught Bill how to ski on two skis. Bill could still remember how tough it was to keep the tips of the wide, heavy wood skis together and pointed up with the rope in between them in the cold water until the Chris Craft pulled him out of the water. It was on the third try that Bill popped out of the water. He could still remember how tall he felt as he skimmed over the churned-up water directly behind the inboard. John, his dad who was driving the boat and John's sister, Rose, who had come along for the ride, all cheered for Bill. For a brief moment, Bill thought about going outside the wake, but when he saw how high it was, he determined it was best for him to stay right behind the boat.

"You had the biggest grin on your face!" stated Rose when they picked up Bill, who had let go of the rope well outside their dock.

"That was so much fun!" gushed Bill. "Thank you so much!"

Bill rode in the boat with Bill's dad and Rose when John skied next on one ski. John sat on the edge of the dock and when there was just a little bit of slack in the ski rope, he yelled, "Hit it!" When the rope tightened, John was up on the water. Bill was so envious of John who had no fear of crossing the tall wake on either side of the inboard, and could send up a wall of spray when he turned. Bill was determined to be able to ski like John some day.

I wonder what John is doing now? I wonder if his sister Rose is still a nun? Two years ahead of Bill and John at St. Charles, Rose was blond and beautiful. Bill was surprised when he found out she entered a convent after graduating from Holy Names High School. *I'm sure I wasn't the only guy who was disappointed to hear that news.*

Now, heading down the hill past Lake Sammamish toward Issaquah, he thought about stopping at Boehm's, his favorite chocolate shop. It was pretty much a must stop on trips to Seattle. He loved the sweet aromas in the shop, and always had a difficult time choosing between their turtles and rocky road. He glanced at his wrist watch. *Humm...better not; it's almost 3:00. Damn!*

His Bug held its own as it began the gradual ascent to Snoqualmie Pass near North Bend. However, the last few steeper miles to the summit slowed its speed to 40 mph in third gear even with a tail wind. *Come on...we're just about to the top. Just get me over the pass.*

The Snoqualmie Summit was the most beautiful part of the trip for Bill, but car worries usually affected his ability to fully enjoy the green and rugged scenery. *Come on…just a few hundred more feet*, he urged now shifting down to second gear. *Still a few patches of snow on some of the peaks.* He glanced at the bare ski slopes to his right. I *wonder how the skiing is here in the winter?*

Bill could almost hear his car gasp a sigh of relief as it began to slowly pick up speed down the east side of the pass. When it reached 50 mph, he put it in neutral so the engine could rest and cool on the long coast down.

Keechelus Lake is still pretty full, he noted gazing across the large lake. He knew by the end of September, however, this reservoir for Seattle would expose hundreds of stumps along its widening shores.

He loved the sweet, spicy smell of the poplar trees along the Yakima River near Cle Elum. By late October, the trees would provide drivers a spectacular display of shimmering gold.

Between Cle Elum and Ellensburg, he was on constant alert for "Staters." On one return trip from visiting Rod, Bill was riding with Ed Lewis in his '61 Pontiac Bonneville. Ed was cruising at about 80 mph when he passed what appeared to be a disabled car stopped on the side of the highway. Its trunk was open revealing sleeping bags and a cooler. But as soon as Ed passed this "disabled" vehicle, it took off in hot pursuit of the Bonneville, its red "cherry top" flashing away. It cost Ed over $75.00 for that ticket. It just didn't seem right to Bill that the State Patrol could utilize such deception to ticket drivers.

The other part of this drive that he enjoyed was the area called Taneum Creek. It looked like it would be perfect horseback riding and hunting country. And the view of the Cascades from the rearview mirror as his Bug neared the top of that summit was breathtaking.

Better top off at Ellensburg and get something to eat; it's going to be a long grind the rest of the way. Ellensburg was one town Bill had no desire to ever live in. The wind was always blowing here as evidenced by the trees that leaned to the east from the constant wind passing through from the Cascades. He hated the wind even back when he was a young kid in Spokane struggling to ride his bike against it.

After topping off, Bill was tempted to go inside one of the air conditioned restaurants to enjoy a bite to eat and cool off, but since he wanted to get back as soon as possible, he ordered two hamburgers, an order of fries and a large root beer with ice to go from the A&W. He missed having Barb to talk with.

The cold liquid and hamburgers and fries took some of the edge off his fatigue as he headed toward Vantage. Flat pasture land soon turned to barren sage brush and rocks. *There must be a ton of rattlesnakes in this area,* he thought coasting down the grade into Vantage to rest his engine.

His mind raced back to the first rattlesnake he saw when they lived in Omak. It was the summer after he'd completed third grade. A friend, Rick Johnson, who lived two blocks away rode his bike to Bill's to tell him they'd found a rattlesnake in their yard. "Come see the rattlesnake! My mom just about stepped on it when she was mowing the lawn."

Bill hopped on his bike and rode up the hill to Rick's house, where he saw Mrs. Johnson and several neighbors standing in a wide circle looking toward her front steps. Bill laid his bike down and joined the circle. The snake was neatly curled up next to the bottom cement step facing the onlookers. Its beady eyes were fixed on them. Its black tongue flicked out every few seconds and its tail rattled whenever someone moved.

A neighbor approached the group holding a shovel. "Okay,

everybody stand back!" When the onlookers moved back, he approached the snake, the shovel extended toward the snake. With lightening speed, the snake struck the shovel; then returned to its coiled position. Everyone jumped when the snake struck and gasped in amazement at its quickness. Then the man raised the shovel and brought it down on the snake severing it in two. The snake's body writhed. The man brought the shovel down again and cut off the snake's head.

"This is where the poison is," he said carrying the head away in the shovel. "I'll be back in a bit to bury the rest, Mrs. Johnson."

Bill remembered staring at the lifeless snake. Its skin had neat patterns on it. Blood and some innards still oozed from where the shovel had cut it in half. It had finally stopped moving.

Bill rode home and described what had happened to his mom as she ironed his dad's dress shirts.

"Yeah, that's why we've always told you boys to be on the look out for snakes when you're out playing. This is rattlesnake country," she added taking a drag from her cigarette and putting it back into the ashtray on the kitchen counter.

A gust of wind jolted Bill's Bug as he drove across the Vantage Bridge and made him concentrate on his driving. As his Bug labored up the gorge on the east side of the Columbia, the intensity of the late afternoon heat off the surrounding rocks increased. He reached over and rolled the passenger side window all the way down to create more of a cross breeze. He wished now he'd brought some water to drink. *I hate this next part of the trip; it's so fucking long and desolate.*

The intense heat today reminded Bill of the day he came in to get a drink of water that same summer before he started fourth grade in Omak. It was a hot August afternoon and his mom was ironing clothes in the kitchen and crying.

"What's wrong, Mom!?"

"Your dad just called and told me that the bank has transferred him to Spokane. I'll...I'll have to say good-bye to all my friends here," she sobbed. Bill went over and touched her arm trying to comfort her, but she just kept ironing. "After five years here, I've made so many good friends...now we'll have to find a new home in Spokane, and I'll have to meet new friends. And you boys will have to go to a new school and meet new friends."

When his mom said this, he began to realize the impact moving would have on his life, too. He liked his school, Christ the King, and he liked the nuns who taught him. He knew they thought highly of him too. They let him leave school early at the end of each day so he could ride his bike to the post office downtown and pick up their mail for them.

"Don't you ever lose that beautiful smile," his third grade teacher had once told him.

Bill looked up at his mom. "I don't want to move either, Mom. I like it here and I like my school. Do we have to go?" His mom, tears running down her cheeks, nodded and kept ironing. Bill had no idea that this was just the beginning of difficult, sad times that would envelop her life for years to come, and change forever the family environment he was used to.

Several miles after he'd climbed out of the Gorge and was heading east on the basin, the exit sign to George, Washington came into view. Bill tried to clear his mind and decide if he should stop and order something to drink at Martha's Inn. *Nah, I think I can make it to Moses Lake,* he determined. He passed the exit and the tiny community of George.

Over the next few miles, Bill struggled to keep his eyes open. He stuck his head out the driver's side window for a few seconds hoping the fresh air would make him more alert; he tilted the driver's seat to different positions in an effort to keep focused on his driving. The heat, his dehydration and the nervous effects of the Benzedrine really began to affect him. *I probably should've stopped at George. Sure wish I'd brought some water.*

He was relieved to see the Moses Lake sign in the distance. *I'll definitely be stopping at the ice cream shop today. A large milk shake cup of ice water and a soft vanilla ice cream cone should get me to Ritzville.* He liked stopping at this ice cream stand because it was right off I-90; you could order and be back on the interstate in minutes.

Bill nodded and smiled at the young high school girl who had taken his order. "Thanks," he said as he headed toward his car with his water in his right hand and his soft vanilla ice cream cone in his left. He placed the cup on the roof of his Bug, opened his door, then grabbing his cup sat down putting the cup on the passenger seat. The vanilla ice cream was already beginning to run down the sides of his cone in his left hand, so he quickly tilted the cone to intercept the tasty drips before they ran all the way down onto his hand. *Oh, man this tastes good!* He restarted his Bug and headed for the I-90 on ramp still doing his best to keep up with the quickly melting ice cream. A blast of hot humid air greeted him as he crossed the bridge spanning the lake. By the time Moses Lake was fading from his rearview mirror, Bill had finished his ice cream cone. He took another drink of his water and noticed the irrigation sprinklers watering crops on both sides of I-90.

The sprinklers reminded him of the summer after his sophomore year at Gonzaga Prep that he spent in Connell,

Washington changing irrigation tubes and bucking hay bales for Clyde Parker.

Bill could still vividly remember riding on the old, noisy swather cutting alfalfa with Clyde, and seeing pheasants attempting to escape the swather's oscillating scythe. Some began their ascent in time and shot out just ahead of the swather. Some unlucky ones, however made their move a split second too late and made a desperate, squawking ascent missing both of their feet. Bill watched them crash land out in the field where they'd try unsuccessfully to escape prowling coyotes during the night.

"I feel bad," shouted Clyde to Bill over the racket of the swather. "But, I can't see them in the alfalfa 'til it's too late!"

Bill recalled plunging into one of the nearby irrigation canals with Tom, Clyde's son after a day of bucking bales in 100 degree heat. It felt so refreshing and minimized the amount of chaff that ended up in the shower at the farmhouse.

He remembered how long it took him to create enough suction in the irrigation tube to begin the flow of water from the ditch to the furrow in the field when he first arrived at the farm. He could still hear Clyde. "Hold the outflow end of the tube between your third and fourth fingers like this," demonstrated Clyde. "Keep your palm away from the end as you push the inflow end of the pipe into the irrigation ditch like this. Now, keeping the inflow end of the pipe in the ditch, pull the tube back toward you while covering the end with your palm. This will create the suction needed to begin the flow of water from the ditch through the tube. Listen…you can hear the water being drawn into the tube. Once you can hear the water filling the tube, lay the outflow end of the pipe into the furrow to irrigate that row of crops—like this." Clyde made it look so easy. He was like a machine that efficiently and steadily worked his way down the irrigation ditch. With only one or two strokes, he created a successful flow of water and placed the tube in its furrow. After several weeks of setting tubes, however, Bill enjoyed competing against Clyde and Tom to see if he could keep up with or even set more tubes than they could.

A lone tumbleweed bouncing across the highway about 30 yards in front of Bill's car brought Bill back to the present. He had to slow down and veer to his left in order to miss it.

Then his mind drifted back again. *I wonder if Clyde and Sara are still farming in Connell? Tom probably went on to college, and Tamara's no doubt married. She was so beautiful.*

Bill forced his tired mind to recall why Clyde had asked Bill to work for him that summer. *Yeah, okay, now I remember.* The Parkers had dry land farmed on Clyde's family farm near Freeman, Washington southeast of the Spokane Valley. When a family dispute came to a head in 1959, Clyde's relatives bought out his share of the farm, and Clyde decided to try his hand at selling cars for a large Ford dealership in the Spokane Valley. But in a short period of time, he missed farm life; so he petitioned the government and was granted a lease on irrigated farm land near Connell, Washington. Clyde's son, Tom, who was a year older than Bill had gotten to know Bill living just a block away on East 20th Avenue.

Seeing that Tom and Bill got along well, Clyde asked Howard in the spring of 1961 if Bill would be interested in working on their farm to earn some money during the coming summer. Clyde knew that moving from the Valley to an isolated farm outside the small town of Connell might be a difficult transition for his son, who would miss his senior year at Central Valley. He hoped Bill would provide much needed companionship for Tom. Of course as a banker, Howard was always glad when his boys earned money, and working far away in Connell would get Bill away from a couple of classmates at Prep that Howard and Rachel believed had become bad influences on Bill during his sophomore year. So, Howard encouraged Bill to take Clyde's offer.

"You've been looking for a summer job, and working on a farm would be a good learning experience for you," Howard pointed out to Bill.

"Sure," agreed Bill.

Clyde left for Connell in March to begin the difficult process of acquiring affordable machinery he would need to operate the farm, and to learn how to irrigate using aluminum tubes. On weekends, he would travel between Connell and Spokane with a flat bed truck so he could move their current belongings to the small farmhouse that would become their home outside of Connell. In late May, Sara sold their home on E. 20th Avenue.

By mid-June, Clyde secured the last load of their belongings onto the flatbed truck. Bill loaded his suitcase into their Ford station wagon and traveled with Sara, Tom and Tamara to Connell following Clyde.

The Parkers were one of those families that you can easily tell are related. Like Clyde and his wife Sara, Tom and his younger sister, Tamara were tall and slender. Both had black hair, dark brown almost black eyes, olive-toned skin, long slender fingers and attractive facial features. Tamara, who was a year behind Bill in high school was quiet and shy. She didn't yet know how attractive she was going to be to guys in high school. Clyde, who was about 6' 4" and possessed the strength that comes from years of hard manual labor, was the most outgoing of the four. He liked to kid and tease; he smiled a lot, had a great laugh and was a tireless worker. Sara was quiet and kind, but had an air of strength and confidence that comes from years of hard work on an isolated farm, and dedication to her husband and family. Tom, who was pretty quiet as well, enjoyed reading books but was glad he'd have Bill as a companion for most of the summer.

Bill slept in the Parker's travel trailer with Tom but ate his meals and used the only bathroom in the small single story house next door. It always amazed Bill that the Columbia Basin, which got so hot during the day could be so chilly at 5:15 AM when he and Tom stepped out of the trailer wearing their sweatshirts to join Clyde in the panel truck. Sitting close to one another in the front seat provided some relief from the morning chill until they arrived in one of the fields and began moving irrigation tubes.

By 8:00 when the three of them came in for breakfast, the sun was already making its daily torrid statement, and by noon, when they ate dinner, it was typically over 100 degrees outside. On super hot days when the outdoor thermometer was stuck at 120 degrees, they remained in the air-conditioned house after dinner until it began to cool off in the late afternoon. Clyde would usually take a nap in his bedroom; Tom and Bill would play games, read or nap. When the temperature began to drop in the late afternoon, the men would finish up projects like bucking bales of hay in one of the alfalfa fields, and setting the irrigation tubes in appropriate furrows before coming in for supper. But even on these extremely hot days, Tamara was expected to help Sara prepare meals, wash dishes, clean, do laundry and shop in town.

I wonder what Tamara ended up doing? Bill thought. He recalled the time he got up in the middle of the night to use the bathroom in the house wearing only his underpants, and was met by Tamara, who was exiting the bathroom. Caught off guard, they both froze and for a few seconds stared at each other without saying a word. Tamara's white bra and panties stood out against her dark tan. Her eyes quickly scanned Bill's near naked body.

Bill broke the awkward silence first. "Hi, Tamara," he whispered smiling at her.

"Hi," she whispered back. Bill quickly entered the bathroom and shut the door. His heart was beating quickly partly because he had been so surprised by Tamara coming out of the bathroom as he was reaching for the handle, and partly because of her beauty. When he returned to his bed in the trailer, it took him awhile to get back to sleep. Images of her shapely, tan body and her short, black curly hair ran through his mind. He wondered if she was lying in her bed thinking of him. The next morning at breakfast when their eyes met, Tamara flashed a smile at Bill then quickly lowered her eyes. The next time she looked up, Bill caught her eye and returned a shy smile.

By mid-August when it was time for Bill to head back to the Spokane Valley to get ready for football season, Bill had become part of the Parker's family.

"Thanks for all your help this summer," stated Clyde handing Bill a check; then giving him a big hug.

"Thank you!" replied Bill. "I really enjoyed staying with you guys, and I learned a lot."

"We'll miss you," added Sara hugging Bill.

Tamara waited her turn to give Bill a hug as well. When she pulled away, Bill noticed her watering eyes.

Bill looked into her eyes and smiled. "Bye, Tamara." Feeling himself getting emotional, Bill looked at Clyde and Sara. "Better watch her this fall; all the boys at school will be in hot pursuit." Clyde and Sara laughed; Tamara blushed and looked down. "Thanks again for everything," added Bill putting the check in his billfold; then grabbing his suitcase.

"Drive carefully," Sara reminded Tom as he and Bill headed for the station wagon. "It's important you return Bill safely to his parents."

"I will," replied Tom.

That was the last time Bill ever saw Clyde, Sara and Tamara. The following summer after Tom had graduated from Connell High School, he stopped by to show Bill the 1957 Plymouth Fury two door hardtop he'd purchased from a guy in nearby Othello. It was in mint condition, and Bill had no doubt Tom would always keep it that way. *I wonder what my life would be like now if I'd stayed in Connell working with the Parkers? Maybe I would've eventually gotten my own farm...even married Tamara....*

—⁓—

About 22 miles west of Ritzville, the exit sign to the Shrag Rest Area came into view. Bill knew he had to stop, drink some water and rest his eyes a bit or risk veering off the highway. He pulled his Bug into a vacant parking stall and headed to the drinking fountain for a long drink. The water tasted kind of metallic but he was too thirsty to be picky. *Must be well water.* He then found a picnic table that was shaded by a nearby tree, sat down and lay his head on his folded arms hoping he could nap for thirty minutes or so. But the best he could manage was once again, a semi-conscious doze. His heart was still pounding from the Benzedrine, and periodically beads of sweat rolled off his forehead and onto his arm. When it was obvious he wasn't going to be able to sleep, he took several more turns at the drinking fountain, filled his water cup, restarted his Bug and merged onto I-90 for the final leg to Spokane.

The effort to stay awake was constant now, and he was

sure of one thing—he'd never, ever again take Benzedrine. He tried to revisit scenes from Rod's party and sights they had shown Barb over the weekend in an effort to keep awake, but it was difficult for him to concentrate on any one thought for very long now. Scenes came and went: Pike Place Market, the Ballard Locks, Green Lake, Ray's Boathouse, racing Barb up the path in the ravine, telling the partiers to leave…. One thought that kept recurring, however was knowing deep down that he needed to keep his commitment to enter the Jesuits in August. *I'm 22 years old for God's sake, and I still don't know what the hell I want to do with my life. I have to figure that out! If I keep running from making this decision, life will happen to me, and the consequences might not be good.* He recalled what Fr. Eric had recommended to him when talking about decision making, *"…try to imagine what your best self would do."*

The warnings of so many of the lifers at Kaiser to not get stuck out there also ran through his mind. He thought about how easy it was to lose sight of loftier ambitions when you worked in the pot rooms. While he enjoyed the workers' down-to-earth antics, by the end of summer, he was always so relieved he wasn't trapped there like some of the young guys his age, who had given up college to stay there, and now regretted it.

He also knew deep down that staying at Kaiser or with Barb would not be healthy for him in the long run. He recalled how uncomfortable she was around his friends at Joe's party. His social life would really be limited if he were married to Barb.

As he neared the small community of Sprague, he could begin to see trees off in the distance, and knew he wasn't far from Cheney…and then Spokane. *I can do this!* he kept repeating to himself.

Heading down the I-90 grade into Spokane, he felt very relieved, but his vision seemed to be impaired as if he were seeing things in a slow motion dream. Surrounding buildings and cars blurred together. He prayed that a Stater wouldn't pull up beside him and notice his fixed gaze and bobbing head. *There's the East Sprague exit—just a few more miles now.*

Thank you, Lord for getting me home safely, he sighed as he parked in front of his parents' house at 8:45 PM and turned off the ignition. He felt dehydrated and weak as he got out of the car. *I am so fucking tired! There's no way I can go to work tonight. I just want to crash in my own bed.*

"Hi, you made it!" welcomed his mom giving him a hug after he entered the front door. "We were just wondering if you'd make it home in time to go to work tonight. Are you still planning on going in?"

"No. I'm too tired to go in tonight. I know I'd fall asleep on the job. I'm going to call in sick. It'll be okay; this will be the first time in five summers I've called in sick. It would just be too dangerous for me to work tonight."

"Okay," his dad responded with a hint of disappointment.

"Did you have a good time?" asked his mom as Rod headed for the basement door.

"Yes, and Rod and I had a good visit. I'll tell you more about it tomorrow? I'm so wiped out and need to get some sleep. I'm sorry I'm so tired, but it's been a looong, hot drive from Seattle, and Rod and I stayed up pretty late over the weekend."

"That's okay; we understand," his mom responded throwing a quick glance toward Howard. "Do you want something to eat before you go to bed?"

"No; I'm just going to crash. I'll call the guardhouse, then give Rod a quick call to let him know I got home safely. G'night."

Bill had to look up the phone number to the guardhouse as he'd never called in. "Hi, this is Bill Roberts, Badge 3961. I won't be coming in tonight because I'm sick." He didn't have to put on an act; his extreme fatigue was convincing over the phone.

"Okay, I'll let the Line Foreman know. Thanks for calling in."

He then called Rod. "Hi, just wanted to let you know I got home okay; thanks again for the great time."

"You're welcome. Your Bug obviously held up okay."

"Well, for the most part. It was really slow on the steep climbs, but it got me home."

"How much did they charge you for the valve adjustment?"

"Eighty-six bucks; it was actually a little less than I thought it was going to be."

"That's not bad at all. Hey, thanks for washing the sheets and making the bed in the basement."

"No problem. Well, I'm going to hit the sack; I'm really beat. Bye."

After Bill hung up, he gave Barb a quick call. He knew his parents would think he was still talking to Rod, but he took the phone into the back room just to be safe. "Hi, just want to let you know I got home okay, but I'm heading to bed. I'm really beat."

"Don't you have to work tonight?"

"Yeah, but I called in sick. I can hardly keep my eyes open. How was your flight?"

"It was sooo much fun; I want to fly again!"

"I'm glad you enjoyed it. Did you make it to work on time?"

"Yeah, no problem at all. Teri was there to pick me up when we landed, so I had time to spare before work."

"Great; I'll give you a call tomorrow afternoon and you can tell me all about your flight. I've gotta crash. Bye."

He fetched his toothbrush from his travel kit, brushed his

teeth, removed his clothes then slid between his cool sheets. His body still pulsed a bit from the Benzedrine and he wondered if he'd be able to sleep. Worries about missing work attempted to occupy his mind, but after a few minutes, his extreme fatigue won out and he fell into a deep sleep.

—⁓—

Roberts? Roberts? Bill struggled to open his eyes.

Bill, it's Fr. Eric…. Again, Bill struggled to open his eyes.

"Bill! Are you going to sleep all day?" his mom asked rapping on his bedroom door. Thought I'd better check on you; you've been asleep for about 13 hours," she announced slightly opening the door and poking her head in.

"Oh, my God, what time is it?" he asked sitting up in bed and trying to focus.

"About 11:00 AM."

"Man, I must have been exhausted. Thanks for waking me, Mom; I'll come up in a bit." He lay back on his pillow and looked at the ceiling. His body wanted more sleep and it would have gotten it had Bill not forced himself out of bed to use the bathroom. *Man, I must have really been dehydrated to sleep that long without peeing,* he thought flushing the toilet. He washed his hands in the sink and splashed water on his face to help him wake up. *There is no way I could have worked last night,* he thought as he looked in the mirror. A weary face with cowlicked hair stared back at him. *Oh, my God, I look like shit.* He dried his face with a towel, then opened the blinds in his room to a sunny day. He pulled on his cutoff jeans, a white t-shirt and headed upstairs.

"Well you were obviously behind on sleep," his mom commented as Bill headed for the coffee pot.

"Yeah. The late nights at Rod's and the long, hot drive over and back really took it out of me, I guess."

"But you had a good time?"

"Yes. It was fun to see Rod and celebrate our graduations together." Bill spent the next hour describing his time in Seattle being careful not to slip up and mention anything about Barb. After two cups of coffee and some scrambled eggs and toast, he felt like he was beginning to recover, but still felt like he was functioning in first gear. He spent most of the afternoon unpacking, doing laundry and washing his car. By 4:00, he finally felt like the Benzedrine had worked its way through his system.

—m—

About 5:30, Bill called Barb. "Hi, how was work today?"

"Not too bad, but I'm still thinking about all the fun we had in Seattle. How about you?"

"Well, now that I've slept for 13 hours, I'm feeling much better. I'm so glad I called in sick last night; there's no way I could have made it through the shift."

"Wow! Thirteen hours! You must've been exhausted. Are you going to stop by before work this evening?"

"I think tomorrow would be better, Barb. Believe it or not, I'm actually still really out of it, and I think my folks would be pretty upset if I went out before work tonight."

"I understand. I think I'm still recovering from the trip as well. Oh, and you'll be happy to know that my period is over. Why don't you come over early so we can spend some time together before you head to work tomorrow?"

"Yes, coming over early would be good!" Bill grinned. "I'll call you before I head over. Bye."

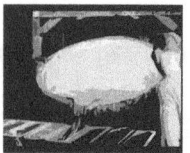

"Roberts?"

"Here!"

"Spare, Line 7."

Whew! sighed Bill as he plodded up the alleyway from Line 4. *Ed Buttenshoen is a pretty low key guy; hopefully he'll assign me somethin' easy like sweeping floors and hauling away butts.*

However, when Bill reported to the Line 7 foreman's office, he was greeted by a sub-foreman he didn't know.

"Hi, my name's Wilson; I'm takin' Ed's place for the next two weeks while he's on vacation. He sure picked a good week to go on vacation; it's been hotter'n hell this week."

Wilson grabbed a black rubber respirator and some ear plugs that were lying on his desk. "Follow me...Roberts, is it?"

"Yes," replied Bill curious and a bit nervous now. The sub-foreman led Bill to a crucible located at the end of Room 13 and off to the side. A jack hammer attached to an air hose leaned against the inside of the crucible.

"Finish jack hammering out this 'cruce'; separate the metal and bath and shovel them into two separate piles," instructed Wilson. "Here are some ear plugs and a respirator. I'll come by during the shift to see how you're doing."

Oh, fuck! Bill thought to himself heading to the nearest waterhole to drop off his sack lunch. Over the past four summers he'd worked at Kaiser, he'd heard from other spares about what a nightmare job this is. He felt fortunate he'd never been assigned this job and had hoped his luck would hold through this summer.

Ed Lewis had explained to him one time why a cruce occasionally has to be sidelined and jackhammered. "The aluminum metal is heavier than the bath so it lies in the bottom of the pot cell below the bath. Experienced siphoners or "tappers" know how far down into the pot to place the siphon and how to control the air flow from the compressed air hose to establish and maintain a good tap of the metal. What little bath typically gets sucked into the cruce can be easily skimmed off the top by the tappers. However, if a rookie or reckless tapper siphons too much bath into the cruce, the cruce is set aside to cool. Then it has to be jackhammered out to separate the bath and metal that have cooled together so the cruce can be reused. If the brick lining of the cruce is damaged in the jackhammering process, the lining has to be repaired before the cruce can be used again. So an inexperienced or careless tapper can cost the company a lot of time and money."

Shortly after Bill climbed into the large circular crucible, he could feel heat from the still hardening bath and metal emanating through his double-soled boots. This added to the already hot pot room temperature. He inserted the small ear plugs, positioned the black rubber respirator over his face and adjusted the straps. It smelled terrible, and Bill wondered who had used it last. *Hopefully not Stretch,* he thought.

He braced himself for the loud rat-tat-tat when he engaged the levers with his hands, and because he was standing inside the crucible, the explosive noise was amplified. The little ear plugs didn't filter out nearly enough of the deafening noise. *Fuck, I'm going to be deaf by the end of this shift!*

As the jackhammer bit attacked the bath and metal, Bill discovered how difficult it was to separate the two substances. The soft, malleable aluminum that was entwined with the bath would simply give with the jackhammer bit rather than break away from the bath. *At this rate, I won't make much progress.*

The walls of the cruce didn't allow the dust caused by the air hammer to readily dissipate, and he could tell the respirator wasn't filtering out all the unhealthy dust. *My lungs will be lined with dust by the end of this shift.* The crucible's walls also prevented the breeze from the open courtyard from cooling him off. These horrible working conditions made frequent breaks a necessity, and during each break as Bill panned the pot room and the casting room across the way, he thought how trapped he would feel doing the same jobs over and over for the rest of his working years. He thought about the warnings many of his colleagues had given him over the last five summers. *"Don't get stuck out here like I did!"* But he also thought about how much he enjoyed being with Barb and recalled Easy Ed telling him how good Kaiser had been to him and his family.

After over two hours of this unproductive, frustrating work, Bill really wished he were carbon setting so he could at least catch some air between his settings. *The time would pass so much more quickly as well.* Twice before lunch break, the sub-foreman walked by to check on Bill's progress, and even though Bill's piles of bath and metal were still quite small, he never said a word to Bill. *He's no doubt done this shitty job at some point in his career and knows what a bitch it is.*

When it was time for his lunch break, Bill leaned the hammer against the cruce's side and climbed out. He removed the respirator from his sweaty face; then took out the ear plugs. The typical din of the pot rooms seemed muted. After climbing out of the cruce, his legs felt wobbly and his feet were hot and sweaty. He glanced at the small piles of bath and metal he had assembled over the last 3-1/2 hours and felt discouraged. He'd always been able to impress foremen with the quantity of his work, but today, the cruce was definitely winning. He spanked the dust from this shirt sleeves and pants, stomped his feet a couple of times and headed for the waterhole to get his lunch. As he passed the foreman's office, he told the sub-foreman he was taking his lunch break and asked him if he could eat his lunch with a friend on Line 2.

"Sure, just be back by 8:00 PM."

"No problem; thanks," replied Bill.

The questions that had been peppering Bill's mind daily, the worries about what to do, the fact that in just a few weeks he would have to give his two weeks' notice were making Bill feel crazy and weighted down. He wanted to talk with Jack Crenshaw and get his advice. He knew Jack would be frank and honest with him, and Fr. Eric was still in California.

He felt nervous as he neared Line 2 and hoped Jack wouldn't be napping when he arrived. Much to Bill's relief, Jack was playing a game of cribbage with two pot men in the waterhole. Jack looked up from his cards as Bill appeared in the doorway.

"Jesus H. Christ, what are you doin' today to look so grimy?" asked Jack.

"Jackhammerin' out a cruce," replied Bill, who beckoned Jack with a nod of his head. Jack could tell Bill needed to talk with him so he put his cards down and headed out of the waterhole.

"What's goin' on?"

"Well…I need to get your advice about some things, Jack."

"Sure," responded Jack, who led Bill to the edge of a nearby breezeway. "Sit down; you look like you need to rest a bit."

"Thanks, Jack. I'm really struggling with some decisions

I have to make within the next few weeks." Bill took a deep breath. "You know about the commitment I've made to enter the Jesuits at the end of August, but you don't know about the girl I've been seeing this summer." He proceeded to tell Jack about how he'd met Barb and how their relationship had developed over the summer and how he now felt so conflicted about the imminent decisions he needed to make. He told Jack about the pressure he felt to not disappoint his family—especially his mom, who had always wanted him to be a priest.

Jack listened carefully to all Bill shared with him then looking into his eyes asked, "What do *you* want to do, Bill?"

Bill did his best to control his emotion before responding. "That's my dilemma, Jack," he answered in a shaky voice looking downward. "I don't really know what I want to do. Part of me wants to stick with my commitment and see if God is truly calling me to be a Jesuit priest, but another part of me wants to stay with Barb and keep this job; it's the only job I have right now."

As soon as Bill mentioned keeping this job, Jack reacted. He leaned down so he could look into Bill's eyes. "Bill, look at me," he instructed. He waited for Bill to meet his gaze. "You would be miserable if you stayed out here. Now that you've expanded your mind in college, you'd be so bored and unchallenged working here. I know—I've seen too many bright, young guys make the mistake of staying here rather than finishing college, and they're all miserable." Jack's lips broke a slight smile. "I must say, I'm glad to hear you've been gettin' a little this summer." Then his look got serious again. "I don't know much about religion...but my advice to you would be this. Enter the Novitiate in August not only to see if God's calling you to be a Jesuit priest, but also to find out if that's truly what *you* want to do. I really believe that God wants us to be happy. If we're happy; He's happy for us. Just like a parent for his children. Now if you discover you don't want to be a priest, you can return and see if Barb's the right girl for you. If she's not the girl you want to spend the rest of your life with, there are plenty of other women out there who would love to spend their life with a guy like you."

Jack then sat up straight and took a deep breath. "You know...you're too young to fully realize this now, Bill, but... you're in the prime of your life. You're at that special, precious time in a man's life that races by so quickly. That time that every older man wishes he could experience again if even for a day. Just enjoy the next few weeks together before you leave; everything else will work itself out."

There was a brief moment of silence as Bill soaked in Jack's counsel; then Bill nodded. "Your advice to enter the Novitiate in August matches what I think is best for me deep down," acknowledged Bill looking at Jack. "It's just going to be very difficult to say good-bye to Barb and leave our relationship behind."

Jack didn't say anything. He simply looked at Bill as if he understood it would be difficult.

Bill flashed Jack a slight smile. "Thank you, Jack. I really appreciate and respect your advice...and...I'd appreciate your keepin' what I've told you to yourself."

"You got it," assured Jack.

Bill stood up. "Well, I'd better head back to Line 7 and to my lonely jackhammer."

Jack stood up so he could be face-to-face with Bill. "And here's my advice regarding that miserable fucking job. It'll take several days of poor spares like yourself hammerin' their brains out before enough bath is out of that cruce for it to be reused. Chances are they'll have to repair the damaged lining anyways.

Someday the brains in the head shed will invent a machine to get all that shit outta there; it's no job for any man. Just go back and take your time, and don't worry about how much bath you get outta there. And if you're assigned that job again tomorrow, I want you to come straight to me, savvy?"

"Will do, Jack," Bill smiled. "Thank you!"

Bill's mind felt more at peace and his step felt lighter as he walked back to Line 7 eating his lunch on the way. When he reached the crucible, he donned the respirator and ear plugs once again, climbed into the cruce and pulled the handle of the jackhammer. For some reason, the job didn't seem so impossible now, and the time seemed to pass more quickly. When the sub-foreman came around near the end of the shift and checked out how much the piles of bath and metal had grown, he gave Bill a thumbs up and signaled him to shut off the jackhammer. Bill removed the respirator and ear plugs.

"You definitely put a dent in this job, Roberts; nice goin'."

"Thanks," replied Bill cracking a smile.

"How'd you like to do this job every shift for a livin'?"

"Not me!" responded Bill unable to tell how loudly he was speaking because of the ringing in his ears.

"Give me the respirator and earplugs; you can call it a night."

"Thanks," replied Bill. "No offense, but I sure hope I'm setting carbon tomorrow." He noticed the smile on the foreman's lips as he turned to head up the pot line toward the waterhole. He was very relieved this shift was nearly over. His ears were still ringing from the jackhammer, and his lungs felt like they were lined with ore dust, but his mind felt more at peace. The nagging questions and dilemmas that had pressed down on him earlier in the shift seemed to have subsided.

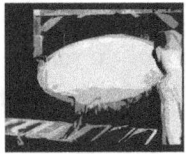

Bill awoke to shouting and foot stomping from upstairs. "Why won't you toss the football with me!?" he heard Don yell. "You never do anything with me!"

Mom must not be home, Bill thought to himself getting out of bed. Rachel typically did a good job of keeping the lid on when Bill was sleeping after a Graveyard Shift. He put on a pair of gym shorts and headed upstairs. "Hey! What's all the fuss about?"

"Phil won't toss the football with me," explained Don. "I want to turn out for football this fall at St. John Vianney and need to start getting ready."

"I'll toss the football with you," offered Bill. "Just let me have a cup of coffee and some breakfast; then we can walk down to Bowdish Junior High and throw the football."

"Thanks!" replied Don, who flashed Phil a dirty look.

—⁓—

"So, what position do you want to play?" asked Bill spinning a football in his hands as he and Don walked east on 21st Avenue toward Bowdish.

"Some line position. They have weight limitations for backs and ends; so I'll have to play a line position."

"You're pretty good-sized for your age; you should do well as a lineman," encouraged Bill. "Don't know what happened to me—I'm kind of the runt of the family."

"But you're so fast," responded Don quickly. "Wish I had your speed."

Once on the football field, Bill showed Don some basic stretches. "Always stretch a bit before practice so you don't pull a muscle," emphasized Bill bending at the waist and touching his toes.

Then, Bill showed Don some basic offensive and defensive stances so Don could get off the ball quickly; he showed him how to move his feet so he could move laterally. Bill "hiked" the football and moved in different directions to give Don practice moving his feet. "When blocking on offense be sure to keep your arms tucked into your chest like this or you'll get called for holding," instructed Bill. "Don't just block the guy across from you, turn him away from where your back will be running, and keep your feet moving until the whistle blows. If you're blocking for a pass, keep blocking your opponent away from your quarterback until the ball is thrown.

"Now on defense, you can use your hands to get rid of your blocker so you can make the tackle. If the player across from you tries to turn you away from the play, roll the opposite way so you can get around him and still help stop the play or sack the quarterback. You'll love defense.

"Now it's time for some running," declared Bill after about 30 minutes of practicing with Don. "Since your season starts in just a few weeks, you should come down here everyday that you can and run so you're in shape when your season begins. First, some ladder sprints." Bill stood at the distance he wanted Don to sprint, and told him which stance to line up with. "Sprint all the way through to me," barked Bill. When Don was pretty winded, Bill took Don over to the hill on the north side of the school and told him to sprint up the hill; then walk back down to him.

"I don't...think...I can...do another...one," panted Don bent over with his hands on his thighs after the second hill climb.

"Give me one more," urged Bill.

"Thanks for all you showed me today," smiled Don, still breathing hard as they walked back to the house.

"You're welcome. Make yourself come down here almost every day to practice these moves and run, and you should be ready for your first practice. You'll have to write me and tell me how you're doin' in football, okay?"

"Okay, I will," assured Don, wiping the sweat from his forehead with his right forearm.

Bill felt good inside. He seldom did anything with his younger brothers just because of the wide age differences. He was glad Don was turning out for football, because he knew the important role sports had played in his life through elementary and high school. Had it not been for hanging out with teammates, Bill knew he would have never gone hunting, fishing or skiing. "You'll enjoy football, Don. It helps you get to know your classmates and their families better."

As a Jesuit, I can coach sports when I'm teaching in one of their high schools, thought Bill. He remembered well the young Jesuit "Misters" who coached him when he was a freshman and sophomore at Gonzaga Prep. It excited Bill to think about coaching football and track.

—॥॥—

For some reason, Bill felt a little nervous as he made his lunch and prepared to head to Barb's before his Graveyard Shift. His drive back to Spokane from Seattle and his talk with Jack Crenshaw had pretty much convinced him that entering the Novitiate on August 29 was the best choice for him at this time in his life. *Should I just come out and tell Barb this evening that I'm leaving for sure on the 29th? If I tell her will this be the last time I'll see her? I do want to spend time with her before I leave.* Then he recalled Jack's advice, *"Just enjoy the next few weeks together before you leave; everything else will work itself out. If she's the right woman for you, you'll return and marry her."*

Bill was definitely looking forward to being with Barb. He hadn't seen her since Seattle, and their last night together had not been very romantic. *After so many wonderful times with Barb, I wouldn't want that to be our last memory together. And, I do want to be with her when my parents are at Newman Lake.* So he decided he wouldn't tell Barb about his renewed decision—at least tonight.

—\\\\\—

"Hi! Long time no see," Barb exclaimed greeting Bill with a long kiss and hug. "Have you finally caught up on your sleep?"

"I'm getting there. Man, I barely made it home Monday evening; I could hardly keep my eyes open the last part of the drive. So, you liked flying, huh?"

"Oh my God, it was incredible! I loved that feeling of acceleration before lift off…and the view from above was amazing! I got a great view of Mt. Rainier when we turned east to head for Spokane. I can't wait to fly again! And I can't stop thinking about all the neat things I saw in Seattle. I really want to move there someday."

"No reason you can't! It's easier to find jobs there than it is here in Spokane." He was hoping their trip to Seattle would inspire her to be a bit more ambitious, and to rise above the survival standard she'd set for herself of working at J.C. Penney in the Spokane Valley for the rest of her life.

"It's so good to have you back!" she smiled as if wanting to change the topic. She moved closer to him. "Thank you so much for arranging my flight back—and for cleaning up that terrible mess. I felt so bad leaving all that for you to clean up."

"Don't worry about it. You tried to tell me and I wouldn't listen. Hey, that room looks cleaner now than when we got there."

She put her hands on his chest. "Well…as I mentioned yesterday on the phone, my period's over, and I've been looking forward to being with you again." She put her arms around his neck and kissed him. "Let's see if you're glad to see me," she said reaching down with her right hand to feel the bulge in his pants. "Oh yeah; you're glad to see me all right." She took his left hand and led him to her bedroom. She turned to him and began kissing him unbuckling his belt and unzipping his cutoffs sending them to the floor. She then pulled his shirt over his head and tossed it onto the floor.

Thoroughly aroused now, he returned the favors sending her clothes to the floor. She pulled him onto her as she lay back on her bed, and wasted no time guiding him to her.

"Oh, God; I've missed you sooo much," she gasped. "Just stay close and move with me." He could feel her tighten around him, and he let her set the pace. He could tell by how she held him with her hands and her tempo that she wanted him to stay at a certain spot with her.

"Yes…yes, right there…Don't stop!" she urged maintaining the close dance.

"Now, Now!" she commanded, as she felt him swell.

"Oh, my God!" Bill grunted releasing his passion. He could tell from Barb's ecstatic gasps that they were both climaxing at the same time. It was wonderful! He went deep now wanting to give her all he had.

"I needed you so much!" she panted between breaths.

"I needed you too, Barb—you make me feel sooo fucking good!" he replied between quick breaths.

When Barb relaxed around him, he retreated from her and lay on his side so he could look at her face. "If I didn't make you pregnant now, I don't think I ever will," Bill said. "I could tell I was at the place you wanted me to be the whole time, and I could tell how much you wanted me. You'll tell me if you get pregnant, won't you?"

"Yes," she replied touching his face with her left hand. "At times like this, I want you to make me pregnant. I just want to be with you forever."

"I know what you mean, Barb. When we're together like this, I just never want it to end."

"Well, it doesn't have to end you know," Barb reminded him looking into his eyes. "We can build our life together here… or…we could both move to Seattle and find jobs. I'm sure Rod would let us stay with him until we find work and a place to live," she added hopefully.

Bill rolled onto his back and sighed deeply. *Here's your opportunity! Tell her now!* Bill's inner voice urged. *No, don't ruin the next few weeks,* another voice warned.

"Barb…I thought about this big decision all the way home from Seattle, and I decided…Barb, I'm going to enter the Novitiate August 29. If I don't go and see if it's for me, I'll always wonder if I should have. I really don't think I'll be able to take being away from you, but I need to find out if God is calling me to be a Jesuit."

The hopeful look that had been on Barb's face vanished and she quietly stared at Bill almost indifferently.

"Barb, I totally understand if you want to stop seeing me, and want to start seeing other guys. I mean, you should."

Barb grabbed Bill's shoulder and pulled him back to her so he was facing her. "Bill, I've known since we met at Jerry and Sandy's that you had committed to entering the Novitiate at the end of August and I've been willing to live with that. I've told myself all along that you would probably not change your mind. Of course, I've secretly hoped you would, but I'm not blindsided or surprised by what you've just told me. And about not wanting to see you anymore...I...I just enjoy being with you, and being loved by you. I really don't have anyone else in my life right now. So, if it's okay with you, let's just enjoy what time we have left together. If we're meant to be together, you'll discover that when you're away from me and come back to me. I told you I'd wait for you for a while and I will. If you decide to stay in the Jesuits, then we'll both know that that's what you want to do."

A tear ran down Bill's left cheek. He smiled at her and kissed her. "Oh, Barb...thank you. I've been so nervous about telling you, and so afraid it would end our wonderful relationship. You don't know what a relief this is to me. I want to be with you too and I don't have anyone else but you in my life now, either. And, if you do get pregnant, I promise I will stay here and take care of you and our baby, okay?"

"Okay," she smiled weakly. She kissed him, then sat up and rolled out of bed. "I'm going to jump in the shower. Care to join me?"

—◊◊◊—

"Remember, my folks leave for Newman Lake on Saturday and they'll be gone until the following Sunday," Bill grinned before heading to Kaiser. "So, I think I'd better stick pretty close to home between now and Saturday so they won't suspect I might have someone over, and to assure them that the house and yard will be in good hands while they're gone."

"Okay," sighed Barb in a teasing manner. "I guess I can wait that long."

"I'll pick you up after they leave on Saturday; so bring what you need for staying over, okay?"

"Will do," Barb smiled. She grabbed his left hand and squeezed. "It will be so nice to wake up next to you. It always feels so empty to wake up and not have you there after making such wonderful love."

"I know; I can't wait. And I'll be on Day Shift that week! See you Saturday."

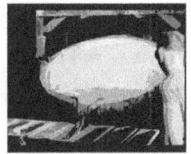

"Roberts!

"Here!"

"Pots, Line 7."

Thank God! thought Bill to himself closing his eyes in relief. *No jackhammerin' today!*

He was relieved to find no bells ringing on his fourth string of pots in Room 14 and to see that all voltage meters were where they should be.

"Well, are you still gonna leave for the Jesuits in August?" asked Don as he began to head up his crane ladder.

"Yes, I leave August 29."

"When's your last day out here?"

"The last day of our next Graveyard Shift."

"Drop by on your last day, will ya? I'd like to say good-bye and give ya something."

"Sure, Don, I'll make a point of it."

Bill utilized all the training tips Jim Bingham had taught him: feeding on the hour, cleaning off carbon anodes to check for red anode connections, maintaining correct voltages, setting new carbon anodes at the right height.

After feeding and checking his pots, Bill would return to the waterhole, chat a bit with the pot man on the 5th string and wait for the next feeding. *Being a pot man on a day like today wouldn't be a bad job at all,* thought Bill looking at one of the brick walls of the waterhole. But when he projected himself sitting there five or ten years from now, staring at the same wall and waiting for the next feeding, Bill knew he would feel greatly underchallenged and unhappy. He pictured himself as a lifer telling young college students, who would come to work during the summer months, *"Don't get stuck out here like I did,"* and wondering if they would heed his advice. Right now it was great to have a good paying job that would allow him to enjoy many of his favorite activities, and that provided him good medical benefits, but he knew this would not be enough to provide him happiness into his future.

All 14 pots ran smoothly throughout the shift much to Bill's relief. *Whew!* sighed Bill with a slight grin as he headed for the shower room at the end of the Graveyard Shift.

—◊◊◊—

"...okay, when you're ready to water the front yard just hit this button," explained Bill's dad showing him the sprinkler controls in the basement. "But remember to insert these sprinklers in the backyard before you water that zone," he instructed pointing to the sprinkler heads he kept in a wooden box nearby. "Other than that, just get the mail and newspaper," he added as they headed upstairs. "We sure hope you can join us some day next week; it could very well be the last time we'll be together at Newman Lake."

"I'll try, Dad. If I'm not able to, I'll see you next Sunday. And don't worry, I'll take good care of everything."

—◊◊◊—

"Guess what—they left for Newman Lake!" Bill announced enthusiastically to Barb from the upstair's phone at 2:15 PM on Saturday.

"Finally!" replied Barb. "My bag's all packed."

"As soon as I'm comfortable they haven't forgotten something, and have had ample time to get to my Aunt's cabin, I'll come over and pick you up—probably in a couple of hours."

"Okay, sounds good; I'll be ready!"

Bill made note of the condition of the rooms in the house—particularly his parents' bedroom and bathroom, as he was pretty sure he and Barb would be using them. *Okay, bed not fully made, two pillows on Dad's side of the bed, his slippers in front of the open closet slider on the right side. Green towels loosely draped over their racks, green washcloth hanging over the bathtub spigot.*

Two and a half hours later, Bill knocked on Barb's door.

"Finally! I thought you'd never get here," greeted Barb after opening her door. She grabbed her overnight bag that was sitting on the living room floor. "This almost feels kind of... naughty," she giggled heading for the door. "I hope they don't drive back to get something they forgot."

"I don't think they will. I gave them plenty of time to get to Newman Lake before I headed over. And we'll put things in order before we leave for work just in case one of them drives back during the week to get something. During all the years we've stayed at the lake, we've never driven back home to get something," replied Bill attempting to put her at ease.

Bill pulled his Bug into the garage so neighbors wouldn't see Barb with him and closed the garage door. "We just won't make ourselves too visible or...too loud," grinned Bill as they entered the kitchen from the garage.

"Wow...this seems so big compared to my place, and so

much cooler; what a nice place!"

He gave her a tour of the upstairs including his parents' bedroom.

"Oh my!" Barb exclaimed. "A queen-sized bed...hmm!"

"I know!" Bill responded, grinning. "And I put clean sheets on it for us. Let's put your bag downstairs in my room just to be safe, but we'll definitely be taking advantage of this big bed."

"Wow, it's so cool down here compared to my hot apartment; you must be able to sleep really well down here," Barb commented placing her bag on his bedroom floor.

"Yeah, it's great when I work graveyard and have to sleep during the hot days."

"So—tell me, Bill Roberts—how many girls have actually been in your bedroom?" she asked coyly her hands on her hips.

"You're the first," he quickly assured her with a smile. She looked at him as if she didn't believe him. "Let's go upstairs and grab a cold beer; then I'll BBQ some hamburgers. We can sit out on the deck and enjoy the evening and then...."

"And then enjoy dessert!" she finished.

—⚍—

By the time Bill put the burgers on the grill, both were on their second beers and feeling more relaxed.

"You're lucky you had a mom and a dad growing up," reflected Barb after another sip of her Bud. "I often wonder what my life would have been like had my dad stayed with my mom?"

"Well, if they didn't get along, it could have been even worse. I'm actually surprised my dad and mom stayed together, especially after my youngest brother, George was born."

"What do you mean?"

"Well, when we lived in Spokane, my mom got pregnant with George shortly after she had Don. George and Don are only 11 months apart. Her doctor had strongly urged her not to have another kid. Well, George was born with several health issues and some mental disabilities, which demanded my mom's attention nearly all the time. After she had George, Mom seemed so unhappy and angry. It seemed like Mom and Dad fought all the time; sometimes there were even loud screaming matches. I remember seeing my dad sitting on their bed upstairs crying after one of their fights. I did my best to comfort him. I really feared they would separate or divorce. Fortunately, for us kids they didn't because Mom didn't have a job, and she really didn't have any job skills. I'm not sure what we would've done.

"When we moved out to the Valley and George grew out of some of his health issues, their marriage improved a bit. But they still don't seem real happy together. I seldom see much affection between them, and my mom sleeps out here on the couch a lot," added Bill nodding to the couch in the family room.

"I wonder if that's how couples get after years of marriage? A friend of mine at work says that's how her parents are now too. Somehow I don't think we'd ever get that way if we were married—you know—based on how much we like to be together and…you know," she added grinning at him.

By the time they had finished their second beers, they were both very relaxed and getting hungry.

"About ready for a hamburger?" asked Bill tossing his bottle into the garbage. *Have to remember to get rid of these before next weekend.*

"Yes, what can I do to help?"

"Well, you can wash some lettuce and slice some tomatoes while I get the coals going."

———〰〰———

"Mmmmm, good job on the burgers," praised Barb looking out over the deck into the backyard. "It's sooo nice out here."

"It really is. We eat most of our meals out here during the summer."

After cleaning up the kitchen, they sat on the deck enjoying the warm summer evening and sharing family stories.

"Did your dad teach you how to play football?" asked Barb at one point.

"No!" Bill snickered. "He never played any sports at all as a kid. But, I was fortunate enough to have friends who liked sports, and they talked me into turning out. If I hadn't played sports in elementary school and high school, I'm not sure how my life would have turned out. Teammates asked me over to their places for dinner and to spend the night. They taught me how to play fun games, to fish, hunt and ski. I wouldn't have learned how to do any of those things had it not been for friends I met through playing sports. Apart from going to Newman Lake for a week during the summers, my folks never took us anywhere. The first time I crossed the border into Idaho was when some friends in high school took me skiing at Schweitzer Basin."

"Tell me what you were like in high school," asked Bill, who didn't want to talk anymore about his family.

"Well, I was pretty quiet. I wasn't very popular, and I wasn't a very good student, either. I just kind of plugged away. My sister, Teri was more outgoing, and had a lot more boy friends than I did."

"You're an incredible lover for not having had many boy-friends," pointed out Bill.

Barb looked down and turned red as if embarrassed. "Well...I've told you about how my mom was when Teri and I were growing up...and...I guess I have a pretty...racy imagination. And, I read a lot of romance stories." She looked back up at Bill, then continued. "After graduation, I got this job at J.C. Penney and have enjoyed living on my own. Meeting you this summer has been so special to me. I have so much fun with you, and you make me feel so special."

"Well, you are special," emphasized Bill reaching over to grab her hand. Bill suddenly slapped his leg, "Oh, oh! Here come the mosquitoes. Guess we'd better go in and...perhaps enjoy some dessert," suggested Bill opening the screen door to the family room.

"Give me five minutes; then come downstairs to your room for dessert, okay?"

"Okay," replied Bill giving her a sideways look, then noting the time on the kitchen clock.

When five minutes were up, he opened the door to the basement stairway and noticed several articles of clothing scattered on the stairs: Barb's shirt, cutoffs, sandals. Then down the hallway to his room: her bra and panties. When he opened the door to his bedroom, Barb was in his bed smiling at him; the top sheet pulled up to her chin.

"What a pleasant surprise," he declared looking at her then pulling his shirt over his head.

"A fantasy come true?" she asked.

"You got that right!" he replied dropping his cut offs and underpants to the linoleum floor.

"Ohhh my!" Barb exclaimed catching a glimpse of his alertness before he joined her in his bed. "Tell me, what do you do when you get horny and you're in your bed all alone?" inquired Barb in a suggestive way. "Do you ever...you know... masturbate?"

"Uhh...I..."

"Do you do this?" she asked stroking him with her right hand. "Or do you do this?" she asked slowly moving him against the top sheet.

"Uhh, I'm not sure...you may have to keep doing that so I can make up my mind," he replied obviously enjoying her hand. "But...nothing can compare to being inside you, Barb."

"Well, that's going to have to wait," she teased now applying some lotion to her hands from a small bottle she had set on the desk next to his bed. She continued to slowly stroke him with her hands that made wet sounds as they moved on him. At one point, she glanced beneath the top sheet to check him out, and then looked at his face to observe his enjoyment.

"Oh, my God! That feels sooo good, Barb. But...if you keep...doing that, I'm going to...come in your...hand," he gasped. "Don't you...want me...to come...inside you?"

"Well, if you insist," she replied wiping her hands on the top sheet. Tossing the covers aside, she straddled him, and raised up enough to guide him to her. Using her legs and arms, she moved herself up and down while tightening around him. The rhythmic wet sounds hastened his surge. He could feel everything rising in him.

"Is this better than my hand?" she asked watching his face.

"Yes, Yes!" he gasped breathing faster.

"Look into my eyes," she commanded him. "Look into my eyes as you come to me."

"Oh, my God," he grunted as he raised up to stay with her and to look into her eyes. As he came, he grabbed her waist to hold her to him; he wanted her to have every last ounce of him.

"You feel sooo fucking good!"

Still straddling him, she bent down to kiss him, then lay down on top of him. "I'll bet you won't get dessert like this in the Novitiate," she whispered in his ear. "This will give you something to think about when alone in your bed," she added.

When he began to retreat from her, she rose up, dismounted and got out of bed.

"Where are you going?" he asked puzzled.

"To take advantage of that queen-sized bed up there," she responded picking up her overnight bag. She threw him a flirty glance. "Care to join me?" she invited scampering down the hall gathering her clothes as she headed upstairs.

"I'll be right there," he called out before heading into his bathroom to wash off, brush his teeth and pee.

Barb was still in his parents' bathroom brushing her teeth and getting ready for bed when Bill leapt into the queen-sized bed. It seemed really weird to be naked in his parents' bed but he quickly put it out of his mind when he saw Barb enter the bedroom dressed only in a t-shirt that barely covered her.

"Does it seem weird to be with a girl in your parents' bed?"

"Kind of, but it's sure nice to be together in a bigger bed isn't it?"

"You mentioned that your mom sleeps out on the couch a lot. Do you think they still...you know...when they sleep together?"

"I have no idea, Barb," Bill chuckled. "I've never heard any squeaky bedsprings or bedroom noises and my room's right below theirs."

Barb asked him several more questions about his parents, but could tell that Bill, now relaxed from his climax was beginning to fall asleep. She watched his peaceful face for several minutes then joined him in slumber.

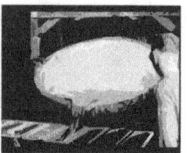

"I can't believe how good I slept last night in this big bed," said Barb sitting up and stretching.

"The passionate lovin' also helps," Bill added grinning up at her. He pulled her to him and kissed her. "I'll go make some coffee; then we can have breakfast on the deck and enjoy the rest of our day together."

"Sounds good; I'll be up shortly," she smiled rolling onto her right side and closing her eyes.

"Mmmm...scrambled eggs, coffee, toast, great lovin'. What a nice morning," sighed Bill as he finished his breakfast on the deck. "What do you want to do today?"

"Just enjoy the day with you." She leaned over the wooden picnic table covered by a red and white plastic table cloth and grabbed his hands. "Maybe sunbathe a bit...make love with you...nap...make love again.... She looked into his eyes. "This may be the last time we have a whole day like this together," she added smiling. Bill thought about assuring her it wouldn't be the last time but remained silent.

After cleaning up the kitchen, they changed into their swimming suits and adjusted the lounges on the deck to face the sun.

This wouldn't be such a bad life, thought Bill enjoying the sun on his back. *If Barb's going to get pregnant, I hope it occurs soon, before I give my two weeks notice to Kaiser. I'd need this job to support her and the baby.*

"Barb, I heard that they screen novices' letters in the Novitiate. So we need to think of a name you can use when we write to one another, and some code you can use in case you find out you're pregnant."

Lying on her stomach, she opened her eyes and turned toward him. "Some code?" she asked puzzled.

"I was thinking…when I was a freshman at Carroll College, I knew a guy whose name was Casey, but we all called him K.C. What if you used K.C. Scott? If they ask me about your name, I can say it's short for Casey."

"Hmmm, I guess that would work," replied Barb indifferently. "And what code could I use if I find out I'm pregnant?"

"Well, with fall not far away, you could mention something about cooler weather. Like…'the mornings are getting cooler now.'"

"Okay…that will work. 'The mornings are getting cooler now,'" she repeated. She then turned away from him again, closed her eyes absorbing the warm sun on her back.

After she had adequately sunned herself front and back, she asked him if she could take a bath before lunch.

"Of course! I'll make sure there's some towels in the master bath for you." He headed for the bathroom and began to draw her bath, making sure the water wasn't too hot for her. "It's all set up for you," he announced returning to the deck. "I'm going to take care of a few things; just let me know if you need anything."

"When you're done with your chores will you come in and…wash my…back?"

"Of course," he replied with a grin.

He walked across the street to the mailbox to get the mail and newspaper. He wanted any vigilant neighbors to see just him taking care of the place while his folks were away. He then turned on the front sprinklers.

After entering the front door, he slowly opened the bathroom door and peeked in. Only Barb's head was visible above the mound of bubble bath. "That looks like fun!" smiled Bill.

"Take your shorts off and join me," she invited. "Here, get in behind me."

"Ohhh, that does feel good," Bill said as he slowly slipped beneath the bubbles behind her.

After snuggling a bit, she took hold of his right hand. "I want to show you something. Did you know that girls also masturbate sometimes when they get horny?"

"No…I…ahh…do they?"

Using her right hand, she guided his right hand below the bubbles. She then grabbed his three middle fingers and pressed them against the area below her softness. She moved her hand on top of his keeping pressure on his fingers. After a couple minutes, she moved his middle finger just inside her, moving it slightly upward to where he felt something round and hard. "Just keep gently pressing right there, she whispered. Periodically, she'd adjust his hand so it was right where she wanted it and his pressure was adequate. As the roundness grew harder and bigger, he could tell that she was enjoying his hand immensely. Using her left hand, she placed his left hand on her left breast.

"Your breast feels so soft but so firm at the same time," Bill murmured. And when his fingers moved over her hard nipple, she would gasp and press her head into his chest.

At one point, she moved two of his fingers inside her. "Press harder," she urged moving against him. He immediately complied wanting to fully contribute to her pleasure. Then she leaned into his chest and gasped, "Yes! Yes!" Her reaction agitated the water in the tub. She moved his hand away and her entire body relaxed against him. "Ohhh, that was very nice, she cooed. Now you know how girls masturbate."

"Do girls always do it in the bathtub?"

"Not always," she chuckled. "Think you can find that spot on your own?" asked Barb attempting to look over her shoulder at him.

"I think so."

"Well, let's go find out."

Barb reached forward and lifted the drain handle to empty the tub. As they rinsed off the bubbles under the shower, Barb glanced at his erectness and flashed Bill one of her quick, sexy glances. "Looks like someone's ready!"

Bill finished drying off first and headed for his parents' bed. When Barb joined him, she had a small jar of petroleum jelly. She unscrewed its lid. "Here, put some of this on your fingers. A little bit more," she added before replacing the lid. She looked at him and grinned. "Let's see if you can find that spot on your own."

Bill proceeded slowly and carefully under the top sheet until he found her. Once inside, he moved his middle finger upward until he rediscovered her hardness.

"Yes!" she breathed nodding. As he gently pressed, she writhed and emitted muffled moans. She tossed her head back and forth on the pillow and slapped her hands against the sheet.

When she couldn't stand it any longer, she moved his hand away and pulled him on to her. "Yes!" she gasped as he entered her. "Just fuck me now!"

Bill loved watching her face as she enjoyed him, and he loved how long he could endure this time. At one point, she locked her legs around his waist to set the pace she was after. Bill could tell from her determined face and her rhythmic movement that she was intent on reaching orgasm. *I hope I can climax at the same time,* he thought. As he concentrated on pleasing her, and listened to the sounds of their love making, he felt his passion beginning to rise, and when she felt it, she frantically commanded, "Now! Come, Baby. Come!"

Secure with the privacy they didn't normally have in her small apartment, neither attempted to muffle their wonderful ecstasies. At one point, their vocalness made them both laugh through their gasps. Together they enjoyed the erotic rush: their synchronized breathing as it slowed, the wonderful exertion that began to set in, then the idyllic peacefulness before sleep overtook them.

—⧖—

"Guess we must have dozed off for a bit," Bill announced as he sat up and peered over at the alarm clock on the bedside table to his left. "It's almost 1:30 in the afternoon."

"I guess so," she replied ending a big yawn.

"I'll go turn off the sprinklers then make us some lunch."

"Wait," she urged grabbing his right arm. I just want to tell you how much I love being with you, and that I'll always remember this special time, and all our times together. Whatever the future holds for us."

"Thanks, Barb, I will too," he replied looking into her eyes and kissing her tenderly.

—ɯ—

"Do you like toasted cheese sandwiches and tomato soup?" he asked when he came back into the house after shutting off the sprinklers.

"I love toasted cheese sandwiches with tomato soup. My mom used to fix that for Teri and me all the time when we were growing up."

As they were finishing lunch, Barb asked him if he had any pictures from when he was a little kid.

"A few, I think."

"Can I see them?"

"Sure, if I can find them." Bill headed to the the hallway closet where his parents kept most of their family pictures, rummaged through some envelopes and returned to the kitchen. "Let's sit over here on the family room couch. Let's see…here's one of when we lived in Omak," explained Bill handing her a picture of three squinting boys sitting on their front porch. "This is me and Rod and a kid who lived up the street."

"Oh, you were so cute!"

Bill grinned. "Here's a picture of Rod and me and Phil one summer at Newman Lake. And, this is me when I played football at St. Charles Elementary school in Spokane."

"What grade were you in here?"

"I think 7th grade…you know…this picture reminds me…I want to give you something. I'll be right back." Bill headed downstairs to get a picture of him in his football uniform at Central Valley. "Here, I want you to have this."

"Are you sure? I mean, I'd love to have it, but someday you might...."

"No, I want you to have it."

"Thank you; this means a lot to me. Hey, speaking of Central Valley do you still have your CV annual from your senior year?"

"Yeah, do you want to see it?"

"Yes...as long as you won't look at my sophomore picture."

"I already have," Bill chuckled heading downstairs again to retrieve his annual. "When Jerry invited me over—the first night we met, I got my annual and checked you out," added Bill sitting back down on the couch. "If you looked that good as a sophomore, I knew I wanted to meet you."

"Oh, what a guy!" Barb began paging through his annual. "You were involved in a lot of activities: student body officer... member of the annual staff...football, track. The only picture I'm in my senior year is my graduation picture in the senior section."

They spent the next couple of hours sharing stories of their experiences at Central Valley, and telling family stories. Bill showed Barb some more family pictures he'd found in the hallway closet.

"Want to take a drive before dinner?" asked Bill.

"Yes, that would be fun. Where to?"

"Well, since we've been reminiscing about CV let's drive out that way."

"OK; how about an ice cream cone at Ron's on the way."

"That does sound good."

As they licked their soft vanilla ice cream cones, Bill headed east on Sprague toward Sullivan Road and headed south up the hill to CV. He pulled into the student parking lot at the lower end of the campus and they walked toward the track and football field.

"Man, I spent a lot of time down here," mentioned Bill as they stood on the track and looked out over the football field.

"Is this where your mom walked out onto the field when you were a sophomore?"

"Yes," replied Bill closing his eyes and shaking his head.

"Which sport did you like better football or track?"

"Oh, man…I really liked them both. I guess I'd have to say football because it's more of a team sport. I have so many good memories of practices and games. We had a pretty good team our senior year, too. We beat Pullman for the league championship in our last game of the season.

"Track was a more individual, low key sport." Bill paused, then chuckled. "You obviously remember Tom Stevens because he dated your sister for awhile. Do you remember Geoff Jensen?"

"Yes."

"Well one day after track practice the three of us drove out to Liberty Lake where Tom's dad had his fishing boat moored. We took the boat out and each of us caught several trout. While we were fishing, a fish and game warden came over in his boat and asked us for our licenses. Well, neither Geoff nor I had a fishing license. The game warden, who could see we were in our track gear gave us a good lecture, wrote down our names and phone numbers, and told us to stop by the Sports Creel across from Ron's on our way home to purchase a fishing license. He said he'd check with the store over the next few days to see if we had, and would issue us tickets if we hadn't."

"Did you go get a fishing license?"

"Yes! It was cheaper than getting fined." A smile came to Bill's face. "We felt pretty lucky that he'd let us 'off the hook' so to speak."

"Argh!" replied Barb getting the pun.

"We actually had a good 880 yard relay team my senior year. We took 5th place at the State Track Meet in Pullman." Bill glanced at his watch. "Well, guess we'd better head back to the house so I can barbecue us some chicken."

They drove slowly past the front of the high school as if giving other high school memories a chance to be remembered. Just past CV which sat on top of a knoll, Sullivan Road descended a ways then flattened out. Gone was the CVTA starting line that used to be spray painted on the asphalt. Bill slowed to nearly a stop where Sullivan Road began to flatten out. "When I was in high school, some guys used to drag race on this quarter mile stretch at night," explained Bill pointing down the road. "The 'Central Valley Timing Association' starting line was about here." Bill paused a second looking down the narrow two lane road and shook his head. "Man, it's a miracle no one was killed racing on this narrow road."

When Bill reached E. 16th Ave., he turned west and headed back toward his parents' place. On the way, he stopped at the IGA and purchased some chicken and a six pack of Bud.

Bill opened a can of Bud and handed it to Barb; then opened one for himself. "I'll light the briquettes if you want to make a salad," Bill suggested. "All the salad fixings are in the refrigerator."

"Did you drink beer in high school?" asked Barb beginning to wash the lettuce.

"Once in awhile—when we could find somebody to buy it for us," Bill grinned. "But the summer before my senior year, I worked at a grocery store in the Valley with Jerry Hendricks. We'd gather up partial six packs, store them back in the cooler then when we had about a case, we'd hide them under some boxes in the back and come back at night to get them."

"What do you mean by partial six packs?"

"Well shoppers would sometimes buy just one beer, or drop a six pack when they were shopping and break a couple of the bottles. We'd just combine different beers into a box until we had about a case.

"But one time when a beer truck driver went up to the front to get paid for the store's order, Jerry lifted a case of beer off his truck and stuck it in the cooler."

"Man, you guys were lucky you didn't get caught!"

"I know! I quit that job when football started near the end of August, and it's probably a good thing because I know our luck would have run out at some point. Did you ever drink in high school?"

"Not very much. Sometimes when my mom had dates over Teri and I would sneak sips of their drinks and their beers. I didn't really like the taste of most of their drinks, but I kind of liked beer—especially in the summer."

They continued to swap drinking stories while they waited for the chicken to cook.

—◊◊◊—

Barb patted her tummy when she stood up to carry her plate into the kitchen from the deck. "Mmmm, that was very tasty; nice job on the chicken."

"Thanks."

"I don't have room for any dessert right now, but maybe later," she smiled back at him from the sink.

Bill walked up behind her, put his arms around her and kissed her on the neck. "I know I'll be ready for some later," he replied squeezing their bodies together. "Want to watch some TV after we clean up the kitchen?"

"Sounds good, but you'll have to pick what to watch. I don't have a TV so I don't watch it much," replied Barb scraping the dishes into the garbage sack under the sink. Bill made sure the coals were extinguished; then helped her load the dishwasher. Barb sat down on the couch and snuggled up next to Bill, who was thumbing through the *TV Guide*.

"How about *Walt Disney's The Wonderful World of Color*?"

"Yes, that is such a good show."

I could get used to this, thought Bill several times during the program. It was so cozy and peaceful to have Barb cuddled up next to him watching TV. Barb must have felt the same way because near the end of the program, she began to nod off.

"I think we'd better hit the sack," suggested Bill turning off the TV. "You're having trouble keeping your eyes open, and we haven't had our dessert yet. And, we'll have to get up by 6:00 because I'll need to drop you off at your place before heading to Kaiser."

Her eyes closed, Barb held her arms up so Bill could pull her up. When she was standing up, Bill turned around and carried her piggy back down the hallway into his parents' bedroom. He backed up to the bed and fell back onto the bed. Barb hooted and they both began to laugh.

"I love you," Barb giggled. "You'd better set an alarm," mumbled Barb brushing her teeth from the bathroom. "I'll be there in a sec."

Bill could tell Barb wasn't interested in any adventurous

dessert tonight. She wanted to have sex so she could quickly fall asleep. "Sleep tight," she said rolling onto her side.

"Oh, you are…I mean I will," Bill chuckled. He loved falling asleep with her in his arms.

—m—

When the alarm went off the next morning, it took them both a few seconds to realize where they were. "It can't be 6:00 already!" mumbled Barb in disbelief attempting to open her eyes.

Bill was already pulling up his underpants. "I'll fix us some coffee while you're getting ready. How about some oatmeal and orange juice this morning?"

"Sounds good," replied Barb yawning. Forcing herself out of bed, she checked around the bedroom and bathroom looking for any clothing—she didn't want to leave anything of hers lying around just in case his dad or mom returned to get some-thing they'd forgotten. She then headed downstairs to shower.

After waking up under the hot shower, she repacked her bag and carried it upstairs. "I double checked downstairs and in your parents' bedroom and bathroom. I don't think I left any evidence around, but you might want to check again. I'm taking my bag back to my place just in case one of your parents returns for something. Sure wish we didn't have to work today."

"I know, me too. But, at least I'm working days this week, and it's so nice to have this uninterrupted time together," Bill noted as he served her oatmeal and toast. He then tossed two peanut butter and raspberry jam sandwiches, an apple and a Snickers bar into a lunch sack with "ROBERTS" written on it.

Barb sat at the kitchen table, crossed her right leg over her left leg and pumped it back and forth as she ate. "Mmmm, thank you! I can't remember the last time I had oatmeal. My mom used to fix it for Teri and me before we left to catch the school bus."

"Yeah, Mom fixed it a lot for us before school, too. It really does stick to your ribs," added Bill poking her in the ribs. Barb shrieked with delight.

After breakfast, Bill put her bag in the backseat of his car before opening the garage door, then drove her to her apartment so she could get ready for work. She exited the car, closed her door, then poked her head through the open passenger window flashing him a sexy grin. "Thanks for the lift, fella."

"Anytime," Bill smiled. "Give me a call after you get off work and are ready to come over okay? I'll come get you. Bye."

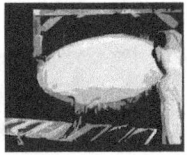

"Roberts!"

"Here."

"Pots on Line 4."

Nice! sighed Bill *This will be a good way to ease back into this week.*

After he returned to the waterhole from the first feeding, he realized that he'd be sharing the waterhole with Stretch, the guy who got his jollies by talking about gross things.

"Hi, my name's Stretch; you must be subbin' for Marv," he said holding out his hand.

"Yep," replied Bill unenthusiastically and making a mental note to wash his hands first chance he got. "My name's Bill Roberts."

"Oh, are you that guy who's gonna be a priest?" asked Stretch spitting through the entryway of the waterhole toward one of his pots. Some Skoal that didn't quite make it hung on his lower lip.

"Well, I'm going to give it a try."

"Man, there's no fuckin' way I could even thinka doin' that," scoffed Stretch. "You know you're givin' up the best thing that can happen to a guy—gettin' laid."

"Yeah, well...I'll see how long I last in the seminary," replied

Bill heading toward the restroom to get away from Stretch and to wash his hands.

Right before lunch out by the pots, Stretch was talking to several other guys about hunting, and how he was loading his own shells these days. He pulled three 30.06 shells from his right front pocket to show them; then removed the shield from a nearby pot and tossed them into the pot. As the other guys scattered for cover expecting momentary explosions, Stretch stood there laughing hysterically. "I didn't load those ones," he roared as the others looked back at him in disgust. One of the men had scraped his shin leaping out into the breezeway and was very upset. "You fuckin' asshole, Stretch!" he shouted limping around out in the breezeway and rubbing his shin.

Unfortunately for Stretch, the Line 4 foreman had witnessed the event, took Stretch into his office, and wrote him up.

"Fucker can't take a joke," complained Stretch returning to the waterhole tossing his gloves onto the table. "What the fuck...I can use the three days off anyway."

Hopefully that'll tone him down for the rest of this shift, thought Bill, who tried to stay out of the waterhole when Stretch came back from feeding his pots. Later that shift, Bill observed Stretch tossing an iron crowbar into one of the Line 4 pots no doubt in retaliation for getting written up. Bill had heard from a lifer once that some guys would toss crowbars and other stuff into the pots on swing and graveyard shifts when the brass weren't around, but he'd never actually seen any worker do so until now.

"It lowers the quality of the aluminum," the lifer had told Bill. "It's some guys' way of getting back at their foremen and the 'pencil pushers' in the head office."

And the other pot men who work that string of pots, Bill reflected at the time. *How selfish and short-sighted.*

—w—

Bill and Barb relished the uninterrupted time they had together for the next few evenings after work. They enjoyed fixing dinner together, sitting out on the deck after dinner and watching TV cuddled up on the couch. But most of all they enjoyed the wonderful space the queen-sized bed offered them, pursuing several new adventures, exhausting themselves with pleasure before falling asleep in one another's arms.

"You know, just to be safe, I think I should drive you back to your place some time this evening," said Bill after they had finished dinner on Friday evening. "My folks said they were coming back on Sunday, but…just in case they decide to come back tomorrow instead, it would give me time to do laundry and make sure everything is in order. We can enjoy the queen-sized bed one more time before I drive you home."

As much as Barb wanted to spend another night together, she nodded, pursed her lips and sighed. "Probably a good idea," she reluctantly agreed. "This week has gone by so quickly…I wish it were just beginning."

"I know, me too. So, let's make tonight special. If you'll double check my room, the bathrooms and my parents' bedroom to make sure you have everything, I'll clean up the kitchen and put our empty beer bottles and cans in a bag. Then…I'm going to fill the bathtub," grinned Bill in a suggestive way.

"Hmmm, that sounds like a plan," agreed Barb. She put her arms around his neck and kissed his lips before slipping in her tongue to alert him to what she really wanted. She stepped back, looked into his eyes and gave him a sexy smile. "I'll give you some of my bubble bath to use while you're filling the tub."

As she repacked her bag down in his room, Barb could hear the tub filling upstairs. A smile came to her face.

"Tub's ready!" announced Bill from the top of the stairs.

"I'll be right there." She paused and looked about Bill's room wondering, hoping but really doubting she would ever be here again. Pursing her lips, she closed her overnight bag and strode down the hall to the stairs wanting to fully enjoy the remaining time they had there together.

When Barb entered the master bathroom, Bill was already in the tub enveloped in bubbles. "Ohh," she smiled removing her clothes. She gingerly stepped into the bubbles in front of Bill, lowered herself into them and sat back against him. "Oh, this feels sooo good!"

"I'll make you feel even better," added Bill wrapping his arms around her.

"Oh, and how do you intend to do that?" she asked grinning.

"You'll have to wait 'til we're in bed to find out."

"Hmmm, I can't wait," she smiled nuzzling into him.

Taking advantage of the warm, relaxing water and their soapy hands, they enjoyed bringing one another to the brink of climax, but backed off in time to delay their ultimate pleasures for the queen-sized bed.

When Barb was ready for what she really wanted, she leaned forward and lifted the drain handle. When the tub was about empty, they stood up, closed the shower curtain, and rinsed off the bubbles. Bill finished toweling off first and headed for his parents' bed.

When Barb joined him, she cuddled up next to him and whispered in his ear, "So, how do you intend to make me feel 'even better'?"

"You'll see," he assured her kissing her neck under her right ear; then kissing his way to her left ear.

"You'll have to do better than that," she teased.

Bill took his time moving southward, kissing around her breasts and hard nipples before placing them in his mouth.

When she'd had enough of that pleasure, she placed a hand on each side of his head and urged him downward. Still in no hurry, he kissed her concave tummy starting at the top of the left side and working down to her softness; then back up and down until he worked his way across her belly. A couple of times, she raised her pelvis hoping he would get the hint and move to her, but he continued to build her anticipation. When she began to move him down with her hands, he instead kissed the inside of her left knee; then kissed her smooth skin moving upward. She desperately wanted him, but he moved to her right knee kissing his way up to her. When he reached the top of her right leg, he finally let her move him to her.

"Oh!" she gasped as he met her. She held him to her panting and moaning as he thoroughly explored her. When the ecstasy became too much for her and she was ready for all of him, she raised him to her lips and kissed him passionately while he entered her. "Yes…that's what I want, just fuck me…Yes! Don't stop!"

Then after a short time had passed, she pushed Bill away and rolled over for him. "I know how to make you feel even better, too," she asserted looking over her shoulder. Bill wasted no time re-entering her. He loved feeling her ultimate tightness again. He was like a wild animal. "Ugh, ugh, ugh," they both uttered each time Bill thrust himself deep inside her. Like the last time he was with her in this way, he felt like he was breeding her, and Barb was remembering what Bill had promised her if he got her pregnant. When she could feel him swell, she put her face into the pillow to both absorb his passion and to secure his seed.

"Oh, my God, Barb!" he gasped burying himself inside her.

"Ohh! ohh!" she moaned as he pulsed deep inside her. He stayed close to her attempting to prolong his intense pleasure as long as he could; then as their breathing slowed, both rolled onto their left sides letting their rapid breathing and heart rates recover together.

As the urge to sleep began to cover them, Bill sighed. "As much as I want to fall asleep with you in my arms and wake up together in the morning, Barb, I'd better get you home—just in case my family comes home tomorrow.

Barb murmured sleepily. "Okay.... Damn...this week went by so fast."

"I know," replied Bill kissing her right shoulder.

"I'll miss waking up with you tomorrow morning," lamented Barb from her living room. "Let me know if your family comes home tomorrow. If they don't, let's go see a movie tomorrow night since we both have the day off," she encouraged wanting to enjoy the rest of the weekend with him.

"Sounds good to me," Bill responded heading for the door to get the bag of empties.

"If they do come back tomorrow, stop by after Swing Shift next week—if you're not too tired," teased Barb following him to her door.

"I'll definitely be stopping by after Swing," grinned Bill. "Oh, that reminds me, I have to give Kaiser my two weeks' notice next week, Barb. So...if you find out you're pregnant over the next few days be sure to let me know, okay? I'll definitely need to keep this job if you are."

She kissed him and flashed him a smile. "Well, my period should begin in the next couple of days—I'll let you know... here give me the bag of empties and I'll put them in our garbage cans out back."

"Thanks; I'll call you tomorrow. Goodnight."

—⁓—

Better park in my regular spot by the curb, thought Bill returning home from Barb's. Once inside, he stripped the sheets from his parents' bed. He could still smell Barb's perfume on them, and flashes of her passion shot through his mind. *I hate to wash away these wonderful memories but washing them tonight will give me a head start on tomorrow.* He tossed the towels and washcloths they had used into the washer with the sheets then headed to his own bed. *I'd better wash my sheets and towels tomorrow morning too,* he thought knowing his mom sometimes washed them to help him out. *If she were to smell Barb's perfume on my sheets or pillow case, she would go into orbit!*

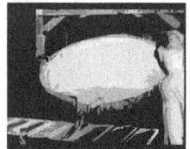

The next morning after drying the laundry, Bill put the sheets on his parents bed, then rolled around on them so they appeared slept on. He then positioned the blankets as they were when his parents left. He made sure his dad's slippers were in front of the open slider on the right side of closet, and that the green towels and washcloths were draped over their racks as he remembered. He double checked all the rooms just to make sure nothing was out of the ordinary; then he watered the backyard.

At about 2:30 PM, he heard the garage door open. *Whew! Thank God I took Barb home last night!* he sighed in relief.

"The place looks great," complimented his dad carrying in the cooler and setting it on the kitchen table.

"Thanks!" smiled Bill. "You're home a day early!"

"Yeah, we needed to buy more groceries if we stayed another day, and everyone seemed like they were ready to come home."

"We were hoping you would make it out to the cabin at least one day," his mom quickly followed in a disappointed almost scolding voice.

"I know, Mom. I wanted to get out there but I was so beat after setting carbon all week. Sorry…. How was the lake?" asked Bill wanting to change the direction of the conversation.

"I caught six fish!" Don announced excitedly.

"That's great," replied Bill trying his best to act excited for him.

"And Dad and I finally got Aunt Doris's outboard to start," bragged Phil.

"Wow, that's quite an accomplishment; I could never get it to run."

After listening to several lake stories, Bill headed downstairs to call Barb from the back room while his family shuttled items from the station wagon to the house.

"It's a good thing you headed home last night; they're back!" announced Bill.

"Oh my! Is everything okay?"

"So far. Dad seems real pleased with how the yard and the house look. Of course they all had to tell me about what they did during the week, and how disappointed they were that I didn't make it out for awhile last week."

"Well, at least they didn't come home to find us in their bed. You'd probably be heading this way with your bags packed if that had happened. Hmmm, maybe that would have been a good thing," Barb chuckled. "Speakin' of coming over here, will you be coming over this evening?"

"As much as I'd love to, Barb, I think I'd better stick around here this evening—just in case they ask about anything. But I'll definitely be stopping by after Swing Shift next week."

"I'll be waiting," replied Barb.

It was difficult for Bill to stay close to home over the weekend but he wanted to be present if his folks noticed anything suspicious and asked him about it. He wanted to be able to quickly ease any suspicions they might have. He could tell his mom was still upset because he didn't come out to the lake while they were there. But he couldn't tell that she had called Rod before they left for the lake to invite him to Bill's going away party in a few weeks, and to convey her suspicions about Bill's seeing a girl over the summer.

"...I don't know for sure, but given how much Bill has gone out on his days off and how late he's come in on his days off, I'm pretty sure he is," Rachel expressed to Rod over the phone. "I think this girl might be a friend of Jerry and Sandy Hendricks. Did Bill mention anything about seeing a girl when he was at your place?"

"No," lied Rod.

"Well, she'd better not show up at Bill's going away party. I won't stand for her being here."

It became obvious to Rod as he talked with Rachel that he had to somehow head off Barb's coming to Bill's party. "I'm sure you don't have anything to worry about," Rod assured her. "And I'll definitely attempt to be at the party. I'll have to ask my new boss if I can take a couple of days off that week. I think Steve, my roommate is planning to drive to Spokane to see his folks about that time. I'll let you know as soon as I find out."

"Okay; hope you can make it work. It would be special to have all of us together that weekend. Bye."

After hanging up, Rod began to formulate a plan.

"Oh, I'm going to be a little late getting home from Swing Shift tonight," Bill informed his mom before heading for Kaiser on Monday afternoon. "A few guys on D Shift want to take me out for a beer before I leave for the Novitiate in a few weeks."

"Okay; see you when you get up tomorrow," replied his mom coolly.

Not having seen Barb for a few days, Bill was eager to be with her after his shift. Memories of last week excited him as he drove to Barb's.

"Hi," she mumbled sleepily when Bill slid in next to her. "I've got good news and bad news. The good news is I'm not pregnant; the bad news is I got my period Friday."

"Oh...darn," replied Bill almost surprised by this news given how rowdy they'd been together during the previous week. He breathed an inward sigh of relief. "I won't try to convince you to make love like I did in Seattle. Do you want me to just let you sleep tonight?"

"No, please stay with me for awhile. And, I do have other ways of taking care of you, ya know," she reminded him reaching for a bottle of lotion on her night stand.

She poured some lotion into her left hand then rubbed her hands together for a bit to warm the lotion. Then moving her hands under the top sheet, she found him. Clasping her hands together, she stroked him tightly and slowly. "How's that?" she asked.

"Oh, my God...that feels so good, Barb," he replied listening to the liquid sounds. He coordinated his movement against hers; at one point she applied more lotion. Then, he could feel the surge building in him, and Barb could tell as well.

"There you come," she said as he gasped with pleasure. He grabbed her hands and stopped her strokes while he climaxed.

"Thank you, Barb," exclaimed Bill still breathing hard. "I really needed you tonight."

"Anytime," she replied reaching for a Kleenex on her night-stand. "My, you made a mess," she commented wiping off her hands. She handed Bill several Kleenex tissues.

After cleaning up, Bill filled Barb in on his family's trip to Newman Lake, and they talked about how wonderful their time was together while his family was at the lake.

"Well, I'd better head for home and let you get some more sleep," Bill said rolling out of her bed and pulling on his underpants. "Friday is my last Swing Shift; I'll tell my folks I won't be home so I can stay over with you."

"Hopefully, I'll be ready for you by then," smiled Barb.

The next day, Bill thought about what Barb had told him last night about not being pregnant. He felt relieved that his plans to enter the Novitiate would not be changed, and that he wouldn't have to break the shocking news of a pregnancy to his parents and friends. Yet, when he thought about the ramifications of giving Joe his two weeks' notice, his gut wrenched. *Is this really what I should do? What if Barb gets pregnant right before I leave for the Novitiate?*

He was still struggling with these questions on his drive to Kaiser that afternoon for Swing Shift. After parking his Bug, he joined other D Shift workers as they headed toward the Guardhouse to punch in. Bill became aware of how quiet it was. There was very little chatter. Few smiles graced men's faces; in fact most looked pretty grim. Many of them looked down at the pavement as they walked. Their gait was slow and plodding as if they were attempting to delay their arrival to the Guardhouse. He pictured himself as one of them in ten more years plodding along, dreading another boring shift, and he knew then that he would give Joe is notice today.

"Okay, I'll let the head shed know," replied Joe making a note on his clipboard. "What is this, summer number four or five for you?"

"Five," answered Bill.

"Well, we'll miss seeing you next summer."

"Thanks, Joe."

I just hope she doesn't get pregnant between now and then, he thought crossing his fingers.

"Oh, by the way, you're setting carbon on Line 3 this evening," added Joe.

For the next few days, Bill continued to keep his fingers crossed about the decision he'd made to give Joe his two weeks' notice. *If Barb gets pregnant before I leave for the Novitiate in a few weeks, I won't have a job to support her, the baby or myself. It would be a disaster! Maybe I should ask Joe how tough it would be to get rehired? He probably couldn't speak for the guys in the head office anyway. And I really don't want to work here for the rest of my life unless I absolutely have to!* He knew he had to make an important decision before he next saw Barb.

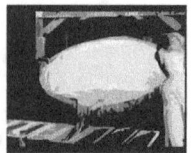

My last Swing Shift—probably forever, thought Bill as he headed home on E. Stoneman Road late Friday night. *And only one week of Graveyard left next week before I'm done there forever!* The cool night air coming in his window felt good after a day of setting carbon. He breathed in the sweet smell of the freshly cut alfalfa.

Then he began to think about what he would do tonight. *Barb's expecting me to show up tonight, and I promised her I'd be there, but I can't get her pregnant now. I should just head home and call her tomorrow. I can think up some reason why I couldn't stop.* He continued to struggle with what he should do as he drove through Millwood. *Of course! The Trojans!* he remembered when he passed the pharmacy. He reached over and opened the glovebox to make sure they were still there. *Whew!* he grinned. *I'll just have to convince Barb we need to use them now.*

At the corner of Argonne and Sprague, he turned west.

—⧄—

"I've missed you coming by these past few nights," Barb said sleepily as she rolled over to greet him. "And I'm so ready for you!" She pulled him to her, eager to welcome him, but Bill hesitated.

"Barb, I gave my two weeks' notice to Kaiser this week; so I think I'd better use a rubber. This would not be a good time for me to get you pregnant."

"Bill, I've told you, you don't need to worry about that," she reminded him.

"I know, Barb...but I am worried now that I won't have a job. Using one will at least help me to not worry when we're making love."

"Okay," Barb agreed reluctantly. "Do you know how to put one on?"

"No, but I'm sure I can figure it out," Bill replied getting out of bed and heading into her bathroom. He closed the bathroom door, turned on the light and tore open the package. He'd never actually seen a rubber before, but it didn't take him long to determine which way it would roll onto him. Shutting off the light, he quickly re-entered her bed.

"Okay, now I'm ready," he announced cheerfully hoping to make her more receptive about using a rubber tonight.

"This is my first time using one of these, too; so go slow for a bit, okay," she cautioned.

Bill could sense Barb was adjusting to the different feel; then she seemed to relax and enjoy him. While some of the intense pleasure he was used to was diminished (*"it's like wearing a glove,"* he recalled Rod saying), the rubber allowed them to enjoy a bit longer than usual, the wonderful climb to climax.

"Well, it certainly didn't keep you from coming," Barb exclaimed still breathing hard. "Just make sure you don't leave it in me when you shrink."

Bill hadn't thought about this aspect of using a rubber. "I won't," he quickly assured her. "In fact...I'll be right back," he added withdrawing and heading back to the bathroom. After flushing the rubber down the toilet, he returned to her bed. She was facing away from him so he nuzzled up to her and wrapped his arms around her.

"How did it feel to you?" he whispered.

"It was okay," she replied quietly and indifferently..."but I like it better when it's just you and me."

"Me too, Barb, but I really think it's safest for us right now. It would not be a good situation for either of us if you got pregnant now."

Barb remained quiet so Bill began to tell her more about giving the line boss his two weeks' notice, and about how good it felt to be leaving his last Swing Shift behind. "I can't believe that my very last shift ever at Kaiser will be next...." Then he felt Barb twitch and realized that she'd fallen back to sleep. While holding her in his arms, he tried to digest tonight's experiences: the relief and joy he felt after working his last Swing Shift, the feel of the cool night air on his face as he drove back to the Valley; remembering the Trojans when he saw the drugstore, choosing to see Barb tonight; her not really wanting him to use a rubber tonight even though he'd given his notice, her aloofness afterwards. *At least it will prevent her from getting pregnant now.* Before long, the warmth of Barb's body against him and her rhythmic breathing lulled him to sleep.

He wasn't sure what time it was when he awoke Saturday morning because he couldn't see his watch, but he could tell it was early in the morning. Barb was still asleep in his arms. He relished her warm body moving in his arms as she slept; it was very quiet except for her rhythmic breathing. He blinked several times to clear his sleepy eyes; her dark brown, disheveled hair came into focus first. Then he looked up at the old, bent Venetian blinds doing their best to hold out the early morning light. As he scanned the room, the walls looked more drab than usual in the dim light. The small open closet across from the foot of the bed displayed Barb's limited wardrobe. He lay there for several minutes surprised at how wide awake he was. It didn't take his mind long to think about giving Joe his two weeks' notice, and as he did so, he felt a quick twinge of nervousness in his stomach. He refocused on Barb's hair to erase this anxiety. *These wonderful times waking up with Barb in my arms will soon come to an end—possibly forever.* Another brief twinge of nervousness.

Then, almost as if she could sense his anxiety through his arms, she stirred and rolled over to him. She blinked several times looking at him and could tell he'd been awake for awhile. "Hi, how long have you been awake?"

"Not very long. I was just…enjoying you sleeping in my arms."

"Oh, how sweet," she smiled at him.

With his arm free now, he could see his watch. "Almost 6:00! Man, I didn't intend to wake up this early, but I feel like I'm wide awake. How about I get up and make us some coffee?"

"Sure; I'll be up soon and fix us some breakfast," she mumbled through a yawn. She managed a sleepy smile then closed her eyes.

After using the bathroom, Bill headed into the kitchen to brew a half pot of coffee. He was confident the smell of the freshly brewed coffee would get Barb out of bed. He added some milk to his cup and walked back to her room expecting to see her awake, but she had obviously gone back to sleep. *She must really be sleepy this morning.*

He carried his coffee into the living room, sat down on the couch and waited for her to stir and get out of bed. While relieved that Barb wasn't pregnant and that she seemed to be okay about using a rubber, he still knew he had to be careful over the next couple of weeks. As he sipped his coffee, he looked around the tiny, bare living room. *This is probably the type of apartment we'd end up living in if Barb were to get pregnant and I didn't have my job at Kaiser.* He envisioned what it would be like living in such a small space with a crying baby while trying to make a living. He and Barb would probably have to work different shifts so one of them could be home with the baby. He knew his parents, especially his mom would be so upset and disappointed in him that they wouldn't want to help them, and neither Barb nor he would want to leave the baby with Barb's mom. He began to get a knot in his stomach. He walked down the hallway to check on Barb again but she was still sleeping soundly. His anxiety level rising, he headed back to the kitchen. It took him several minutes to find a pen and piece of paper in one of the kitchen drawers.

"Barb, you fell back to sleep and I didn't want to wake you; so headed home. Coffee's made; will call you later. Bill."

———※———

"Hi, what time did you finally wake up?" Bill asked from the downstair's phone about 10:00 AM.

"Not 'til about 9:00," replied Barb sleepily. "You should have woke me up."

"Well, I thought about it, but you must have needed the

sleep, and I knew you needed to work this afternoon."

"Well, I feel bad that I didn't get up and fix you breakfast."

"That's okay; don't worry about it. I have a lot things I need to get done here today anyway. Hey, before I forget it, a long time friend of mine in Spokane is having a BBQ next Friday afternoon about 6:00 and wants me to stop by; would you like to come with me?"

"Sure! Will beat hanging out here."

"Great; we'd probably leave from your place about 5:15, but I'll call you before heading over. Don't work too hard today. Bye."

—⟋⟍—

"Have you determined your last shift?" asked Howard after dinner on Sunday.

"Yes, at the end of this coming graveyard shift. That will give me a couple weeks to wrap things up and pack for the Novitiate."

"Good idea. Hopefully you can sell your car easily, and pay off any outstanding bills," added his dad in his usual serious banker voice. "Then, just put what's left into your savings account for now. If there's any unexpected expense that comes up after you leave, I can take care of it from your savings account."

"Thanks, Dad. I appreciate your help."

"Oh, your mom and I would like to throw a going away party for you on Saturday, the 19th of August. Invite any friends you want to come; we want to invite some family friends as well. We called Rod the other night and he said he'd be here for sure. He's going to drive over with his roommate, Steve."

"Oh, great! I'm glad Rod can come. That's nice of you to do

this for me. I'll be done with work so I'll certainly have time to help you get ready for it."

"Great! Once we know how many of your friends will come, we'll make a guest list; if it's quite a few, I'd like to order a keg. Any ideas where I might order one?" his dad asked with a rare grin on his face.

"Yeah, Joey's by Gonzaga. I'll be happy to order it for you; just let me know."

"That would be helpful," smiled Howard heading for the couch to read the newspaper.

Sitting out on the deck enjoying the warm evening and looking up at the big Ponderosa pines in the back yard, Bill thought about the fact that in just a few days, he'd be clearing out his locker for the last time at Kaiser. Near the end of his previous four summers, he'd really looked forward to his last work week before heading back to classes. But this summer, he had mixed feelings. Of course, it would be nice to be done with the rotating shifts, the heat, gas and dust. But he knew when he punched out after his last Graveyard Shift, it would close this chapter of his life forever.

He thought of his neighbor, Mr. Jacobs, who had gotten him the job five summers ago, and he felt grateful to him, and to Kaiser for hiring him back each summer. There weren't many summer jobs in Spokane that allowed you to make enough money during three months' time to attend a private university like Gonzaga, and not have to work during the school year.

He was also grateful to the men he'd worked with during the past five summers. They had encouraged him to finish college so he wouldn't have to work out there for the rest of his working life like they did. Those men and the tough working conditions taught him how to endure difficult, scary probationary periods, and how to earn the respect of veterans when starting a new position. He knew he'd probably never see most of them again, and wondered how long they'd live. The unhealthy working conditions there really took a toll on their health. Guys who were 35 years old looked 45. But behind those tough exteriors were warm, generous hearts.

"Whacha thinkin' about?" his mom asked sliding open the screen and coming out on the deck to join him.

"Well, I was just thinking that this will be my last summer working at Kaiser. I can't believe it's almost the end of my fifth summer there. Looking back on it, it all went by sooo fast."

"You'll be saying that very same thing more and more as you get older," she replied. "I can't believe you kids are as old as you are now. I can remember so clearly when you were just little boys running around with so much energy. It seemed to go by slow enough at the time, but now when I look back on it…it went by so quickly." She struck a match once, twice and lit up a Winston. "You'll be startin' a new chapter in your life in just a couple of weeks. How do you feel about that?"

"It makes me nervous to think about giving up the life I'm used to living. I don't know if I'll be able to adjust to such a different life. But deep down, I feel it's what God's calling me to do, and I know it's what's best for me now. Even if I don't end up stayin' it will help me clarify what I want to do with my life. So many of my friends have jobs lined up now that they've graduated from college, but I really don't know what I want to do."

"Yet!" she quickly added with emphasis. "I just have a feeling that you'll stay in the Jesuits and become a fine priest."

"Well…I hope so…we'll see." Bill stood up. "I'm going to leave for work a bit early tonight so I can stop by and visit with some friends; see you when I wake up tomorrow after shift."

"Okay, Hon. "There's sandwich stuff in the fridge for your lunch."

—ᴍ—

On the way home from his pharmacy job near Bothell the following Tuesday evening, Rod finalized his plan to head off the possibility of Barb coming to Bill's going away party. He did not want Barb to show up not only for her sake, but also to prevent a scene at the party that could be very embarrassing to Bill and all present there.

"Hi, Barb, this is Rod—Bill's brother. How are you?"

"Fine…gosh what a surprise to hear from you."

"I know. Am I interrupting your dinner?"

"No, I've already eaten."

"Well, I wanted to call and run an idea by you. My folks are organizing a going away party for Bill on Saturday, August 19. I know that Bill will want to invite you but as you know, my parents don't know that you and Bill have been together over the summer. Well…I'm worried that if you come to this party…it could end up being pretty awkward for you, Bill and others there."

"Yeah, I know. Bill's been pretty worried that his folks… especially his mom would find out that we've been dating all summer."

"Well, here's my idea. When Bill invites you to this party, I'd suggest telling him that you don't feel comfortable coming, but tell him you'd like to organize a going away get together at Rathskeller's the next week. My boss has given me a few days off the week after Bill's party so I'd definitely go to Rathskeller's for that, and maybe Jerry and Sandy would want to go and Ed Lewis too. Steve, my roommate whom you met at my party would probably want to go as well because he'll be here visiting his folks. What do you think?"

"You know...that sounds like a good plan. I definitely want to see Bill before he leaves but I don't want to cause him any embarrassment at his party."

"Okay, great! So you'll organize the trip to Rat's the week after the party?"

"Yes. I'll take care of it. Thanks for your call, Rod, and I'll see you...I guess in just a couple of weeks. Bye."

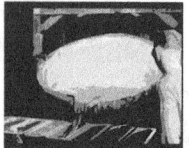

Even though Bill hated working Graveyard Shift, he intention-
ally thought about each aspect of his work experience at Kaiser
as he headed to his last shift Thursday evening: the drive out
to work and the smell of the alfalfa, walking from the parking
lot to the guardhouse, the walk from the locker room past the
carbon plant down to Line 4 to find out what he'd be doing
that day; the dirty, smelly exhausts roiling up to the ceiling
vents, the noise of the moving cranes, the conversations in the
waterhole. He knew he'd probably never set foot in this plant
again after this shift. He was glad he was leaving this behind
but was a bit sentimental in that this place had made it possible
for him to finish college. It also made him think about all the
guys who would have to endure these conditions for the rest of
their working lives.

"Roberts!"

"Here."

Joe looked at Bill and smiled. "Line 2 carbon setter!"

Great! thought Bill as he headed to Line 2. *This will give me
a chance to work with Jack Chrenshaw one last time. Man, it's
almost symbolic; this is where I got my carbon setter's training, and
where I earned my stripes with Jack and the carbon setting crew.*

"Well, look who's here!" Jack broadcast as Bill approached
the foreman's office. "I was wondering if I'd get a chance to

give you shit one more time."

Then it occurred to Bill—*I'll bet Jack spearheaded my being assigned to Line 2 tonight.* "Well, you got it," laughed Bill. He could tell Jack and the other carbon setters were glad to work with him on his last shift at Kaiser. Ed was the only regular carbon setter missing, as his foot was still healing up.

"Well, what did you decide?" asked Jack before he headed to his crane.

"I'm heading to Oregon August 29," replied Bill.

"Good, I think that's the right decision for you, Bill. So what are you gonna do for the next couple of weeks before you leave?"

"Well, mostly get ready to leave for Oregon. I have to sell my car, do some shopping, say good-bye to some friends."

"I hope you're gonna get laid a few more times before you leave."

Bill laughed. "Well, that too, Jack. I'll come find you at the end of this shift."

Even though it was a Graveyard Shift and the crew wanted to finish the first room so they could take advantage of a longer break between rooms, they wanted to make sure Bill didn't get off too easily on his last shift at Kaiser. Jack deliberately brought the new carbon to the wrong slot a few times just to make Bill work harder. "Sorry about that," Jack smiled from the crane.

When one of the other carbon setters found a burn off, he yelled for Bill to come help him pull it out. "See what you'll be missing," teased the crew member as Bill struggled to get the tongs around the red hot carbon butt.

"Don't think I'll ever miss pulling hot burn offs out of a pot," returned Bill as he tossed the carbon unto the pot room floor.

After the crew finished the first room on Line 2 and headed

for the waterhole, Bill announced that he wanted to walk up the line and say good-bye to a few guys he'd worked with over the summers. The first stop he made was at Line 4 to see Joe, his assigning foreman. "Joe, just wanted to stop by and thank you for all your support and patience with me over the past 5 summers, and for assigning me to Line 2 tonight," he smiled. "Take care of yourself."

"You too," replied Joe, shaking Bill's hand. "It'll seem like someone's missing next summer when you're not here. I hope that seminary thing works out okay for you."

"Thanks, Joe; me too. Oh, is Jim Bingham here tonight?"

"No; he called in tonight. He'll be disappointed he didn't get to see ya."

"Darn. Please tell him I stopped by to say good-bye. Sure glad I got my pot training from him. Bye, Joe."

Bill made a couple more stops on his way to Line 7 to see Don Wilson, the crane driver Bill had promised to see on his last shift. "Good, I was hopin' you weren't nappin'," stated Bill as he approached Don in the Line 7 waterhole.

"Bill! Glad you remembered to say good-bye," replied Don as he stood up. He grabbed something from the shelf, and motioned for Bill to exit the waterhole. "I've got somethin' to give you. It ain't much, but I thought it would be appropriate, and that it'll remind you to pray for me."

Bill opened the blue box to find a ceramic statue of Mary, the Blessed Mother. "Oh, it's beautiful!" Bill said as he removed it carefully from the box. "Don...this is so thoughtful of you. Thank you so much!" Bill could see Don's eyes watering-up, and he extended his hand to Don.

"Good luck to ya; we'll miss seein' ya next summer, but I'm glad you have sense enough to not stay out here like we all did. Take care."

"You too, Don," replied Bill before heading back to Line 2. Bill would never forget Don's thoughtfulness and sincerity.

When Bill returned to the Line 2 waterhole, he put the blue box on the shelf above the table, ate his lunch and chatted with the pot men. The other carbon setters had all already eaten and were curled up next to the pots sleeping. But Bill was too wound up to nap so he visited with the pot men until it was time to set carbon in the second room.

After the crew completed the second room, Bill waited for Jack to climb down his crane's ladder. "Jack...I'll always remember that I survived my carbon setting training under you," said Bill extending his hand to Jack.

"Yes, you did, and you were one of the best summer kids I ever trained," declared Jack firmly shaking Bill's hand. "I'm confident you'll find out what you want to do with your life while you're in the seminary, Bill, and whatever it is, I wish ya the best. At least you're getting outa this hell hole." Jack looked Bill in the eye, then looked quickly away to hide an emotion Bill had never seen on Jack's face before. Then, much as he had done Bill's first summer there, Jack turned away and headed for the shower room.

Word had gotten around that this was Bill's last shift, and while Bill was waiting to clock out that morning, several guys he had worked with during the summers came up to wish him well.

This is it, thought Bill as he placed his card in his 3961 slot after clocking out. He felt a sense of freedom and happiness as he walked through the parking lot to his car, but also a bit of nostalgia. He was leaving behind the job that had gotten him through his college years; he was leaving behind this stage of his life, and saying good-bye to guys he'd probably never see again.

He pulled out of the gate and turned left onto E. Hawthorne Road. The guardhouse, the cyclone fence, the pot lines disappeared from view as he headed for E. Stoneman Road. *Thank you, God for all you given to me during my time at Kaiser, and please keep all these guys safe.*

Turning right on N. Bruce Rd., he felt a sense of peace and happiness. He knew his decision to not stay at Kaiser was also a decision to honor his commitment to the Jesuits in August. *"Ask yourself how you feel when you're making a difficult decision,"* Fr. Eric had told him. *"Which choice gives you a sense of peace, joy, happiness; which choice makes you feel anxious, stressed, unhappy? Remember, God wants us to be happy in life."*

As he neared his parents' house, he knew it was going to be very difficult to say good-bye to Barb and to give up their relationship and all the pleasures she gave him. But he was confident that the thirty day retreat in the Novitiate would help him decide what he wanted to do with his life, and that gave him a great sense of relief. *Thank you for helping me make this decision, Lord, and please help me get through these next couple of weeks.*

"So, who's your friend?" asked Barb as they headed for Spokane about 5:30 on Friday evening.

"Oh, a guy I've known for years; his name is Greg Raines. I knew him in grade school, and we went to Gonzaga Prep together—well, for a year anyway. Greg was a real screwball in high school and Prep told him they didn't want him back after his freshman year. We've kind of stayed in touch over the years, and he wants to see me before I head for the Novitiate."

"Is he married?"

"No, but he's been living with this gal for about three years now. Not sure how she puts up with his shenanigans. He probably keeps her in stitches most of the time; he still is a really funny, crazy guy."

"Bill! *Dominus Vobiscuit*!" greeted Greg as he opened the door. "And who is this? A date? Guess I'll have to entertain her since you shouldn't be going out with girls now."

"This is Barb," introduced Bill laughing. "And I'm not in the seminary yet; so hands off!"

"That's the Bill Roberts I know. Come out back and I'll introduce you. Just help yourselves to the pony keg. Hey, do you remember your ol' neighbor, Lynda Brown?"

"Yes! Oh, my God, I haven't seen Lynda since 8th grade."

"Well, she's here; she lives just across the street—small world."

"Oh, my God, Bill Roberts!" screamed Lynda as Bill entered the backyard. "It's been ages since I've seen you." She ran up to Bill and gave him a big hug.

Lynda's still as beautiful and sexy as ever, thought Bill. He'd never thought girls with red hair were very pretty, but Linda was an exception—auburn colored hair, green eyes and flawless, clear skin. She was a knockout back in grade school, and she still was.

"Lynda, it's so good to see you! You look great! I think the last time I saw you was the summer after 8th grade." Barb nudged Bill. "Oh, I'm sorry, Lynda, this is Barb Scott."

Lynda shook Barb's hand. "Pleased to meet you, Barb. You guys go get a beer; then we'll have to catch up."

On the way over to the keg, Bill's mind raced back to the time he and Lynda were in 7th grade in her basement. Her mom was gone; it was just Lynda and him. While Bill was playing their piano, Lynda came up behind him and tried to look down the back of his pants.

Bill quickly stood up. "Don't, Lynda!" She ran from him into her bedroom, and Bill chased after her. She turned and faced Bill looking into his eyes.

"Have you ever kissed a girl before?"

"No," Bill replied quickly embarrassed and intimidated by Lynda's aggressiveness.

She stepped toward him. "Would you like to kiss me?"

"Well…I…"

She kissed him on the lips before Bill could change his mind. He stood there dumbfounded for a second trying to figure out what had just happened. He wanted to get mad at her but he kind of liked it.

"Now you kiss me," she demanded.

He felt nervous now and didn't know exactly how to kiss her; so he kissed her on the lips quickly and backed away.

She smiled at him. "I'll let you see my private parts if you'll let me see yours," dared Lynda.

"No!" Bill responded. "I…I can't…." He knew he was getting hard, which he felt embarrassed about and certainly didn't want her to see.

Giggling, Lynda stepped toward him and grabbed his belt.

"No, Lynda don't!"

He released her hands and backed away from her. When she made another attempt to grab his belt, he turned, ran up the stairs and out the back door to the driveway where his bike was parked. He could hear her calling his name and asking him to come back saying she was sorry, but he rode home not even looking back.

What an opportunity I missed, he thought to himself as he filled Barb's Dixie cup from the keg.

Bill and Barb returned to where Lynda was sitting and resumed their visit. "Does your mom still live on Riverview Drive?" asked Bill.

"No, she remarried and now lives north of Spokane. How about your folks?"

"They still live out in the valley. What are you doing these days?"

"Well…not much right now." She paused and looked down. "My husband, Steve…we got married three years ago…he was killed in a head on collision on I-90 coming back from Rathskeller's in Coeur d' Alene. About four months ago…."

"Oh, I'm so sorry, Lynda—I didn't know." Bill put his arm

around Lynda and hugged her.

"Oh, my God, that must have been devastating!" gasped Barb. "I don't know how I'd be able to cope with a loss like that."

"The past four months have been pretty rough," replied Lynda trying to force a smile. "Right now I'm just in the process of putting my life back together. Of course having Greg as a neighbor helps me from getting too serious." This brought a subdued chuckle from Greg and his girlfriend who were close by.

"Hey, don't let your cups get empty," reminded Greg wanting to change the subject. He headed for the keg hoping others would follow.

"See what I mean!" said Lynda.

Greg always threw fun parties and this was no exception. It wasn't long before both Bill and Barb had enjoyed several cups of the ice cold Bud and were feeling right at home. Bill shared some of Greg's antics when they attended Prep as freshmen. "At the end of each day, one of the Jesuit priests would get on the intercom to make some announcements, including which students had earned 'jug' and had to stay after school to complete missed assignments. He'd also announce which students had 'rock pile.' Rock pile was given to students for disciplinary infractions. Students had to stay after school and help maintain the grounds—like cleaning out flower beds, sweeping walkways, washing windows, etc. Well, almost everyday the priest would end his rock pile list with '…and Greg Raines.'" This story brought laughter from everyone there, for they knew Greg's nature.

"Speaking of Prep, Greg told me that you're entering the Jesuit Novitiate at the end of August," said Lynda quietly to Bill, flashing a glance at Barb.

"Yes. I decided to enter the Jesuits during second semester this year at GU. Then I met Barb this summer—so, I'll see how long I last."

Lynda took a sip of her beer then grew a bit quiet, as if disappointed Bill wouldn't be available in the future.

About 9:00 PM the pony keg ran dry. Most guests began departing shortly after that because they had to work in the morning. Barb had to work as well, but seemed in no hurry to leave.

On her way out the door about 10:00, Lynda gave Bill a long hug and told him how great it was to see him again. "Best wishes in the Jesuits, Bill. I hope it works out for you if that's the life you really want." She smiled at him almost sadly, then turned and walked out the door.

"Thanks for coming over Lynda," said Greg closing the screen door. "Well, I think we're going to head to bed too," yawned Greg. "You guys are welcome to stay here if you don't want to drive back to the Valley tonight. That's a big soft leather couch," invited Greg nodding to his left.

"Thanks, Greg, we just may take you up on that. I probably shouldn't drive...at least for awhile."

As soon as Barb heard their bedroom door shut, she pulled Bill over to the couch and started to kiss him passionately.

"Barb, let's wait to make sure they're in bed," whispered Bill. But Barb, buzzed from the beers she had downed over the evening, and wanting to make sure he quickly forgot about Lynda, had only one thing on her mind. She unbuckled his belt, unzipped his jeans and pushed them and his underpants to the floor. "Barb, I need to go get a ..." Before Bill could adequately gather his thoughts and self-restraint, she'd stepped out of her sandals, unbuttoned her shorts and slid them and her panties to the floor. She put her arms around him and pulled him to her as she lay down on the plush leather couch. She was desperate for him. He made a brief attempt to get up but the cushy couch, her secure hold on him, the feel of her silkiness against him, and the buzz from the beers he'd drank prevented him from doing so—he surrendered to her wonderful warmth. The intense pleasure of not wearing a rubber overwhelmed any iota of reason or hesitation on his part. There was no turning back for him now. He quickly joined her passion. Both of them were like animals wanting, needing to satisfy their needs, neither caring about privacy. They didn't even hear Greg, who came out of his room intending to offer a blanket. As he later informed Bill over the phone, "...all I saw was your bare ass moving on top of her." Their intense rhythm on the supple, deep leather couch created a luxurious, undulating wave that allowed them to move together exactly where she wanted him. When Bill's passion climaxed, she accommodated all of him capturing everything he had to give her.

When he was done, there was no gradual recovery as there usually was—both of them fell asleep almost instantly.

Bill awoke to his own snoring. He was still on top of Barb, who was snoring as well. He could tell he'd been drooling. He raised up and wiped his mouth with his arm. He tried unsuccessfully to read the time on his watch; so he withdrew from her and headed for the bathroom. Completing a much needed pee, he checked the clock on the kitchen wall. *Twelve fifteen! Fuck, we need to get out of here,* thought Bill. After dressing, he tried to wake up Barb by lightly shaking her, but she wanted to sleep more. "Barb...Barb, we have to get going. I need to get you home so you'll be ready for work in the morning."

Unable to get her upright and moving, Bill found her panties and began to dress her. When he had fastened her shorts and put her sandals on her feet, he stood her up, and supported her out the front door to his car. She quickly fell back to sleep as soon as she was seated in his car. *Just hope I don't get pulled over…I hope she doesn't get sick on the way back to her place…and I hope to God I didn't get her pregnant.*

—⟐—

"Oh, my God, how did we get back here?" Barb slurred as he pulled her from his car and began walking her toward her apartment. He held her left arm around his neck to keep her upright as they teetered to her door. He used his key to open it, ushered her down the narrow hallway to her bed, where he eased her down to the mattress. He removed her sandals and covered her with the top sheet.

"Try to sleep it off," he urged. "I set your alarm for 7:00; I'll call you tomorrow."

—⟐—

The next day, Bill called Barb about 5:30 in the afternoon.

"I was sooo fucking hung over today," Barb moaned, "and the day just crawled by. I don't even remember leaving your friend's house or driving home last night."

"I'm not surprised. You were pretty shit-faced. You'd better catch up on sleep tonight, I'll stop by tomorrow evening."

"Okay. I'm going to eat something and head right to bed. See you tomorrow night."

—ˠˠ—

"Hi," greeted Bill as Barb opened her apartment door Sunday evening. He looked at her face evaluating her condition. "Have you recovered yet?"

"I think so," she replied looking down and stepping back so he could close her door. "I'm sure sorry I got so drunk at Greg's. I hope I didn't do anything stupid."

"No, you didn't. In fact Greg didn't even hear us leave," Bill lied not wanting Barb to feel worse than she already did.

"I must have been really tired or something for me to crash like that."

"Don't worry about it, Barb; the same thing's happened to me before. At least you didn't get sick—that's the worst.

Speaking of partying…my folks told me this evening that they want to have a going away party for me on Saturday the 19th. Rod and his roommate Steve are going to come over for it. I want you to come…but I want you to feel comfortable, too."

Barb sat down on the couch and looked down like she was pondering this invitation for the first time. "You know…I'd like to come…but I don't think I'd feel comfortable, and I wouldn't want to cause a scene. Your folks don't really know that we've been together this summer and…you know…I just don't think it would be a good idea. But, I do have another idea…."

"Oh…what's that?"

"Well, I could organize a little get together at Rathskeller's the week after your party. You could invite anyone you want to like Jerry and Sandy, your friend Ed Lewis…maybe Rod and Steve could come if they're still here. And this will give me a chance to see you before you leave," added Barb wiping a tear from her right cheek.

Bill sat down beside her and put his arm around her. "What a great idea, Barb; I like it! I mean, I'd love to have you at my party on the 19th, but your idea makes a lot better sense given the circumstances."

Barb smiled at Bill, wiped another tear away and stood up. "Thanks…. Well, it must be a great feeling to be all done at Kaiser!" she added wanting to change the topic.

"It is!" he nodded. "And it will be so nice to not have to work those rotating shifts and work in those unhealthy conditions." Bill stood up, looked at her sad face and took her hands in his. "Hey, do you want to get out of here for awhile—maybe go get something to eat or get some dessert before I head to work?"

Barb nodded, "That would be great. You know what really sounds good to me is a bowl of homemade chicken noodle soup…like the kind they serve at the sandwich shop at the Mall.

"You got it; let's go get you some soup," replied Bill smiling.

"Just give me a minute to freshen up a bit," Barb urged heading to her bathroom. "We can always come back here for dessert," she suggested from the bathroom.

Bill grinned as he made sure the Trojan was in his pocket. "Sounds good to me."

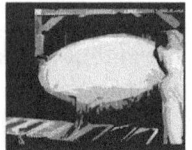

Instead of sleeping until 11:00 or noon as he typically did after working graveyard shifts, he was up by 8:00 the following week making his "to do" list at the kitchen table: shopping for clothes he needed in the Novitiate, advertising his Volkswagen Bug, paying outstanding bills. He couldn't believe how upbeat he felt. The twinges in his gut and the worry were gone. He felt at peace about the tough decision he'd made to quit Kaiser and move forward with his commitment to the Jesuits.

On Thursday, he sold his Bug to Tom Blair, who would be starting classes at Spokane Community College in a few weeks and needed a car for commuting. Tom's folks were close friends of his parents so Bill reduced his asking price. "It doesn't handle trips over the pass very well, but it should be a good commute car for ya, Tom" noted Bill handing him the keys. "Good luck in college."

"Thanks, Bill, and best wishes to you in the Jesuits."

"Well, no changing my mind now," declared Bill to his mom and dad after Tom drove off. "I've quit my job and sold my car. Hope it'll be okay to borrow one of your cars to do some shopping over the next few days before I leave? I'll be sure to put gas in it."

"No problem," replied his mom. "Let's go take a look at the friends your dad and I have invited to your party."

Bill noted that most of them were neighbors they had gotten to know since moving to the Valley nine years ago. He winced a little bit when he saw the Hintons' name. He knew they didn't think very highly of him ever since that New Year's Eve get together with their twin daughters over at their house when he was a junior in high school. *I wish they weren't coming,* thought Bill. *But my folks want them to come...and maybe by now they've gotten over that unfortunate incident.*

"Guest list looks good," assured Bill. "I would say no more than ten of my friends will attend for awhile; so looks like about 40-50 people will be here over the course of the evening. Just remember, Rod and his roommate Steve will be here—I'd say we'd better get two kegs the way they go through the beer," Bill added grinning.

"When the keg's empty, people will leave," Bill's dad assured him. "And between the hors d' oeuvres, BBQ'd hamburgers and potato salad and a piece of your cake, no one should go away short-changed. So, if you'll order a large keg from Joey's, Bill, that would be great. Tell them we can pick it up the morning of the 19th."

"Will do."

Later that afternoon as Bill lay in the sun in the backyard, he looked over at the Hinton's house and let his mind take him back to that embarrassing New Year's Eve party with their twins, Beth and Linda.

During Christmas break his junior year, Bill had run into Beth at University Mall and mentioned to her that he and another classmate, John Jacobs had acquired a bottle of vodka for a New Year's Eve party they'd been invited to.

"Why don't you and John come over to our house before you head for your party and give Linda and me a New Year's Eve drink? I could call you after my folks head out for their New Year's Eve party."

"Okay," agreed Bill. He knew John wouldn't mind as he and Linda were good friends at school.

"Did Beth call you yet?" asked John after arriving at Bill's on New Year's Eve.

"Yes, their parents left about thirty minutes ago."

Both girls were so excited to see Bill and John when they entered the front door carrying a brown paper bag.

"Here, I'll take your coats," offered Beth. Both girls were wearing sweaters, jeans and slippers. Each had pinned their dark red hair up into a small bun.

"Well, I made some orange juice; did you bring the vodka?" asked Beth.

Bill pulled the full bottle out of the paper bag. "Yes," he replied smiling.

"Come into the kitchen and I'll get you some glasses."

While Beth was getting the glasses from the cupboard, Linda removed a plate of cheese and crackers from the refrigerator and took it into the family room.

Bill and John mixed four drinks and handed two of them to the twins.

"Cheers," offered Bill holding his glass up.

"Cheers," the others echoed clinking their glasses together then taking a sip.

Both girls were inexperienced drinkers and had finished their drinks well ahead of John and Bill.

When John took his last sip, he looked over at Bill. "Well,

we'd better get goin' if we're gonna make that party."

"What!? You guys just got here; you can't go yet! Can we have just one more drink? Here, have some cheese and crackers," offered Beth holding up the plate.

Bill looked at John. "The evening's still pretty young; I think we have time for one more drink," suggested Bill.

While he and John were refilling glasses in the kitchen, a Sam Cooke song began to play from the family room. Beth and Linda whispered something to one another, then giggled before entering the kitchen.

"Okay, last one," announced John handing them their refills. "Then Bill and I have to get to that party."

"Okay," replied Beth looking at Linda, who moved closer to John.

Beth edged closer to Bill and smiled at him. "Let's go sit on the couch," she suggested heading for the family room. When Bill sat down next to Beth, he noticed that Linda and John had not followed them and were no longer in the kitchen. *Divide and conquer,* thought Bill. Beth took a sip from her drink, set it on the coffee table in front of the couch and shifted closer to Bill. She began asking Bill what he had done over Christmas Break and sharing what her family had done. *She doesn't want me to leave,* thought Bill.

Beth finished her second drink well before Bill had consumed his, and he could tell she was pretty buzzed. He was feeling pretty relaxed as well. At one point, she leaned toward him, looked at his lips and kissed him. Bill didn't shy away and kissed her back. *I wonder how John is making out with Linda?*

When the Sam Cooke album was done, Beth put on a Henry Mancini record and returned to the couch. She repositioned herself leaning back against one corner of the couch and pulled Bill to her. She began kissing him again. *I don't think*

John and I are going to make it to that other party, thought Bill as he made out with her. *John hasn't returned so he and Linda must be enjoying themselves. What the heck, we're both doing pretty well here!*

During the evening, Bill got up to use the bathroom right off the kitchen. When he exited the bathroom, he saw John refilling his and Linda's glasses. Bill looked at him and gave him the thumbs up sign. John nodded, picked up the glasses and headed into the other room. Bill took this opportunity to pour himself and Beth another drink.

Now into her third drink, Beth was enjoying Bill's body pressed against hers; she even let him feel her breasts through her sweater. Suddenly, Bill heard a noise. It sounded like a garage door opening.

"Oh, my God, your parents are home!" exclaimed Bill. As he attempted to roll off Beth, his foot accidentally hit a large wooden bowl of mixed nuts that was on the coffee table and sent it crashing to the hardwood floor. Nuts scattered in every direction across the family room floor.

"They said they wouldn't be home until after midnight," Beth slurred looking very disheveled and drunk as she sat up.

When her parents opened the door from the garage into the family room and saw Bill attempting to pick up the nuts, they stood there for a minute trying to figure out what the heck was going on.

"I'm sorry, I accidentally knocked the bowl off the table," apologized Bill. "I'll make sure they're all off the floor." By this time John and Linda had re-entered the family room and began to help Bill pick up the nuts. Bill glanced back at Beth still sitting on the couch. She had her right hand over her mouth, and was swallowing attempting to delay getting sick. Fortunately, the girls' parents, who had obviously enjoyed a few drinks announced that they were going next door to Bill's parents' house for a New Year's Eve drink. Mr. Hinton shot a stern look at both girls; then at Bill and John before heading out the front door.

As soon as the door closed, Beth dashed for the bathroom off the kitchen and began barfing her guts out. Linda left to assist Beth. Within minutes, the Hintons' phone rang.

"It's for you, Bill. It's your mom," announced Linda from the kitchen.

"Okay…thanks, Mom…I'll ask them," responded Bill.

When John and Bill entered his parents' house about fifteen minutes later, Mr. and Mrs. Hinton both glared at them and asked, "Where are the girls?"

"Aaa…they said they were really tired, and were just going to go to bed," replied Bill on their behalf. He looked at his mom. "Is it okay if John spends the night here? I think we're going to crash as well."

"Sure," replied Rachel no doubt relieved they wouldn't be out driving on New Year's Eve. "Remember to let your folks know you're staying here, John."

"I'll call home right now," assured John. "Happy New Year," he added following Bill downstairs.

"Happy New Year," replied the adults looking at one another perplexed.

"Whew!" sighed Bill after John entered his bedroom after calling home. "Did you see the looks Mr. and Mrs. Hinton gave us when we walked in the door!?"

"Oh, my God—if looks could kill…."

"Good thing we both made out well with Beth and Linda tonight 'cause I don't think we'll be asking either of them out anytime soon," chuckled Bill. "Speaking of making out, you and Linda must have hit it off okay!"

"Man, a lot better than I expected—thanks to all the vodka. She even gave me a hand job! How did you and Beth do?"

"Not bad. We were dry bangin' on the couch when I heard the garage door open. Thank God we had all our clothes on."

"Fuck, I wouldn't want to be those girls tomorrow when they have to face the music—especially Beth."

After getting into their twin beds, Bill and John continued sharing details of their impromptu evening with the twins.

"Hey, why don't you sneak out that window and spend the night with Linda; I think I'll stay here," snickered Bill.

"Yeah, right," laughed John. "Well, g'night and Happy New Year."

"Happy New Year, John; see ya in the morning."

Bill remembered how glad he was that John was there the next morning when his parents began asking questions about their party with the girls. Between the two of them, they were able to minimize the questions and divert the conversation.

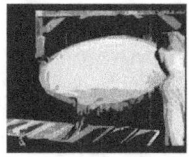

Rod and his roommate Steve arrived late Friday afternoon from Seattle.

"I'll be sure to come by and raise a glass to you at your party tomorrow," Steve assured Bill before heading out the door to drive to his folks' place.

"I'm glad you can come," responded Bill.

When Steve drove away, Bill gave Rod a big hug. "Sure appreciate you travelin' all the way from Seattle for my party, Rod. How was the drive?"

"Looong, but it sure goes faster when you have someone to talk with. Oh, and I don't have to be back to my job until next Friday. I told them about the occasion and they were great about giving me a few days off. My boss is Catholic and thinks the world of the Jesuits."

"How nice!" rejoiced Rachel smiling. "Dad is barbecuing some steaks for dinner shortly; wanna beer?"

"I'll never turn down a beer," Rod grinned.

Rachel was in heaven having both her oldest boys home. She asked one question after another just to hear their voices. "How's the new job, Rod? Any steady girlfriend at this time? Show Rod the guest list, Bill."

Even Howard after consuming a couple of beers seemed to enjoy having both boys home. This certainly hadn't been the case before Rod left home to attend the UW. Rod and Bill had been hard to handle for Howard. There had been alter-cations—even physical confrontations with both boys, and Howard was pretty intimidated by both of them. But not tonight. Tonight provided them this rare opportunity to all be together and enjoy this family visit. *And after the going away party, I'll be in Oregon and Rod'll be back in Seattle. Dad's house will be more peaceful than ever—just the way he likes it,* thought Bill.

—⁓—

"Ready to get the keg this morning?" asked Howard pouring himself a cup of coffee.

"Yep. Joey's opens at 11:00," replied Bill. "We can stop at Rosauers on the way home and pick up some ice so we can get it real cold before we tap it."

"Great, I'll make you a list of a few more things we need to get for tonight," Rachel added. "Is Rod still sleeping?"

"Yeah, I figured he probably needs the sleep after working all week and after the long drive over the pass," responded Bill, who was enjoying a breakfast of scrambled eggs, ham, toast and coffee with his parents.

—⁓—

"It's hard to believe the party's today," reflected Bill as he drove his dad's red and white '56 Chev Nomad into Spokane to pick up the keg. "All summer it seemed like this day was so far off; and now it's here. I can't believe how quickly this summer flew by."

"Yeah, that's how life is as you get older, Bill," his dad

replied. "I try not to let myself think about how fast you and Rod, and now your brothers, have grown up.

"You know…as you were growing up, I wasn't very good about telling you and Rod that I love you. Maybe it's because my dad was that way. He was from the old country, and he just never told me or my older brother that he loved us when we were growing up. But I want you to know that…I do love you and Rod, and I am very proud of you both."

Bill noticed a tear running down his dad's left cheek. "Thanks Dad…I know we haven't been the easiest boys to raise, either."

"Well, just want you to know that I'm proud of you and think you're making a good decision at this time of your life. And remember…if you decide the Jesuits aren't for you, you're welcome to move back home until you find a job and a place of your own."

"Thanks, Dad; that means a lot to me to know that."

Bill exited the freeway onto N. Hamilton and headed to Joey's Tavern.

"Wasn't Joey August a pretty successful boxer?" asked Howard.

"Yes, back in his day. And as boxing coach, he led his GU team to the National Collegiate Boxing Tournament where they were co-national champs in 1950. I'm not sure how he got his start in the tavern business, though." Bill turned right on E. Sharp and parked the Nomad next to Joey's tavern.

"Can I help you?" asked Joey from behind the bar.

"Yes, my name's Bill Roberts; I'm here to pick up a keg and tap."

"Yes…that was a big keg wasn't it?"

"Yes."

"That'll be $35 for the keg, and a $20 deposit on the tap."

Howard wrote a check for $55 and handed it to Joey.

"Thank you," Joey replied placing the check in the till. He headed toward the back of the tavern. "Where ya parked?"

"On Sharp," replied Bill nodding to his left.

"What's the occasion, Bill?" asked Joey wheeling the keg on a dolly toward the car.

"Well, my folks are throwing a farewell party for me today. I'm leaving for the Jesuit Novitiate on August 29. By the way, Joey, this is my dad, Howard Roberts."

"Pleased to meet you, Mr. Roberts," replied Joey shaking Howard's hand.

Bill helped Joey load the keg into the back of the Nomad. "Well, best wishes to you, Bill; keep us in your prayers. And no hurry on returning the keg and tap—Monday or Tuesday afternoon is fine."

"Thanks for buying the keg, Dad; that's very generous," Bill expressed heading south on Hamilton.

"Well, you're welcome. Mom and I wanted to have a party for you." Howard glanced back at the keg. "Just don't slam on the brakes or that keg'll pin us against the dash," grinned Howard.

—m—

"We have a good five hours before folks start arriving; so the keg should be settled down by then," assured Rod arranging ice in the metal wash tub surrounding the keg.

Rachel looked down at them from the deck. "If you and Rod will clean the downstairs and your bathroom that would be great. "That's the bathroom many of the guests will probably use as it's the closest to the back yard."

"No problem, Mom," responded Rod.

"You know, every time I walk by our bathroom now, I think of you screwin' that girl on the bathroom floor last summer," Bill pointed out to Rod on the way to their bedroom.

"You heard that!?" asked Rod surprised.

"Yup. Just be glad that it wasn't Mom or Dad who walked by at the time."

"Man, she was somethin' else," reminisced Rod shaking his head. "All she wanted to do was fuck."

"Well, I know Mom and Dad were relieved when you broke it off with her. They weren't real excited you were going with her. Speakin' of which…you can clean the bathroom since some of you and her may still be on the floor! I'll clean up our bedroom in case anyone pokes their head in during the party."

For the next few hours both Bill and Rod helped their folks clean, set up the backyard, and prepare the food and the grill.

"Well, let's see how much foam we got," suggested Rod tapping the keg about an hour before guests were scheduled to arrive. "Not bad…not bad…always get some foam after you first tap it," he added looking at the first pour in his glass. He took a sip. "It's sure cold; tastes good on such a warm afternoon!"

"Ah…yes!" agreed Howard sampling the second pour of cold Bud. A rare smile of satisfaction came to his face.

He can finally relax a bit now that all the planning's over, thought Bill as he looked at his dad, who was smacking his lips and enjoying another taste of the cold beer. *He deserves to be happy; it hasn't been easy raising two hellions like Rod and me.*

—⁓—

Neighbors began arriving first around 5:00 hoping to wish Bill well, have a beverage or two, some food and leave before things got too rowdy. Both Rod and Bill had reputations in the neighborhood of being wild partiers.

The keg spigot kept busy filling guests' glasses, and the noise level rose with each refill. When Bill's friends began arriving about 6:00, the revelry increased significantly. He was pleased to see so many of his high school and college friends drive out to the Valley to wish him well before he headed to the Novitiate.

"Hey, Bill!" announced Rachel about two hours into the party. "You need to open this present from Mary Ann." Rachel had a devilish grin on her face.

Put on the spot, Bill opened the package to discover three pair of white underpants all hemmed with small red tassels. Bill held one pair up for all to see, which brought a roar of delight from the guests.

"I'm sure they'll be well-received in the Novitiate," Mary Ann giggled. After thanking Mary Ann with a hug, he took them into his room where Rod was telling Steve something about Rathskeller's.

"You ought to put them on!" urged Rod, who knew Bill would do darn near anything after a few beers.

Now dressed only in his tasseled underpants and a white t-shirt, Bill re-entered the party to the gasps and howls of the guests. Some of the more proper guests, who came early so they could leave early did so; others entered more fully into the now loose party atmosphere. Embarrassed, his mom directed him to go back inside and put on some shorts.

"Oh come on, Rachel, we don't mind him dressed that way," some of her lady friends objected.

Bill obeyed his mom, and returned now wearing the tasseled underpants on the outside of his khaki shorts.

"Bill...please," Rachel groaned rolling her eyes. "Go in and take them off!"

About this time, Mr. O'Reilly, Bill's favorite English teacher at Central Valley and a member of St. John Vianney parish, walked into the backyard to wish Bill well. He surveyed Bill's outfit. "I see you're all prepared to enter the Jesuits," he quipped in his typical dry wit. Bill chuckled and led him over to the keg and food.

"Please help yourself, Mr. O'Reilly...I really appreciate you coming." Bill looked down at his tasseled underwear. "I was just headed in to change outa these when you arrived; when I come back out, I'll introduce you to other guests."

Looks like folks are havin' a good time, thought Bill to himself surveying the back yard scene as he headed inside. People were refilling their cups, enjoying the food, talking with one another, laughing. Even the Hintons looked like they were having fun. *After I take these off, I'll go over and thank them for coming.*

"Well, it will probably be a lot quieter around here after I leave," submitted Bill a bit sheepishly to the Hintons, extending his right hand to Mr. Hinton.

"Probably," chuckled Mr. Hinton shaking Bill's hand. "But it makes us feel old to see you kids grow up and move away. We hope this works out for you, Bill," he added. Mrs. Hinton then gave Bill an efficient hug.

"Thanks so much for coming to my party, and be sure to tell Beth and Linda hi for me."

"We will," replied Mr. Hinton. "Don't know if you know,

but Linda's engaged to Keith Smith, whom you probably know from your Prep days, and Beth's engaged to John Hill, who graduated a couple years ahead of your class at CV. So this next year could be a very exciting one for our family."

"I'll say! Please tell them congratulations for me."

As keg parties typically go, when the keg goes dry most of the guests decide it's time to go. Before Mr. O'Reilly left, Bill gave him a leather-bound copy of *Kidnapped* by Robert Louis Stevenson, a book that Bill's grandfather had given him during his sophomore year in high school.

"I can't take this," argued Mr. O'Reilly, knowing that Bill was feeling no pain and might later regret this offer.

"Please take it," insisted Bill. "I want you to have it."

"Well, thank you, and best wishes in the Jesuits," replied Mr. O'Reilly no doubt convinced Bill wouldn't last too long in the Novitiate.

"Good luck to you Bill," offered Jeff Zarillo giving Bill a big hug. "If you're ever assigned to GU or Prep at some point, call me and we can play some handball." Other Gonzaga buddies who had driven out with Jeff also wished Bill the best as they exited the backyard.

About 9:00 PM it was just Bill, his folks and brothers, and they began to clean up the now very quiet backyard.

"Thanks for the great party," slurred Bill rounding up used Dixie cups and paper plates. "It was very thoughtful of you, and it was great to see all the folks who came by. Seemed like everyone was having a good time!"

By the time left over food had been put away, tables and chairs moved back to their normal places, and the tap removed from the keg and brought inside, Bill was ready to hit the sack. "Thanks again for the party," Bill yawned. "I think I'm gonna crash." He hugged his mom and dad before heading downstairs.

On his way to his bedroom, Bill glanced at the phone. He decided to call Barb to tell her about the party, and to see how she was doing. He let the phone ring several times; then hung up. *Hmmm, she must be out—maybe she has a date!?* For a few minutes this thought bothered Bill, but he realized she had every right to proceed with her life without him. After all, he was proceeding with his, and there was a good chance his future wouldn't include her. He headed for bed and was soon fast asleep.

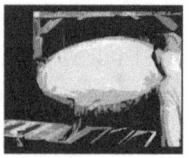

On Monday afternoon, Bill called Barb about 5:30 assuming she'd be home from work, but she didn't answer. He wondered where she could be and began to worry about her. As Bill and his family were finishing up the party leftovers for dinner out on the deck, the phone rang.

"Bill, phone's for you," announced his younger brother, Phil.

"Hi," greeted Jerry in his low monotone voice when Bill answered the phone. "Great party Saturday; thanks for inviting us. Ah…Barb told us about her plan to take you to Rathskeller's for one last fling before you leave for Oregon. Because she wasn't at your party, she really wants to see you before you take off, and Sandy and I would like to go, too. So, if you're up for it, we'd like to drive you and Barb up to Rats tomorrow night."

"That would be great Jerry! I'm definitely up for that. Is Barb there now?"

"Yeah. She spent most of Sunday with us, too."

"Oh, that explains why she hasn't answered her phone. I've tried calling her several times. Ah…I can't talk with her right now," whispered Bill looking around to make sure his parents weren't listening, "but…can you tell her I've been trying to call her?"

"Sure. She has to work Wednesday morning, but I'm sure we can get her home at a decent hour Tuesday night. We'll leave from our place about 6:00. I talked with Ed Lewis and he wants to come. If Rod's home, he'll no doubt want to come as well, knowin' him."

"I'll definitely be at your place at 6:00 tomorrow evening, and I bet Rod will as well. Thanks for doing this, Jerry…and thanks for looking after Barb."

"No problem; see ya tomorrow."

"Hey, Rod. That was Jerry Hendricks. He's invited us to a farewell get together at Rathskeller's tomorrow night. Wanna go?"

"Yes! I haven't been to Rat's in so long. I'll call Steve and see if he wants to come along as well."

"Rathskeller's!? I don't know, you guys. Seems like every time you guys go up there, something bad happens. And Bill you leave in just a few days," cautioned Rachel.

"Don't worry, Mom; I'll watch out for Bill," assured Rod.

"I don't know…I'd rather you wouldn't go. But if you do… just be careful…promise me?"

"Yes," they responded in unison.

Bill and his folks continued visiting on the deck well into the evening enjoying the warm August evening. Rod told them about his new job at Bartell Drug in Kirkland, what his plans were for buying a reliable car and for finding a place to live near his store.

"Ouch! Here come the damned mosquitoes!" exclaimed Rod slapping his leg, then heading for the screen door. "Think it's time for me to hit the sack anyway."

"I'd better as well," added Bill. He wanted to update Rod regarding Barb and share a request before heading to the Novitiate. "G'night, Dad; night, Mom. Thanks for dinner."

"Are you still seein' Barb?" asked Rod from his bed as Bill turned out the bedroom light.

"Yeah, but the relationship has kind of cooled down in the past couple of weeks. She knows for sure now that I'm leaving for Oregon on the 29th; so reality's begun to set in with both of us. On a positive note, she's talked more about maybe going to a community college, and she really would like to get out of Spokane and live in Seattle if she can."

"She should; both of those experiences would be good for her."

"I agree. In fact, I'd like to ask you for a favor. If I'm still in the Jesuits at Christmas time, I'll tell Dad to withdraw $300 from my savings and give it to you. I'll tell him you loaned me the money some time ago. But I'd like you to give it to Barb for me. Tell her I hope it will allow her to go back to school or to get a job in Seattle."

"Are you sure!? Won't you need that money if you decide to leave the Jesuits?"

"I'll still have enough in the bank to help me restart my life if I leave. Will you do that for me?"

"Sure, if that's what you want then. But to be honest, I'll be surprised if you're still in the Novitiate at Christmas. Well, see you in the morning. Night."

"G'night," Bill replied, forcing a big fart.

"God, some things never change!"

Both enjoyed a final laugh before falling asleep.

Bill arrived at Jerry and Sandy's house a bit early on Tuesday evening because he wanted a chance to talk with Barb before heading up to Rathskeller's. The first thing he did was give

Barb a long, firm hug. "How are you?" he asked her.

"Okay," she replied trying not to cry and forcing a quick smile.

"I tried to call you after my party and the next day but you evidently weren't home."

"Yeah, I came over to Sandy and Jerry's. Even though I understood why I shouldn't come to your party, I was pretty down about it, and just needed to be with someone."

"I understand, Barb, and I'm so sorry," replied Bill hugging her again. "And I'm glad you arranged this special get together with Jerry and Sandy so we could all celebrate together tonight."

Bill made all the needed introductions when the others arrived at Jerry and Sandy's.

"Nice to meet you, Steve," Ed responded removing his unfiltered Pall Mall cigarette from his lips with his left hand to shake Steve's hand. "Bill's told me about some of your wild parties at the UW."

"Don't believe him. Rod and I were very serious students," chuckled Steve looking at Rod. "Man, what a beautiful Bonneville you have," Steve gushed moving closer to it and looking it over. He glanced over at his '61 Chevy still dirty from the drive over the pass. "I was going to suggest you ride up with Rod and me in my beater, but it would sure be a lot more fun to ride in your Bonneville."

"I don't mind drivin' at all," replied Ed. "Hop in; let's go!"

Bill and Barb rode with Jerry and Sandy, who led the caravan east on I-90 toward Coeur d' Alene.

"We've enjoyed some wild and crazy times at Rathskeller's over the last four years, Bill, and this could very well be your last visit there," declared Sandy from the front seat looking back at Bill. "Remember last year's Diamond Cup?"

"Well, some of it," laughed Bill. "I remember the people lined up around Rathskeller's trying to get in. And the endless pitchers of beer on tables…and people passed out. I don't think we ever actually bought any beer; we just helped ourselves to pitchers sitting on tables—that is until we had to punch our way outta there."

Barb looked at Bill with alarm. "You got in a fight inside Rathskeller's!?"

"Yeah, but the other guy started it, so they held him for the cops and told me to get the hell outta there."

"God, remember the National Guard and cops trying to control the crowds of people on Sherman Ave?" reflected Jerry.

"Yes, and the guys in the Coeur d' Alene jail yelling to their friends from the barred windows in the basement of the jail to bail them out," added Bill. "No wonder they're not having the races again this summer."

"Was that the same Diamond Cup that you ended up running from the cops?" asked Jerry.

"What!?" exclaimed Barb looking at Bill with raised eyebrows.

"Yes, it was! A girl I knew invited me to a party at her mom's house for that weekend. Her mom was on a trip some place. A bunch of us headed to Rat's, where I got caught up in some skirmish. When someone yelled, 'cops,' I ran up an alley and down some side streets back to her mom's place. I was hot and sweaty and pretty drunk so I jumped in the shower. Well, guess who came back from her trip early? Yep, her mom comes into the bathroom and discovers this strange guy in her shower. She was going to call the police, but when I begged her not to, and told her that her daughter had invited me up to her party, she decided not to call the police. I don't think she wanted her daughter answering to the cops. Anyway, when her daughter returned from Rathskeller's with a bunch of her friends, her mom really unloaded on her. Needless to say, I headed for Spokane."

"God, I'm sure glad I didn't know you then," exclaimed Barb moving slightly away from him in the back seat.

"Man, I'll never forget the night Rod, Ed and I were coming out of Rathskeller's after they closed down, and these two guys in a red MG convertible swerved at us like they were trying to run us down. They took off, and we jumped in Ed's Bonneville and chased them to a gravel pit outside of town. We thought we had them trapped but there was just enough room for them to squeeze around us through the entrance. As they headed for us, Rod chucked a full stubby of beer at them. Thank God he missed! If that bottle had hit one of them in the head, it would have killed him."

"You guys were so lucky that night!" exclaimed Sandy. "Remember the night we were up there and you and Rod got up on stage and danced when Paul Revere and the Raiders were playing?"

"Yeah, the band and crowd loved it, but not the bouncer who escorted us to the door."

"Probably a good thing it's a Tuesday night tonight; should be a fairly quiet night," Jerry commented looking at Bill through the rearview mirror.

"I hope so. Don't let me get thrown in jail tonight," pleaded Bill. "My folks might have a difficult time explaining to the Novice Master why their son didn't make the plane on the 29th."

The sight of the nearly block long Rathskeller Inn on Sherman Avenue always amazed Bill. Not too many years before, it was just a small tavern on the corner. As it grew in popularity, it expanded to its current, impressive size.

After finding a parking place on a nearby side street, they entered the tavern where as usual, a bouncer checked their ID's.

Bill turned to Jerry as they entered the tavern. "I'm sure a lot more relaxed comin' to Rat's now that I'm legal." During Bill's first three years of college, he'd been frequenting Rathskeller's with a fake student ID card that a classmate had made for him during his freshman year at Carroll College.

Shortly after finding a table, Rod, Steve and Ed joined them, and in short order the cold tap beer and live music had them animated, laughing and dancing. Rod wasted no time getting into his typical party groove. Excited to be at Rat's again with friends, listening to live music and watching gals in cutoffs and t-shirts workin' it on the dance floor, he just wasn't able to pace himself. Before long he was slurrin' his words, asking girls to dance, and blurting out whatever came to mind. "God, look at that nice ass!"

Barb looked at Bill, "Oh, my God, he'll be passed out before the evening's over—just like at his party in Seattle."

During one dance, Rod bumped into a gal on the dance floor, and the guy she was dancing with shoved Rod. When Rod confronted the guy, Bill and Steve quickly intervened and pulled Rod over to the table.

"Just relax, Rod!" Bill told him sternly. "The evening's young and we're just here to have a good time—remember!? Just back off on the beer for awhile."

But the challenge had been initiated. Over the next couple of hours, Rod exchanged stares with the other guy sitting several tables away even though Bill and his friends did their best to distract Rod.

Steve, who was seated to Barb's left, eventually struck up a conversation with her about coming to Seattle. "Bill tells me you'd like to live in Seattle at some point; maybe even go to school."

"Yes! It is so much more alive there than Spokane."

"Well, if you come over to scope things out, you're welcome to stay at the house where you stayed for Rod's party. I've got a year of school left and will be living there during this next school year. We always have room for someone to stay for a few days."

Barb smiled at Steve. "That would be great!"

Bill was keeping a pretty close eye on Rod to make sure he didn't do anything stupid, so Steve at one point asked Bill if it was okay to dance with Barb.

"Sure," replied Bill. When he glanced at them on the dance floor, he could see they were having a fun time together. A twinge of jealousy briefly touched Bill. But it helped him to think that after he left for the Novitiate, Barb would be able to move on with her life—who knows, maybe even with Steve in Seattle.

About 10:30, Barb announced that she would need to head back to Spokane soon because she had to work early the next day.

"I should get going as well; I'm working Day Shift tomorrow," Ed added.

Bill wanted to stay longer, but he knew given Rod's condition and the staring that had been going on throughout the evening, he should get Rod home. Bill turned to Jerry. "As much as I'd like to stay, I think I'd better get Rod out of here before he and that other guy get into it. They've been glarin' at each other all evening."

"I think you're right," replied Jerry. "No problem; it wouldn't hurt Sandy and me to get home a bit early either."

When the group exited the tavern door, turned left and headed up the side street for their cars, the guy Rod had been staring at ran up to Rod pushed him, then punched him in the face. The guy's friends standing in back of him cheered him on. But when Rod went down, Bill was on the guy like a flash. He launched a quick, solid left jab into the guy's nose, which exploded and sprayed blood in all directions. Before the guy could react, Bill quickly followed with a right cross to his chin sending him to the sidewalk like a dropped sack of potatoes. Bill stood over him poised to throw more punches if the guy got up. Then one of the guys' friends hit Bill in the back of the head with something. A sickening "thunk" could be heard as the back of Bill's head hit the sidewalk. Ed and Steve quickly subdued the guy, and held him down.

Barb rushed over to Bill, who was staring at her blankly and moving his mouth as if trying to say something. "Bill! Bill, can you hear me?" Blood oozed onto the sidewalk from the back of his head. "Oh my God, I think he's hurt really bad," cried Barb. "Somebody call an ambulance!"

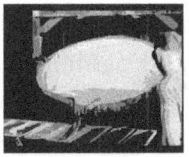

October 5, 1967

"Bill? If you can hear me open your eyes," pleaded his mom bending over Bill's hospital bed at Sacred Heart Hospital in Spokane. The pulsing noise of the ventilator clicked on and off, and the heart monitor beeped in the background.

"Mr. and Mrs. Roberts, I think we need to discuss removing Bill from life support," counseled Dr. O'Brien, the neurosurgeon. "It's been a little over six weeks now since Bill came to us in a comatose state. He's in what we call a 'persistent vegetative state,' and we believe his vegetative state will be permanent. I know this is a very difficult decision for you to make, but based on my experience and that of my colleagues, I think it's the right decision. Please…think about my recommendation over the next 72 hours; then let's talk about your decision," advised the doctor before leaving the room.

Rachel shook her head and began to sob. She leaned closer to her son and pleaded, "Bill, Bill if you can hear me just…just squeeze my hand."

—◊◊◊—

Barb had just finished flushing her breakfast down the toilet and was rinsing out her mouth with scoops of water from the bathroom tap when she heard a knock at her door. She quickly dried her face and hands, straightened her hair and headed for her door. She was puzzled as she wasn't expecting anyone. When she opened her door, she was surprised to see Bill's brother, Rod. He looked thinner than when she'd last seen him; he appeared tired and dejected. "Oh, my gosh, Rod—what are you doing here?"

"Well, I just flew into Spokane last night and wanted to come by and bring you something."

"Come in," Barb invited closing the door behind him. She pointed toward the couch. "Have a seat."

Rod handed Barb a white business envelope. She took the envelope, looked at Rod confused; then opened it. Inside were six fifty dollar bills. "What's this!?" asked Barb looking up at Rod.

"When I was here for Bill's party, he asked me to give this to you if he was still in the Jesuits at Christmas…but…I think now is the time to give it to you. He thought it would help you move to Seattle or go to school if you wanted to. And…the reason I'm here today is…Barb, tomorrow the doctors are going to disconnect Bill's life support."

Barb stared at Rod and shook her head. She put her hands to her face, burst into tears and ran into the bathroom where she cried uncontrollably for several minutes.

"Can I get you anything, Barb?"

"No…I'll be out in a minute."

After washing and drying her face, Barb emerged from the

bathroom. "Oh, I'm so sorry to hear this news," she sniveled holding a Kleenex to her nose. "I knew it could happen at some point, but…at least there was some glimmer of hope while he was on life support. Now it's so final…and…Rod…I'm pregnant with Bill's baby," she announced tearfully.

"Oh, my gosh, Barb…did Bill know?"

"No, I think I got pregnant the last night we were together…the week before his party. I didn't really know I was pregnant until after we were at Rathskeller's."

"Oh, Barb…what are you going to do?"

"Well, for now just keep working at J.C. Penney. I certainly won't be moving to Seattle or going to school at this time…but this money will definitely help me prepare for the baby."

"So, the baby would be due in…"

"Mid-May."

"I'll keep in touch with you to see how you and the baby are doing, if that's okay."

Barb nodded.

"Barb, I should let my parents know—they would want to know."

"No! I don't want them to know. I don't want them to be disappointed in Bill, and I don't want them to blame me." She grabbed Rod's hand. "Please…promise me you won't tell them."

Rod looked at her intently and could see her determination. He nodded. "Okay, I promise I won't tell them."

"Thank you…. What time tomorrow are they going to remove his life support?"

"About 10:00 AM. I think they want to give us ample time to be with Bill before they…you know. And I understand it can take several hours before he's gone."

"Will you please let me know when he's gone?"

"Yes."

"How are you doin', Rod?" Barb asked studying his face.

"Not very good," admitted Rod glancing at her; then at the floor. Tears ran down his cheeks; he clasped his hands together and rocked back and forth as if attempting to comfort himself. "I keep thinking that if I hadn't gotten drunk and caused a fight with that guy…this would never have happened…." He looked at her. "If I hadn't called you with the idea of going to Rathskeller's this wouldn't have happened. It's all my fault! And I don't think I'll ever be able to forgive myself."

She reached out and put her left hand on his hands. "You're going to have to find a way to move forward with your life, Rod. I'd give anything to have Bill here right now too." She placed her right hand on her tummy. "But it helps me to know he'll always be with me now."

A brief silence ensued then Rod stood up. "I should probably get going. I'm staying with my folks for the rest of the week to be with them and help them make funeral arrangements."

"Will you let me know when Bill's service is going to be?" Barb asked standing up.

"Yes," Rod assured her opening the door.

"I'm glad you came over today rather than afterward, Rod. Thank you."

Rob gave a slight nod then closed the door behind him.

At 9:00 AM the entire Roberts family gathered in the hallway outside Bill's hospital room in Spokane.

"Can I have just a few minutes with Bill by myself?" asked Rod. Rachel and Howard nodded and Rod entered the room. He stared at Bill, who lie in the same fixed comatose position.

The ventilator clicked on and off at regular intervals. Rod pulled up a chair on Bill's left and took hold of his hand. "I gave Barb your gift yesterday, Bill; she was so grateful to get it. She's going to use it to take care of your baby." Rod put his head down on the bed and began to sob. "Bill...I am so sorry for what I've done to you. Please forgive me. Hopefully some day, I'll be able to forgive myself...but it's so hard...."

Several miles east in the Valley, Barb sat on her couch clutching the silver and turquoise cross Bill had bought for her in Seattle. She looked at it, kissed it, then held it to her chest. "You'll always be with us, Bill."

About 9:10, the hospital door opened and the rest of the Roberts family entered the room. Rod dried his eyes with his left sleeve, stood up and motioned Rachel to come take his chair.

Rachel held Bill's left hand in hers watching his face carefully, hoping, praying to see the slightest glimmer of hope. Howard, tears running down his cheeks had his right hand on her shoulder. Bill's younger brothers stood behind them staring blankly. Don was wearing his St. John Vianney football jersey and was carrying the football he and Bill had practiced with at Bowdish.

Fr. Eric, who had given Bill the Last Rites at the hospital the night of the fight at Rathskeller's using the Last Rites crucifix Rachel and Howard had brought to him, arrived a few minutes later. He stood next to Bill's bed closest to the life-support machines and placed on Bill's chest the crucifix from his Jesuit House room at GU that Bill had admired so.

Dr. O'Brien entered the room at 9:45. He comforted each family member, reviewed the disconnect procedures with them and answered their questions.

"We will make sure Bill is comfortable," assured Dr.

O'Brien, "but it may take hours before he's gone. It will probably become difficult for him to breathe—so we strongly recommend you wait out in the waiting room or even go back home. I will call you when he's gone; you will be able to see him again at that time."

Fr. Eric bent over Bill. "Bill, this is Fr. Eric. It's time to head for the Novitiate now. Are you ready to go?"

Then Eric raised up and led the family out of the room.

Bill breathed in the fresh, cool air after emerging from the steamy shower room at Kaiser. He smiled as he listened to the banter of the men on D Shift, who like him were waiting to clock out after Swing Shift.

"Hey, Slim, I'll bet I know where you're headed tonight," someone blurted. A gush of laughter followed.

The line began to move toward the guardhouse. Bill removed his time card from its slot and placed it in the machine which made a loud clunk...

Bill sat on the edge of his aunt's dock with Barb, a towel wrapped around them. A star shot across the night ski. He smiled and turned to kiss her...

The jet engines began to roar as they propelled the plane down the runway faster and faster and faster. Gripping the arm rests a bit tighter, Bill recalled what Rod had told Barb about the incredible feeling of acceleration right before takeoff. Airport scenery whizzed by as the plane gained speed; the tires rumbled underneath, then went silent as the plane left the runway.

—ɯ—

Acknowledgements

SPECIAL THANKS to my wife, Polly, who not only patiently supported my hours and hours of writing, but provided me invaluable feedback. Thanks to my friend and teaching colleague, Glen Baron, who edited my first draft, gently provided me needed direction and encouraged me to proceed.

Thanks to the following men who worked in the pot rooms at the Kaiser Aluminum Mead Works at various times and helped me remember the details that had faded from my memory since the mid-1960s: Ralph Rice, Terry Luding, Barry Hullett and Dan Cosby; thanks to my brother Dennis Rae who worked at Kaiser Aluminum Trentwood Works in the Spokane Valley.

About the Author

BRIAN RAE was born and raised in Spokane, Washington. He worked at Kaiser Aluminum Mead Works north of Spokane during the summer months of 1963-67 to pay for his tuition at Gonzaga University. He earned his undergraduate degree from Gonzaga in 1967 then entered the Jesuit Religious Order which provided him important direction in his unfocused life.

He earned a Masters of Education degree at Seattle University in 1987. A retired high school English teacher, coach and administrator, and retired adjunct professor in the Secondary Education Department at Western Washington University, he currently resides in Lynden, Washington. He and his wife Polly have two daughters. When not writing, he loves to backpack, hike, hunt and snow ski.